THE *PECAN SPRINGS ENTERPRISE* TRILOGY

THE *PECAN SPRINGS ENTERPRISE* TRILOGY OMNIBUS EDITION

DEADLINES, FAULT LINES, FIRELINES

SUSAN WITTIG ALBERT

THORNDIKE PRESS
A part of Gale, a Cengage Company

GALE
A Cengage Company

LIBRARY OF CONGRESS CIP DATA ON FILE.
CATALOGUING IN PUBLICATION FOR THIS BOOK
IS AVAILABLE FROM THE LIBRARY OF CONGRESS.

ISBN-13: 978-1-4328-8812-1 (hardcover alk. paper)

Published in 2021 by arrangement with Levine/Greenberg Literary Agency, Inc., d.b.a. Levine Greenberg Rostan Literary Agency

Printed in Mexico
Print Number: 01   Print Year: 2021

CONTENTS

■ ■ ■ ■

DEADLINES:
BOOK ONE

■ ■ ■ ■

Deadline. Noun US [C] /'ded‚laɪn/:
a time or day by which something
must be done.
— Cambridge Dictionary

Are you aware that rushing toward a goal
is a sublimated death wish? It's no
coincidence we call them deadlines.
— *Tom Robbins,*
Half Asleep in Frog Pajamas

A NOTE TO READERS

Deadlines is the first novella in a trilogy that focuses on Jessica Nelson, the crime reporter for the *Pecan Springs Enterprise.* You may remember Jessica as a central character in *Mourning Gloria* (book 19 of the China Bayles series) and in *Out of BODY* (the third novella in the Crystal Cave series). I became so interested in her as a person and her work as a crime reporter and true-crime author that I wanted to learn more about her and share what I've learned with you. I hope you will enjoy getting deeply acquainted with Jessica — her backstory, her professional challenges, her friendships and love life — as much as I have.

As a writer, I've also enjoyed telling Jessica's stories as *novellas,* which are about half the length of a novel. I think of the novella as an opportunity to work out a full-size story in just half the space, requiring me to "write tight" (as one of my teachers always advised) and strip the narrative down to its basic necessities. And the trilogy form (three linked novellas) gives us time to get to know the central character deeply, as she deals with three very different kinds of challenges, each one revealing more of what makes her tick. The novella trilogy is the best of both worlds, it seems to me: the shorter, tighter form embedded in the longer linked format.

Thanks for being a reader. I appreciate each one of you!

Susan Wittig Albert

PROLOGUE

Christine couldn't sleep.

She had tried everything — yoga, meditation, deep breathing, turning off the TV so the screen's blue light wouldn't suppress her melatonin, even drinking banana tea (which she detested), because Dr. Oz called it a sleeping pill in a peel. She had talked to the pharmacist. She had even been to a sleep clinic, and when they gave her prescriptions, she followed instructions and took the pills, all but Ambien. She refused to take Ambien, for reasons she would not discuss.

Most nights — early mornings, really — she finally fell asleep. But when that happened, when she at last lost her tenuous perch on the cliff of uneasy wakefulness and fell into the black void below, the dream was waiting for her, just one dream, always the same dream.

The woman, the pills, the pillow — except

15

that now she was the woman in the bed and the pillow was over her face, covering her nose and mouth so that she couldn't breathe, couldn't cry out, could only wait to die.

And then she would wake with a gasp and lie in the dark, clinging again to the cliff above the void, the dream waiting like a malignant dragon below, eager for her to fall into its clutches.

The woman, the pills, the pillow.

And the killer. Yes, that one.

Yes.

CHAPTER ONE

Deadlines, deadlines. Always deadlines.

Deadlines were the name of the game in Jessica Nelson's life. Meet one, and there was another one waiting. Meet that one, and *wham-bam,* here comes a third.

But deadlines came with the territory. And deadlines made things happen, as her editor Hark Hibler liked to remind everyone in the newsroom. Jessica knew it was true. Left to her own manic devices, she would rewrite every story endlessly, improving each paragraph (as Hark once remarked drily) one comma at a time. The only cure for her rewrite habit was to bang out the story fast, while the facts were still fresh in her mind and their taste — sweet, sour, bland, bitter — was still on her tongue. When she got to the end, she'd give the story a quick once-over, swallow hard, and force herself to submit it, so she wouldn't be tempted to do just one more rewrite.

That morning, for instance, five minutes ahead of the deadline, she had finished a piece about an insurance fraud scheme that involved a couple of staged car crashes on I-35, just outside of Pecan Springs. She wrote the final word in the final paragraph, added her byline (Jessica Nelson, Police and Public Safety), hit *save,* and emailed the file to Francine Fenner, who edited the *Enterprise*'s monthly magazine supplement, where it would appear. The story didn't have far to go. Francine's computer was in her cube just across the aisle in the newsroom.

And now it was 4:40 in the afternoon and the deadline clock was still ticking. This time her story was aimed for the Breaking News segment of the online edition, one of Hark's continuing attempts to push the *Pecan Springs Enterprise* into the fast-changing world of the internet, Twitter, Instagram, and Facebook. Jessica had spent the earlier part of the afternoon hanging out at the Adams County courthouse, cattycornered from the Enterprise building. Along with a handful of reporters from San Marcos and New Braunfels and a camera crew from KVUE-TV in Austin, she had been waiting for the district attorney, Margo Henderson, to announce the grand jury's indictment of

Howard Byers, the serial killer who called himself Azrael, the Angel of Death.

But Jessica's personal stake in the story was bigger than that of the other reporters. She was the one who had stumbled across Byers' terrifying trail of bizarre murders. She had spent months pursuing him with all the investigative skills she could summon, a few lucky breaks, and some just-in-time help from her somewhat-psychic friend, Ruby Wilcox. What's more, she had done it in the face of Hark's obstinate editorial opposition, the disapproval of her boyfriend (now her *ex*-boyfriend) Kelly, and her own personal demons.*

And she was right to be terrified of Byers, for she had nearly become one of his victims. In fact, she would likely be dead right now if it hadn't been for Ruby and her detective friend, Ethan Connors, who showed up just in the nick of time. If there was any justice in this misbegotten world, Byers would soon be on his way to prison. And Jessica could finish the book she was writing about his homicidal career.

How many people had Byers killed? Nobody knew for sure — and the actual num-

* Read Jessica's story in *Out of BODY,* the third book in the Crystal Cave trilogy.

ber might never be known. Before his attorney muzzled him, the man had claimed twelve murders, although Jessica had been able to identify only eight and the police were still trying to come up with an accurate body count. So as far as she was concerned, the three indictments that DA Margo Henderson had announced that afternoon were just another chapter in a tragic story whose end was not yet in sight. But those indictments were the subject of her story, so she shut out the newsroom's wraparound noise, opened a file, and began typing her first sentence, her lede, as journalists called it.

And there was plenty going on. In Denise Sanger's office at the far end of the newsroom, an ancient computer printer was spitting out a staccato print job. Copy editor Becky Compton's phone was ringing (her ringtone was "I Can't Get No Satisfaction"), and for some unexplained reason, somebody was hammering on a wall in the break room.

In the cube next to Jessica's, sports editor Will Wagner was on his speakerphone with an irate reader who was mad at the Pecan Springs city council for approving a new soccer field on the south side of town, rather than on the east. Will, in response, was repeating, in detail and at length, why the

Enterprise had endorsed the council's decision.

Across the aisle, Francine was debating Heather McNally about the placement of Virgil Osborn's photographs in the next *Magazine* insert. Heather seemed to be coming down with a cold, for she was coughing her head off. Of course, anybody else would have stayed home instead of coming to work and spreading germs to everyone within sneezing distance. But Heather — who did obits as well as covering general assignments — couldn't bear to be out of the newsroom for even a day. Jessica suspected that it wasn't dedication to truth, justice, and the American way that kept her on the job, though. Heather was afraid she might miss a chance to move in on Jessica's cops-and-crime beat.

Not that Jessica blamed her. Pecan Springs was a small town without much in the way of big-city excitement. A week's news budget — the stories they would be covering — might include a wreck on I-35, a case of food poisoning at a local restaurant, a seven-foot alligator captured in the Pecan River, and the city council's latest drought contingency plan. Jessica's beat, however, included not only Pecan Springs and its cop shop (headed by chief Sheila Dawson) but sprawling Adams County. There was enough crime to keep law enforcement busy twenty-four-seven.

Which meant that Jessica was on call twenty-four-seven. She was dispatched to cover meth busts, pot grows, oil property thefts, and cattle rustling (still a thing in Texas). She had a police scanner app on her phone, so she could pick up both the Pecan Springs and the Adams County live law enforcement feeds. She kept tabs on the police blotters at both the PSPD and the sheriff's office, visited the jail to interview prisoners, and listened to the prosecution and the defense stake their disparate claims to justice in front of a jury. Pecan Springs didn't have a lot of crime, but the cops-and-crime beat was a window onto an ugly, often brutal part of the community that most Pecan Springers didn't see.

Not that they wanted to, of course. When Jessica did her job, they read all about it in the comfort and safety of their living rooms, where they could experience the crime in all its gory grittiness and be grateful that the cops and the courts were taking care of all the brutal bits.

Jessica's concentration wasn't marred by Will's speakerphone, Heather's coughing, or somebody's hammering, for she had learned to work through all kinds of newsroom interruptions — the telephone, email, somebody's urgent request for information, somebody else's need for a shoulder to cry on. So she kept her fingers moving until she had eight solid paragraphs, starting with a who-what-when-where lede:

The Adams County Grand Jury for the 507th District Court today indicted Howard Byers, the so-called Angel of Death, for the murders of three people . . .

And ending with a quick quote from the defense, which Jessica had snagged on the way out of the courthouse this afternoon:

"I expect the trial to begin in the next few months," Howard Byers' attorney, David Redfern, said.

David Redfern. Now, there was an intriguing puzzle.

Jessica leaned back in her chair and stretched her arms toward the ceiling, unkinking her fingers and elbows. Redfern was a definitely hunkish guy in his early thirties, with an engaging personality and a sharply penetrating intelligence. He had become a partner in Charlie Lipman's law firm last year and was already recognized as one of

Pecan Springs' most promising young attorneys. Jessica had interviewed him a few days ago for background for her book on the Byers case. She had asked him how he planned to manage Byers' defense.

"Do you expect to plead him? If you go to trial, won't you have to put on an insanity defense? Are you considering any other options?"

For a moment, Redfern fixed her with an intensely questioning gaze. Then he grinned and said, in a mock-regretful tone, "For that, Ms. Nelson, I'm afraid you'll just have to wait. But I can tell you right now that I'll be on my A game, especially for you. Especially since you're writing that book. Your second, I understand." He was still smiling, but she thought she could hear the snark in his tone. "True crime pays, does it?"

She was about to retort, "Writing true crime pays a lot less than defending the criminal," but she bit it back, not wanting to antagonize him further.

Snarky or not, Redfern's smile was certainly intended to be charming. He was a supremely attractive guy — oh, absolutely, no question — and Jessica had definitely felt attracted. But that was silly. He was already taken: she had heard he was seriously dating Carla Morgan, a local doctor with a successful pediatrics practice.

Still, there was that unsettling gaze and those challenging gray eyes. As a witness for the prosecution, she would be called to testify about her months-long investigation, which had led directly to Byers' arrest, and about his attempt to kill her. Nervously, she wondered how well she would hold up under his cross examination, if it came to that. It might not. Each of the three indictments announced that afternoon carried the death penalty, so Byers might plead down to life without parole, and there would be no trial.

But the larger question, as far as Jessica was concerned, was *why*. Why in the world would a man like Redfern agree to defend somebody like Byers, who had taken advantage of the sick and vulnerable? By her count, the Angel of Death had killed eight terminally ill people, each one murdered days or weeks before they were expected to die a natural death. Byers wouldn't be charged with all of his crimes, for several were unprovable and she suspected that more — perhaps many more — would never be known. But he was sure to be convicted of the three murders for which Margo Henderson, Adams County's district attorney, had won grand jury indictments. David

Redfern was successful enough to pick and choose the people he wanted to defend. Why would he —

Her reflections were interrupted by her cellphone's ringtone: the theme from *The Good, the Bad, and the Ugly,* which pretty much summed up her view of a crime writer's life. It said something like *Get over it, Jessie. The good stuff will be bad and the bad stuff will be ugly. That's what you signed on for, isn't it?*

She peered at the phone to see who was calling and flinched. It was Kelly Rifkin.

Kelly. Her ex-boyfriend. Again.

They had broken up several months before, but she was just beginning to get over the disappointment and the pain. They had practically lived together for almost a year, until Kelly decided that he was tired of playing second fiddle to her job and specifically, to her investigation of the Angel of Death murders. In their final stormy encounter, he'd growled that she was totally obsessed with the story.

"There's no room in your life for anything — or anyone — else," he said. "I am *done,* Jessica."

What could she say? It wasn't as if she hadn't been here before. Kelly wasn't the first of her boyfriends to object to the way she got involved in her work. But he was the first to accuse her of something else, which had made her feel like a . . . like somebody she didn't want to be.

"You know what you're doing?" His tone had been cruel. "As a crime writer, you are exploiting the criminal's evildoing. You are trading on the victim's suffering. You're turning it into a story — for its entertainment value." *Entertainment.* He had made the word ugly.

She was horrified. "That is absolutely not true!" she exclaimed. "I —"

"For its career value, too," he went on brutally. "Truman Capote and Ann Rule found out that there's no better way to attract readers than to drench a boring story in blood. If one murder is good, three or four murders are a dozen times better. More dramatic. More *sensational.* You are using this stuff to get ahead in the newspaper game."

That had rocked her. "Hey, wait!" she protested. "I'm not interested in murder. I'm interested in what's behind it. In human complexities and human frailties and the uncertainties and ambiguities — and yes, the *failures* of law enforcement and the justice system. And I refuse to buy the assumption that, as a writer, I have to choose

27

between being authentic and being boring!"

But even as she heard her words — big words, abstractions — she couldn't help wondering if Kelly had a point, and she filed it away, to think about later. She already knew that he was right about obsession. When she was on a story, any story, she was *on* it, with a laser focus and a jaw-clenched determination that shoved everything else into second place. For months, she had been completely and utterly engrossed in the Angel of Death story. It occupied her to the point where she could barely spare the time to eat and sleep. She didn't blame Kelly for giving up on her. He wanted more, and it was her fault — not his — that she didn't have more to give him.

Still, she missed the good sex, which had held them together even after they began coming apart. She missed the comfort of knowing there was somebody to come home to after a tough day. And there were some very tough days — ugly, brutal days — on the cops-and-crime beat.

Most of all, though, she missed the companionship. Kelly taught literature at CTSU — Central Texas State University, on the hill north of town — so they were both in the business of words and stories. Both of them had a lively interest in climate change and politics, local and national, and in what was going on at the university and at the *Enterprise.* There was always something interesting to talk about. Or argue about, when they were on different sides. She missed that, too.

Lately, Kelly had started calling again, wanting to talk, to hear how she was doing. Then, just last week, he'd suggested going out to a movie. She was surprised at how easy it would have been to say yes. She hadn't — and now, here he was, again. And again, it would be so easy to say yes. But nothing fundamental had changed. She would continue to be stubbornly dedicated to her work and he would be jealous of it. And then they would have to do it all over again. What was the point?

She took a breath, and her resolve wobbled, like a kid's top running out of spin. What if she was wrong? Maybe Kelly would be willing to let her have what she needed — space and time for her work. Maybe he was ready to —

She picked up the call. "Hey, Kelly," she said, making her voice carefully neutral. "What's up?" She glanced at the clock over the break room door. 4:53. Seven minutes. "I'm on deadline," she said. "I don't have a lot of time."

"Happy Valentine's Day," he said.

"You're kidding." She made herself sound surprised, although she wasn't. You couldn't overlook Valentine's Day. The world was submerged in a tsunami of flowers and chocolate hearts. "I guess I got busy and forgot."

"That's because I wasn't there to remind you," he said matter-of-factly. "But now that I have, how about dinner tonight? A new Thai restaurant just opened up near the campus." He chuckled. "We can celebrate your forgetting that it's Valentine's."

He didn't add *It's also our anniversary.*

But it was. She and Kelly had started going together two years ago today. He wouldn't mention it because he wouldn't want her to think he'd remembered. And she wouldn't mention it because she didn't want him to know she hadn't forgotten.

"Tonight?" Well, that made it easy. "I can't, Kelly. Chelsea emailed me this morning. She pitched the Byers book to the True Crime Library editor at St. Martin's, and he's asked for a proposal. I've pulled my notes together, but Chelsea wants it tomorrow, so I have to work on it tonight. I'm calling it *Not Only in the Dark.*"

Chelsea was her literary agent. Knowing how Kelly felt about her work, she should probably have found a different excuse. But she had been really excited when she read the email about Chelsea's conversation with the editor at St. Martin's.

"He's ready to hop on it," Chelsea had written. "True crime is super-hot right now. What's more, St. Martin's is producing a new true-crime podcast series, and your Angel of Death story would be perfect for it. If you can get your proposal to me this week, I think we'll see an offer before the end of the month."

Reading that, Jessica had to pinch herself. St. Martin's True Crime Library would be the perfect home for the Byers book. But Kelly wasn't ready to congratulate her.

"Byers is in jail, and the *Enterprise* published your four-part series on the case a couple of weeks ago." His voice was thin and hard. "Now you're telling me there's going to be *more*?"

"Of course there'll be more." For crying out loud. Didn't he remember that she'd had a book in mind, all along? She took a breath.

"The grand jury indictments came down just today, Kelly. The trial won't begin for a couple of months, and there's still a *lot* of work to be done. Interviewing the victims' families and people who know Byers, researching his backstory, tracking down sources, collecting documents and interviews. And the trial could go on for weeks, given the extent of the charges. I can start to write anytime, but I can't finish the book until the trial is over." Writing a true-crime book required miles of legwork, piles of research, and months of writing time. There was nothing glamorous about it.*

"I see." Kelly's sigh was intended to convey his disappointment. "I guess I thought that story was all wrapped up. Especially after I heard the DA's announcement this afternoon."

So that was what was behind the phone call. Kelly figured that once the indictments were in, she would have time for *him.* She took a breath and squared her shoulders.

"We're talking about a *book,* Kelly, and I'm the logical one to write it. The investigation was mine from the get-go, and I know more about the killings than anybody, except for the cops, maybe. But there's always the possibility that somebody else —"

---

* Jessica knows this already because she's written another book. For her first big story, read China Bayles #19, *Mourning Gloria.*

"Will sneak in and steal the idea," he said curtly.

"It wouldn't be the first time an aggressive writer grabbed a juicy story from a journalist who was already on it," she replied. "As you know, I've invested a lot of time in this project already and —"

"You're right. I know. I certainly do." He cleared his throat. "So how about if I get takeout and bring it over to your place? I could leave after we eat and you could work on your proposal."

"I don't think that would be such a good idea," she said cautiously. "You know how I work. I need —"

"Yeah," he interrupted brusquely. "You need time and space. And deadlines, plenty of deadlines. Face it, Jessica. If somebody took your deadlines away from you, you'd be freaking *lost.*" He clicked off.

She stared at her cell for a moment. Why was she making this so complicated? She already knew there wasn't any future with Kelly, so there was no point in tying herself in knots over a stupid phone conversation. Next time he called, she just wouldn't pick up, damn it.

He was right about deadlines, though, she thought ruefully. She could whine about them, but she needed the structure they imposed. Without them, she felt depressed and directionless. Without them, she would get nothing done.

Thinking of deadlines, she glanced at the clock. Four-fifty-seven. She glanced through the story quickly, then typed -30- below the final paragraph, the way Hark liked it done, and emailed the file to him. As usual, she also copied it to Denise Sanger, the assistant editor, who was definitely not her favorite person. Denise took enormous pleasure in giving her a hard time.

But another deadline was history, and she could afford to reward herself with a couple of minutes of feel-good time. She stood up and glanced over the wall of her cubicle toward the editor's office, up three steps from the newsroom and with a large glass window that looked out over the two rows of cubicles. Through the window, she could see Hark running his hand through his dark, shaggy hair and scowling through nerdy black-rimmed glasses at something on his computer monitor. Whatever he was look-ing at — probably not her story, not yet — must be giving him heartburn.

It was likely another financial report, she thought with regret. She liked Hark person-ally and respected his principled stand on community journalism. She sympathized, too. Everybody on the staff knew that the *Enterprise* was in deep financial trouble. Although he usually tried to disguise his anxiety with a *what-me-worry?* grin, she knew Hark spent a lot of time wrestling with some pretty fierce alligators: the payroll, printing costs, advertising revenues, the competition. He had bet his career and a sizeable cash investment on his ability to keep a small-town newspaper alive. And it looked like he was about to lose it.

She turned back to her desk and opened her email inbox. As usual, it was a hodgepodge of press releases, solicitations, work-related emails from colleagues, reminders from Hark, and complaints from Denise. Sometimes there were comments on her blog, *Crime and Consequences,* or story tips from readers. Just keeping up with the email was a full-time job.

But Jessica didn't mind. It came with the territory. She agreed with Hark. It was important for reporters to respond to readers' queries and complaints. "The *Enterprise* is a community newspaper," he liked to say. "Emphasis on 'community.' Answer every letter, every email, no matter how wacky. Let people know they're being heard. And you never know. You might stumble into a good story."

So that's what she did. She replied to all her emails and letters. She kept an eye out for anything interesting, anything juicy, anything that might lead to a story. After all, her first acquaintance with the Angel of Death had come via an email — from Azrael himself, no less.

Today, not so much.

She replied to a reprint request, thanked Virgil for his comic valentine, and replied to somebody who was looking for a photo from a story she'd done the previous month. She forwarded a press release from Texas' medical commissioner on the alarming increase in the number of measles cases to Francine Fenner, who handled health and wellness stories. Fran was a fitness freak who ran every local marathon she could cram into her weekends. Sometimes they met in Pecan Park after work and ran the hike-and-bike trail along the river. Fran held back so Jessica could keep up.

She reached for the small stack of mail that Coralee, the mailroom manager, had left on the shelf over her desk while she was at the courthouse. Not much there, either. Three or four advertising mailers, a dues reminder from Sisters in Crime, and one square white envelope, hand-addressed to her in blue ink and postmarked in Pecan

Springs. It had no return address.

Curious, she pulled out and unfolded the single thick sheet of pretty stationery, which had ferns and tiny dried flowers embedded in one side of the paper. The letter was written on the other, plain side, in the same tidy hand as the address on the envelope. It was brief, only two short paragraphs. When she read it — and read it again, and then read it a third time — she could feel the skin prickling on her shoulders.

She frowned. Was it credible? If it was, it could lead to a big story — a shocking story with many different angles. An *interesting* story that could take her just about anywhere.

Or it could take her down a rabbit hole. You could never tell with these things.

First things first. She kept a supply of plastic zipper bags in her desk drawer. The chances of fingerprints on the letter were probably pretty remote, but she supposed it wouldn't hurt to try. Carefully, handling the letter by the corners, she inserted it into a bag and zipped the bag shut. Then she leaned over and riffled through the Rolodex on her desk. The well-thumbed cards were decorated with colored sticky tabs in pink, blue, yellow. It was her admittedly messy system for keeping track of sources, informants, and helpful people, more visual and easier to use than her phone or her computer. When she got to the Ps, she paused, flicked two more cards, and found the one she was looking for.

Porterfield, Maude, Judge. There was an office number and a private number. Maude Porterfield had retired as a justice of the peace the previous year, so it was the private number Jessica put into her cellphone. But she wasn't going to call the judge just now. She wanted to do a little research first.

"Jessica, if you have a few minutes, I have something for you to do."

Denise was standing in the doorway of Jessica's cubicle. Denise, whose main job as assistant editor was keeping reporters' fingers collectively, on their keyboards, racing to beat deadlines. And to keep Jessica, individually, from going rogue — important (as far as Denise was concerned) because Jessica spent a good part of her day out of the newsroom, at the courthouse or the cop shop, where Denise couldn't keep an eye on her.

Jessie glanced at the clock. "A two-minute-and-thirty-second job?"

Denise arched a meticulously pruned brown eyebrow and pursed her lips, carefully detailed with lip liner and filled in with a glossy peach. The other women in the newsroom (Francine, Heather, Becky, and Jessica) were content with the *au naturel* look, which sometimes meant that they'd barely had time to dab on some lipstick. Denise obviously spent hours on her makeup and hair, which she wore slicked back in a stylish chignon. And her clothes. Today she was wearing a cropped maroon jacket and a short maroon pencil skirt, with maroon heels. Next to her, Jessica felt grubby and definitely under-accessorized.

"I suppose you have a hot date," Denise said. She had not been lucky in love and harbored a deep resentment of anybody she imagined having a love life.

Jessica didn't, but she wasn't going to disillusion Denise. She closed her laptop, stood, and reached for her coat. "Well, it *is* five o'clock. On Valentine's Day."

"I suppose this will have to wait until tomorrow, then," Denise said reluctantly. "But please see me first thing."

"Oh, I will," Jessica promised. She slung her bag over her shoulder and picked up her laptop. "Happy Valentine's Day, Denise."

And then, of course, Jessica's office phone had rung again.

CHAPTER TWO

The incoming email signal dinged, and Hark Hibler left the financial spreadsheet on his computer screen — definitely not a comforting read — and clicked over to his inbox.

It was Jessica Nelson's story on the Byers grand jury indictments, just three minutes under the deadline. He scanned it quickly, deleted an extra space and a hyphen in the third paragraph, added a pair of commas to a sentence in the sixth, changed two words, and forwarded it with a note to Allan Hodge, the production manager. Allan would insert it into the layout of the print edition. It would also appear online, in the breaking news section of the digital edition.

While he tried to pretend otherwise, Hark wasn't crazy about the digital edition, which was managed by his assistant editor, Denise Sanger. At first, he'd been concerned about the extra workload involved in producing an online newspaper — but since it was a digital replica of the print edition, there wasn't much extra work involved. Still, it was expensive, and so far, it hadn't brought in enough new subscribers or advertisers to justify the cost.

That wasn't the real reason, though. Fundamentally, Hark was a print guy. His dad had been a pressman at the *Galveston Daily News,* which published its first issue back in 1842, when Texas was still an independent republic. As a kid, Hark had hung out in the pressroom the way some kids hung out at the mall. He loved the sound of the presses rolling, the intoxicating smell of freshly inked newsprint, the crisp smoothness of the off-the-press pages, and the thought that he was holding history in his hands, a present record of the soon-to-be-past, preserved for the future. Even now, a word impressed in black ink on white paper seemed to Hark to have a tactile weight that pinned it to the page, while pixels — weightless, inconsequential, easily altered or deleted — floated in cyberspace, unmoored to any kind of reality.

Sure, he worked with computers all the time. He had to. But a newspaper — a book, too — was still *print,* damn it. Digital didn't do a thing for him. He didn't understand it and didn't care to.

He glanced through the glass window that gave him a view of the newsroom below and saw Denise, hips swaying, heading to Jessica Nelson's cubicle, no doubt with a late assignment. Denise liked to use deadlines to bully people, and Hark (who had inherited her from the earlier publishers) hadn't figured out how to get her to stop doing it.

And as usual, Denise was all dolled up, as if she was in the lineup for a major runway attraction in a Parisian style show. Jessica, on the other hand, was wearing her usual work uniform: a plain khaki blazer over a yellow top and dark slacks. Sometimes the blazer was black or red or blue, and the tank top was blue or black or red. But it was almost always the same. Blazer, tank, slacks. A neat, professional look.

Hark cupped his chin in his hand and watched as Jessica exchanged a few words with Denise, then reached down to pick up the phone as Denise spun on her heel and marched off. An energetic young woman with girl-next-door freckles and boy-cut blond hair, Jessica had a quick smile that might be mistaken for flirtatious and a probing intelligence that she disguised as curiosity. But if you watched her for a while, you'd notice that her breezy casualness was at odds with the watchful resolve in her brown eyes. She was an uncompromising competitor who knew what she was after and how she intended to get it — excellent qualities in a reporter, although they might not fit very comfortably into everyday life.

Hark had hired her, so he knew Jessica's story. A journalism student at Central Texas State University, she had studied the 1966 true-crime classic *In Cold Blood* and decided she was going to be Truman Capote when she grew up. She started with the *Enterprise* as an intern and quickly distinguished herself, scoring a big story — a *national* story — when she foiled her own kidnapper and helped solve a particularly ugly murder.

With an eye on the end game, she capitalized on the national attention, got a book contract, and — just like *that* — produced *Mourning Gloria,* which CNN called one of the best true-crime books of the year. When she was asked how she could write it so quickly, she always said, "I didn't. The experience was so powerful that the story wrote itself. I was just the typist."

Which made it, in Hark's considered opinion, the best kind of story to write. A reporter who stumbled into a story like that was not very likely to screw it up.

But *Mourning Gloria* hadn't been Jessica's

first introduction to crime. Jessica's parents and twin sister had died when their house burned in the little town of Georgia Shores, about thirty miles east of Pecan Springs. A high school freshman, Jessica had been away on a school trip when it happened. The investigators called it arson and the police interviewed a handful of suspects. But no charges were ever brought and Jessica — who went to live with her grandmother in Louisiana — was left to get on with her life alone, her questions unanswered. Hark knew the permanent scars that such an incomprehensible event could inflict on a young kid. Her chances for psychological survival must have been pretty damned low. Nobody would have been surprised if she'd spun out into drugs and a wild, rollercoaster life.

But the tragedy had toughened her instead, and he had to admire her for that. When she finished her journalism degree at CTSU, he'd offered her the police-and-public-safety beat he knew she wanted. Still, he was surprised when she'd said yes. He'd figured that when she had her diploma, she would leave Pecan Springs and head for a big-city newspaper with a decent-sized newsroom and a daily brew of strong story material. And even though Jessica seemed to be content enough at the *Enterprise,* he always had the feeling that today was the day she would announce that she had taken a job at the *Dallas Morning News* or the *Houston Chronicle* and was moving to a city where there was enough crime to keep her busy.

Hark frowned. On the other hand, maybe she would hang around until she finished her book about Howard Byers, the serial killer who called himself Azrael, the Angel of Death. Hark still felt uncomfortable about that, for he had told her over and over to knock it off with that story. Denise had given her a hard time about it, too. Both of them thought she was barking up an empty tree, when there were plenty of other stories to be written.

Which reminded him of his real frustration with her. Jessie might be the best reporter in the newsroom, but she wasn't a team player, as Denise often pointed out. When Jess got the ball, she ran with it. She didn't watch the coach for signals. She played her own game, paying no attention to the game her editors wanted her to play. If she weren't so damned good, this would be a more serious matter.

But she was, so it wasn't. Until it was.

Jessica Nelson wasn't Hark's biggest

problem. That, of course, was the *Enterprise's* bottom line, and the note that was coming due at the bank. Unfortunately, it was a note that he'd already rolled over twice, along with the interest. The bank was saying a flat no to his request — no, his *plea* — for a third rollover. It had to be paid off.

He left his inbox, clicked back to the financial spreadsheet that Kate Rodriguez, the accountant, had emailed him, and tried to concentrate on the bottom line, which was more bad news. The same bad news as last month and the month before that, but worse. The *Enterprise,* for the first time in its long life, was not going to make the next payroll. And there wasn't a penny to pay that freaking note.

Hark felt a tug of despair. The *Enterprise* wasn't alone, of course. It was damned near impossible to keep a small-town newspaper afloat these days, what with competition from cable news, the internet, and better-funded newspapers in the larger nearby cities. Anybody who invested career time and (God forbid) serious money in a small newspaper was risking a swift, hard kick in the teeth.

Hark had been willing to risk it. He had left Dallas and come to Pecan Springs for the same reasons lots of people did. He needed to get away from the fast-track, big-city world, where he and his wife Caren had both been driven by their careers — his at the *Morning News,* hers at Frost Bank. He needed a quieter, slower life, with less pressure. Newspapering was in his blood, so when he came to the fork in the road and knew he had to take the less-traveled one, that's the kind of work he was looking for.

But when push came to shove, Caren couldn't bring herself to give up the bright lights of Dallas. When he took the editor's job at the *Enterprise,* he came to Pecan Springs by himself. They called it a "commuting marriage" for a few months, but that had about as much promise as a snowball in hell. The divorce happened quickly, and he reverted to the bachelor existence he'd led before he met Caren: a small apartment, takeout in front of TV, nights at the desk. He repeatedly fell in and out of love with Ruby Wilcox, dated other women occasionally, and finally decided that a single, no-drama life was preferable to dealing with somebody else's angst. The last he'd heard, Caren had married and divorced an investment banker and was now married to the owner of a big PR firm. He wished her joy and dug a little deeper into the piles on his desk.

The new job was a seismic shift, for both Hark and the *Enterprise.* The newspaper had been in the Seidensticker family since 1903, and a succession of long-lived but short-sighted Seidensticker editors had made it their mission to portray Pecan Springs as the sweetest small town in Texas. Before a story saw print, every potentially embarrassing, uncomfortable, or incriminating fact was airbrushed. Oh, there was always enough crime to fill the *Enterprise*'s weekly "Police Blotter" column, but it was usually of the entertaining goats-on-the-loose, Uncle-Joe-shooting-fireworks, escaped-python-returned-to-owner variety. Everything unsavory was scrubbed, and the newspaper's pages were full of gossip and local club news.

That wasn't the way Hark thought a newspaper ought to be run. "Cozy is comforting," he told his reporters darkly, "but not when it's a lie. The local paper has a responsibility to inform its readers of the truth. Every story has to be factual and accurate. What's more, every story has a backstory — the details nobody sees, the details nobody *wants* to see. Whether it's pretty or ugly, whether it makes us proud or makes us want to cry, it's up to us, as journalists, to get it. And print it."

As a friend, Hark was gentle and easy-going, a shy, mild-mannered man with a soft voice, rumpled dark hair, and shambling gait. As a journalist, he was fierce. He hated fake news of any kind. He believed in facts. He didn't mind devoting sections of the paper to club updates and ribbon-cuttings and homecoming-queen coronations — the bread and butter of small-town life, the schmaltzy kind of stuff that people loved to read. But as far as real news was concerned, Hark was determined that the *Enterprise* would tell it like it was, no matter whose sacred ox got gored.

So the stories Hark ran revealed the town's gritty underside. He wasn't afraid to cover the grade-changing scandal that knocked several top athletes off the high school basketball team, or the bribery at the city council, or the Medicare fraud at a local hospice. Like everywhere else, Pecan Springs had a drug problem, of course, and there were too many opioid addictions. There was domestic violence, sadly, and child abuse and, occasionally, a homicide. The Seidenstickers would have papered over these dark-side stories. They got the *Enterprise*'s full-on, no-holds-barred attention.

This dramatic change in editorial policy did not go over well with those who had a vested interest in making their little town look like the golden village at the foot of the rainbow. Members of the Pecan Springs Chamber of Commerce, for instance, or merchants in the tourist trade, along with some of the town's older citizens. For them, reality, as it so often does, felt uncomfortably edgy.

So some merchants found other places to spend their advertising dollars and some subscribers tuned into other news sources that told a more pleasant story, and all of this took place at a time when, across the country, television and the internet were delivering the news and small-town newspapers were dropping like flies. At the *Enterprise,* circulation fell off the cliff and kept on falling. And now, with the note coming due, Hark knew he had to find a savior.

The year before, he had approached several wealthy businessmen who, he thought, might understand the importance of keeping the local newspaper alive. They had turned him down flat.

He had consulted a firm that specialized in newspaper acquisitions and stock purchases, but the *Enterprise* profit margin was too small. They weren't interested. And even if they *were,* he'd be selling out to managers outside of Pecan Springs. To investors who lived in Dallas or Houston or on the East Coast. The *Austin American-Statesman,* for example, had recently been bought by Gatehouse, a massive New York holding company that owned over 140 local newspapers — except they weren't exactly local anymore. A few months after the purchase, Gatehouse merged with Gannet, which owned over 400 newspapers, and the new company began laying plans to cut the newsroom staffs.

Austin wasn't the only city where this had happened. There was New Orleans, where all 161 staffers of the *Times-Picayune* were fired when the newspaper was sold to an out-of-town buyer. And Denver, where the New York hedge fund that bought the *Denver Post* had slashed its newsroom by a third. And Chicago, where the *Tribune* was left with a $350 million debt after being acquired by a group of investment firms. Among them, the three papers had won forty Pulitzers. Forty Pulitzers! How many would they win going forward?

So to keep the *Enterprise* in Pecan Springs, Hark had concentrated on cutting expenses, making up a list of the costs he could cut. He could cut one of the print days, although reducing from three papers to two a week might alienate some subscribers. He could also drop the internet edition, which — to his mind, anyway — cost more than it was worth.

But those cuts wouldn't pay off that damned bank loan, which was barreling down on him like an EF5 tornado.

Which is where Jeff Dixon came into the picture.

That would be Jefferson Davis Dixon III, scion of the powerful Dixon political family and heir to the multinational Dixon beer and wine distributorship.

Who was interested in buying a piece of the *Enterprise* — or so he said. In fact, he had already made a preliminary offer, and Hark was supposed to meet him to talk about it.

Desperate as he was for money, Hark considered the offer a nonstarter. He had known Dixon since their days as journalism students at the University of Texas at Austin, where they worked on the staff of the *Daily Texan* and where it had quickly become evident that their styles were totally different.

Hark was a head-down-let's-get-it-done-damn-it kind of guy who bulled his way through a challenge on sheer guts and determination. Dixon (as Hark saw him) was glib and agile — slick, even. He was always looking for ways to cut corners, shortcuts that would make the job easier. But more than that (and the thing that frosted Hark the most), Dixon was a guy who had always had things easy because he'd always had the Dixon family money to paper over any little difficulties.

There weren't many little difficulties, of course. Jeff had been the star of the men's golf team, Delta Tau Delta president, and Phi Beta Kappa. He dated a couple of beautiful Alpha Phi girls and married a Texas cheerleader named (naturally) Tiffani. After college, he took control of Dixon International, which — along with his yacht and his business jet and Tiffani — should have been all the toys anybody needed to stay productively occupied.

So, Hark asked himself, why was Dixon interested in buying a stake in the *Pecan Springs Enterprise?* Why did he want to put his money into a teetering two-bit newspaper in a two-bit Texas town?

But Hark didn't need a degree in rocket science to figure that one out. Jefferson Davis Dixon was bored with the family empire and itching to acquire a newspaper, or maybe two or three, on which he could slide into the governor's mansion and beyond. Bush the Younger — George W. Bush, son of George H. W. Bush — had done it on baseball and oil and the family name. Why not newspapers and the family name? Pour enough Dixon beer and wine money onto the playing field (to mix a couple of metaphors), and anything was possible.

But however desperate Hark was for money, he had no intention of letting Dixon into the *Enterprise* wheelhouse. Nobody was going to tell him how to report the news, especially somebody with political ambitions hiding like a greedy ghost behind the curtain of newspaper ownership. If Jefferson Davis Dixon III wanted to climb on board, he would have to agree that he was a silent partner, with no participation at all in the daily life of the newspaper.

That he was not, under any circumstances, going to use the newspaper as a pawn in his political game.

And most of all, that the *Enterprise* would have only one guy's hand on the helm, one editor-in-chief in the newsroom, and one publisher charting the newspaper's course. That guy was Hark Hibler.

Which Dixon would never agree to, of course. Why should he? Playing second fiddle wouldn't get him where he wanted to go.

So no deal. That was it.

Period. Paragraph.

But as Hark returned to the spreadsheet on his computer monitor, he could see that, while the near term looked survivable (if you didn't count the freaking bank note), the long term looked pretty damned grim. There were no two ways about it. The *Enterprise* was going down for the count. It needed a cash infusion, and a big one. But without more subscribers *and* more advertisers, money might not save it.

Not even Dixon's money.

CHAPTER THREE

That late-afternoon phone call had been an unsettling surprise, and an hour later, at home, Jessica was still trying to comprehend what she had heard.

Years ago, when she was a girl, her life had been irrevocably scarred by the devastating loss of her family — her father, mother, and twin sister Ginger — in an arson fire in their little town of Georgia Shores. Jessica had been away on a school trip that weekend and had come home to a pile of smoldering ashes and a huge and awful emptiness. The police investigated, of course, but they had never found the arsonist. The case was still unsolved.

The unsettling phone call had been from Officer Walter Riley of the Georgia Shores PD. He'd said that there was a possibility that the GSPD would reopen the investigation into the fire and asked Jessica a few questions about friends of the Nelson family. And then, specifically, about boys who might have been interested in her or Ginger.

"*Interested* in us?" she asked blankly. "Ginger and I were in our first year of high school. We hadn't started dating yet."

"Well, think about it," Riley said. "I've gotten a tip and I'm looking into a new lead. I may want to talk to you again." He was obviously trying to keep his cool, but a note of excitement had crept into his voice. Still, he warned her not to get her hopes up and promised to keep her informed.

Jessica had been trembling when she hung up the phone. Losing everyone she loved in a single horrible night had created a black hole in the center of her life. It had sucked in everything bright and good and sustaining, crushed it, and left her with only lingering fears and anguished questions: *Who had done this? Why?* Her father had been a legal officer — an Army judge advocate, stationed at Fort Sam Houston, in nearby San Antonio — so the police had decided that maybe the fire had been set by somebody who had a grudge against him. It seemed the likeliest explanation, anyway. But the questions still bedeviled Jessica, almost fifteen years later.

And there was something else. Panic attacks.

Several years after the fire, in her first year

of college, Jessica had been diagnosed with a severe case of pyrophobia, a fear of fire. She could tolerate candle flames and gas burners on the kitchen stove, but a fire in the fireplace and sometimes even the smell of smoke could send her spiraling into a physical panic that seemed to get worse every time it occurred.

The doctor had explained that this was a kind of post-traumatic stress disorder. Quite understandable, really, he had reassured her, caused by what had happened to her family and probably sharpened by the strain and anxiety of going away to college. At first, it was just a sense of uneasiness and apprehension — nothing she couldn't handle by telling herself sternly that there was absolutely nothing to be uneasy about. She was strong, she was in control, nothing was going to happen. But the next few times it happened, she couldn't talk herself out of it. She grew lightheaded and dizzy and her pulse banged in her ears. Her hands grew icy. Her legs trembled. She couldn't catch her breath. She felt as if she was going to pass out.

And one night when she was still in college, that's what happened. The pizza shop next door to her apartment building had gone up in flames and everybody was evacuated. Jessica was frightened but more or less okay — until she got out on the street, saw the flames lancing up into the sky, and got a whiff of acrid smoke. Swept by panic, she couldn't catch her breath, her heart hammered erratically, and the world whirled around her. She fainted into the arms of a confused and deeply concerned boyfriend. He was even more concerned when, after he'd helped her up, she fainted a second time. The EMS crew on the scene took her to the hospital, where the doctors examined her and then sent her home. She was fine, they said.

Physically, maybe. But no, she wasn't fine. For Jessica, fainting had been a frightening experience, even more terrifying than the fire. As she came to in her boyfriend's arms, she had felt utterly helpless, vulnerable, undefended. She began visiting Dr. Pam Neely, a therapist recommended by her friend, China Bayles. Dr. Pam had suggested that Jessica write about the fire and its long-term after-effects in her journal.

"You're a writer," she'd said. "Writing about what's happened can help you come to terms with the unanswered questions. And I have some suggestions for exposure therapy, as well."

"Exposure therapy?"

Dr. Pam had smiled. "How about if we start with a fire in my fireplace and work our way up to a bonfire. I'll bet you'll have those panic attacks under control in no time."

The writing helped, and the exposure therapy, too. Jessica had persisted with both, and as Dr. Pam had predicted, things improved to the point where she could manage to be in a room with a blazing fireplace without feeling lightheaded. Even better, she could cover a fire when she had to, like the recent arson fire at Joe's Tavern, near the campus. She didn't like to do it, of course, and she was always uneasy, afraid she might be swept by one of those awful, debilitating panics. Still, the attacks had happened less frequently in the past two years, and Jessica knew she could do the job when she had to.

But today's unexpected phone call — Officer Riley's hopeful tone, the half-promise that *this* time, they would catch the arsonist and make him pay — had yanked everything back into her awareness, bringing with it a jolt of something close to panic. Her breath had come short, the blood had pounded in her ears, and she'd had to sit down abruptly.

Then the still-unanswered questions, like

sharp-pointed spear thrusts, had followed: *Who murdered her family? Why? Why, why, why?*

And another question, urgent for her as a crime reporter: What kind of lead could the police possibly have, after so much time had passed? She remembered Georgia Shores as a very small town on the western edge of Texas' Lost Pines forest. There were only a handful of police officers, most of whom spent their shifts monitoring the speed trap across from the drive-in movie theater. All she had ever heard from the GSPD was how impossible it was to solve arson cases, because the evidence was destroyed by the fire.

And now the phone call, with its hopeful half-promise.

It was unsettling. Very.

A February day in the Texas Hill Country can be sunny and pretty and warm, with crystalline skies, a benevolent breeze off the Gulf, and the red-buds offering the pink-purple promise of an early spring.

Or it can be a gloomy reprise of winter: gray and bitter cold, with a frigid wind sweeping down from the Panhandle, heavy with freezing rain, peppery sleet, or even snow. Not enough snow to be pretty, usually. Just enough to snarl traffic and make everybody testy.

Today — Valentine's Day — had been wintry, and a chilly twilight was falling over the hills when Jessica parked her silver Kia in her driveway after work. She hadn't felt safe in her condo after the night Howard Byers — the Angel of Death — had attacked and threatened to kill her. She had changed all the locks, of course, and the condo management had beefed up security.

But she couldn't lock out the pain and the bone-numbing terror that enveloped her every time she stepped through the front door and into the hall where Byers had grabbed her from behind and held a chloroformed cloth over her mouth and nose. If it hadn't been for Ruby, who was tuned into some sort of psychic messaging service that Jessica didn't understand but for which she was eternally grateful, she probably wouldn't be alive today.

That had been Halloween night, just three-and-a-half months before. By Thanksgiving, Jessica knew that she couldn't live comfortably in the condo. So she negotiated an early end to the lease, rented a small frame house in the hills on the other side of the CTSU campus, and escaped there the week before Christmas.

It felt very different. The condo had been upscale, occupied mostly by millennial singles. The houses in her new neighborhood were modest, and her new neighbors were mostly seniors or young marrieds with babies in strollers and kids on trikes. Her house was modest, too, just two bedrooms and a single bath. When it was built in the 1940s, Pecan Springs had been little more than a village on a narrow two-lane highway, halfway between Austin and San Antonio. Central Texas State had been a tiny teachers' college, and the biggest event of the year was the Fourth of July community picnic and fireworks.

All that had changed. The two-lane now was a six- to eight-lane interstate in a concrete corridor of shopping malls and business parks, called "Innovation Corridor" by the area-wide economic development council. Now, when people talked about the Corridor, they meant the fast-developing, seventy-mile area along I-35, between south Austin and north San Antonio. And the small college had morphed into a university with fifty-plus graduate programs and faculty doing far-out research in materials science, life sciences, computer science, and something called nanotechnology that Jessica couldn't get her head around.

But in spite of all this change, Jessica's new neighborhood still felt, well, neighborly. The neighbor in the tiny cottage on her left was Mrs. Robertson, a widow with two iguanas, a cockatoo, and a daughter who dropped in every few days to make sure her mom was okay. On her right, in a bigger house, lived the seven members of the Knight family: mom and dad, three adopted kids and two fosters between the ages of two and twelve, plus four hens and a rooster who felt duty-bound to wake the neighborhood at the crack of dawn. On the other side of the street lived a leather-jacketed Harley jockey, an African American math professor, and a Latina nurse who worked nights in the hospital ER. It was a neighborhood that valued diversity.

Jessica's small house had a big backyard shaded by large live oak trees and a kitchen garden in a sunny patch near the back screen door. It also had a real front porch with a real porch swing and honeysuckle growing up the trellis. Inside, there were wood floors, a red-brick fireplace in the little living room, and a pleasant sunporch off the kitchen where she could put her pathetic collection of hard-to-kill houseplants — a ragged fern, a drooping spider plant, a mother-in-law's tongue. Pets had been outlawed at the condo, but the day after she moved into her new house, she stopped at the Humane Society and was adopted by an orange tabby cat who went by the name of Murphy. She wouldn't ever forget the nightmare of Byers' violent attack, but every day in her new house brought her a little closer to something that felt almost like happiness.

This evening, on her way home from work, she had stopped at Cavette's Market (which she preferred to the huge supermarket a few blocks away) and picked up some mixed greens, a couple of tomatoes, fresh mushrooms, and an avocado. The large salad — with hot bread and olive oil dip (just oil, garlic, rosemary, thyme, and some freshly grated Parmesan cheese), as well as a cup of the chicken soup she had made the previous weekend — was a good meal for a wintry night. Not as exotic as that new Thai restaurant, of course, but since she wasn't seeing Kelly, her evening would be much less complicated.

Murphy was waiting for her at the front door. An affectionate cat, he wound himself around her ankles while she reset the alarm system — Byers' attack had taught her to take precautions — and hung up her jacket and woolly hat. She scooped him up, holding him close and rubbing her cold cheek against his warm, ginger-colored fur.

"Missed me, did you, Murph?" she crooned. He patted her cheek with a paw, rumbling a warm, welcoming purr. Murphy obviously regarded her as somebody he had rescued off the street and had to take care of. He regularly plied her with little love offerings — crunchy giant tree roaches from the yard, mice from the kitchen pantry, and even (once) a fuzzy orange sock studded with grass burrs. Heaven only knew where *that* came from.

Murphy's kibbles came first. Then she ran upstairs and changed into jeans and a sweater and turned on the gas log in the living room fireplace. She would have supper on a tray in front of the tidy gas fire, toasting her toes and watching the PBS *NewsHour* while she ate. Afterward, she would settle on the sofa with her laptop and draft the book proposal. She felt a shiver of excitement when she thought of a contract with St. Martin's, a perfect home for *Not Only in the Dark.*

Jessica had something else to do that evening, but she put it off until the *NewsHour* was over and she had finished eating.

Sitting in front of the fire, she took out the plastic bag containing the letter that had come in the day's mail and read it again. She wasn't sure how seriously she should take it, but the writer had certainly wasted no time getting to the point.

Dear Ms. Nelson,
Just about a year ago, Judge Maude Porterfield ruled that the death of Lilia Thompson was a suicide. The judge got it wrong. Lilia didn't kill herself. She was murdered. I can't tell you how I know, but believe me, I know.

You seem to have had a pretty good track record when it comes to investigating crimes. I hope you will look into this and let people know what really happened.

Sincerely,
A concerned citizen

Frowning, Jessica got up from the sofa and went to get her laptop. In the old days, journalists used the newspaper morgue and the phone book and the reverse directory to track down information. But now, the answer to any question you could think of (plus the answers to questions that hadn't yet crossed your mind) could be found online. And in the rare event that you came up totally empty-handed . . . well, that would tell you something, wouldn't it?

So Jessica fetched her laptop, and — as Murphy jumped up and inserted himself between her and the keyboard — googled Lilia Thompson. Thankfully, the woman's first name was uncommon, but why didn't it ring a bell? There weren't *that* many suicides in Pecan Springs. It would have been noted on the police blotter. Jessica would have covered the story. She should remember.

But when she found the two-paragraph story in an old issue of the *Enterprise* online, she realized why she hadn't recognized Lilia Thompson's name. The story was dated a year and a half ago and had run under Heather's byline. Jessica had been in the hospital at the time, recovering from an appendectomy. There had been complications, and it was a while before she was back on the job.

Which explained why she didn't recognize the name of Lilia Thompson, who (as she learned from the *Enterprise* story) had died from a fatal mix of zolpidem (under the brand name Ambien) and alcohol. As Concerned Citizen had written in the letter, Justice of the Peace Maude Porterfield ruled the death a suicide. Unfortunately, Heather's story was bare-bones. It offered a minimum of details, except to say that a note had been found and that the family had requested that no autopsy be performed.

There was a little more information in the brief obituary that ran a few days later. Lilia Bakke Thompson had been a librarian at the Pecan Springs Library, a member of the Myra Merryweather Herb Guild, and a volunteer at the Adams County Hospital. She had been married to Samuel Thompson, who was the principal of one of the local charter schools, and was survived by her husband and a sister, Margaret Bakke Nichols. There were no children.

Jessica glanced down at the letter and reread the second sentence. *The judge got it wrong.* If that were true, it would be a surprise. Justice of the Peace Maude Porterfield had been on the bench for over fifty years and knew everything there was to know about the law, her job, her neighbors, and Pecan Springs. Her rulings were seldom appealed and almost never overturned. If Judge Maude said it was suicide, it was suicide.

But still . . .

Jessica sat back, thinking. Adams County

operated under the Inquest Law, an old section of the Texas Code of Criminal Procedure that made justices of the peace responsible for determining the cause when a death occurred outside of a hospital. But Judge Maude was getting older, and her arthritis and her poor hearing had finally persuaded her that it was time to retire from the bench. Was Lilia Thompson's death one of her last rulings? Had the judge been entirely . . . well, on top of things? Was it possible that Concerned Citizen was right and the judge was wrong?

Jessica checked the time. It was only a few minutes after seven — not too late. And Judge Maude lived just four blocks away. There was no point in putting her question off until tomorrow if it could be asked — and answered — this evening.

What's more, the judge's phone number was already in her phone. She dialed it.

CHAPTER FOUR

Judge Maude opened the door, leaning on her cane. She wore gold-rimmed granny glasses and a hearing aid, but she was dressed in a burnt orange track suit (she was a passionate Longhorns football fan) and her crisp silver hair was done in a lacquered bouffant that reminded Jessica of Ann Richards, Texas' smart, gutsy former governor. When the judge saw Jessica, she held out her hand.

"Come in, child," she said. "It's cold as a witch's heart out there." The old lady had grown up on the high plains of the Panhandle, and her speech was flavored with a tangy West Texas drawl. "My creaky old bones say it's fixin' to freeze tonight — mebbe even snow."

"Thank you," Jessica said with a shiver, stepping into the warm house. She was thinking that the judge's old bones were correct, especially since they agreed with

Jim Spencer on KXAN, who was predicting snow tomorrow for parts of the Hill Country — unusual but not unheard of.

"And thank you for seeing me tonight," she added, as a gray Scottish terrier trotted briskly up and gave her ankles an exploratory sniff. "On short notice, too. Sorry to be a bother."

"No bother at all." The judge hung Jessica's down jacket on an old-fashioned coat tree. "Docket and I are here all by our lonesome tonight, and we're always glad for comp'ny. You've had your supper, I reckon?" When Jessica nodded, she said, "Well, then, how 'bout a cup of hot cranberry tea? I'll rustle us up a cookie or two."

Jessica had met the judge a number of times during the four years she'd been a reporter for the *Enterprise*. In fact, just the week before, they had encountered each other in the courthouse, where Judge Maude had complimented her on the outcome of her investigation into the Azrael murders.

"My kind of woman," she'd said. "You got onto that murdering sonofabitch when nobody else had any idea he was doin' what he was doin'. That took brains. And *cojones*." The judge was such an authoritative figure in Pecan Springs that nobody objected to her salty language. Not out loud, anyway.

"Tea and cookies sounds terrific," Jessica said, bending to stroke Docket's perky ears. The Scottie's full name was Rocket Docket, a term used to describe a court that had a reputation for getting the job done expeditiously. Judge Maude had handed out her rulings under a gilt-framed "Don't Mess with Texas" sign on the wall behind her bench. Her court was all business, all the time. Late filers and lazy litigants knew better than to ask for any favors.

"Well, come on, then," the judge said, heading for the kitchen. Favoring an arthritic knee, she leaned heavily on her cane. In a few moments, they were sitting at the kitchen table with a bright blue pottery teapot, a pair of matching mugs, and a plate of peanut butter cookies in front of them. On the wall above the kitchen stove, a row of copper-bottomed pans gleamed. On the window sill over the sink, pots of red geraniums bloomed cheerfully against the wintry darkness outside. Docket politely accepted a share of Jessica's cookie and took it to his wicker basket beside the pantry door, under a yellow warning sign with a silhouette of a small Scottie and a legend that cautioned "Don't trip over the guard dog."

Judge Maude poured, then set the teapot down. "Now, Jessica, tell me what brings you out on such a chilly night. Today is Valentine's Day, isn't it? Why aren't you out with your young man?" She frowned over the top of her glasses. "You *do* have a young man, don't you?"

"Not at the moment," Jessica replied. With a half-smile, she added, "I'm a reporter, you know. Which means I'm on the job twenty-four-seven. Guys seem to want more time and attention than I can manage." She bent over and picked up her shoulder bag.

The judge frowned. "There are some out there that don't. Not many, maybe, but a few. Keep your eyes open. You'll find one." She nodded at the plastic zipper bag that Jessica was taking out of her purse. "What d'you have there?"

"A letter." Jessica slid it across the table. Half-sheepishly, she added, "I bagged it to preserve any fingerprints."

"Fingerprints?" The judge gave an amused chuckle, adjusted her glasses, and held up the bag. "Pretty stationery," she said, looking at both sides. "Handmade, wouldn't you say?" She began reading the letter through the plastic, silently. When she finished, she went back and reread two sentences aloud, musing. "Lilia didn't kill herself. She was murdered."

After a moment, she pushed the letter back across the table. "Horsefeathers," she said crisply.

Jessica wasn't surprised. "Do you remember the case?"

"Of course I remember it." Judge Maude lifted her chin. "Lilia Thompson used to check out my books from the library once a week. I know Sam, too. Sam Thompson, her widower. He's everybody's idea of a real good guy. Her dyin' was a tragedy, nothing less. I'll give you that. But it sure as hell wasn't *murder.*" She put down her mug and squinted at the letter. "Who is this 'Concerned Citizen,' anyway? Some kook, I reckon. Lookin' to cause trouble."

"I don't know who it is yet, but I will." Jessica spoke with more confidence than she felt. It wasn't easy to trace a letter with no return address. "I was out when this happened and I didn't remember it, so I pulled up the *Enterprise* story. Unfortunately, there weren't many details. I also found the obituary, but it didn't tell me much more." She took out her notebook. "There was no autopsy. I wondered why."

"Well, that's easy." The judge picked up a cookie. "Lilia Thompson and her husband were both Christian Scientists. Her sister, too."

Jessica frowned. "I didn't know that Christian Scientists objected to —"

"These did. Both of the Thompsons had recently made wills, sayin' that for religious reasons, they didn't want to be autopsied. So I took the recommendation of the detective who answered poor Sam's 9-1-1 call. I ruled it a suicide. No need for an autopsy, especially seein' as how there was that will."

Jessica opened her notebook. "Okay if I make a few notes — on background," she added hastily. "I'm just trying to inform myself, since I missed this case." If the judge was speaking on background, anything she said would be paraphrased, not quoted. And she wouldn't be identified by name as a source.

"I don't know how come you're taking this letter seriously." The judge sounded peeved. "Anybody wants to be taken seriously, they should sign their name, damn it."

Jessica gave a little shrug. "I guess you could call it a reporter's curiosity. We get paid for being nosy, you know."

"Hmmph." The judge sniffed. "Well, in my opinion, Concerned Citizen is talking through his hat. And you probably won't get much out of me. My memory isn't so good these days, which is one of the reasons I stepped down." Resigned, she added, "If you want to take notes, go ahead. You might as well get it right."

"Thanks." Jessica dated her page. "So tell me what happened."

There seemed to be nothing wrong with the judge's memory. Samuel Thompson had reported that he and his wife Lilia had gone out to dinner that evening. She said she wasn't feeling well, and when they arrived back home to Saratoga Drive about eight-thirty, she went right to bed. He got in the car and drove to his office at Cedar Ridge School, to clean up some paperwork.

When he got home a little after midnight, he couldn't get into their bedroom. The door was locked from the inside, and although he knocked and then banged on it and yelled, Lilia didn't answer. He considered spending the night in the guest room, but he was worried about his wife. Their only child — a daughter — had died two years before, an accidental drowning. Lilia blamed herself, he said. She couldn't seem to get past it. She was despondent. She'd been having difficulty sleeping.

When more knocking couldn't rouse her, he got a screwdriver out of the toolbox under the kitchen sink and used it to remove the door hinges. That's when he found her, not breathing. On the bedside table, he saw a bottle of Ambien and an empty bottle of Southern Comfort — Lilia liked to drink a glass of it before she went to bed. There was a note, too. He called 9-1-1 and tried CPR, but she was unresponsive. The police and the EMS arrived at the same time. A little later, Detective Carl Foster, who had been called to the scene, phoned Judge Maude to report the unattended death. By that time, it was nearly two a.m.

"I'd just been released from the hospital," the judge said. "I'd been down for a couple of days with pneumonia, and I was still pretty doped up. Jim Crawley lives next door. He also happened to be there."

"Jim Crawley," Jessica repeated. "That would be Dr. Crawley?" He was a widely respected doctor in Pecan Springs.

"Yes. When he heard the emergency vehicles arriving, he got up and went over to the Thompson house, so he was the one who actually pronounced her dead. When Carl Foster called me, Jim came to the phone and told me that he had prescribed the Ambien when Lilia asked him to get her something to help her sleep. She had just bought a bottle of pills and it was empty, as well as a bottle of Southern Comfort. He didn't seem terribly surprised by her suicide. And she had mentioned to him that she didn't want to be autopsied. He said she seemed quite firm on the matter and thought her wishes ought to be respected."

"You know Dr. Crawley, I assume," Jessica said.

The judge nodded. "Jim and I — and his wife, Christine, too — go back a long ways. Same with Carl Foster, the detective. After Carl read me Lilia's note and gave me the details, I felt he could deal with the situation without my getting dressed and driving over there in the pouring rain. And Jim said that he thought it would be a real bad idea, seein' as how I was just out of the hospital."

The dead woman, the husband, the cop, the doc, and the judge. It sounded as if everybody knew and liked everybody else, Jessica thought. But that's how small towns operated. And as a matter of fact, while Jessica didn't know the Thompsons, she had met Dr. Crawley and liked him. She also knew the cop, Carl Foster, although she couldn't say that theirs was a very congenial acquaintance. Foster didn't like reporters. He considered them the enemy.

Jessica looked up. "The note. What did it say?"

"That, I don't remember. Not exactly, anyway." The judge's brow furrowed. "Something to the effect that she couldn't stop feeling responsible for her daughter's death."

"Handwritten? Signed?"

"No," the judge said, slowly. Another frown. "Lilia had broken a couple of bones in her right hand and it was in a cast. She couldn't write, so she typed the note. On the portable typewriter in the bedroom."

"Do you have a copy?"

"I never saw it. After Carl read it to me, he said he felt, out of respect for the woman's wishes — and her husband's standing in the community — that an autopsy was unnecessary." She glanced at Jessica. "In case you don't know him, Sam's the principal over at Cedar Ridge Charter School. Also sings in the Choral Society. Oh, and he's president of the local Kiwanis Club."

"And you agreed about the autopsy?"

"I told Carl I'd rule on it later." Judge Maude turned her mug in her fingers. "Lilia's parents are dead, but the next morning, I called her sister, Margaret, to get her feelings on the matter. She's Christian Science, too. She said she didn't want her sister autopsied. And there was the will, of course. It's pretty hard to argue with that."

Margaret Nichols. The sister, who had been named in the obituary. Jessica made a mental note to look her up. "Did *you* see the body?"

The judge shook her head. "As I said, I was still dopey from the pneumonia, even the next day. Carl said there was no need. And since Doc Crawley had been there, too, the situation seemed straightforward." She looked at Jessica over the rim of her glasses, and her voice took on some of it usual crispness. "Texas law doesn't require a JP to actually see a person's body or even to visit the scene, you know. When there's a high degree of medical certainty about the cause of death, an autopsy isn't required. All that's necessary is to file an inquest report with the date and the findings."

"Does the inquest have to be public?"

Another shake of the head. "Only when the public's interest is at stake. In the case of a violent death, for instance."

"A murder, that is."

The judge was silent a moment. Then, "Yes. A murder."

Jessica was scribbling. "And Lilia Thompson's death certificate? Do you remember how you listed the cause of death?"

"An overdose of Ambien, combined with alcohol. Pretty lethal."

Jessica looked up from her notebook. "Did you ever have second thoughts about not ordering an autopsy?"

"Nope." The judge shook her head emphatically. "And over the years, I've ordered more than my share." She pursed her lips. "Given Carl's report, Doc Crawley's information about the pills, the recent will, and the sister's feelings, an autopsy wasn't called for. I didn't think so then. I don't think so now."

Jessica considered. Was the judge's tone defensive? Yes, definitely. Maybe she didn't like it that Concerned Citizen was saying she had made a serious mistake in judgment.

Or maybe she was afraid that an accusation like this could damage her reputation. That was natural enough, wasn't it?

She had one other question. "What about life insurance? Was there a policy? Who was the beneficiary?"

The judge smiled thinly. "Can't help you there, I'm afraid. I think we're done. Don't you?" She leaned forward and pushed the plate across the table. Her smile broadened.

"Have another of my peanut butter cookies, Jessica. They're Docket's favorite, you know."

"Wow. Look at those gorgeous yellow roses," Francine said, coming into Jessica's cubicle. "From Kelly, huh? What happened? He did something that requires forgiveness? Like maybe he forgot about Valentine's Day?"

Jessica pulled off her woolly green hat and ran a quick comb through her hair, grateful for a cut that a winter hat couldn't damage.

Judge Maude's creaky old bones had accurately predicted the temperature. It was hovering around freezing and the heavy gray clouds scudding across the sky were producing a few snow flurries, with "some accumulation" predicted. Snow flurries happened once or twice each winter, but serious snow — enough snow to dismiss school, for instance — was unusual. In 1937, a blue norther had raced down from the Panhandle and dumped a record eleven inches on Austin. Ten years ago, San Antonio had gotten thirteen. In the same storm, Pecan Springs got twelve, and so many people were snow-bound that CTSU had to reschedule second-semester registration.

"Not Kelly," Jessica replied. He'd once said that sending flowers was a barbaric tradition. She glanced at the flowers, wondering. Aloud she added, "Your guess is as good as mine."

The three yellow roses in the cute red ceramic cowboy boot had been on her desk when she came in. Sherry, the perky blond intern who handled reception, said they'd been delivered by a local florist and hadn't included a note.

"Woot!" Francine rolled her eyes. "A secret admirer."

Tall, willowy, and long-legged, with a runner's body and dark hair skinned back tightly into a single thick braid, Fran was wearing a red Austin Marathon T-shirt over black jeans. She had run the marathon the previous weekend, finishing back in the pack but with the very respectable time of 4:22. Jessica had run the half-marathon once. Once was enough. Now, she stood at the finish line and cheered for Fran.

Remembering her exchange with Denise at the end of the day yesterday, Jessica glanced in the direction of the assistant editor's office, next to Hark's on the far side of the room. It was still dark, so Denise hadn't come in yet. Jessica wanted to be gone when she did.

She sat down at her desk and opened her laptop. "It's pretty silly to send somebody flowers and not include your name," she said, bringing up the Pecan Springs Police Department's website. "Why wouldn't you want the other person to know?"

She hadn't slept well after her conversation with the judge the evening before. She kept dreaming of the sentences in the letter from Concerned Citizen, like a chyron crawling across the bottom of a television screen, endlessly repeating *The judge got it wrong. Lilia didn't kill herself. She was murdered. The judge got it wrong . . .*

But if Concerned Citizen had it right, the judge wasn't the only one who got it wrong. So did the cop and the next-door doc, both of whom had been on the scene. What did Concerned know? Why was he — or she — so certain that Lilia Thompson had been murdered? Why bring it up now, after all this time? And in an anonymous letter? If you were serious about the charge, wouldn't you want to put your name on it?

The PSPD website came up and Jessica clicked on the Criminal Investigation Division tab. A few weeks before, she had heard that Carl Foster was retiring from the force after thirty-seven years of service. However, his name was still on the CID list as one of the two sergeants in the division. So either the website hadn't been updated or the big day hadn't happened yet.

But she wouldn't call to find out which it was. Her questions weren't the kind she could ask over the phone. In a face-to-face, she might surprise Detective Sergeant Foster into a straight answer or two.

"If it wasn't Kelly, who was it?" Still thinking about the flowers, Fran flicked her ponytail. "You're an investigative reporter. Investigate. Talk to the florist. Find out who he is."

"What makes you think he's a guy?" Jessica tilted her head. "I have female admirers too, you know."

Fran snorted a laugh. "Listen, Jessie, I've got a problem. Heather was supposed to come up with a piece for the next issue of the magazine, but she called in sick this morning. She says she'll be out for at least a week, maybe more. I'm remembering that you interviewed David Redfern last week. Could we use that interview instead of Heather's story?"

"Heather's out for a whole *week*?" Jessica shook her head. "That girl must be on her deathbed. She's never missed a day on the job."

"Doctor's orders," Fran said. "She's contagious. She should have stayed home yesterday, but she was afraid it might be a black mark on her record. She was the last one hired in the newsroom, and she knows she's at the top of Hark's first-to-be-fired list." She regarded me. "So you're okay with my using the Redfern interview? He volunteers a day a week for Big Brothers, I understand. That's a big plus in his favor. And by all reports, he's a terrific lawyer. He's been here a year and we haven't done anything on him."

Jessica frowned. "That interview was a backgrounder for my book, but I don't think Redfern will object to using pieces of it for the magazine. I'll have to cover some additional territory with him, though. He's also on the board of the animal shelter and the Family Violence Center. We'll need an intro and a wrap-up. And photos."

"And his family," Francine said. "Get something on that. Is he married? Kids? Do we want a family photo?"

"I don't think he's married. I didn't see a wedding ring." Jessica grinned. "And I looked."

Fran grinned back. "I'll bet you did.

Could you check with him now? I can send Virgil over to get the photos this afternoon. My deadline is five tomorrow, so I'll need whatever you've got by three. Fifteen hundred words."

"Works for me." Jessica glanced up at the clock. "I'll check with Redfern later. I need to go over to the cop shop first thing." But there was something else. "What was it you said about Heather being on Hark's first-to-be-fired list? What's that about?"

Fran put her hands on her waist, inhaled, and dove into one of her favorite yoga poses, a forward fold. She bent over from the waist and dropped her head until her nose was almost touching her knees in what looked to Jessica like an impossible bend. *She* couldn't do it, anyway.

Fran's voice was muffled. "You haven't heard about the list?" She dropped her hands until her palms were flat on the floor beside her feet.

"If I'd heard about it, I wouldn't be asking you, would I?" Jessica knew that her failure to do a halfway decent forward fold was no measure of her worth, but there it was. Francine could do it and she couldn't. "So what's this about Heather being the first to get fired?"

There was a moment's silence while Francine contemplated her knees. Then she raised her torso until it was horizontal, lifted her head, and looked at Jessica. "The *Enterprise* is in trouble. Hark has to make some cuts."

"Your shoulders aren't straight," Jessica said critically. "And this isn't news. The *Enterprise* was in trouble last month. And six months ago. And six months before that."

Which didn't mean it wasn't true, of course. The leaky roof that was giving the business office fits still hadn't been repaired. There had been an Out of Service sign on the elevator for the better part of a year, forcing everybody to take the stairs. And when the refrigerator in the break room conked out and the staff asked Hark for a new one, he turned them down. The one they were using now was on loan from Virgil's sister.

"I know it's not news." Fran straightened her shoulders. "But this time, the paper's in *real* trouble. Ethel told me. Hark has already made a list of people he plans to fire. Heather heard that her name's at the top."

Jessica looped the lanyard of her press credentials around her neck. "Ethel's mouth has a big problem." She reached for her down jacket. "It flaps. Constantly."

Ethel Fritz had worked in the *Enterprise* business office since she graduated high school some thirty years before. She viewed the newspaper as her second home, and the chief asset she brought to her job was her intimate knowledge of native Pecan Springers. She knew their family trees, all their in-laws and outlaws and secret sins and vices — a storehouse of bare-boned fact and juicy rumor. Jessica hated to admit it, but she often consulted Ethel for deep background when she was working on a local news story.

But anybody who went to Ethel for information had to remember that she lacked what sports editor Will Wagner called the "bullshit filter." Anything (well, almost anything) she heard, she believed. And anything she believed, she considered worth passing on. What's more, she thought it was her *duty* to pass it on.

Fran straightened her torso, raised her arms to shoulder height, and swung them to the left, holding her hips in place. "You're right. You have to take everything Ethel tells you with a grain of salt. But this time, it's the truth, Jessie."

"Really?" Jessica was skeptical.

"Yes, really. The accountant sent Ethel a copy of the same spreadsheet Hark got yesterday. It was bad news. *Really* bad news.

90

Unless Hark can come up with some money somewhere, it looks like we won't get paid this month." She bent over again. "I can't afford to miss a paycheck. Can you?"

Jessica felt a niggle of worry. She knew that circulation and advertising were both down, but wasn't it like that for newspapers everywhere? It was also a bad year for journalists — layoffs were higher than at any time since the 2009 recession. If the *Enterprise* went belly-up, it would be damned tough for the journalists in the newsroom to get another job.

Jessica forced herself to smile. "Well, I refuse to worry until I have to," she said, zipping up her jacket. She had learned a long time ago that it wasn't worth worrying about things that *might* happen, when things that had already happened or looked like they were definitely going to happen required her full attention.

She wrapped her green scarf around her neck. "Hey, Fran, do you happen to remember a woman named Lilia Thompson?"

Fran dropped her arms. "You're talking about the woman who killed herself?"

"Yep. That one. About a year and a half ago, when I was in the hospital with that appendectomy. Heather covered the story. Sort of."

"Lilia worked at the library, didn't she? My mother knew her mother. She said she was very surprised. About the suicide, I mean."

"She who?" Jessica frowned. "Lilia's mother?"

"No. My mother. She used to see Lilia at the library every time she went — and my mother goes to the library a *lot*. She said Lilia was always a very cheerful person. Plus, she was all excited about a volunteer project at the Merryweather House — you know, the herb guild's house. Mom said she didn't understand how somebody could kill herself when she was managing a big garden project and had people depending on her."

That's the thing about Pecan Springs, Jessica thought. Everybody knew everybody else. And sometimes someone knew something relevant, like the fact that Lilia Thompson had been involved in a big project.

A light came on in Denise's office, and Jessica picked up her shoulder bag. Time to get out, before Denise came looking for her. "I'm going over to the police station," she said. "And then I'll talk to Redfern."

She would talk to China Bayles, too. China owned an herb shop and belonged to the herb guild. If Lilia Thompson was a volunteer at the Merryweather House, China would have known her. And while she was visiting with China, she would drop in on Ruby, at the Crystal Cave, next door. Jessica had never been much of a believer in psychic phenomena, but Ruby's unusual gift had been undeniably helpful in the Azrael investigation.

Maybe Ruby would have an idea about how Lilia Thompson had died.

CHAPTER SIX

No two ways about it, it was *cold.* Stinging ice pelted Jessica's face, and the wind whipped around her jeans-clad legs and suede boots. She pulled her wool cap down over her ears as she left the Enterprise building and crossed Alamo Street. The Pecan Springs Police Department was only a block away on West San Marcos Street, where it shared an asphalt parking lot and a brick-and-glass building with City Hall and the municipal court. The county courthouse was another block away on the square, so on any given workday, Jessica could find herself trekking from the newsroom to the courthouse to the police station and back again half-a-dozen times. She was some-times tempted to rent a scooter.

But the idea of a scooter wasn't very invit-ing today, with the street glazed with ice. Picking her way cautiously, she crossed the parking lot, went into the police station the back way, and walked down a short hall lined with photographs of cops and first responders receiving medals for doing brave things.

At the information desk, she unzipped her jacket and held up her press credentials to the young officer, whom she knew. She knew most of the cops on the force, actually, and had good working relations with all but a few.

"Hey, Dale," she said. "I'd like to see Detective Sergeant Foster."

Dale was tall and thin, his dark hair regulation-cut and carefully slicked down. He was growing a moustache. "You sure about that, Jess? Today's kind of a bad day back there."

She smiled. "Thanks. But yes, I'm sure."

"Don't say I didn't warn you." He scribbled her name on a pass and handed it to her. "Guess you know the way."

If there had been a problem in the Criminal Investigation Division that morning, there was no sign of it now. The room — a modest-sized windowless bullpen just large enough to include five desks and chairs, a couple of tables, and a whiteboard — was empty except for two men.

One, Ethan Connors, in shirtsleeves, sat staring into his computer monitor. He looked up and smiled and Jessica smiled back. Connors and Ruby Wilcox had come to her rescue when Howard Byers had her pinned to her bed and was trying to kill her. He had led the investigation that picked up where Jessica's own investigation had left off and built the case that concluded with yesterday's indictments. He would be testifying at Byers' trial. And he and Ruby were seeing one another pretty seriously. Jessica was glad. Ruby hadn't been lucky in love. Maybe this detective would change that.

The other man was older, in his sixties, and nearly bald, with a barrel-like torso and the thick neck and forearms of a wrestler. The sleeves of his white shirt were rolled up and his tie was loose. He was leafing through a stack of paperwork on his desk.

Jessica swallowed. She wouldn't have admitted it, but she was a little afraid of this guy. "Good morning, Detective Foster," she said brightly. "I'm working on a story and I hope you can help."

Looking as if his breakfast hadn't agreed with him, Foster glanced up from the papers. "What story?" he growled.

Jessica sighed to herself. Foster wasn't going to make it easy. "Judge Porterfield suggested I talk to you." Not strictly true, but close enough. "About the death of Lilia

Thompson."

"Ancient history." He went back to riffling the papers. "Suicide. Sleeping pills and alcohol, as I remember. Happened a couple of years ago, maybe three."

"A year-and-a-half ago."

He glanced up sharply. "Okay, so a year-and-a-half. Doc Crawley was there, neighbor from next door. Mrs. Crawley was there, too, half-hysterical — she was a friend of Mrs. Thompson. When the EMS boys showed up, it was a real crowd scene. Not to be disrespectful, but the judge is an old lady, and she was just home from the hospital. I didn't think she needed to drag herself out of a sickbed and drive over just to look at the body." He straightened. "So what else you want to know?"

Jessica took out the plastic zipper bag containing Concerned Citizen's letter. "I received this yesterday." She put it in front of him. "The writer says it wasn't suicide."

He read the letter and shrugged. "Garbage. Somebody looking to get his fifteen minutes of fame. No story here. Keep your nose out of police business."

Taking the bag back, she said, controlling her voice, "If you still have Ms. Thompson's suicide note, I'd like to see it."

He shook his head. "Case closed. Once

the judge ruled, that was it. Ask her. She's got a copy."

"Judge Porterfield never saw the note. She never saw the woman's body, either, or spoke to the husband." Despite her efforts, her voice rose, trembling a little. "She ruled it a suicide on your say-so."

Foster's bald head came up sharply. His eyes were narrowed and flinty. "Don't you take that tone with me, missy. The judge ruled suicide because she decided it was suicide. End of story. And ancient history, way I said."

Jessica wasn't about to be bullied. That Foster was adamant about this proved something, didn't it?

"There was no autopsy, either," she said flatly. Do you remember why you recommended to the judge that she not order —"

Foster stood up suddenly, pushing his chair back with such force that it hit the wall with a loud bang. "Because the dead woman had a will that said no autopsy, that's why! And I'm busy, so you go on back to your newspaper and let the dead rest in peace." He slapped the desk with the flat of his hand.

At the other end of the room, Ethan Connors looked in their direction. But Jessica persisted. "Under the circumstances,

Detective, don't you think an autopsy would have been —"

"I said I'm *busy*," Foster roared. He was leaning on his desk on the palms of his hands, his head lowered like a bull getting ready to charge. "You just trot right on out that door, young lady, before I —"

"Maybe I can help."

Connors' voice was cool and even. His dark hair was a little long for a cop, but he was wearing a businesslike shoulder holster under his left arm and a badge clip and handcuff on his belt. His face was craggy, his eyes ice-blue and steady. It was true that he had been a lifesaver when Byers attacked her and Jessica was grateful. But she wasn't going to let that affects what was going on here.

She turned to give him a straight, hard look.

"I doubt it," she said deliberately. "Unless you can tell me why an unattended death that could have been either a suicide or something else didn't have a JP's eyes on it, or an investigation, or an autopsy. On top of which, the suicide note was typewritten. Glad to hear your ideas, Detective."

Connors' glance shifted to Foster, and one eyebrow went up. In answer to the unspoken question, Foster raised both hands and let them fall. His face was red, but when he spoke, his voice was less harsh.

"Just one of those things, Connors. I've known the husband for years — from Kiwanis and his school. That's where my grandkids go. The doc lives next door, Doc Crawley. He gave Ms. Thompson her Ambien prescription, which she refilled at Walgreen's the day before. Most of the pills were missing, and she'd drunk a good half bottle of Southern Comfort. No monkey business. Guy loses the woman he's lived with for fifteen years. There's a doc handy and the JP is just out of the hospital with pneumonia, not to mention it's raining like a son of a bitch. Suicide, plain and simple. We had a good look at the scene, got photographs and everything. No need to complicate it further. Everything's cool."

He directed a malevolent glance at Jessica. "Everything's cool," he repeated, and sat back down. "Now, get her out of here. I got work to do."

Connors regarded him thoughtfully. After a moment, he took Jessica's elbow. "Come on. I'll walk you out."

She wasn't ready to go, but she could see that she wasn't going to get anything out of Foster. They went out into the hall.

"I'm sorry," Connors said. "Foster's had a

100

bad day."

"Already?" Jessica asked sarcastically. "It can't be more than a few minutes past nine."

"Sometimes bad stuff kinda jams up in the morning. The captain reamed him out for something he couldn't help and there wasn't much he could say besides *yessir*." He paused. "How about letting me see that letter."

She frowned. "Why?"

He gave her a crooked grin. "Based on what I know of your work on the Byers case, I'm thinking you intend to investigate the Thompson suicide. I'd like to make sure that you don't get yourself into the kind of trouble you did with your Angel of Death." That eyebrow went up again. "Remember?"

She lifted her chin, refusing to take the bait. "*My* Angel of Death?"

"Whatever." Connors' lips twitched. He held out his hand. "The letter."

Reluctantly, she took out the plastic bag. When he raised an eyebrow, she muttered, "I thought it might have fingerprints."

"A possibility," he said mildly. He read the letter and handed it back. "What have you turned up so far?"

"I talked to Judge Maude last night." Jessica kept her expression neutral. "Next up, I'm ordering a copy of Lilia's death certificate and talking to somebody who knew her."

"The husband? Relatives?"

"A sister." She had searched for Margaret Nichols on the internet before she went to bed last night, but without success. "I'm putting the husband off for now."

"Yeah? Well, he sounds like a reputable guy," Connors said evenly, with no sarcasm in his voice. His eyes met hers. "School principal, Kiwanis, etcetera. Sure you don't want to talk to him up front? Get his side of the story?"

"I'm sure," she said, just as evenly. She was thinking: The husband's usually guilty. Isn't that what they say? Foster could have intentionally looked past Sam Thompson because he was a fellow Kiwanian and the principal of his grandkids' school. Connors could be discounting him because he's a "reputable guy." The old boys' network doing what old boys do best.

She looked down at the letter in her hand. "I'd also like to find out who wrote this and why. Unfortunately, there was no return address." She was suddenly conscious that she hadn't been properly grateful for Connors' intervention a few minutes before. She straightened her shoulders.

"Thanks," she added. "If you hadn't

stepped in, I might have . . . well, said something. I don't like being bullied."

He regarded her thoughtfully. "Foster is retiring at the end of the week. If you've got a question a cop can answer, try me. I'm available."

"I'll do it," she said. Then, thinking quickly: "Foster mentioned photographs. Do you suppose you could round them up for me?"

"I can try," he said. "I'll give you a call and let you know." He smiled. "I admire your work on the Byers case, Jessica. You've got a sharp eye. You know what you're looking for. Far as I'm concerned, it's good that you're interested in this. Deal me in if you pick up anything significant. Okay?"

She nodded. And she would, once she got all her ducks lined up and understood what was going on here.

But for now, there was no reason to get the cops involved. For now, it was her story.

Her story.

CHAPTER SEVEN

The wind was still cold but the ice pellets had stopped coming down, so Jessica decided to walk to China Bayles' herb shop, Thyme and Seasons, a couple of blocks off the square. Her route took her past the courthouse, where she put in a request for Lilia Thompson's death certificate, which the clerk said she could pick up in a couple of hours.

And then, since she would be going right past the law offices of Lipman and Redfern, she decided that a drop-in would be as quick as a phone call. She could get Fran's question about the magazine interview out of the way. But if there was another reason for wanting to see David Redfern, she put it out of her mind quickly, remembering that he was dating Dr. Morgan, who had absolutely everything — glamour, a great body, a sharp intelligence, and a going-somewhere career. There was no point in thinking of

David Redfern as anything more than a source for the legal chapters of *Not Only in the Dark* — chapters that would trace out the whys and wherefores of Byers' defense, assuming he didn't plead. Anything else was out of the question, anyway, because journalists weren't supposed to go out with their sources. Jessica knew that there weren't many hard-and-fast rules in the reporting business, but that was one of them.

It was still early and there was nobody at the reception desk, so Jessica went down the hall to Redfern's office and rapped on his open door. He looked up from his computer keyboard and peered at her through black-framed glasses.

"You're out on a cold morning, Ms. Nelson," he said. The glasses made him look like Gregory Peck in that old movie, *To Kill a Mockingbird.* They set off his dark hair and eyes and softened his face, which featured sharp planes, a cleft chin, and a strong jaw. "Take off your coat and sit down. Can I get you some coffee? Hot tea, maybe?"

"Thanks." Jessica sat down on the edge of the chair, pulling off her hat but keeping her coat on. She stuffed her gloves in a pocket, suddenly aware of her own heartbeat. Really, the guy was just too sexy. "I'll only take a minute of your time," she said, and quickly outlined her request. "The magazine piece is likely to go a full page. We'd like to feature your volunteer work — Big Brother, the Family Violence Center, the animal shelter."

"Sounds good," Redfern said approvingly. "Thanks for putting in a word for me. I appreciate it."

"Actually, I didn't," Jessica said. "It was Fran's idea — she's the editor." She added, "I'll also need something about your life outside of the office and community work. Girlfriend, hobbies, dogs, cats, goldfish, whatever. We can cover that on the phone later today or tomorrow. Oh, and Fran would like to send a photographer this afternoon. That's Virgil. He'll be quick."

He smiled. "I'm always glad to talk about the volunteer work, but I'm afraid there's not much of a life otherwise. No girlfriend, no kids." Crinkles appeared at the corners of his eyes. "But I do have an aquarium full of fish, which is sort of a hobby, I guess. And a monitor lizard named Darwin. He likes to have his picture taken. He'd be glad to pose for Virgil."

No girlfriend? Jessica blinked. What happened to Dr. Morgan?

"That's great," she blurted, and then, thinking how that might sound, added, hurriedly. "I mean, about Darwin. And the fish. People like to read about pets, especially weird ones." She could feel herself flushing. "Not that Darwin is weird. A lizard is just . . . well, different."

"That's Darwin, for sure. He's different." He laughed, and heart-stopping dimples suddenly appeared. "Did the flowers get there okay?"

"The flowers?" Jessica blinked again. *He didn't mean . . . he couldn't . . .* She tried to control her voice. "The yellow roses? In the cowgirl boot? You mean, those are from *you*?"

He nodded. "I enjoyed our earlier interview and felt that you were making a serious effort to inform yourself about Howard Byers' defense." His gray eyes darkened. "I appreciate how hard it will be for you to write about the trial in your book, given what is said to have happened in your apartment. I just wanted to say . . . well, thank you." He frowned. "The florist didn't include the card?"

She shook her head mutely. David Redfern had sent her flowers. Which meant that he must —

Feeling the muscles tighten in her midriff, she stopped herself. No, she told herself sternly. It did *not* mean that he was interested in her. Of course not.

It meant that he knew he could be facing a tough trial, and he was angling for favorable coverage in her book. Her flush deepened. And the magazine piece — he must think she had arranged it in return for the flowers! His little investment was already paying off.

But this man was a lawyer, for Pete's sake. Didn't he know that, as a journalist, she couldn't accept a gift from a source? Doing so might compromise her objectivity. And if it didn't, there was always the question of optics — what somebody might think about such a transaction. Even something as innocent and inconsequential as a drink or dinner or tickets to a concert could be construed as quid pro quo. It could open a reporter to charges of bias.

She forced a bleak smile. "Thank you for the flowers, Mr. Redfern. They're lovely. But if I had known they came from you, I would have returned them. Journalists can't accept gifts from subjects of their reporting. The flowers won't make any difference in what I write about you or about the trial."

There was a moment's silence. Then, "Of course they won't," he said. "You're a professional. If I've seemed to suggest otherwise, I do apologize. I saw that boot in the florist's window and ordered the flowers on impulse. I only wanted to —"

"And thank you for taking the time to see me this morning." She pushed her chair back and stood. "I think, instead of phoning, it would be better if I emailed my questions. I won't need your answers until tomorrow morning, when I'll be working on the story."

"Damn," he muttered. He stood too, his mouth tightening. "Jessica — Ms. Nelson — please don't misunderstand me. I sent you the flowers out of admiration for your *courage*. It had nothing at all to do with anything you might write or say about —"

"Thanks again, Mr. Redfern." She pulled her gloves out of her pocket. "I'll donate the flowers to the children's wing at the hospital. I'm sure they'll be glad to have them."

Chapter Eight

China Bayles' Thyme and Seasons was only a couple of blocks down Crockett, not far from the law office of Lipman and Redfern. Head down and gloved hands in pockets, Jessica walked the distance quickly, glad for the wind that pushed icy fingers down the back of her neck. It helped to cool off some of her heated annoyance at what had just happened. Even so, there was plenty left.

David Redfern claimed to have sent her flowers out of admiration for her courage?

Really?

Oh, come on. That made no sense at all. She was the one who was responsible for his client's arrest and indictment. If it weren't for her, Howard Byers would still be a free man and the Angel of Death a dark, deadly secret. And it wasn't just the book, either. She would be a witness for the prosecution and David Redfern would be cross examining her. The man knew exactly what he was doing. The flowers were intended to influence the way she spoke and wrote about the Azrael case. And what made it even more insulting was his idea that she would be stupid enough to accept his little bribe — or foolish enough to be flattered by his attention.

"Grrrr," she muttered. And the rough sound felt so good in her throat that she raised her head and announced to the wind, "I'm no idiot, Redfern. You're not fooling me."

She was still muttering to herself when she opened the door and stepped into Thyme and Seasons. The shop bell tinkled overhead and she was immediately enveloped by the warm and pleasantly fragrant air, spiced with cinnamon and cloves and the faint scent of orange. Jessica loved coming here. The two shops — the herb shop and Ruby Wilcox's Crystal Cave, as well as the tea room and Lori Lowry's textile studio in the loft — were her very favorite places, quiet retreats from the hectic *Enterprise* newsroom. The building itself, constructed of square-cut limestone blocks in the style of Pecan Springs' German settlers, was well over a century old. The floor was polished pine, the ceiling was old-fashioned pressed tin, and the windows were tall and narrow.

The shop was crowded with shelves and racks and attractive displays of herb products. Dried flower wreaths and swags decorated the old stone walls.

China had opened the herb shop after leaving a successful career as a criminal defense attorney in Houston. A few years later, she and Ruby Wilcox opened the tea room — Thyme for Tea — at the back of the building, as well as a catering service called Party Thyme. With Cass Wilde, they also owned The Thyme Gourmet, a meal-delivery business that served working people who were too busy to cook for themselves but too health-conscious to eat out every night. Jessica admired the team's can-do spirit — and their stamina. China often said that running their businesses was like managing a three-ring circus and a zoo full of wild animals, but nothing seemed to faze them.

At the sound of the bell, China poked her head around a shelf with a glass jar of cinnamon sticks in her hands. "Oh, hi, Jessica," she said with a wide smile. "What brings you out on such a cold morning?"

"I need your help with something," Jessica said. "Do you have a few minutes?"

China put the jar back on the shelf. "Sure thing. Take off your jacket and hang out for a while. You're my first customer. Everybody else is staying home where it's warm."

China was in her forties, with a pleasant face, steady gray eyes, and straight brown hair cut short and streaked with a wide swath of gray down the left side. She was wearing jeans and her usual green Thyme and Seasons T-shirt, topped with a woolly green cardigan sweater with big pockets. Jessica couldn't remember ever seeing her in a skirt. In fact, she had once heard China say that she felt as if she was cross-dressing when she wore something with a ruffle.

Unzipping her jacket, Jessica hung it on a hook beside the open door to the Crystal Cave. The lights were on over there and she could hear the haunting melody of Celtic flute music that Ruby loved to play. But the shop seemed to be empty.

"When will Ruby be in?" she asked, thinking that it might be better if she could talk to both China and Ruby together.

"Not today, I'm afraid. She left yesterday for Dallas. She's giving a talk at the Texas Business Women's conference. I'm keeping an eye on the Cave until she gets back. Not that there'll be much traffic," she added. "With this storm."

"Sorry I missed her," Jessica said. "Will she be home this evening?"

"Nope. She's staying with friends in Fort Worth over the weekend. Won't be back until Monday." China gestured to a slow cooker on a table against the back wall. Beside it were a plate of cookies and several colorful mugs. "Help yourself to some mulled cider and some cookies and come and sit with me at the counter. We can talk there — I don't think we'll be interrupted."

Jessica picked up a blue-and-red pottery mug and ladled it full of cider, sniffing deeply of the cloves-and-cinnamon fragrance. She put several cookies on a plate and carried it to the cash register counter, where China was perched on a stool. Jessica sat down on the other stool and put the plate on the counter between them.

"I'm glad you came in this morning, Jessica." China pulled her sweater closer around her. "I've been wanting to ask you about something. McQuaid tells me that the *Enterprise* is in trouble." Mike McQuaid — a former Houston homicide detective, now a private investigator — was China's husband. "Financial trouble, I mean," she added, a serious expression on her face. "He heard from one of his clients that Hark wants to sell. Is that true?"

"I don't think Hark *wants* to sell," Jessica said, sipping her cider. She was remembering what Fran had said that morning, and the niggling feeling of worry returned to tighten her stomach muscles. If the *Enterprise* went under, she'd lose her job. And Pecan Springs would lose something very important. "As I understand it, he's looking for money to keep the newspaper going. If he can get it any other way, that's what he'll do."

"But if he's forced to sell?" China asked quietly. "What happens then?"

Jessica made a face. China was a business owner and understood that sometimes you needed outside cash to keep a business going. If you couldn't borrow it — well, there weren't many other options. Especially if your business was a small newspaper. Especially these days.

"Let's hope it doesn't come to that," she said. "But Hark hasn't talked to us about it — to the newsroom staff I mean. I suppose he's hoping to get things resolved before he has to break the news, whatever it is. But I'm afraid that's it, China. I don't have any more information."

China looked troubled. "I just wish more people understood how important the *Enterprise* is to Pecan Springs. Hark has brought it up to date and made it relevant — a real community newspaper. If it folds or is bought by an out-of-town holding company that doesn't give two hoots about the local community, we'll never be able to replace it." She shook her head. "Sorry. I'm ranting. And I'm preaching to the choir. You said you needed help. What's up?"

"I wanted to ask you whether you know someone who died a while back. A woman named Thompson. Lilia Thompson. I've heard that she was involved with the herb guild here in town." Jessica took a bite of cookie and felt it immediately warm her mouth. "Wow," she said. "Cool! No, hot, I mean." She swallowed. "Not too hot, though. Delicious. What *is* it?"

"Ruby calls them Hot Lips Cookie Crisps," China said. "A plain vanilla sugar cookie with a habanero pepper kick." Her face darkened. "And yes, I knew Lilia. We were working on a wildflower project when she died. Losing her was a tragedy."

At that moment, Khat, China's elegant Siamese shop cat, paused in the door to Ruby's shop and gave an inquiring *mrrrow*. A moment later, he was rubbing against the leg of Jessica's stool.

"Hello, Khat," Jessica said, bending down to pick him up. Ruby had named him Khat K'o-Kung, after her favorite fictional cat in the Cat Who mysteries. Stroking his charcoal-colored ears, she went on. "I don't know much about Lilia Thompson's death. What can you tell me?"

"Not a whole lot, actually," China said. "I only know what I read in the *Enterprise,* plus the rumors that were floating around town at the time. I understand that she killed herself — alcohol and Ambien." She frowned. "I only knew Lilia through the herb guild, but I have to say that was hard for me to believe. She was always cheerful, rarely depressed. Not in a million years would I have guessed that she might commit suicide." She picked up a cookie and nibbled at one edge. "Your question didn't come out of the wild blue, Jessie. Why are you asking?"

With a loud, throaty purr, Khat rubbed his head in the crook of Jessica's arm, indulging in the scent of her cat, Murphy. Still holding him close, she reached into her shoulder bag and pulled out the letter in its plastic bag. She slid it across the counter.

"This is why. It came to me yesterday, at the office."

As Jessica cuddled Khat, China leaned on her elbows, reading. After a moment she said, "Wowza," very softly. "Imagine Judge Maude making a *mistake.*" She looked up. "Have you talked to her about this?"

117

"I saw her last night," Jessica said. "She told me that Sam Thompson telephoned 9-1-1 when he found his wife unresponsive, sometime after midnight. The EMS came, and a detective named Carl Foster and a neighbor, Doctor Crawley — the doctor who prescribed the Ambien. Judge Maude had just gotten out of the hospital after a bout with pneumonia. Foster called her at home, described the circumstances and read her the suicide note, which was typed. He recommended that she rule the death a suicide. She didn't see the body, or the note. And she didn't require an autopsy."

China's eyebrows went up. "A *typed* suicide note — and no autopsy?" She seemed genuinely surprised. "That's not like Judge Maude. She must have been pretty sick."

Jessica nodded. "Detective Foster told the judge that Thompson had injured her hand and couldn't write — that's why the note was typed. I haven't seen it and I'm not sure I will. Foster isn't very cooperative. As for the autopsy, the judge said that Lilia and her husband had both executed wills stating that they didn't want to be autopsied. Judge Maude ruled on the strength of Foster's recommendation, the doc's say-so, and Lilia's will."

"Ah." China looked troubled. "Foster isn't cooperating? You've talked to him?"

"This morning. It turns out that he and Sam Thompson are friends." Jessica smiled crookedly. " 'No story here' is a direct quote. He told me to keep my nose out of police business."

Khat decided that he'd had enough lap time. He jumped onto the counter, walked to the end, and stationed himself so that he could look out onto the street, where the snow was beginning to fall in earnest.

"Keep your nose out," China repeated wryly. "The old boys' network in action." She looked down at the letter again. "Too bad Ruby isn't here," she said, flipping the plastic zipper bag and glancing at the other side of the letter. "She could channel the writer's identity for us. A name and a phone number, plus maybe an email address." She added. "I'm not being snarky, either."

"Actually," Jessica confessed, "I was thinking the same thing. I know she always says that her gift isn't very reliable, but if it hadn't been for her, I might not —"

"Hey," China said abruptly. She was looking at the reverse side of the letter. "Hang on a sec."

She got up from her stool, walked across the room to a shelf, and came back to the counter with a small cardboard box. Opening it, she pulled out a thick sheet of stationery embedded with bits of dried flowers and herbs. "We might not need Ruby." She handed the paper to Jessica. "To put it a different way, we can channel some bits of info ourselves."

With a disbelieving gasp, Jessica took it. "It's the very same paper, China! Where did you *get* this?"

"It's handcrafted," China said. "It's made by a paper artist who lives south of town, near Gruene, on the river. Maggie — the papermaker — was in one of my workshops a couple of years ago, and she fell in love with the craft. Last fall, she created her own business, the WildTexas Paper Company, she calls it. She has a very nice line of notecards, stationery, invitations, giftwrap, drink coasters, and other paper goods. It's all handcrafted from plant materials she gathers around her studio." She pointed. "Look — you can see bits of bluebonnet and bee balm petals, and some rosemary and sage. And here are a few tiny fern fronds. Maggie has also done some really interesting collage work. She's becoming quite an artist."

"Wait." Jessica held up her hand, feeling the hope rising inside her. "You're saying that Concerned Citizen — the person who

120

wrote this letter — may have bought this handmade paper right here in your shop? Can you tell me who?"

"Afraid not," China said ruefully. She held up the box. "I had a dozen of these to start with, and I ordered another dozen. This is the last one from the second order. I might be able to name three or four of the people who bought this, but not everybody. And I'm sure Maggie sells her work in other shops, in other towns."

"But she might know *something* that would help," Jessica said. "I'd like to talk to her. Do you have her address? Phone number?"

"Hang on," China replied, and pulled out her cellphone. After a moment, she said, "Yes. I'll write them down for you." She picked up a scrap of paper, scribbled fast, then pushed it across the counter. "Here."

"Maggie Nichols, WildTexas Papers," Jessica read, and then the phone number. She sucked in her breath. Shocked, she repeated, "Maggie *Nichols*? China, Lilia had a sister named Nichols. Margaret Nichols!"

China's eyes widened. "Really? Omigosh. You're saying that the woman who made this stationery is Lilia Thompson's *sister*? I had no idea!" She stopped, her eyes fixed on Jessica. "Are you thinking that Maggie wrote this letter?"

"It's too big a coincidence to ignore," Jessica said. "I was going to interview her anyway." She paused. "Look. You know this woman and I don't. Would you go with me?"

China frowned. "When?"

"Now," Jessica said without hesitation. "This morning. Before the day gets any older. This might be an important story, China. I don't want to put it on hold."

"Sorry." China shook her head regretfully. "I wish I could help, but I'm here by myself — and I'm watching Ruby's shop, as well. But you should talk to Maggie. I think you'll like her. She's smart, thoughtful, and sympathetic. She may be surprised to see you, but tell her how you tracked her down and that I hope she'll be willing to answer your questions."

"I will," Jessica said, standing. "And you've already been hugely helpful, China. You've given me the first real lead I've had on this story." She went to get her jacket. "If Lilia's sister wrote that letter, I want to know what evidence she has. And why she's waited so long to do something about it."

China came around the counter and gave her a hug. "Good luck, Lois Lane," she said with a laugh. "The *Daily Planet* is depending on you!"

122

Before Jessica got in her car and started for Gruene, she stopped in the newsroom to let Hark know where she was going. He gave his reporters the discretion to follow leads that might turn into important stories. But if a lead took them out of Pecan Springs, he liked to be informed. And if the lead was likely to turn into something important, he needed to know.

"Gruene?" he asked, looking up from some papers on his desk. "What's going on over there?"

"I want to check out a letter that came in yesterday," Jessica replied. "About Lilia Thompson's suicide. Do you remember it?"

"Of course I remember it. Sam Thompson and I have been friends for years, and Lilia was his wife." Hark's chair squeaked as he leaned back and clasped his hands behind his head. "Losing her was the worst thing that could have happened to him. I was afraid the poor guy would never get over it." He ran a hand through his dark hair. "But I was glad to hear last week that he's remarried. Grace Mannerby, her name is. She teaches biology at the college."

The poor guy? Jessica's investigative antenna went up with a snap. It sounded like Sam Thompson was thought of sympathetically by just about everybody in Pecan Springs, everybody who mattered, anyway. Detectives Foster and Connors, Judge Maude, now Hark — they were all friends. Was that why none of them had taken a hard look at his wife's death?

And now Thompson had remarried? Lilia had been dead for a year, which Jessica supposed was enough time to establish a new relationship, even if you loved your wife. But had he known Grace Mannerby when Lilia was still alive? Had they been lovers? Could this be a motive for —

"Which is good news, if you ask me," Hark added. "Sam is the kind of guy who needs a wife." He gave Jessica a curious look. "A letter, you say? About Lilia's suicide? Who wrote it?"

Jessica thought quickly. Given his friendship with the husband, Hark wouldn't be too happy to hear what she was up to or why she planned to have a conversation with

Margaret Nichols. She wasn't about to lie to him, but she wasn't sure she should level with him, either.

"Lilia's sister," she said casually. "It was just a note, but I thought I'd talk to her. If it looks like there's a story, I'll let you know." All true, and all designed not to raise any red flags. "Unless you've got something else for me," she added, mentally crossing her fingers that he didn't.

"Nothing going on here," Hark said. "Slow news day, at least for now." He glanced out the window beside his desk. "But be careful out there. It's snowing, in case you hadn't noticed. The roads are getting icy."

"Sure thing," Jessica said. She gave him a curious look. His face was puffy and his eyes were red, as if he hadn't had enough sleep. And he definitely wasn't his usual hard-punching self. "Everything okay with you, boss?"

"More or less." His tone was careless. "Why wouldn't it be?"

"No reason." She gave him a slight smile, but she knew there *was* a reason, and she wondered whether it had anything to do with what Fran had said this morning about Hark's to-be-fired list. Was he looking at the upcoming payroll and figuring out who he

125

would cut if he had to start cutting staff positions in the newsroom? If the *Enterprise* was about to fold, that would surely be keeping him awake at night. But maybe that wasn't the reason. Maybe —

"I suppose you've been vaccinated for measles," he said.

"Measles?" Well, that question came out of the blue. Jessica blinked. "Gosh, I don't know, Hark. I suppose I must have been. Where Ginger and I were concerned, Mom was pretty conscientious about our health. But I don't remember."

"Ask her, why don't you?" Hark said impatiently. He stopped, then grimaced. "Oh. Jeez, Jessie. Sorry. I'm so sorry. I forgot about all that. I apologize."

"That's okay," Jessica said. "There are lots of things I wish I could ask my mom. I'll add measles to the list. But all our records were destroyed in the fire, so I don't know for sure about vaccinations." She frowned. "How come you're asking?"

"Because Heather broke out with the measles last night. She saw a doctor this morning. He put her under quarantine."

"Quarantine!" Jessica breathed. "Oh, wow! No wonder she didn't show up this morning."

"Yeah. But the doc says she was contagious for at least four days before she broke out in a rash. So it's not just Heather, it's the rest of us. Everybody in the newsroom, that is."

"Oh, no!" Jessica exclaimed.

"Oh, yes. We've all been exposed. As has anybody who has been within sneezing distance of her. And the measles are no joke, in a working situation like the one we've got here. We can't put out a newspaper if we're all sick." Hark rubbed his eyes. "I need to call the county health department to find out what's next. Do we all get vaccinated or what?"

"Well, I don't want to hear that *I'm* supposed to be quarantined," Jessica said briskly, turning toward the door. She was not going to tell him that she and Heather had eaten their lunches at the same table for the past several days. "I feel perfectly well. And I've got reporting to do."

"Yeah. Well, what you want and what you're going to get may be two different things," Hark said. "Stay in touch — we may need you. And before you go, check in with Denise. She was looking for you a few minutes ago. Said you were supposed to meet with her early this morning."

"Aargh," Jessica muttered.

"Do it," Hark instructed, reaching for his

phone. "Part of the job."

On her way out of the newsroom after reporting to Denise (an unpleasant encounter that took all of ten minutes), Jessica stopped at her desk to pick up the messages on her answering machine. Most people phoned her cell these days, so there wasn't much. Just a call from a reporter at the *Austin American-Statesman* asking for background on the Byers indictments and a reminder about a meeting of the American Civil Liberties Union later that week on criminal sentencing reform, always a hot topic.

Fran poked her head around the cubicle door. "I saw you talking to Hark. Did he tell you about Heather's measles?"

"Yeah," Jessica said, making a note about the ACLU meeting. "Quarantine."

"Yes, damn it." Fran made a face. "I was hoping she could work from home, but she says she's feeling pretty rocky. Which means we'll be short-staffed for at least the next week. You'll have the Redfern piece ready tomorrow?"

"It's in the works," Jessica said, mentally reminding herself that she had to come up with the questions she had promised to send. She could dictate them to her phone and then email them. "He's cool with it.

And he's expecting Virgil. He has a pet lizard named Darwin," she added. Her glance fell on the cowgirl boot filled with yellow roses, and she picked it up.

"Awesome," Fran said, satisfied. "I'll tell Virgil to be sure and shoot Darwin." She glanced at the roses. "Where are you going with those?"

"The children's wing at the hospital," Jessica said, and ducked out before Fran could ask any more questions.

CHAPTER TEN

The village of Gruene (Texans long ago anglicized the German pronunciation from *Gru-en* to *Green*) is about ten miles south of Pecan Springs, on the banks of the Guadalupe River. It was established in the decade before the Civil War by a small group of German immigrants and quickly grew into a prosperous settlement. There was plenty of flat land along the river for farming, and cotton became the warp and weft of its economy. The village was located on the San Antonio-to-Austin stage line, which stopped for a change of horses and a hot meal of ham, eggs, biscuits, and red-eye gravy for the passengers. A bank, a mercantile store, three cotton gins, and a dance hall and saloon were built, along with two railroad depots and a cluster of turn-of-the-century Victorian and German-style homes.

But around 1900, the railroad killed off the stage coach line. The boll weevil destroyed the cotton in the 1920s, the Great Depression closed both railroad depots in the 1930s, and the highway bypass dealt its final bitter blow in the late 1940s. Tucked into a quiet bend in the river, Gruene became a ghost town, populated by a few older folk living in the still-older houses, now pretty dilapidated.

The early 1970s, however, brought a renaissance. The village's attractive German and Victorian buildings and its picturesque setting caught the attention of the Texas Historical Commission, which put the entire village on the National Register of Historic Places. The six-thousand-square-foot open-air dance hall, the oldest in Texas, gave real-life cowboy George Strait his start and welcomed such country-and-western stars as Willie Nelson and Kris Kristofferson. The old Gruene mansion blossomed into a thirty-room inn, and antique shops, art galleries, a half-dozen restaurants, and a tasting room for Texas wines and craft beers popped up among the native wildflowers. Movie crews arrived, and John Travolta showed up at the dance hall to film a couple of scenes for a movie about an archangel. Flotillas of people on inner tubes and rubber rafts floated down the Guadalupe River on blistering summer weekends, and tourists flocked by the thousands every month of the year.

But there would be no rafters on the river and few tourists on the streets today, Jessica thought, as she drove her silver Kia south on Hunter Road. Her cellphone weather app had issued an unusual region-wide winter weather warning, with ice accumulations predicted to be a half-inch or more, enough to bring down tree limbs and cause power outages. The temperature was just below freezing, and the road surface was glazed here and there with patches of treacherous, almost invisible ice.

But it was beautiful. The snow was coming down harder now, fat flakes falling from the pewter gray sky and curtaining the trees on either side of the road. The ground had been cold enough for long enough to keep the snow from melting, and it was beginning to drift against the fences. If it snowed this steadily for a couple of hours, Jessica thought, Hark would put everybody on standby, anticipating emergency callouts. Of course, this storm wouldn't be anything like a fifteen-inch snowstorm in Wisconsin or Michigan, but Texans don't see snow often enough to know how to drive in it. She would likely find herself out on I-35, covering multiple-vehicle pileups.

There was nobody on the street as she drove into Gruene — past the Fickle Pickles antique shop, the old general store, and the dance hall (both built by Henry Gruene for his cotton hands in 1878) — and crossed the Guadalupe River on the concrete bridge that had long ago replaced the shallow stagecoach ford. Using the map on her phone, she navigated west to Edwards Bluff Road, which curved along the river.

She hadn't phoned Maggie Nichols to make an appointment. She usually learned more from a source if she caught the person at home, by surprise. And she suspected there was plenty to learn. There was a better-than-good chance that Maggie was Concerned Citizen. If so, who did she think had killed her sister? Why?

And now that Hark had told her that Sam Thompson had remarried, Jessica thought that the situation had the potential to be an ugly extramarital triangle. Maybe Sam Thompson had been having an affair with Grace Mannerby. Lilia found out about it and objected, perhaps even threatened him with public exposure — which he couldn't afford professionally, as a school principal. If that were the case, Ambien in a favorite bedtime drink would take care of the problem wife, perhaps assisted by a pillow over the face.

The more Jessica thought about this, the more convinced she became that this was what Maggie Nichols was going to tell her — if she could get her to talk. As a reporter, she'd had a lot of experience interviewing reluctant witnesses, so she had a reason to hope. But you never knew. Nichols might just clam up.

And if the sister *did* have a story to tell and evidence to back it up, then what?

Jessica tried not to think about that question, because she didn't have an answer. The case had long since been closed — in fact, it had never been opened, really. Detective Foster, Judge Maude, and Dr. Crawley had seen to that. Sam Thompson's powerful friends were all on his side, helping him to get through the tragic loss of his wife. Bringing him to justice at this late date might prove difficult, if not downright impossible. But that didn't mean she couldn't take a few initial steps in that direction. Who knows what she might turn up?

Edwards Bluff Road wound along the river, with sprawling houses on generous lots on either side of the road, most concealed discreetly behind stylish fences or screens of native landscaping. Margaret Nichols' house was a compact ranch-style dwelling set well back from the road on the river bluff in a cluster of cedars and young live oak trees, leaves glittering with a coating of ice. A wooden sign beside the drive directed visitors to the WildTexas studio entrance at the back of the house, where Jessica rang the doorbell and stood, the chill north wind running cold fingers through her hair and down her neck.

Inside, a small dog yapped excitedly, and a moment later, the door opened. The woman was in her forties, dark-haired, with a sculptured face and remarkably large dark eyes. She was wearing a canvas apron over a black turtleneck top, black yoga pants, knitted blue leg warmers, and Sherpa boots. The dog was a gray miniature schnauzer with a mop of silver whiskers and a sharp, snappy bark.

"Margaret Nichols?" Jessica asked, unzipping her coat a few inches and pulling out the press badge that hung around her neck. "I'm Jessica Nelson, from the *Enterprise*. I'd like to talk to you for a few minutes."

Apprehensive, the woman bit her lip. "About what?"

Jessica took out the plastic zipper bag containing the letter and held it up. "About this. And about your sister."

The woman jerked back, clearly startled.

135

"How in the world did you — I mean, I didn't . . . I don't —" Her mouth tightened. "That's enough, Max," she said to the dog, who obediently stopped barking. To Jessica: "I don't have any idea what you're talking about. Go away." She began to push the door shut.

But Jessica had had doors slammed in her face before, and she had already planted her boot on the threshold to keep this one from closing.

"Look, Ms. Nichols. I know that you're Lilia Thompson's sister. China Bayles showed me the stationery she's selling in her shop — the same paper you used when you wrote this letter to me."

"You're a friend of China's?" The woman's voice was wary.

"Yes," Jessica said, and smiled. "She said to tell you that she has only one box left from her second order and she'd love to have more. And that she hopes you'll be willing to talk to me. She doesn't believe Lilia killed herself, either."

The woman stood there for a moment, hesitating, her shoulders slumped. At last, she opened the door. "I was hoping not to get involved," she said reluctantly. "But now that you're here . . . well, I guess you'd better come in."

"Thank you," Jessica said, and followed her into the studio.

The large room was windowed along its north side and suffused with a pearly light reflected from the falling snow outside. Its walls were lined with paper collages in all colors, sizes, and shapes, some framed, some unframed. Shelves held boxes, rolls, and sheets of materials and tools, and what looked like paper works-in-progress were spread out on a couple of work tables under hanging lights. Other shelves held sculpted paper figures and forms made, Jessica guessed, of papier-mâché. It was the studio of a serious artist.

"We might as well sit down," the woman said, gesturing toward two upholstered chairs on either side of a small coffee table in front of the window. She took Jessica's jacket and scarf and hung them on a peg beside the door. "I was about to get a cup of coffee. Would you like one?"

"Thank you," Jessica said, rubbing her chilly hands together. "Coffee would be wonderful." Outside the window, a bright red cardinal flashed, brilliant against the snow. Through the trees and down the steep hill, Jessica could see the glint of light on the Guadalupe River. "What a terrific view."

"The snow makes for a nice change in the

winter," the woman said, "but it's prettier in the spring. The hill is full of wildflowers, all the way down to the water." She went to a shelf that held a coffee urn and several cups. "Cream, Ms. Nelson? Sugar?"

"Black is fine. And I'm Jessica, if I may call you Maggie." When the woman nodded, Jessica gestured to the shelves of paper figures, most of whom were gracefully, delicately female. "Your work is lovely — quite unusual."

"Thank you," Maggie replied, pouring coffee. "Unfortunately, my most interesting work sells only occasionally. The stationery line is the most reliable income-producer — production stuff like notecards, paper, invitations, giftwrap. It's carried in quite a few shops now." She smiled briefly. "China has been a strong supporter since the beginning. In fact, I made my first batch in one of her paper workshops. I'm grateful to her for getting me started."

"She has helped a great many people," Jessica said. She was remembering how China had given *her* a hand, when she was a new intern at the *Enterprise*.

A moment later, they were seated with their cups, Max on the floor at Maggie's feet, his eyes, alert and watchful, on Jessica. Sipping her coffee, Jessica was grateful for its warmth sliding down her throat. She didn't waste time with small talk.

"It's been quite a while since your sister's death." She was aware that her questions would be confrontational and tried to soften her voice. "I'm wondering what prompted you to write to me. And why now, so long after the fact? Why didn't you say something when it happened? Why haven't you gone to the police?"

There was a long silence. Cradling her cup in her hands, Maggie was gazing out the window. "There's a hawk out there," she said finally. "On that mesquite tree. See him?"

"I do," Jessica said. The hawk was large, almost the size of an eagle, with a sharply hooked beak, a silvery breast, and dark wings. "He's a splendid fellow. Fierce."

"I'm sure he's hungry. There's not much to eat out there in the winter. He'll be lucky to catch a mouse once every couple of days, or maybe an unwary sparrow. But he watches and waits. He sees every tiny movement out there in the grass and undergrowth. He's incredibly patient."

Still holding her cup, she turned to face Jessica. "I wrote to you because I read about your investigation of the Angel of Death — Howard Byers, I mean — in the *Enterprise.*

When I read that, I thought you must have spent a great deal of time sifting through evidence others had overlooked, noticing the patterns, watching and waiting. Waiting for Byers to reveal himself. Like that hawk. That kind of patient investigative work isn't the sort of thing the police are equipped to do. I wrote because I was hoping the letter might attract your attention. That you might want to investigate the way Lilia died." She nodded toward a framed photo on a nearby shelf. "That's my sister. Isn't she beautiful? I miss her so very much. I would give anything to know what really happened that night."

Jessica turned to look at the photo. Lilia *was* beautiful. Dark-haired, like Maggie, with the same large, dark eyes. Head cocked, she was regarding the camera with a lively curiosity, about to ask a question. Jessica's heart twisted painfully. She knew what it was like to miss a sister. Ginger, her twin, had died in the fire that killed their parents. What wouldn't *she* give to know what really happened that night: how the fire got started, who started it, why? In the silence, she wondered whether Officer Riley was really onto something — or whether it was going to turn out to be nothing but a false alarm.

Pulling her thoughts back to the present, she cleared her throat. "In your letter, you say that Judge Porterfield was wrong when she ruled that your sister killed herself. How do you know that?"

Another long silence. "I guess I don't really *know*," Maggie said slowly. "I just suspect." She stared down at her cup, turning it in her fingers. "Actually, I was hoping you could find out. Whether Lilia killed herself." She dropped her voice to nearly a whisper. "Or was . . . murdered."

So Maggie only *suspected*? Jessica felt a sharp stab of disappointment. This was a cold case — no, it wasn't even a *case,* as far as the police were concerned. It was going to take more than suspicions to get anybody's attention. The cops had to have facts. Clear, cold, confirmable facts.

"Something must have made you suspicious," she said. "What was it?"

Maggie hesitated so long that Jessica began to think she wasn't going to answer. When she spoke, it was with an evident reluctance. "Well, if you must know, it was the letters. The . . . love letters. The ones that Lilia hid."

The love letters? Jessica felt an intense surge of energy. Concealing it, she bent over and took her phone out of her shoulder bag.

"Do you mind if I record this?" she asked, holding it up. "I don't have a photographic memory, and I want to be sure to get the details right."

Another hesitation. Then: "As you might guess," Maggie said, "talking about this is painful for me. But if it's got to be done, let's not make any mistakes. So yes, it's okay to record."

Jessica liked the way she said that. As she set her phone to record, Maggie leaned forward and put her cup on the table. Max cocked his head alertly, looking up at her. She took a breath and began, haltingly at first.

"Late last fall, Sam — Lilia's husband — sold their house on Saratoga Drive. As he was moving stuff out, he came across some boxes of art materials that Lilia had stashed in an upstairs closet. I do hands-on paper workshops with kids, and he thought I might be able to use some of it. So he brought the boxes over and stacked them in my garage. After Christmas, I started going through them, sorting out what could be used and what should be given away. That's when I found them." She shifted uncomfortably. "The letters. Hidden at the bottom of a box full of origami materials."

Now they were getting somewhere, Jessica

thought. She spoke eagerly. "Letters. Letters to Sam?"

Of course. There was the fact she needed! Letters to Sam, from the woman he had been seeing, would prove that there had been a relationship. What's more, they would prove that Lilia (who had hidden them) had known what was going on. Maybe she had threatened to use the letters to expose Sam's relationship with the woman. Maybe —

But Maggie was shaking her head. "No. Not to Sam. They were letters to Lilia. From her lover."

Jessica's eyes widened. "*Her* . . . lover?"

Just two words. A seismic shift.

"Yes." Maggie pulled up her legs and tucked them under her in the chair. "There were six, written over the course of four or five months." She sighed. "Lilia was a wonderful sister and I adored her. But she wasn't a terribly happy person. She was . . . she was carrying a lot of emotional baggage."

"What kind of baggage?" Jessica asked, still trying to cope with this new revelation. Her question was intrusive and not necessarily relevant. But she wanted to know. Sometimes the past was more than just a ghost.

Maggie's voice was matter-of-fact, but her mouth trembled and she looked away. "Lilia and I were . . . molested by an uncle when we were girls. It had a terrible, long-lasting effect on both of us. Lilia's marriage wasn't perfect, and I understood that she was deeply unhappy after her baby died. But marriages go through hard times, as I know from my own experience."

"All relationships do," Jessica murmured, thinking of Kelly. "Some of them don't survive."

Maggie made a wry face. "I was hoping the trouble would blow over — and I actually thought it had. About six or seven months before she died, Lilia began to seem happier and . . . well, more stable. She was looking forward to some things that were going on at the library, where she worked. And she was involved with a project at the herb guild."

"With China Bayles," Jessica murmured, picking up her coffee cup.

"Yes, that's right. She and China were working together. Anyway, whatever the difficulty between Lilia and Sam, I thought it must have straightened itself out." She shivered and wrapped her arms around herself. "I was wrong. That's the irony of it, I'm afraid. She seemed happier because she was in love. But not with Sam."

Jessica put her cup down. Maggie's story was compelling and she found herself deeply involved with it. "Who?"

Max got to his feet, put his paws on Maggie's chair, and jumped into her lap. She began to stroke his wiry gray fur. "That's where the letters come in," she said slowly, "but it took me a while to figure that out. The man was being very careful, you see. All of the letters are signed with a little drawing of a heart. He never wrote his name, not even any initials."

"But you eventually learned who it was," Jessica said hopefully. Of course she did. And the answer might reveal —

"Yes, I pieced it together from clues in the letters themselves," Maggie said. "Little bits here and there. Lilia was having an affair with her next-door neighbor, Jim Crawley. To judge from the letters, it was quite passionate."

Dr. Crawley? Jessica pulled in her breath. "He was there that night. After your sister died, I mean. He came over from next door and pronounced her dead."

A look of deep sadness crossed Maggie's face. "So I understand," she said. "It must have been extraordinarily difficult for him, wouldn't you think? When I finally figured

145

it out, I understood why Lilia was attracted to him."

"Why?" Jessica asked. "I'm just trying to understand," she added, not wanting Maggie to think that she was prying — although of course she was. That was her job.

Maggie sighed. "Well, Sam is a very nice guy, but he let Lilia call all the shots, which isn't always good in a marriage — and it especially wasn't good for Lilia. She needed someone strong and definitive, and Jim Crawley certainly fit the bill. For one thing, he was older by about fifteen years, and I'm sure he must have been a kind of authority figure for her. From something he said to me at the funeral, I understood that he cared for her. At the time, I didn't understand — I thought it was just a neighborly fondness. Now, reading his letters, I believe he loved Lilia deeply."

But Lilia was married, Jessica thought, and their affair couldn't go anywhere. Secrets can be dangerous, especially when reputations are at stake, or when the spouse is jealous. Maybe — She frowned, trying to remember. "Dr. Crawley is married, isn't he?" Hadn't the judge mentioned his wife? And Detective Foster had said that Mrs. Crawley was there, on the scene. She was half-hysterical.

146

"Oh, yes, he was married," Maggie said grimly. "And Lilia and his wife were close friends. I know that they went out to lunch together frequently. Mrs. Crawley even had a key to Lilia's and Sam's house so she could feed their cats when they were gone. In fact, the doctor mentioned his wife a couple of times in his letters. He seemed anxious to protect her because he thought she was emotionally fragile. He said that if she knew about the affair it would . . . destroy her."

Jessica shivered. She could understand that. It was a double betrayal — not only her husband, but her friend. "How about Lilia's husband? Did Sam know?"

"I'm not sure," Maggie said, "because I don't have Lilia's letters. But there are suggestions in Dr. Crawley's letters that Lilia *thought* Sam knew, or at least suspected. She felt guilty, it seems, maybe even to the point of wanting to break off the affair. She also wanted to tell Crawley's wife — Christine, her name is."

"But why?" Jessica asked, surprised.

"To get it off her chest, I suppose." Maggie made a wry face. "Maybe she thought confession was good for the soul. Maybe she thought Christine Crawley deserved to know. Whatever, the doctor was apparently trying to talk her out of it." There was a momentary silence. "I just wish I knew what was in Lilia's mind. Was she going to tell the doctor's wife? Tell the doctor she was through? Or tell Sam?"

"Maybe she did," Jessica said.

"Did what?"

"Confess to her husband," Jessica hazarded. "And Sam killed her for it."

"No. No!" Maggie shook her head vehemently. "He couldn't have, Jessica. I know that, just as surely as I know that Lilia didn't kill herself."

"Why?"

"Because he . . . he doesn't have it in him." She held up a hand. "I know, I know. When a wife is murdered, it's usually the husband who does it. But I've spent a lot of time with my brother-in-law, and I can tell you that Sam Thompson is an easygoing guy with a mild temper and the patience of a saint. He couldn't harm *anyone.*"

Jessica had heard several versions of this story before, most recently from the sister of a man who had confessed to brutally stabbing his wife with a butcher knife. But there was no point in contradicting Maggie, who seemed to have her mind made up.

Instead, she said, "If your sister didn't kill herself, then somebody else killed her. If it wasn't her husband, who . . ." She let her voice trail off.

"I don't know," Maggie said. "And I hate to point fingers especially when I'm really just guessing. But maybe it was . . ." She faltered. "Maybe it was Mrs. Crawley."

"Mrs. Crawley?" Jessica was surprised. "Why? What makes you say that?"

"Well, mostly the process of elimination, I guess. You can read the letters for yourself and make up your mind. To me, it seems that Dr. Crawley loved Lilia too much to have harmed her. I am positive that Sam didn't do it. And the doctor himself said that his wife was . . ." She hesitated. "Unbalanced."

"Unbalanced?"

"Actually, I think the word he used was 'unstable.' Maybe she found out about the affair — not from Lilia, but from somebody else. It's pretty hard to keep a secret in Pecan Springs. Maybe Mrs. Crawley saw Lilia and her husband together, or even spied on them. Or she might have intercepted a letter. There's probably no way to know, short of asking her." She looked at Jessica. "You could do that, you know. Ask her. See what she says."

Jessica frowned. "But say that Mrs. Crawley knew that her husband and Lilia were having an affair. Then what?"

"Lilia never made any secret of the fact that she always had a glass of Southern Comfort at bedtime. She thought it helped her sleep. She didn't drink otherwise, but she made a big thing about her Southern Comfort. Mrs. Crawley would have known that. It would have been easy for her to have entered the house while nobody was there. She could have crushed a handful of pills and put them into the bottle." She looked at Jessica, hoping for agreement. "It makes sense, doesn't it?"

"Well, sort of, I guess," Jessica said slowly, thinking that Sam Thompson could have done the very same thing. He could have seen the illicit lovers together, spied on them, intercepted a letter, overheard a phone call. But there wasn't any point in insisting. Maggie's mind was made up. She moved to a different topic. "It's too bad that there was no autopsy."

"That was a mistake," Maggie admitted. "Sam said it was what Lilia wanted."

"I understand that it was in her will."

"Well, that's what Sam said, and Dr. Crawley, too. I didn't look at Lilia's will. And when Judge Porterfield called me to ask my opinion, I think I must have been in shock. I know I wanted just to get it over with. That was wrong. I should have asked that Lilia be autopsied."

Jessica frowned, wondering whether *anyone* had bothered to look at Lilia's will. Maybe Sam had planted the no-autopsy idea and everybody had taken his assertion for granted, without checking. She hesitated. "Have you thought of exhumation?"

Maggie shuddered. "That's pretty extreme. We'd need other evidence, wouldn't we? That she didn't kill herself, I mean."

Jessie gave her a straight look. "If there *is* any other evidence, would you be willing to ask for an exhumation? And an autopsy?"

Maggie took a breath. "Well, I suppose. It's not the cost, of course — it's the idea of it. But if that's the only way to get to the bottom of this, then yes." She hesitated. "How is that . . . how would I go about doing that?"

"I'm not sure," Jessica said. "But I'll find out and get back to you." She paused. "About the letters. I would like to borrow them — although if there is reason to believe that Lilia was murdered, the police will want them."

"The police, yes. I've given a lot of thought to that." Maggie sighed. "If you'll agree to investigate Lilia's death, I'll give you the letters. If the police need them, that's between you and them. If nothing comes of it, I'll want them back."

"I have to be careful, you know," Jessica said cautiously. "One detective has already told me to keep my nose out of police business."

"But you *will*?" Maggie asked. "Right away? I don't know why, but now — here, talking with you — I have the feeling that this is urgent."

Jessica didn't hesitate. "I'll get on it today. And I'll take it as far as I can."

"That's a promise?" Maggie asked.

"It's a promise," Jessica said.

When she left, she had the letters, six of them, each in a separate plastic bag, tucked securely into her purse. And she had a plan. She would read them as soon as she got back to Pecan Springs. And then she would talk to Mrs. Crawley, to the doctor, and to Sam Thompson.

But like everyone else's plans that day, Jessica's would require a re-do.

Mother Nature had other ideas.

CHAPTER ELEVEN

The drive back to Pecan Springs was harrowing. Hunter Road was now a sheet of ice, and the combination of a gusty north wind and a heavy ice load had brought limbs and whole trees down across the narrow road. The fifteen-mile trip took forty minutes, Jessica's police scanner app buzzing with accident reports. Clearly, the storm was going to be this week's big news. She was anxious to get to the doctor's letters, but Hark was mobilizing the newsroom staff by the time she got back to the *Enterprise,* so they would have to wait.

Jessica was dispatched to I-35 to report on an accident involving a snowplow, an auto, and a pickup truck, which snarled traffic for a couple of hours while the tangled metal wreckage was cleared. Virgil went with her to take pictures, and they were on scene for a good hour before she'd gotten the story she was after. As usual, the drivers offered radically different explanations of how the wreck happened and who was at fault, a reminder (if Jessica needed one) that her job was to assemble the information and report all sides of the story. The "true" story would likely be a matter of debate until it was settled by the insurance companies or in a courtroom — and even then, it would be a negotiated truth.

She went back to the newspaper, but Hark waylaid her before she could reach her desk and sent her up to the campus to report on the failure of the main heating unit in one of the dorms. She was on her way back when Denise, the assistant editor, phoned to direct Jessica to a water main break on Galveston Street. It had happened the night before and hadn't yet been repaired. When she arrived on the scene, the main was still producing an icy fountain. The street was submerged to the curbs in what resembled a glacial lake, and the sidewalk on one side was a solid ribbon of ice. Some kids had put on skates and were enjoying themselves.

"Happens every time we get a damned winter storm," the Pecan Springs water supervisor growled. "Some of these pipes are eighty, ninety years old. They don't like cold weather any more than the rest of us."

Jessica could have gone back to the newsroom, but something told her that if she did, Hark or Denise would have her out on the street again in a hurry, chasing another emergency. She needed some time and space to get her work done.

So she parked in the next block of Galveston and sat in her car with the heater running, using her iPad to write about the dorm heat failure and the water main break and email the stories to Hark, with copies to Denise. She wrote a half-dozen questions for David Redfern and emailed them to him. She checked her inbox on her phone and replied to the most urgent messages.

And then she realized that she'd missed lunch altogether, an omission she remedied by driving a couple of blocks to Delilah's Deli. She ordered a bagel with lox, cream cheese, and onions and a pot of hot Earl Grey tea and took the food to a back table, where she opened her shoulder bag and pulled out the six letters Maggie had given her.

They were all dated in the four-month period before Lilia's death, and Jessica read them in order. All were typed, fairly short, and, yes, passionate, florid but heartfelt and full of declarations of enduring love. Each was signed with the same hand-drawn heart. She noticed the brief comments that had led Maggie to conclude that the letters were written by a neighbor (a remark about a noisy party across the street from both their houses, another about a downed willow tree in the garden) and by a doctor ("seeing patients," "coming back from the hospital"). And another, in the final letter, that caught her attention.

I know you're deeply troubled by this development, Lilia. I've told you how I feel and what I think — what I know — needs to be done, and swiftly. You have already been a mother, and you've already known tragedy. Believe me, my darling, unless you do as I advise, this is not going to turn out well. Not for you, not for me, not for both of us.

Jessica finished the last of her bagel, frowning at the passage.

What was "this development"? What was the significance of "you have already been a mother"? What had the writer — Jim Crawley, she was sure — advised Lilia to do? And what wasn't going to turn out well? Those five sentences seemed to her to have their own special urgency, their own commanding voice. They were different than anything else in the letters. She looked at the date. They had been written just a week before Lilia died.

Jessica folded the letters and put them back in her bag. When she left Maggie's house (and before the storm intervened) she had planned that — after reading the letters — she would talk first to Dr. Crawley's wife and then to the doctor himself.

But a quick online search on her cellphone browser revealed that Dr. and Mrs. Crawley no longer lived on Saratoga Drive, next door to the house Sam Thompson had just sold. They — maybe just Christine Crawley, since the telephone was now listed in her name only — lived on High Ridge Drive. Had the Crawleys separated? Divorced?

Hurriedly, Jessica drained the last of her tea. It was now a few minutes past three and she really ought to get back to the newsroom. But if Hark had another assignment for her, he could text her. This story felt just as urgent as the demolition derby out there on the icy interstate or malfunctioning dorm heating units and elderly water mains.

Five minutes later, she was back in her car, headed west on San Marcos Avenue.

The snow had been coming down for hours, and now it was three or four inches deep, drifting deeper against the trees and bushes. Pecan Springs saw snow so infrequently that the city didn't have snowplows and the streets were a mushy mess — an icy mess, where the traffic was light enough for the pavement to start freezing.

High Ridge Drive was notoriously steep and twisty, with houses on one side of the street and a fifty-foot cliff on the other, a sheer drop to the Pecan River. Now, with the storm, there was only a narrow, icy lane in the middle of the street, and no room for mistakes. Jessica hunched over the wheel, clutching it in both white-knuckled hands, feeling her little Kia's rear end fishtailing when she tried to speed up enough to get up the hill.

She flicked the wipers faster to keep ahead of the snow that was piling up on her windshield, asking herself what in the world she was doing up here on such a rotten day. She wasn't under a deadline for this story. Lilia Thompson's death was old news and her lover's letters were even older (and secret). Even Lilia's sister had kept her concerns to herself until recently. Surely the story could wait for another day, another week, even. It would be smarter to take the first right, go two blocks to San Jacinto, then right again and back down the hill to the safety of the newsroom.

But if Jessica were honest with herself (she rarely was), she would have to admit that she was operating under the same obsessions that had driven her to seek out and reconstruct Howard Byers' hidden crimes. Hark had told her several times to back off and had even threatened to fire her if she didn't. Kelly had complained that once she got her teeth into an investigation, she was like a dog with a bone in its jaws. She couldn't let go, even if she wanted to. And the more somebody tried to get her to let it go, the harder she hung on.

She had to agree. There was something in her that wouldn't let the puzzle rest until she had solved it. Or — with a different metaphor — wouldn't allow her to abandon the trail until she had reached the end. Or something.

But Jessica had no idea what that something was. And since she didn't, all she could do was clear her mind of everything else and focus on keeping her wheels on the street.

Christine Crawley's condo was discreetly tucked behind a screen of yaupon holly shrubs, their red berries bright as drops of fresh blood against the snow that lay thick on their branches. Jessica rang the doorbell, thinking that on a day like today, only crazy people were out on the streets. Someone should be at home here.

Someone was. The door opened on a chain and a woman's voice said, "Who is it?"

"Jessica Nelson, from the *Enterprise.*" Jessica pulled out her press badge and held it up. "I'm doing a story on the death of Lilia Thompson, your next-door neighbor on Saratoga Drive. I'd like to talk to you about it."

A startled intake of breath. "Talk to *me*? But I don't —"

"I'll only take a few minutes, Mrs. Crawley. I have some questions about —"

"I am *not* Mrs. Crawley." the woman said sharply. "That bastard and I are divorced, as of last week. I'm Christine Perkins now."

Jessica processed that fact, realizing that it substantially changed her approach to this woman. "I see," she said. "Well, something's come up about Mrs. Thompson and I was hoping you might be able to help me out. I promise not to take too much of your time, but this is important — to you, I think. May we talk?"

The door opened an inch or two wider. "Help you out how? That woman is dead. I can't tell you anything." Her voice was thin and brittle. "I don't *know* anything."

Jessica pulled her coat closer around her. "Could we talk inside?" she asked plaintively. "It's pretty cold out here."

There was a silence. Somewhere in the distance, Jessica heard a siren wail, and then another. A car wreck, maybe, or a fire. She shuddered. After a moment, the chain rattled and the door came open.

"I suppose it's okay," the woman said, sounding resigned. "For a few minutes."

Christine Perkins was a small, slender woman, with delicate features, china-blue eyes, and frosted hair, carefully arranged in a stylish cut. Her silky blue dress clung to her slender figure as she led the way into the all-white living room: white walls and ceiling, white carpet, white sofa and chairs, brightened only by the heaps of colored pillows on the sofa and chairs and several large modern paintings on the wall. But these barely warmed the room, whose whiteness made the air seem as frigid as the snowy outdoors. Jessica shivered as the doctor's wife — the doctor's *ex*-wife — took her jacket.

The woman gave her a wary look. "Help

you out how?" she repeated, gesturing to a chair. She perched on the edge of the sofa, precariously poised, like a bird ready to take flight.

"I received a letter claiming that your neighbor didn't kill herself," Jessica said quietly, taking out her notebook. She wasn't going to make this easy. She was depending on shock to shake something loose. "The writer believes that Lilia Thompson was murdered by someone who had easy access to the house. That person put a fatal dose of Ambien into the Southern Comfort Lilia drank before bedtime every evening. I wondered if you had any thoughts about this that you would be willing to share."

Christine stifled a gasp. Her face had gone as white as the walls of the room. "A letter? Who — who sent it?" Her voice was thin and high-pitched, like a stretched guitar string, and barely under control.

Jessica was surprised by the strength of the woman's reaction. "It was signed with a pseudonym, but I was able to learn the identity of the writer. This morning, I spoke at length with that person." She paused deliberately. Christine's eyes were growing larger and darker. "It's someone who knows both you and your ex-husband. That person recently came into possession of several letters that reveal a great deal about his relationship with Lilia Thompson."

"Letters?" Christine cried. "You say there are *letters*?"

"Yes," Jessica said steadily. "I've also spoken with the detective who came to the house that night and the judge who ruled —"

One hand had gone to the woman's mouth. "Letters to Lilia?" Her fingers were trembling.

"Yes. To Lilia. Love letters."

"From . . ." She clenched her small hands so tightly that the knuckles turned white.

"I think you know," Jessica said gently. "Don't you?"

She was utterly unprepared for what happened next.

CHAPTER TWELVE

When she finally returned to her car, Jessica texted Hark to let him know that she would be late getting back to the newsroom. It was just four-thirty, but she was so drained that she was ready to go home and flop for the rest of the evening. That wasn't in the cards, though, because she had to talk to Ethan Connors, who had texted her midway through her conversation with Christine Perkins, asking her to call him. She hadn't replied, not wanting to interrupt Christine's deeply disturbing story.

Now, she dialed the detective's number. Without preamble, he said, "I have the photos."

Jessica was still trying to deal with the mind-numbing story that Christine had just told her. For a moment, his words didn't register. "The photos?"

"The photos of Lilia Thompson. Taken the night she died." His voice was unexpectedly taut. "You haven't forgotten that you asked for them, have you?"

"Of course not," Jessica lied. The morning seemed a century ago. "I've just . . . been occupied."

"Well, get unoccupied. You need to see these." He was brusque. "Where are you?"

She turned the key in the ignition. The Kia hesitated, then turned over, and the wipers struggled to clear the windshield of snow. "I'm on the other side of the river, about to head back to town. Something's come up. I need to see you, right away. Where can we meet?" She thought of Detective Foster, whom she didn't want to include in the conversation. "Not at the station, please."

"Roger that," Connors said wryly. "Foster is still on the warpath. How about Bean's?"

"Meet you there in twenty," Jessica said, and clicked off.

Bean's Bar and Grill was named for Judge Roy Bean, who held court in the pioneer town of Vinegaroon, on the Pecos River. It was a couple of blocks off the square, next door to Purley's Tire Company and across the street from the Old Fire House Dance Hall. Inside, it was a throwback to the last century, featuring a down-home-Texas bar on one side of the room, dining tables and chairs in whatever color was on sale at Banger's Hardware the week they were painted, and a couple of pool tables in the back. The owner, Bob Godwin, served Tex-Mex and barbecued brisket and cabrito, which he grilled on the smokers behind the restaurant, a stone's throw from the Missouri & Pacific railroad tracks. Bean's was a good place for a private conversation, as long as you sat shoulder-to-shoulder with your friend and talked under the buzz of loud voices, the clatter of dishes, the sharp *crack!* of cue balls, and the sweet sound of Tanya Tucker and her classic "Delta Dawn" on the jukebox. And every couple of hours, the earthquake-like rumble of a passing Union Pacific freight train.

Jessica didn't make it in twenty. "Sorry to keep you waiting," she said, pulling out the chair next to Connors at the back-corner table he had claimed. "High Ridge Drive was closed while I was up there — too dangerous to drive down. I had to find a detour that was still passable. And a couple of traffic lights were out, so it was slow and go on San Marcos Avenue the rest of the way."

"We'll be lucky if the power stays on," Connors said. "With all this ice, it's off in a dozen places around town." He pointed to his longneck. "Beer? Wine?"

"Coffee for me," Jessica said, and signaled to the waitperson.

Connors pushed a large manila envelope across the table. "Copies. I think you should have a look."

"I'll do it later," Jessica said, picking up the envelope and starting to put it in her bag. "I have something to tell you. It's pretty —"

"No." He raised his hand like a traffic cop. "Now, Jessica." His voice was gruff.

Puzzled, Jessica opened the envelope. There were three photos, all in color. In the first, Lilia was lying in bed, flat on her back in a white nightgown. She had been an attractive woman in life, as Jessica knew from the photo she had seen at Maggie's, and she was still attractive in death. Her oval face was framed in dark hair, with delicate dark, arched brows and smile marks on either side of her mouth. Her eyes were closed, her lashes sooty against pale cheeks.

"Look there." Connors pulled a pencil out of his shirt pocket and pointed to the woman's lower lip. "And there." To the tip of her nose.

Jessica bent closer. "Looks like her lip might be bruised," she said. "And there's a spot on her nose. But both are barely visible. You'd have to know what to look for or you wouldn't see them."

"An abrasion," Connors said. "And her lower lip *is* bruised, maybe by contact with her teeth. And you're right. I could see them because I once saw similar marks — on a woman who was asphyxiated." He gave Jessica a straight look. "In that case, the autopsy surgeon found fibers in her lungs consistent with fibers in the pillowcase on her bed. Her husband had smothered her with a pillow." He pulled out the second photo. "Here. This one is better."

Jessica studied the photo. "Yeah," she said softly. This was one of those times when being right really sucked.

"I'm reopening the case," Connors said. "I'm going to bring Sam Thompson in and have a talk with him. But I wanted to check with you first, to see if you've made any progress in finding out who wrote that letter."

"I have," Jessica said, as her coffee arrived. "And I've brought you something." She took the letters out of her shoulder bag and put them on the table. "Here. Read."

Five minutes later, Connors looked up. "Where did you get these? Do you know who wrote them?"

The jukebox was now playing Willie and

Waylon singing "Mamas, Don't Let Your Babies Grow Up to Be Cowboys." Jessica moved her chair closer to Connors. In a low voice, she said. "Concerned Citizen turned out to be Lilia's sister Margaret Nichols. A few weeks ago, she found those letters in a box of art supplies, where Lilia apparently hid them."

She reached for the last letter. "They were written by Lilia's next-door neighbor. He was also her doctor. And the man who pronounced her dead."

"Son of a —" Connors broke off, shaking his head. "Are you freakin' kiddin' me?"

"Nope." She pointed to the five sentences that had attracted her attention earlier. "You have to read this."

Half under his breath, Connors read the sentences out loud. "I know you're deeply troubled by this development, Lilia. I've told you how I feel and what I think — I know — needs to be done, and swiftly. You have already been a mother, and you've already known tragedy. Believe me, my darling, unless you do as I advise, this is not going to turn out well. Not for you, not for me, not for both of us."

"This development?" He stopped, frowning. "What is that supposed to mean?"

Jessica sat up straighter. "I just came from

talking to Christine Perkins — Doctor Crawley's ex-wife. She's no longer using his name."

His eyebrows went up. "His *ex*-wife? When did that happen?"

"Last week. According to her, 'this development' was an unplanned pregnancy — *Lilia's* pregnancy."

"Pregnancy!"

"Yes. Lilia told Dr. Crowley that the child was his, and that she wanted to keep it. That's when he wrote this letter." She pointed to the one Connors had just read aloud. " 'You've already been a mother, and you've known tragedy,' refers to Lilia's and Sam's daughter, who drowned. The operational word here is 'mother.' "

"So the doctor was advising . . . what?" His eyes went back to the letter. "Abortion?"

"That's what he wanted. According to Christine, Lilia refused. She wanted them to divorce their spouses so they could marry and raise their child."

"Pregnant by another man." His jaw was working. "If the husband knew, that's a pretty compelling motive for murder."

"Wait. It wasn't the husband." Jessica leaned closer and lowered her voice even more. "While they were separated, Crawley confessed to Christine that *he* killed Lilia — he doped her with Ambien and alcohol, then smothered her." She pointed to the photographs. "That's why the bruise on the lip and the abrasion on the nose. And an autopsy might have shown fibers." She leaned back. "He was the one who first began arguing that an autopsy wasn't necessary."

"Crawley's wife told you *that*?" Connors asked, surprised.

"Ex-wife," Jessica reminded him. "She's pretty fragile right now. Ever since Crawley told her what he did, she's been dreaming about it — dreaming that he suffocates *her.* She can't get it out of her mind. She's afraid and angry and . . ." She paused. "She actually recorded his confession. On her cellphone." She shuddered. "She played it for me. I *heard* it."

"Sweet Jesus," Connors said reverentially. "Did you —"

"Yes," Jessica said, taking out her phone. "I recorded it while she played it. But you'll want to talk to her right away — and get that cellphone. She's wound pretty tight. And she's not sure whether she can testify against him. That's what has kept her from going to the police." She made a face. "That, and the fact that he's paying substantial alimony. If he goes to jail, she's afraid it will stop."

"I can get a warrant for her phone." Connors took a long, careful look at Jessica. "In Texas, spousal privilege doesn't apply when there's a crime involved. And if Lilia Thompson was actually pregnant, the charge will be capital murder. The ex-wife can be compelled to testify."

"Lilia's sister is ready to request an exhumation and an autopsy. Since Sam Thompson has remarried, it can be argued that she is Lilia's next of kin. Even if Sam wanted to, he probably can't quash the exhumation."

"Porterfield will want to have a say in this, since she skipped the autopsy in the first place."

"If we give her all the facts, I think she'll tell Arthur Davidson to order both an exhumation and an autopsy, to confirm whether Lilia was indeed pregnant and obtain the fetal DNA." Davidson had been elected to replace Judge Maude as the justice of the peace. "We need to ask her. The sooner the better."

"Let's do it," Connors said, pushing back his chair.

A half hour later, they were in the judge's

kitchen, which was warm and steamy after the frigid dusk outdoors. Connors and the judge were already acquainted, and he was matter-of-fact as he laid out the photos on the kitchen table.

"This is the deceased," he said. "Lilia Thompson. The photos were taken at the scene by one of the EMS guys. As you know, the death has been assumed to be a suicide — until Ms. Nelson began asking questions."

"Nosy young lady, aren't you?" Judge Maude said. She was scowling, but there was a glint in her eye.

"I'm paid to be nosy, remember?" Jessica replied. "My questions were prompted by that letter I showed you last night. Which turned out to have been written by Lilia Thompson's sister, Margaret Nichols. I spoke to her this morning, at her home in Gruene. She very much regrets that she didn't insist on an autopsy."

"Which we need," Connors said. "And the sooner the better."

The judge frowned. "I'm afraid I don't see why you're —"

"Look here," Connors said, and pointed with his pencil to the photograph. "And here."

"Ah," the judge said, bending closer. "Jessica, there's a magnifying glass in the living room beside my recliner. Please bring it." When she had it, she examined both photos for a moment and straightened. "I see what you're getting at, although I have to say that if I had seen the body on the night of her death, I might not have noticed either the bruise or the abrasion. So I'm not sure my ruling would have been any different."

"There's more," Jessica said, and told her about the doctor's letters, Lilia's alleged pregnancy, and Crawley's confession to his ex-wife. As she talked, the judge's eyes got larger and larger. She was shaking her head.

"Jim Crawley?" she said, incredulous. "Why, I wouldn't have believed it of him. Are you *sure*?"

"And as soon as we're done here," Connors said, "I'll be speaking with the ex-Mrs. Crawley."

"Better not call her that," Jessica cautioned. "She might refuse to talk."

There was a silence. Finally, the judge sighed. "I guess I'll have to say I was wrong," she said. "I should have ordered the autopsy. But it's not too late. I believe we'd better have another look. Remind me of when this death occurred."

"A year-and-a-half ago," Connors said.

The judge turned to Jessica. "And the

sister is ready to request an exhumation and an autopsy?"

"She is," Jessica said. "What's more, the husband — Sam Thompson has remarried. He may no longer be considered a next of kin."

"Remarried?" The judge brightened. "Has he now? Good for Sam. He's the kind of man who gets along better married." She thought for a moment. "I'm no longer on the bench, but that doesn't mean I don't have any authority. And it was my ruling that caused the trouble in the first place. I'll talk to Judge Davidson. Here's what you should tell the sister to do." She outlined the steps.

"Thank you," Jessica said. "I'll telephone her tonight. Maybe she can get started on that tomorrow."

"It would be a good idea if she could," the judge said. She paused. "You tell her I'm sorry I didn't do it right the first time," she said. "We should be glad that Ms. Thompson wasn't cremated. At least we've got the opportunity for a do-over."

CHAPTER THIRTEEN

Jeff Dixon leaned back in his luxurious leather chair and stretched his long legs toward the fire.

"So. You want to discuss my offer?" He regarded Hark curiously.

"It's still on the table, you know."

"Yeah, I guess. Yeah. Let's discuss it."

Hark flushed at his feeble reply and turned his glass in his fingers, trying to forget that he was drinking Elliott's Select bourbon, which he knew for a fact went for $350 a bottle — when you could find it, which definitely wasn't anywhere in Pecan Springs. And that he was a guest in the palatial home of Jefferson Davis Dixon III, where a hundred-inch flat screen silently displayed a video of Dixon in scuba gear filming a reef, flamboyantly colored fish darting through the coral. The flat screen was part of a massive teak entertainment center, which also included a yard-long replica of Dixon's sleek, forty-foot sailing yacht, a collection of baseballs (one, worth something north of $50K, was autographed by the Babe in 1927), and signed photos of Dixon with golf legends Tiger Woods, Jack Nicklaus, and an aging Arnold Palmer. It sat opposite a fireplace with a crackling fire and shelves of books on either side, not just bestsellers but classics. Dostoevsky. Dickens. James Joyce. They looked well-thumbed, too. Hark wouldn't put it past Dixon to have read them. All of them. And not the Cliff Notes versions, either.

Hark shifted in his chair. He knew he was a first-class editor, but he wasn't good at stuff like this. Trying to score points, raise money, negotiate a deal. He was a lousy bluffer who hated to pretend he had a decent hand when he didn't. All of which put him at a definite disadvantage with Dixon. When it came to financial wheeling and dealing, he had the feeling that Dixon knew every trick in the book and exactly when and how to play each one.

He looked the part, too. Dressed in gray wool slacks, a camel-colored cashmere sweater, and St. Laurent loafers, Dixon was a Nordic type with thick blond hair, shrewd blue eyes in a tanned face, muscular arms, and a lean build. Now in his mid-forties, he

177

hadn't changed much since the nights the two of them had put in on the *Daily Texan,* where Hark had been news editor and Dixon had handled sports and politics, which in Texas, weren't far removed from one another.

Well, of course Dixon hadn't changed, except that he and his wife Tiffani had gone their separate ways. That build of his was the product of yachting in the summer, skiing in the winter, and golf all year. The way Hark saw it, guys like Dixon had all the time in the world to keep fit, all the money to stay that way, and all the women who were looking for a lifestyle of sybaritic pleasures.

Unlike Hark, who was far more of a monk than a sybarite and spent his days herding reporters to their deadlines, corralling enough advertisers to pay the month's bills, trying to squeeze out a few bucks for deferred maintenance on the old newspaper building, and wrestling with the bank over the line of credit. Worrying over what it cost to run a newspaper was enough to give a guy PTSD.

Dixon gave him a measuring glance. "Well, as I said when we talked last week, there are private equity guys out there who might want to take a look at the *Enterprise.* Have you explored that possibility?"

Hark shuddered. He knew all about the private equity appetite for community newspapers. He had already "explored that possibility," which was a stupid way to put it, anyway. Exploring anything with a PE firm was like exploring a swamp in the company of a hungry alligator. You'd be the first victim. He set his glass down with a thump on the polished coffee table in front of him.

"Here's the thing, Mr. Dixon."

"Jeff." Dixon pushed an engraved silver coaster toward him. Hark snatched up his glass and replaced it on the coaster.

"Jeff." There wasn't any way to say this but say it straight out and be damned. "It's not a pretty picture. I need money to clear the note at the bank and meet the payroll. If I can't get it, I'll have to start making plans to fold the paper."

Half-guiltily, as if he were betraying a sister or a daughter by discussing her faults and shortcomings with a prospective suitor, he pushed a printout of the spreadsheet and a copy of the profit and loss statement across the table.

"This is the latest. I've included the bank note on this page." Full disclosure. "The due date is final. They won't let me roll it over again." His mouth was dry and he took another sip of Elliott's Select, conscious that he was making a mess of this. But it didn't much matter. The damned thing was hopeless, anyway.

"Thank you." Dixon went to his desk, opened a drawer, and took out a pair of reading glasses and a classic silver Meisterstück fountain pen, which must have cost as much as four or five loan payments on Hark's used Chevy. Back in his chair, glasses on the end of his nose, he picked up the P and L and studied it, Meisterstück in hand.

On a shelf, an ornate antique clock ticked loudly. In the fireplace, a log fell in a cascade of sparks. Dixon's pen made soundless scratches on the paper. Hark sat, not sure what to do with his hands, feeling like a kid called into the principal's office to confess that he was the one who heaved the rock through the girls' restroom window so he could sneak a peek. Dealing with Dixon was *not* a good idea, damn it. He gritted his teeth. It was like dancing with a devil who called all the tunes. And had all the hot moves.

But he was fresh out of ideas. If this didn't work, there were no more options. The bank would foreclose on the Enterprise building and the other property on Alamo Street. They might let him lease it, at least until they sold it. But he couldn't manage the lease and the payroll, too. Hobson's dilemma. Lease the building or fire the newsroom. Either way, the *Enterprise* was screwed.

At last, Dixon spoke. "This the latest P and L?" Scratching his nose with his Meisterstück, he peered critically at Hark. "The whole thing?"

"You got it," Hark said, with a half-assed attempt at jocularity. "We're down to the nut-cuttin'."

He waited, bracing himself against what he knew would be a refusal. Dixon might be community-minded enough to consider bailing out the local newspaper if it was in a temporary bind. But the P and L told a different story. Nobody with any business savvy would be interested in what was clearly a failing operation. And Jeff Davis Dixon was obviously a man with a great deal of business savvy.

Of course, Hark reminded himself, if Dixon really was operating with a political agenda, maybe he'd be willing to invest in what he thought was a failing newspaper — *if* it would give him the chips he needed to buy into the political game. But Hark wasn't going to sell to a man who would use the paper for political gain. That would be like torching the *Enterprise* to save it.

"Seems like you don't have a lot of time," Dixon added. "Bank's breathing down your neck." He riffled the papers with his thumb, pulled one out to examine, then another. "You've got a couple of pieces of valuable real estate. But it's fair to say that the rest of it doesn't look too promising. You agree?"

Hark wanted to point out that if the note wasn't paid, the bank would take the real estate, but he thought Dixon was probably smart enough to figure it out for himself. "Yeah. I agree," he said reluctantly.

Another couple of minutes, then Dixon put the papers down. "How's that online edition working out? Bringing in many subscriptions?"

Hark tried not to show that he was surprised by the question. He didn't know that Dixon knew that there *was* an online edition.

"Some," he replied cautiously. "It's bringing in more local advertisers. It's cheap online advertising, comparatively. And the advertisers can see the click-throughs to their websites, which they like."

All true. But he was avoiding the harder truth, that the digital edition was bringing in almost no new print subscribers, which in his view was what the *Enterprise* desperately needed. But the play gets over the...

"Look. Here's the bottom line." Dixon took off his glasses. "I'm a big fan of community-supported journalism. I believe in local newspapers that bring local problems to the attention of the local folks. I've been watching what you've been doing with the *Enterprise,* and I like it. You don't duck the hard stuff. You've made an honest newspaper out of a cozy little sweet sheet designed to make the chamber of commerce look good."

"Thanks," Hark said, now even more surprised. Who knew that Dixon could give this kind of thought to the situation? Or that he understood anything at all about community journalism?

Dixon leaned forward, elbows on knees. "That's dangerous, though — you know? What you're doing, I mean. Truth telling may produce good copy, but it doesn't always produce love and kisses. Readers may not appreciate the truth — not all of them, anyway."

"It was worth it," Hark said defensively. "Every word of it."

Dixon nodded emphatically. "I'm remembering something I heard once in a journalism class. The owner of the Lerner neighborhood weekly newspaper chain used to say, 'Let the big guys cover the international news; a fistfight on Clark Street is more interesting to our readers than a war in Europe.' I think you're doing a premier job of covering the fistfights. That young crime reporter you've got — Jessica Nelson — is as good as anybody in the business. I've been watching her investigative work on the Angel of Death. And your features editor. Fran Fenner. She's good, too."

Another surprise. Hark hadn't known that Dixon read the bylines or paid any attention to the reporters in the newsroom.

Getting up, Dixon went to the desk and picked up a gold cigarette box. He offered one to Hark, who shook his head. Giving up cigarettes had been the hardest thing he'd done in his whole life — harder even than giving up trying to save his marriage. He damned sure wasn't going back there again.

Dixon sat down and used a heavy gold lighter to light his cigarette. He leaned back in his chair and stretched out his feet. "So here's the deal, Hark. I want to help you get where it looks like you want to go. I'll finance the bank note repayment with the accrued interest, plus twelve months' payroll and all the digital expenses. Judging from your P and L, that should pretty much give you a clean start."

Hark pulled in his breath. The bank note *and* payrolls for twelve months? That would save both the real estate *and* the jobs in the newsroom. It was more than he was expecting, much more. But for this, the devil would demand his due. He would want —

"I want a thirty-percent share." Dixon gave him a straight, hard look. "And a title. Co-publisher."

Thirty was the number Hark had been thinking, but an actual management job? Forget it. Out of the question.

"A title is not on the table," he said shortly. "I'm not going to let anybody —"

Dixon raised his hand. "Hold on. In that position, my responsibility will be limited to the digital and social media side. You're the boss where print is concerned. I may have some proposals about using some of the staff to create original content. I will also propose that we ditch the digital replica edition in favor of a digital-only edition. It will have some of the same content as the print, but many more digital-only features, aimed at a different audience. A wider, younger, more diverse audience. A Corridor audience."

Diverse? Younger? Corridor? That would attract more advertisers. Still . . .

Hark frowned. "But won't that cost —"

"I'll fund the cost, which might include bringing in a few new journalists. I think digital is where small-town newspapers are headed in the long haul, and I have some ideas I want to experiment with. I want the freedom to do that. No rules, no restraints." He pulled on his cigarette. "That's the deal, Hark. Your fiscal problems are solved for at least a year. I won't tell you how to manage the news, or what to print, or how, or when, or why. I stay out of print. You stay out of digital. Deal?"

Hark stared at Dixon. This was nothing like what he'd expected. Clenching his jaw, he did a quick mental calculation. The bank note plus twelve months of payroll — that was a much bigger cash infusion than he'd dared to hope for. To tell the truth, it was the answer to his prayers. It was like winning the Triple Crown or a Mega-Bucks record lottery. It would see the *Enterprise* entirely out of debt for the first time ever.

And all for just thirty percent? Not nearly as bad as he had feared. He'd been sure that Dixon was going to demand a controlling interest. And as far as digital was concerned —

Yeah. That could be a problem. Hark didn't know enough about digital to guess where Dixon was going with it. And what about his political ambitions? What tricks did the man have up his sleeve?

He narrowed his eyes. "Exactly what sort of experiments are you thinking about? 'Digital ideas'? What's that?"

"If I knew, I'd tell you." Dixon gave him a candid smile. "News as it happens, maybe, with rolling deadlines. Maybe Snapchat's Discover program. An online advertisers' gallery. An active Facebook page. Certainly a larger internet presence, with maybe a marketplace that generates online affiliate revenue. And intersections with other media outlets along the Corridor — radio, television, newspapers. I'm also thinking that there may be some folks in journalism at CTSU who might like to get involved. It could be a good place for students to get some real-world experience."

"Affiliate revenue?" Hark blinked. "You thinking of selling — what? Like T-shirts and stuff?"

"Can't say yet. I won't know what's possible until I get in and get a good look." Dixon gave Hark a crooked grin. "I'm putting my money where my mouth is, Hark. I think there's potential here and I'm willing to pay to play. I'm also willing to fail, if that's in the cards. Bottom line, you'll have my money. For the rest of it, I guess you'll just have to trust me."

Trust him? Hark turned down his mouth. Trusting somebody — especially somebody like Dixon — was like handing over your wife's private phone number or the password to your computer. Trust wasn't something he did, especially where the *Enterprise* was concerned. This guy had some clever moves, that was for sure. But what kind of game was he playing? What about the political angle? What about —

"Okay, I get it." Dixon tossed the papers onto the coffee table. "I'm wasting my time. You don't need my money that bad. You've got some local investors who will come in with more cash for less control. You've got a couple of PE firms waiting in the wings."

Hark pressed his lips together. He needed the money like he needed to take another breath. He had no local investors, and he wouldn't let a private equity firm touch the *Enterprise,* even if it meant pulling the plug tomorrrow. Dixon's money would keep them going for another year. And if that digital stuff didn't work out, if the whole thing crashed and burned — well, he'd done what he could. At worst, he would have bought another year. At best —

But maybe he could dicker down the cost.

"Twenty and digital," he said. "In return for covering the note and fifteen months' payroll. I'll have my lawyer draw up the agreement."

"Thirty and twelve," Dixon said firmly. "Any more haggling and it goes to thirty-five and nine. And I'll have *my* lawyer draw up the agreement."

"I need some time to think," Hark said.

"Take all the time you want. You're the one with the bank breathing down your back." Dixon shook his head. "This is a no-brainer, Hark. You're either ready to deal or you aren't. It's as simple as that."

"Yeah," Hark said dispiritedly. "Simple as that."

But it wasn't. It wasn't simple at all.

The devil was in the details.

CHAPTER FOURTEEN

Texas weather is utterly inconstant. Bone-chilling cold one week, spring-like warmth the next. The thaw set in after Valentine's Day, and before long, the daffodils, early iris, and forsythia were blooming in people's gardens. The mountain laurel outside Jessica's kitchen door (which wasn't a laurel at all and smelled exactly like grape Kool-Aid) was decorated with clusters of purple blossoms, and bluebonnets were only days away.

It had been an eventful couple of weeks. At Ethan Connors' request — his order, really — Jessica had not told Maggie what she had learned about Lilia's pregnancy, her desire to keep the baby, and her insistence that she and the doctor divorce their spouses and marry. She hadn't mentioned Crawley's confession to his now ex-wife, either.

But she did give Maggie Judge Maude's instructions for filing the exhumation request, and Maggie did what had to be done. Judge Davidson granted the exhumation order, and Maggie asked Jessica to go to the cemetery with her. Jessica found the small, impromptu ceremony deeply moving and found herself hoping that Lilia — silenced for too long — would at last be able to tell them what they needed to know.

And all this while, she couldn't stop wondering what was going on with the arson investigation in Georgia Shores. Officer Riley had promised to call her, but she'd heard nothing from him, which was no great surprise. She hadn't actually expected anything, although she alternated between hoping that the cops were onto something and fearing that they weren't. She figured that Riley's promising lead, whatever it was, had fizzled out. He didn't want to tell her that the investigation had gone nowhere. Again.

But that wasn't it. After several more days went by, she called the Georgia Shores PD and asked for Officer Riley. The call was referred to Officer Hapgood, who wasn't there. And then to Officer Beverly Loomis. When Jessica repeated her request for the third time, Loomis hesitated. Then: "You haven't heard?"

"Haven't heard what?"

"Officer Riley was shot."

"Shot!" Jessica could feel her heart constrict and something — shock, disappointment, fear? — flooded, cold, through her veins. Had he been murdered? Was the murder related to the case he'd been working on? Her family's case?

But her unasked question was answered in the next breath.

"It was a routine traffic stop that went bad." Loomis said flatly. There were a few other details. The shooter, a parole violator, had fled and been apprehended, hiding in the Dumpster at a nearby Dairy Queen. Riley's death was all the more tragic because he had left a wife and a three-year-old son.

"If you'll tell me why you're calling," Loomis said, "maybe I can help."

Hesitantly, Jessica told her about Riley's phone call and his report of a possible lead in her family's arson deaths. But Loomis didn't seem to know anything about it. She said, "I'll check with Riley's partner, Officer Hapgood. He's out on sick leave for a couple of weeks, but maybe he knows something. I'll give you a call."

Sure you will, Jessica thought as she clicked off the call. *But I won't hold my breath.*

The newsroom had been even busier than

usual. There had been the measles scare, with Heather out for over a week and Denise out the week after that — she had caught Heather's measles. That hadn't been much of a loss, as far as Jessica was concerned. When Denise was gone, things always seemed to run more smoothly.

More importantly, Jessica had met several times with Hark to update him on progress in the Lilia Thompson story. She had written several brief pieces on the exhumation, the autopsy, and the pending report, noting that these were part of a developing story. But Connors and his team were expecting that their investigation would result in Dr. Crawley's arrest, and premature publicity might throw a monkey wrench in the works. She had drafted the full story for release when she got a green light.

It had been a little hard to talk to Hark, though. He was distracted. Jessica suspected that it had to do with his attempts to get funding for the *Enterprise.* Everybody in the newsroom was worried and on edge, and unsettling rumors were flying. The newspaper was going to be sold. The bank was going to repossess the building. The paper was going to go to one issue a week and half the newsroom would be fired.

Her story on David Redfern had appeared

in the weekend magazine. On Monday evening, just as she was about to make a grilled cheese sandwich for her supper, David had called to say that he liked the story very much — especially the part about Darwin, his monitor lizard, who lived in a three-by-five-foot glass enclosure, six feet high and furnished with floor-to-ceiling climbing branches and a small, green forest of live plants. Fran had featured a large photo of Darwin and his owner.

"Darwin has never had his photo in a newspaper before," he said, "and he's already hearing from fans. I'd love to take you out to dinner as a thank-you."

"I'm sorry." She put slices of cheddar and mozzarella cheese between slices of bread. "I can't."

"Look, Jessica," he'd said firmly, "The interview has been published, so you're done writing about me. Right? Let's have dinner — say, tomorrow night." His voice was warm. "There's an Indian restaurant in one of the malls on the interstate. I haven't been there yet, but I've been told it's good. And I definitely owe you."

"The interview was one thing," she said. "But I'm writing a book about Byers' crimes, and next week, I'll be covering his preliminary hearing." Feeling awkward, she cleared her throat. "Thanks for asking, David. I really do appreciate it and I'm sorry to say no. A reporter can't have a personal relationship with a source. Period. Paragraph. End of story."

"Jeez," he said, sounding pained. "Is this the way it's going to be from here on out? You're off limits — I mean, *we* are off limits? The only place I get to see you is in the office or the courtroom?"

"Not necessarily," she said cautiously. "I have an appointment with the DA to talk about her plans for the preliminary hearing." She buttered both sides of the sandwich and slid it into the skillet on the stove. "I'll also be glad to hear the plans for your side of the prelim. We can do this over the phone . . . or whatever."

There was a silence. "Okay," he said finally. "I get it. No date. But sure, I'd be glad to tell you what I've got in mind for the prelim — what I want people to know, that is. How about doing it over lunch instead of over the phone? Tomorrow. At that Indian place."

She didn't hesitate. "I can do that." She paused and added firmly, "Dutch treat."

He chuckled. "You are a *hard* woman, Jessica Nelson."

"Just playing by the rules."

"Tomorrow, then," he said, and clicked off.

She was flipping her sandwich when her cellphone rang again. This time, it was Connors.

"The autopsy report on Lilia Thompson came back this morning," he said. "This afternoon, we charged Dr. Crawley with her murder. I thought you'd like a heads-up, since you jump-started this investigation."

Jessica pulled in her breath. "What did the autopsy show?"

"The abrasion on her nose and the bruising on her lower lip were both consistent with being smothered with a pillow. There were cotton fibers in her lungs that could have come from a pillowcase. But the most important fact: Lilia was fifteen weeks pregnant. And the doctor's DNA was a match for the fetal DNA." His voice was triumphant. "It's a slam dunk, Jessica."

"The doctor's DNA?" Jessica let out her breath again. "Can I ask how you got that, or is it a deep, dark secret?"

Connors chuckled. "You've heard of Starbucks?"

Jessica wondered briefly how many criminals had been identified by DNA left on coffee cups, tissues, drinking straws, or cigarettes. It might make an interesting piece for the weekend magazine.

"That, plus the confession Christine recorded on her phone, have gone to the DA. Henderson says it's a strong case." He paused. "I'll let you know when the arraignment is scheduled. I assume you'll want to be there."

"You bet," Jessica said fervently. "I wouldn't miss it for the world."

She clicked off, finished grilling her sandwich, and took it into the living room. She planned to eat her dinner in front of the television, with her feet on the coffee table and Murph purring on the sofa beside her. She had met all her deadlines for the day. Tonight, she could kick off her shoes, sit back, relax, and —

The phone again. This time, it was Hark. "Hope you're not busy," he said. "We have a developing hostage situation at Dinky's, that joint on Redbud Trail, just across the river. Virgil's got his cameras and he's on his way. How quick can you get there?"

Jessica glanced at the clock on the shelf over the television. "Fifteen, tops," she said. "Tell Virgil I'm already out the door."

"Great," Hark said. "Be safe over there." He paused, adding almost (but not quite) apologetically. "Sorry for busting up your evening. Hope you weren't doing something exciting."

"Who, me?" Jessica chuckled wryly. "Do I ever?"

■ ■ ■ ■

FAULT LINES:
BOOK TWO

■ ■ ■ ■

Tomorrow, every fault
is to be amended;
but that tomorrow never comes.
— Benjamin Franklin

There's enough grief in this
world without always getting into
whose fault it is.
— Lisa Samson

A NOTE TO READERS

Fault Lines is the second book in a trilogy that takes us into the newsroom of the *Pecan Springs Enterprise,* a small newspaper that is facing an enormous challenge — the same challenge faced by communities all over America. Their newspapers are disappearing at a phenomenal rate, leaving behind vast "news deserts" served by local television channels with national news prescribed by out-of-state network owners. The *New York Times* sums up this national crisis:

School board and city council meetings are going uncovered. Overstretched reporters receive promising tips about stories but have no time to follow up. Newspapers publish fewer pages or less frequently or, in hundreds of cases across the country, are shuttered completely. All of this has added up to a crisis in local news coverage in the United States that has frayed communities and left many Americans woefully uninformed . . . and without access to crucial information about where they live.

The dangerous and very real plight of community newspapers and the journalists they employ has been much on my mind for the last few years, which is why I chose to make it one of the major plotlines in the *Enterprise* trilogy.

When Hark Hibler became the editor of the *Enterprise* back in *Chile Death* (book 6 of the China Bayles series), he began introducing us to the newspaper's role in the fictional community of Pecan Springs. Now the owner-publisher, Hark is facing new and more formidable challenges: the competition of the internet, the loss of local readers and local advertising, and the possibility that the newspaper may have to close.

Whose fault is this? What can be done to prevent it? What will it cost to fix it — if it *can* be fixed? Who pays — and why?

These are some of the important questions I wanted to bring up in *Deadlines* and *Fault Lines*. But in this second novella, I also wanted to explore the resolution of the intriguing mystery that has troubled Ruby

Wilcox for the past couple of decades. And to consider an interesting dilemma that Jessica Nelson faces: Is it ever okay for a journalist to enter a romantic relationship with one of her sources?

Thanks for being a reader. You're what it's all about.

Susan Wittig Albert

Jessica pulled out an empty chair and sat down at the large round table at Bean's Bar and Grill. "Green beer?" she repeated with a skeptical glance. "Ugh."

"Hey, it's everyday draft beer," Francine Fenner said. "Bob just puts a few drops of green food coloring into it. Perfect for St. Pat's Day." She stuck out her tongue. "Does turn you green inside, though."

"No booze for me tonight, anyway," Jessica said. When she came in, she'd stopped at the bar and picked up a Virgin Mary — a Bloody Mary minus the vodka. "Has anybody ordered nachos?"

"A couple of plates, on the way," Will Wagner told her, leaning back in his chair. Will looked the part of sports editor in an olive green Pittsburgh Steelers T-shirt and a shamrock-colored Boston Celtics baseball cap. As usual, the cap was on backwards, and his straggly blond hair was sticking out on all sides. He grinned at Jessica. "Wouldn't be a party without nachos."

"At least, not a party at Bean's," Jessica said.

Bean's Bar and Grill (named for Judge Roy Bean, who named *his* saloon — the Jersey Lillie — for Lilly Langtry) was Pecan Springs' favorite Tex-Mex place. Today, it was even more crowded than usual, since the crowd was celebrating St. Patrick's Day. People lined the old-fashioned saloon bar and filled most of the tables in the room. Over their heads hung antique wooden wagon wheels studded with red and green chili-pepper lights, and a carved wooden Indian stood in the corner. The walls were studded with posters of famous Texas politicos and the posters, also used as targets for dart games, were studded with tiny holes. People could throw darts at Lyndon Johnson on a horse; white-haired former governor Ann Richards on a white Harley, wearing white leathers; and George W. Bush on a riding lawn mower, wearing a cowboy hat and a business suit.

"No booze on St. Pat's?" Francine asked curiously. "Are you on the wagon?"

"Nope." Jessica made a face. "But I have to go back to the newsroom and finish the piece on the Angel of Death. Denise wants it first thing tomorrow." Jessica, the *Enterprise*'s crime reporter, had recently uncovered a string of serial killings committed by Howard Byers, who called himself Azrael, the Angel of Death. She was writing a book about his crimes, as well as some articles for the newspaper.*

"You have to work tonight?" Francine asked sympathetically. "That sucks, Jessie. There's live Irish music coming up. Should be fun." Her long dark hair was snugged tightly into a ponytail and cinched with a green ribbon that matched her black-and-green luck-of-the-Irish T-shirt and her green jeans.

"Blame Denise," Jessica said, stirring her drink with a celery stick. "It's her fault, for moving up the deadline." She had spent the afternoon at the courthouse, so she was wearing a businesslike blazer over a silky green blouse (her nod to St. Pat's) and a gray pencil-slim skirt. She lowered her voice. "Denise — the slave driver from hell."

Denise Sanger, the assistant editor, was universally disliked by the staff. At the mo-

* For Jessica's investigation, read *Out of BODY,* book 3 in the Crystal Cave novella trilogy. The story is updated in *Deadlines,* the first novella in the *Enterprise* trilogy.

ment, togged out in dark green yoga pants and a flowing green tunic patterned with shamrocks, she was sitting at the bar, flirting with a half-bald guy in jeans and a brown leather vest.

"Slave driver from hell." Fran repeated with a crooked smile. "You got that right." She lifted her mug of green beer. "Well, here's to St. Paddy."

"And to the *Enterprise*," put in Hark Hibler, the newspaper's publisher and editor, on the other side of the table. He hoisted his bottle of Guinness. His green sweatshirt featured a tipsy leprechaun with the caption, "Drink the fook up."

Jessica picked up her glass and joined in the chorus of voices. "To St. Paddy and the *Enterprise*!"

The group around the table was large and congenial, and Jessica felt very glad to be one of them. In addition to Fran (features) and Will (sports) there were Angie and Heather (staff writers) and Becky (copy editor). The tall, skinny guy snapping candids with his Nikon was Virgil Osborn, the paper's photographer. Len Hopkins from Advertising was having a serious conversation with Allan Hodge, production manager, and Coralee Moore, from the mailroom, was listening, a bored expression on her freckled face. Not there, Jessica noticed, were several people from the business office and the newspaper's community columnists: her friend China Bayles, who wrote the gardening column, and Jeannine Benson, who covered nearby Wimberley and San Marcos.

Hark pushed back his chair, got up, and came around to the empty chair next to Jessica. "How you doin', Jessie?"

He turned the chair around, straddled it, and folded his arms across the back. Hark was dark-haired and stocky with black-rimmed glasses, sloped shoulders, and a permanently rumpled look. Nobody would call him handsome, but he was a top-flight editor, stood by his staff, and was totally dedicated to the idea of community journalism as a way of helping small towns cope with change. Give him half a chance, and he would lean in close and explain in passionate detail why the *Enterprise* was vitally important to the health of Pecan Springs and why every community needed a strong local paper to survive and thrive.

Several years before, Hark had moved from Dallas to Pecan Springs to take over the editorship of the Pecan Springs *Enterprise,* a cozy little weekly paper that rarely printed the *real* news, only the good news.

Not long afterward, he arranged to buy it from its longtime local owners, the Seidensticker family. His goal: to reinvent the *Enterprise* as a modern newspaper that served every citizen, not just the chamber of commerce, the business owners, and the real estate developers, all of whom had a stake in making Pecan Springs look like the cleanest, coziest little town in Texas.

But these days, people didn't get all their news from newspapers. Now, the internet and the twenty-four-hour cable news cycle were making things difficult for newspapers everywhere, rural or urban, small or large. It was hardest for small local newspapers, most of whom (if they were still in business) were operating on a very thin, very frayed shoestring.

Things were extremely difficult for the *Enterprise.* Circulation was down and ad revenue was at a low ebb. Even the classifieds, which used to take up a couple of pages, had shrunk to a single column. Got something to sell or trade? A job to fill, a house to rent, a request for a daily ride to San Antonio or Austin? Forget the *Enterprise.* It was quicker and more effective to post whatever you needed on Craigslist online.

This wasn't any secret, of course. From

the newsroom to the business office to the local delivery kids, every employee understood that the *Enterprise* was bleeding and that its publisher, their boss, was facing a mountain of insurmountable financial challenges. A couple of people had already left for jobs outside of journalism, and the most recent hires (Heather and Coralee) worried that they were at the top of Hark's to-be-fired list. Jessica couldn't blame people for wondering just how the *Enterprise* could manage to survive. And what they would do if it didn't.

Which made this evening's St. Patrick's Day party all that more important, Jessica thought. As several plates of nachos arrived and people started helping themselves, she stole a glance at Hark, thinking that he looked even more troubled than usual. Maybe he'd gotten more bad news from the accountant. Maybe he was trying to come up with a last-ditch way to save the paper, like Superman saving the *Daily Planet.* Maybe —

But Hark had something else on his mind. He took a nacho off the plate, then leaned toward Jessica and whispered, "Have you seen Ruby lately?"

Ruby was Jessica's friend Ruby Wilcox, the owner of the Crystal Cave, Pecan

Springs' only New Age shop. Hark and Ruby had dated each other for a while, but Ruby had moved on. Her current romantic flame was a detective on the Pecan Springs police force. And although Hark wouldn't want to admit it, Jessica suspected that he still carried a torch.

"Yes, I've seen her," Jessica said. "Last weekend, actually. Why? Is something the matter?"

"I'm afraid so." Hark thumbed his glasses up on his nose. "I ran into her in the grocery yesterday and she seemed . . . well, a little more flaky than usual. She told me something that's bothering me."

Jessica refrained from rolling her eyes. Hark was a thoughtful guy. She liked him as a person and respected him as an editor. But he had a pronounced judgmental streak and a tendency to look on the dark side of things — and people. She had never been certain how much he knew or suspected about Ruby's unusual . . . gifts, so she wasn't sure how to answer him.

"I wouldn't call her 'flaky,' " she said defensively. "It's true that she's sort of out there sometimes. And her sister can be a little bit wacko. But Ruby is a —"

"What Ruby told me," Hark broke in, "is that she's going to that parapsychology lab at the university. Twice a week." He frowned. "Given her tendency to go off the deep end, I wouldn't say it's very healthy for her. The lab, I mean. Mentally."

Go off the deep end? In the newsroom, Jessica always maintained a professional distance when she talked to her boss. But they were at Bean's, and this was a personal matter. She put a reassuring hand on his arm.

"I know where you're coming from, Hark. But if I were you, I wouldn't worry. There are no mental issues here. Ruby is just doing what's good for her."

That was true, Jessica knew. For years, her friend Ruby Wilcox had thought that she was the only one in the world who had a special talent — a curse, as she viewed it — for seeing and hearing things that others couldn't. (Except for her sister Ramona, of course — but Ramona was a whole other story.) Like many people with genuine psychic abilities, Ruby had spent her life hiding out, pretending she was every bit as normal as the person standing next to her at the checkout register in Cavette's Market.

But some of Ruby's recent experiences had made that hopeful pretense impossible, jarring her into the uneasy awareness that she was far more *different* than she had ever imagined.* On the heels of that recognition, she had learned about Dr. Scott's parapsychology lab at Central Texas State University, one of the few such programs operating anywhere in the country. While Dr. Scott worked primarily with students, she had quietly opened the lab to others who demonstrated what the professor called "unusual gifts." Meeting Dr. Scott, who was gifted in some of the same ways, was helping Ruby make sense of what was happening in her life. Which was why Jessica thought it was good for her.

But Hark obviously thought otherwise.

"Good for her?" he hooted skeptically. "Cripes, Jessica, what makes you think that? I've heard some pretty damned unsettling things about that lab. Lots of ridiculous woo-woo stuff going on up there. I have some friends on the psych faculty, and they think that lab makes them look like a load of loonies. They'd like to put it out of business and send Dr. Scott back to teaching the intro courses."

Jessica sighed. Her beat as the *Enterprise* crime reporter gave her unusual access to

* For the full story of Ruby's experiences, read the Crystal Cave Trilogy: *NoBODY, SomeBODY Else,* and *Out of BODY.*

the underworld of bad people. Dr. Scott was not one of them. "That would be unfortunate," she said soberly. "I've met the professor. She's a very —"

"Difficult woman to work with," Hark inserted. "She has some exceptionally creepy ideas, I'm told." He pulled on his Guinness. "I don't feel like I have a lot of influence over Ruby these days, or I'd tell her what I think. But maybe you can persuade her to drop out of this nutty lab situation — before she gets herself into trouble."

"Before she gets herself into trouble?" Jessica echoed, frowning. "What the dickens is *that* supposed to mean?"

Hark smiled enigmatically. "You're the investigative reporter, Jessica. I'll leave it to you to find out."

Before Jessica could answer, Denise Sanger appeared behind them. "Oh, *there* you are, Hark," she cooed, in what Jessica thought of as her sex-kitten voice. Neatly inserting herself between Hark and Jessica, she leaned over his shoulder. "I was wondering if I was going to have to drag you away from the meeting with Mr. Dixon. How did it go?"

"Got postponed," Hark said shortly. "Rescheduled for tomorrow morning."

"Oh, good," Denise said brightly. "That

leaves us plenty of time for fun." She gave Jessica a meaningful look.

Jessica understood. Denise was recently divorced and now had her eye on Hark, who was also divorced and — supposedly — available. Far be it from her to stand in Denise's way. She pushed her chair back and picked up her drink.

"You can have my seat, Denise. I'll move over there." She pointed to the chair Hark had vacated on the other side of the table, next to Virgil. "I have to leave in a few minutes, anyway."

"You can't stay and party with the rest of us?" Hark asked, frowning. "Why the hell not? You got a hot date?"

Jessica smiled. "I truly *wish.* I have to go back to the newsroom. Denise wants my Angel of Death story first thing tomorrow. But that's okay," she added hastily. "I really don't mind, Denise. Glad to do it."

"Is that so, Denise?" Hark looked over his shoulder at her, frowning. "You must have forgotten that we moved Jessica's story."

Denise was flustered. "Oh, gosh, you're right," she said, stepping back. "Sorry." She didn't say it as if she meant it, though.

"So no deadline," Hark said to Jessica. "We don't need it tomorrow." He gestured at her chair. "Stick around. I need to ask you a couple of things about your story on the Crawley arraignment." He added, reaching for a napkin and a pen. "Which was good, by the way. I like your opening sentences, but I think you might want to expand the third paragraph. Like this, maybe."

So Jessica sat back down while Hark told her what he thought and Denise moved to the seat on the other side of the table. The glare she aimed at Jessica was so laser-fierce that it might have scorched a hole right through Jessie's silky green blouse. Clearly, this little episode would not be forgotten.

A moment later, Hark's and Jessica's cellphones dinged, both at the same time. There was a two-alarm fire in a laundromat a couple of blocks from the *Enterprise* building, threatening a Chinese restaurant on one side and a copy shop on the other.

Hark looked at her, eyebrows raised. "Sounds like it might be a big one," he said. "You okay to handle this, Jessica?"

Jessica pushed back her chair and stood up. Hark knew her story. He understood that — while not even the bloodiest shooting scenes could faze her — she had a problem covering fires. When she was a girl, her mother and father and twin sister had died when their house burned. Jessica had been away on a school trip that weekend, and when she returned, there was nothing left but a pile of smoking embers. The fire was ruled as arson, although nobody was ever charged with the crime. And because no one was charged, there could be no closure. The pain and the loss would never go away.

Jessica went to live with her grandmother in Louisiana. She was sad and bereft, but she seemed — at first, anyway — to handle her loss fairly well. But as time went on, she began suffering from fire-related panic attacks. She could deal (more or less) with candle flames, and gas burners on the kitchen stove, but a big bonfire could send her spiraling into panic mode. And when the fire alarms went off at school — even when she knew it was a drill — she felt suddenly paralyzed. It was as if time stood still, and the fire that killed her family was still blazing now, right this minute.

The first few times this happened, she tried to deal with it by telling herself that there was nothing to be afraid of. She was strong, she wasn't in real danger, everything was going to be just fine.

Really. Just. Fine.

Whatever this feeling was, it was all in her head. It was silly.

Be strong. Ignore it and it would go away. Right?

Wrong.

After a while, lecturing herself on being strong was no help at all. The smell of smoke and the sight of flames — by or sometimes even on television — made her feel lightheaded and her skin grew clammy. As it got worse, her vision would begin to blur and she couldn't get her breath. Her hands felt icy and her legs were like spaghetti. If she couldn't escape, she was afraid she would pass out. The only way to be safe was to avoid fire altogether, which meant that she had to miss the big homecoming bonfires and the Fourth of July celebrations — and pray that she wouldn't encounter a fire she couldn't avoid.

And then one night, it happened. She had moved to Pecan Springs to go to college. In her senior year, the pizza shop next door to her apartment had burned, and all the residents were told to evacuate the building. She was scared but more or less okay — until she got out on the street and saw the blaze lighting up the black sky. The air was filled with smoke and suddenly, the fiery tentacles of the flames seemed to reach out searing arms for her, threatening to pull her into the white-hot heart of the fire.

Blindly, she stumbled away as a darkness enveloped her and sound seemed to fade away. She couldn't breathe. She was dizzy. Her heart pounded in her throat, and the next moment she was fainting into the arms of her alarmed boyfriend.

This was frightening enough, but when she came to and he helped her get to her feet, she fainted again. The standby EMS crew gave her oxygen and bundled her into an ambulance. She spent the night in the hospital, where she was finally pronounced well enough to go home — but not back to the apartment. The smell of smoke made her panic again. She went home with Charlie, her boyfriend, and stayed there for the next couple of weeks.

Which proved to be a bad idea. Jessica had always thought of herself as tough, self-reliant, and independent, and she was deeply shaken by what had happened. Charlie was sweet, even tender, about the whole thing. In fact, he seemed almost to have enjoyed playing the role of the manly male who rescued his fainting damsel. For weeks afterward, he watched her carefully, as if he expected her to pass out at any moment.

But Charlie's solicitude only made things worse. For Jessica, the episode had been terrifying — and it wasn't just the fire. Fainting had felt like a complete loss of control, a betrayal by her own body that left her vulnerable and undefended. She was embarrassed that she couldn't handle something that everybody else handled just fine, as if she were the hypersensitive princess who could feel a pea even when it was under twenty mattresses.

And anyway, that kind of way-out panic reaction wasn't just scary, it could be downright dangerous. What if she fainted in the middle of a street, in front of a car? The fear itself became obsessive. She couldn't get it out of her mind.

That's when she went to see Dr. Pam Neely, a therapist who was suggested by her friend China. Sympathetic and helpful, Dr. Pam (as she preferred to be called) diagnosed her as suffering from a severe case of PTSD — post-traumatic stress disorder — and prescribed journal writing and a series of "therapeutic exposures" that helped her to gradually lose at least some of her fear of fire. The situation had improved to the point where she could enter a room with a burning fireplace without being overcome with dizziness — and the fear of falling into a dark place.

And she had even disciplined herself to cover a fire when she had to. It wasn't on her list of favorite things, and she was still apprehensive that she might be overtaken by a panic she couldn't control. But she kept on seeing Dr. Pam and her apprehension eased. She felt she was getting better.

Hark was watching her cautiously. "You okay to check out this fire?" he asked. "Want me to send Heather?"

"No, I can do it." She managed a smile. "On my way."

"Atta girl." Hark lifted his Guinness in salute.

Denise smiled archly, gave her a little wave, and got up to take her empty seat.

CHAPTER TWO

"I'm sorry I couldn't come to the St. Pat's party yesterday evening."

China Bayles put three bowls of jalapeño cheese soup on the table in the tearoom. One was for her and the others were for Ruby Wilcox and Jessica. "McQuaid and I were talking about the financial crisis at the newspaper over supper last night," she added, sitting down. "It sounds pretty grim."

"I've been thinking about this, too," Ruby said. "Does Hark have a plan?"

Jessica pulled her bowl toward her. Small local newspapers all over the country were in serious trouble — including the *Pecan Springs Enterprise,* which had been a community institution since Teddy Roosevelt was president. It was no surprise that concern about the financial health of the *Enterprise* was being felt in the community. Some people were wondering whether it was going to survive and what they would do if it didn't. Sadly, too many others took the paper for granted and forgot to renew their subscriptions. If it went under, they would be the first to complain, of course — and the loudest.

Jessica unfolded her napkin with a sigh. "If Hark has a plan, he hasn't told the rest of us yet."

Jessica, China, and Ruby were sitting down to lunch in the tearoom behind China's Thyme and Seasons herb shop and Ruby's Crystal Cave. The tearoom had the same limestone walls, wooden floors, and painted tin ceiling that appeared throughout the old building. But it was distinguished by its green-painted wainscoting and tables, colorful chintz table mats and napkins, and terra-cotta pots of rosemary and thyme on the tables. The noon lunch rush was over, the other diners had left, and the three of them had the place to themselves.

"The newspaper staff must be really worried," Ruby said, taking a piece of hot herb bread out of the basket. She'd had her hair cut earlier in the week, and it frizzed out in thick red curls all over her head. As usual, she was wearing an eye-catching outfit: peacock-blue harem-styled pants and a tie-dyed purple tank top with chunky strands of green and blue pottery beads. "After all, if the paper goes away, jobs will disappear, too."

"Yes, people are worried." Jessica picked up her spoon and began on her soup. It was a blustery March day and the wind was chilly, so the jalapeño cheese soup — hot and pleasantly spicy — warmed her all the way through. "This morning, we heard a rumor that Hark is trying to work out a deal with a guy he knows. Jeff Dixon. Nobody knows the details, though. And it's probably just wishful thinking."

"I heard something about that," China said, starting on her salad. She was dressed in her usual casual work outfit — a green Thyme and Seasons T-shirt, jeans, and sneakers. "Jeff Dixon is the heir of Dixon International. Not the kind of guy you'd think would be interested in buying a news-paper."

"As long as he has plenty of money," Ruby remarked archly. "That's the bottom line, so to speak."

"You think?" China asked. "I have the feeling that Hark won't make a deal just based on money. There's got to be some-thing else — some advantage for the news-paper." She sighed. "I don't know why people aren't jumping in to help out. This is a *community* thing we're talking about."

"I hope the paper can stay afloat." Jessica made a face. "I love my job — most of the time, anyway."

But not the night before. The laundromat fire had been a bad one. The owner's mother lived in an upstairs apartment and had to be rescued from the burning building in a close call that saw both her and a fireman sent to the hospital for smoke inhalation. The acrid smell of smoke and wet ash and the sight of lancing flames had made Jessica feel queasy and lightheaded, an unsettling reminder of the awful night the pizza shop caught fire. But she felt better when she could retreat to a place where she could fill her lungs with fresh air. She had even managed to write a halfway decent story.

She changed the subject. "I've been meaning to ask — how's Sheila's new baby? Or not so new, I guess. Noah must be . . . what? Five months old now? Six?" Sheila Dawson was a mutual friend — and Pecan Springs' chief of police — who had just had a baby.

"Almost six months," China replied with a smile. "He has a full head of dark hair, just like his daddy. He rolls over, tries to sit up, and eats like a little pig." She put her spoon into her soup. "Sheila and Blackie are over the moon, naturally."

"Naturally." Ruby speared a sprig of arugula, "But we hardly ever see Sheila these days. Not that we blame her," she added. "She has her hands full."

"If anybody can manage a new baby and still keep her cops in line," Jessica said with a chuckle, "it's Smart Cookie." The three of them were in awe of Sheila, who sailed serenely through difficulties and even danger without ruffling a hair of her beautiful blond head.

China turned to Jessica. "We're not seeing much of you either, Jessie. How's your book coming along? You must have a couple of chapters done by now." China was talking about *Not Only in the Dark,* Jessica's true-crime book about her investigation into the Angel of Death murders, a string of serial killings that had taken place, undetected, in six counties across Central Texas.*

"I've got a draft of the first chapter," Jessica said. "And a publishing contract with St. Martin's. *And* a deadline, of course," she added ruefully. "And at some point, I'll need to start interviewing Byers." Howard Byers, the Angel of Death.

Ruby pushed her empty soup bowl away.

* For this story, read *Out of BODY,* the third novella in the Crystal Cave Trilogy.

"Is that gorgeously hunky guy with the odd name still defending Byers?"

Jessica glanced at Ruby, who already knew the answer to that question, as she knew the answers to most questions she asked. She just didn't want to let you know that she knew. It was part of her cover. Part of being strongly telepathic but wanting to seem . . . well, normal.

"Yes, he is," she said.

That hunky guy was David Redfern, Charlie Lipman's law partner. As Byers' lawyer, David was not only a source for the book but would be a major character in it — which put him off limits. He had sent flowers and even asked her for a date, but developing any kind of personal relationship with him would be massively unethical. Journalists were supposed to maintain a professional relationship with their sources. So she had given the flowers away and said no to the date. Their one lunch together had been a working lunch, Dutch treat.

Still, Jessica had to admit that she was attracted to David Redfern. He was dark-haired, tall, and good-looking, a sharply intelligent man with an infinite collection of conversational topics. When she was with him, his smile made her skin tingle and her heart hopped and skipped like a jubilant girl on a bright spring day.

But dating was definitely off limits. Byers' trial likely wouldn't begin for months and months, and whatever the verdict, there would likely be an appeal. And she had to finish her book, which — given the fact that she had a day job — would occupy all of the year's nights and weekends, and the following year's, as well. Jessica had the feeling that David Redfern wouldn't be content to wait around on the off chance that she might be available to go out on a date with him sometime in the next decade.

China chuckled. "Well, I'm sure that Redfern understands the ethics of the situation as well as you do, Jessie. He must be pretty smitten if he keeps on asking." She sipped her iced tea. "I know we have things to talk about other than your crime beat, but I'm curious. Has Lilia Thompson's murderer been arraigned yet?" She corrected herself. "*Alleged* murderer." China had been a criminal defense attorney before she opened Thyme and Seasons.

"Scheduled for tomorrow," Jessica said. "I've heard there's a plea deal in the works."

"That would be a good thing," China said seriously. "A trial would be terribly painful for a great many people." The much-discussed case involved an admired Pecan

Springs doctor, a beloved (but deceased) librarian, and the librarian's sister.*

From there, the conversation skipped through the classes and workshops China and Ruby had scheduled for the spring, a couple of garden makeovers China was working on, the May Eve Fairy Festival Ruby was planning — the events that usually kept both shops busy until things slowed down in the simmering summer stretch of July and August. Then the talk segued to the doings in China's family: her husband, Mike McQuaid (a former cop turned private investigator) and their kids, Brian and Caitie. And to Ruby, who was still dating Ethan Connors, a detective with the Pecan Springs police force.

"Don't forget to tell Jess about Dr. Scott's psych lab," China said teasingly. To Jessica, she said, "Before we know it, Ruby will be selling tickets to her crystal ball readings." China supported Ruby's psychic activities, but she couldn't help being a little snarky about them.

"That reminds me, Ruby." Jessica said. "Hark wanted me to tell you that he's worried about that lab. He's afraid it's not good

* Jessica works on this story in *Deadlines,* book 1 in the *Enterprise* trilogy.

for you."

"What?" China raised her eyebrows. "Hark thinks our Ruby will turn into a vampire and invade his nightmares?"

Ruby frowned. "Hark should stop worrying about *me*. His newspaper is about to go down like the Titanic. He has his priorities all wrong!"

Jessica laughed. "Well, if you happen to run into him, don't offer to read his palm. He's already convinced that Dr. Scott is reinforcing all your wacko tendencies." She cocked her head. "You're still going to the lab, then?"

"Twice a week." Ruby leaned forward and lowered her voice. "Once for testing and the second for counseling sessions with Dr. Scott. I wouldn't tell anybody but you and China, Jessica. Dr. Scott is really helping. For one thing, she's asked me to keep a dream journal." In a softer, more wistful tone, she added, "I've been dreaming about Sarah — whatever that means."

Jessica nodded sympathetically. Ruby had told her about Sarah Gellner, the friend — her *best* friend — who had disappeared when they were juniors in high school, leaving a host of nagging questions behind her and opening a ragged hole in Ruby's life.

"Nobody has ever discovered what happened to her?" she asked.

"Not really." Ruby sounded pragmatic. "The cops decided she ran away, although her parents said she would never do that. I was sure she'd been kidnapped, and I even dreamed of the place where she'd been taken — an old abandoned house outside of town. But by the time I got up the courage to go to the police, she wasn't there. My fault," she said sadly. "If I had been more sure of myself, if I had trusted my intuition, who knows? I might have saved her."

"Don't beat yourself up, Ruby," China said, reaching across the table to touch Ruby's hand. "It wasn't your fault."

"But it *was* my fault," Ruby insisted. "The night she disappeared, she called and wanted me to go out with her. But I'd been grounded for staying out too late the weekend before, and I couldn't. If I had been with her . . ."

Jessica wanted to point out that if Ruby had been with her friend, they might *both* have disappeared. But instead, she said, "Remember Jaycee Dugard? She was eleven when she was kidnapped on the way to her school bus stop. But she survived and came home — eighteen years later. She's even written a book. So there's always hope." A disappearance might be as bitter as death, but at least it was open-ended.

Ruby brightened. "You're right," she said. "I need to remember Jaycee's story. It's just that . . ." Her voice trailed away.

Jessica understood, for her own life had never been the same since she had lost her parents and her twin sister. Like Ruby, she had struggled for years with the sense that she had been somehow at fault for being away that weekend. If she had been home, she might have wakened in time to get everyone out of the house before it burned. People called it survivor's guilt, but that didn't make it any easier to bear or even to explain. It was still just *guilt.*

And regardless of who set the fire and why — questions that would never be answered now — it was still her *fault,* irrational or not, that everyone else had died and she was still alive. Dr. Pam had suggested that this terrible sense of guilt might be one source of her panic attacks. She herself wondered if it was the reason she had become a crime writer, making amends by sharing the stories of victims and the impact of crime on their lives.

Jessica's phone pinged, and she jumped. "Oh, sorry," she said, pulling it out and turning it off. "I set an alarm to remind me of a call I need to make. Let me help you with the cleanup, girls, and then I have to go."

Ruby pushed back her chair and stood up. "You go on and make your phone call. We'll take care of things here."

"Thanks" Jessica said. "And thanks again for the lunch. That soup was totally awesome. It warmed me from the inside out."

China grinned. "Next time you're coming, we'll double the jalapeños. That'll warm you even more."

Ruby understood how Jessica felt and wished she could help. But survivor's guilt was something that each person had to work out for herself. Jessica was a strong young woman. She was on the right track.

Back in the Crystal Cave after lunch, Ruby thanked Laurel Wiley, her longtime helper, for keeping an eye on the cash register. She took a call from Ethan Connors, reminding her that they were going out to dinner that weekend, as if she needed a reminder. An evening with Ethan — perhaps a whole night together — was something she looked forward to and thought about long afterward. They had both been scarred by previous relationships, but this felt different. And special. Even his phone calls were enough to make her heart beat a little erratically. She found herself smiling dreamily as she clicked off.

But it was time to settle down to the job she'd planned for the afternoon. She was inventorying the book section and deciding which titles she needed to reorder. She made sure to order both new books and classics on important metaphysical topics: astrology, dreams, divination, meditation, shamanism, past lives, Wicca and the Craft, and more. She had also received a catalog from one of the book distributors, with several new books she wanted to order because she wanted to read them *herself* — definitely one of the perks of owning the shop.

In fact, while Ruby had been modestly successful at any number of things, she had never felt quite comfortable with any of it until she opened the Cave. She took an almost physical pleasure in the shelves of glittering crystals, candles, smudge sticks, and incense, like the patchouli she was burning behind the counter just now, its distinctive scent infused with jasmine, soft musk, cedar, and fragrant frangipani. She delighted in playing with the rune stones, the Ouija boards, the I Ching's yarrow sticks and coins, the shimmering crystal balls, and the mysterious obsidian scrying bowls. She admired the oracle cards and angel cards and tarot decks, and enjoyed playing meditative music, like the delicate George Winston piano music that was on her CD player just now.

To tell the truth, Ruby's life got easier after she opened the Cave. As a child, she had worked hard (and it *was* work!) to suppress the knowledge that she saw more, heard more, understood more, and *felt* more than other people. Her intuitions had often caused trouble, especially when she saw something ominous just around the corner. She was always tempted to share what she knew, but when she did, things usually went haywire. Before she graduated from kindergarten, she had learned that too much knowledge in the wrong hands could be damaging, even destructive — hard lessons for a young girl.

Here at the Cave, though, being different was perfectly okay. That was because Ruby's customers and friends liked to imagine that a shop that specialized in crystal balls and magic wands might be the Pecan Springs campus of Hogwarts School of Witchcraft and Wizardry, or an enchanted outpost of the Dominion of All Souls. For them, it was a magical space, somewhere between normal, down-to-earth life and the wide, wild universe of the imagination. For them, Ruby was the center of this charmed world, an enchantress who could perform *real* magic.

But for Ruby herself, it was a whole other story. The Crystal Cave was a place where she could allow herself to be totally different, but in a normal sort of way — if that made any sense (which it did, to her). She could indulge in spells and incantations. She could wear her red-orange hair in whatever outrageous style she chose. She could dress like a witch or a magician, and nobody would raise an eyebrow. Like the peacock-blue harem pants, tie-dyed purple tank, green and blue beads, and purple sandals she was wearing today, for instance. A bizarre outfit for the streets of Pecan Springs, but everyday attire for the Cave.

Ruby was sitting on the floor, checking the books on the lower shelves against the inventory list on her iPad, when the front door opened. She looked up to see a woman enter the shop and glance around, frowning. She was about Ruby's age, but heavyset and conservatively dressed in a navy blazer and skirt, white blouse and pearls, and navy pumps. Over her arm, she carried a large navy purse. When she saw Ruby in her blue harem pants and purple top, sitting cross-legged on the floor, her mouth made a surprised O and her eyebrows flew up under her dark Mamie-style bangs. She looked as if Aladdin's genie had just jumped out of the bottle right in front of her.

Ruby waggled her fingers in greeting. Without getting up, she said, pleasantly, "If you're looking for something in particular, I'm the one to ask. If you're just looking, make yourself at home. And take your time. There's lots to see."

"There certainly is," the woman muttered, eyeing a feathered dream catcher that hung from the ceiling a foot from her nose. "But I think I must be in the wrong place. I'm looking for —" She consulted a business card, holding it out at arm's length to squint at it. "Victoria's Vintage Crystal and Lace. I want to get an appraisal on my mother's Waterford."

"You *are* in the wrong place," Ruby said. "Victoria's is a block or so away."

The woman was peering at her. "Excuse me," she said. "Wait a minute. I know you, don't I? Aren't you —" Staring at Ruby, she pursed her lips, cocked her head, and then suddenly pointed her finger. "Why, you're Ruby Gifford!"

"Ruby Wilcox," Ruby corrected her, rising to her feet.

240

"But you *were* Ruby Gifford," the woman said accusingly, as if Ruby had forgotten her own name. "When we were in high school."

"Yes, I was," Ruby said. "And you are —"

She stopped, bracing herself against the unwelcome recognition she had been pushing away. The woman had gained forty pounds or more since Ruby had last seen her, and her features, once childlike and unformed, had sharpened. But Ruby knew.

"And you are Leslie Newell," she said.

"That's me," the woman said in a sprightly tone, but her smile was thin. "I'm back here for a few weeks to settle my mother's estate — sell the house, get rid of the ugly old furniture, that sort of thing." Chin raised, mouth slightly pouting, she looked around. "This your place?"

Without waiting for an answer, she added, "I must say, times have changed. I wouldn't have guessed that Pecan Springs would actually tolerate a shop that catered to the . . ." She sniffled. "The *occult.*"

Vintage Leslie, Ruby thought, half-amused. "I read about your mom's death in the paper," she said. "I'm sorry. She was greatly admired here." An outgoing, energetic woman with many friends, Karen Newell had been a major supporter of the

241

arts in Pecan Springs.

"Mother lived a full life," Leslie said in a tone that was almost dismissive. She regarded Ruby curiously. "I suppose you married that kid with the pimples. Stewart? Wasn't that his name?" The eyebrows arched into the dark bangs again. "What a naïve little dork he was."

"No," Ruby said. "I didn't marry Stewart."

Stewart's parents still lived in Pecan Springs and she saw his picture in the newspaper sometimes. He had outgrown his pimples, graduated *summa* from Harvard Law, and now headed up a large New York legal firm. So much for the "naïve little dork."

"I married Wade Wilcox," she added, "but we divorced years ago."

"Wade Wilcox!" The eyebrows again, disbelieving now. "Senior when we were sophomores? Tall, blond, good-looking?" Leslie's tone implied that Ruby couldn't have married *that* Wade Wilcox.

"Yes." A thought pulled itself out of the periphery of Ruby's consciousness and pushed itself into speech. "What do you hear from Brittany?"

Brittany. Why in the world was she asking? Brittany Morrow had been Leslie's friend, never Ruby's — especially after Sarah disappeared. And then Brittany had —

"Brittany?" Leslie shifted her purse from one arm to the other. "I suppose you know that Brit and Ted got married after college. Ted Stevens. Remember him?"

Of course Ruby remembered. She nodded.

"Well," Leslie said, "they had a little girl right away and a boy when Ted was in medical school. Another girl when Ted opened his practice in Houston. That's where Brit —" Her mouth twisted.

"That's where Brit what?"

"You don't know?"

Ruby tightened her jaw. She didn't need to hear it, but she wanted Leslie to say it. "Where she what?"

"Where she killed herself. I guess the story didn't get covered over here, huh?"

It had been covered. "Why?" Ruby pressed her lips together. "I mean, why did she do it?"

It was a real question, for while Ruby knew some things, many things, other things were still a mystery. Brittany was one of them. She had gotten everything she ever wanted. She had Ted. Two girls for her and a boy for Ted. Plenty of money, a storybook life as a doctor's wife. What had happened?

"Who knows?" Leslie glanced sharply at Ruby. "She was always terribly impulsive — maybe she never outgrew it. And of course, we never know what goes on in the minds of other people, do we?" Her smile went crooked. "But then of course, *you* do."

Ruby took a deep breath. "I don't know what you mean."

"Of course you know what I mean. Don't you remember? Once, when we were eating lunch in the cafeteria, you told Brittany that she was thinking about a contest that she'd entered at Radio Shack. You said she was going to win the transistor radio. Nobody believed you, not even Brittany. But she won. So you not only read Brittany's mind, you read her future. That wasn't the only time, either." She gestured toward a shelf of crystal balls, gleaming softly. "I suppose that's why you have all this woo-woo stuff." She gave Ruby a wary look. "Do you still know what people are thinking?"

Ruby managed a shrug. "High school was a long time ago. I've grown up. You have too. We're different people now."

Or not. Something told her that Leslie was still the same competitive, envious creature she had been as a young girl. "I don't suppose you've heard anything from Sarah," she heard herself say.

"Sarah?" Leslie blinked. "Oh, Sarah Gellner. Your friend. The girl who ran away midway through our junior year." She shook her head. "Nope, not a word. Have you? I've always wondered where she went. Kids were a lot more free back then, don't you think? She probably met some guys and headed out to the West Coast. That's what I heard, anyway."

Ran away? Numbly, Ruby shook her head. But of course that was what the police had decided, too. They had asked Ruby all kinds of silly questions based on their assumption that Sarah was just another teenage runaway. Questions about boys Sarah had known, other than Ted. About friends she might have gone to visit. About rock groups she followed and drugs she had taken and whether she'd ever yearned for adventure in LA or New York.

"Pecan Springs is nothing but a Podunk little town," one cop had said. "Of course she wanted to get away."

Sarah's parents knew better, of course. They organized searches for her, but that was back in the days before the internet and social media, when it was much harder to organize anything. Still, they put up flyers on utility poles and handed them out in the mall, advertised in area newspapers, and tried to get coverage on the TV news in Austin and San Antonio. In fact, Sarah's father and mother were coming back from KSAT-TV in San Antonio when they died in a car wreck. Their deaths had put an effective end to searching for Sarah.

"Poor Ted." Leslie heaved a dramatic sigh. "The cops questioned him awfully hard about that girl's disappearance, you know. Of course, he couldn't tell them a blessed thing. He had been with the high school debate team in Houston that week, so he had a . . . a whaddya-call-it, an alibi. But that didn't stop the cops. Or the gossip. Even after Ted and Brit got together, people kept on saying he must have had something to do with Sarah's disappearance." She gave a brittle laugh. "Is Pecan Springs the same old rumor mill it used to be, or do people have better things to do with their time these days?"

"I think it's pretty much the same," Ruby said.

"Well, if you ask me," Leslie went on, cheerfully now, "things have definitely changed for the better. The outlet malls along the interstate are great, and I was glad to see that most of those pokey old mom-and-pop shops have closed. And house prices are up, which is definitely good. I hope Mom's place brings a good price."

Ruby tilted her head. "That's the house on Mesquite Street, where you lived when you were in high school?" It was across the street from Brittany's and just a few blocks from the house where Ruby lived now.

"That's it," Leslie said comfortably. "It's not in tiptop shape, of course — Mom left a lot of repair work undone. Still, the realtor tells me that the Pecan Springs market is hot and it's a desirable neighborhood. But I've got to get it cleared out first. Some of the stuff is probably worth a little money — the Waterford and the silver. But my mother liked to think she was an artist, so she accumulated a lot of art supplies and stuff, over the years. I've got one of those big Dumpsters almost filled."

"Your mother *was* an artist," Ruby said. "I remember seeing her paintings at local art shows. They were very good."

"I suppose." Leslie gave a dismissive wave of her hand. "Anyway, I've hired a guy who's coming in next week to tear down that old shed she used as a studio. The floor has pretty much rotted away, so the realtor said it should come out."

Ruby nodded, remembering. One of Mrs. Newell's neighbors had once hosted an art show in her backyard, and people were invited to go next door to visit Mrs. Newell's little studio.

Leslie looked at her watch. "Well, speaking of the Waterford, I'd better try to find Victoria's Crystal and Lace. You wouldn't happen to —"

"You're almost there," Ruby said. "One block east and turn left at Howard Drive. It's about halfway down the block on the left."

"Oh, good," Leslie said. She smiled, showing all her teeth. "Well, I'll be on my way, then. It's nice to have seen you again, Ruby."

"Yes, of course," Ruby echoed. "Nice." Feeling obliged to say more, she added, "Come back anytime. It's always good to see an old friend."

But when Leslie left the shop, a smudge of darkness hung in the air where she had stood.

CHAPTER THREE

Hark Hibler hadn't been able to put his St. Pat's party conversation with Jessica out of his mind. He had gotten nowhere in his effort to get her to persuade Ruby Wilcox to stop fooling around with that psychic stuff.

He knew, of course, that whatever went on with Ruby Wilcox — no matter how it messed with her pretty head — was absolutely no business of his. He had to face facts, and the fact was that he and Ruby were no longer a couple. However she wanted to mess herself up, she was free to do it. He didn't expect her to ask his advice.

But he had loved her once. And if he were more candid than usual with himself, he'd have to admit that he probably still did. That aside, though, what he had heard about the weird doings at Dr. Scott's lab would be enough to keep any normal person awake at night. How seriously involved was Ruby? How could that stuff affect her brain?

Ruby was . . . well, *highly intuitive* was how he put it to himself. Empathic, perceptive, sensitive. She thought she was psychic, but he'd never believed there was anything to that — anything more, that is, than a powerful empathy and what Hark thought of as a seriously spooky spidey sense about ten times stronger than Spiderman's. Her poltergeisty sister (probably not the right word and of course it was all a stunt) was totally off the rails. He fervently hoped that whatever was going on up at that lab wouldn't push Ruby to become another Ramona.

But Hark had other things on his mind. He shoved his apprehension about Ruby aside and focused on the meeting ahead of him, one that promised to be about as pleasant as getting a leg or two amputated. He was about to sign over thirty percent of his newspaper to Jefferson Davis Dixon III, along with the title of co-publisher and a major position on the editorial team. He hated like hell to do it, but he had come to the reluctant conclusion that he had no other choice. If he wanted to keep the *Enterprise* alive, he had to let go of a piece of it.

The problem Hark was facing, of course, was bedeviling every newspaper in the country, even the big guys — the *Times,* the *Globe,* the *Chicago Tribune.* Competition from the internet and cable TV was eroding readership and advertising revenues — a death by a thousand cuts that added up to a bloody bottom line. The *Enterprise* was in worse shape, for Hark had bought it with borrowed money several years before and the note was coming due. If he couldn't meet it, Ranchers State Bank would move in and seize the collateral: the *Enterprise* building and its adjacent lot, which were among the most valuable properties in downtown Pecan Springs.

And while the newspaper might be able to lease the building from the bank, Hark knew he couldn't make the lease payments and the payroll, too. The newspaper would close and there would be no local news, big or small. No reports on the sometimes shady shenanigans at the city council meetings, or the arrest of a school counselor for doctoring student test scores, or the cleanup of the homeless camp under the I-35 bridge. No intercity sports scores, no ladies club notes or church announcements, no arrest logs, no lists of blue ribbon 4-H winners or spelling bee champs, no obituaries. The news desert that had overtaken so many small towns would engulf Pecan Springs and all of Adams County.

Hark hadn't shared his apprehensions

with the staff — if he told them, morale would drop like a box of rocks. But he knew they knew. He had felt their eyes on him for weeks, whenever he walked through the newsroom. He wished he could tell them that he was trying his damnedest to get the money together to save the paper — and their jobs. But he didn't want to raise their hopes. He couldn't tell them until he had *some* good news, and there wasn't any. Yet.

He had begun seriously attacking the problem a couple months before, looking around for an investor who would be willing to drop a hunk of cash into the *Enterprise* in return for a percentage of the stock. He'd started by approaching several Pecan Springs businessmen. But they weren't interested, probably because when Hark took over the paper, he'd changed the previous owners' editorial policies. The *Enterprise* was no longer a cozy little newspaper that swept the dirty dealings of prominent townspeople under the rug. Hark put an emphasis on investigative reporting. He made sure that every story told the truth. No making it pretty. The bare truth, no matter whose ox was being gored.

Having struck out on the local scene, he consulted with a private equity firm that specialized in buying faltering newspapers.

But it was located in Chicago, which meant that control over the *Enterprise* would be in another city, in the hands of fund managers who didn't give a damn about local issues.

So he'd talked to a Texas PE firm located in Dallas. He was told that the *Enterprise*'s profit margin was too small to interest them, but they *would* be interested in the building and its adjacent lot. "The real estate is worth more than the newspaper," they'd said bluntly. "Sell that and close the paper. That's the smart move."

And that was it. That was his last option. There was no Hallmark happy ending to this story.

Until Jeff Dixon stepped into the batter's box.

Jefferson Davis Dixon III, son of a Texas senator, grandson of a Texas political power broker, heir to the multinational Dixon beer and wine distributorship. Dixon was no stranger. Hark had known him since they were journalism students at the University of Texas, working on the staff of the *Daily Texan,* the student newspaper where Hark was news editor and Dixon had edited sports and politics (in Texas, two sides of the same coin). They got along, more or less, but it was evident that they were completely different personalities who went about getting things done in radically different ways.

Hark constantly pushed as hard as he could, depending on instinct, dogged determination, and sheer force of will. He preferred to work on one problem at a time, grabbing it by the scruff of the neck and hanging on like a bulldog until it gave up. Dixon, on the other hand, liked to sit down with a beer and think about the easiest, smoothest way to confront a crisis, then solve it quickly and with as little effort as possible.

These styles were the product, Hark thought, of the way they'd grown up. His father had been a pressman at the *Galveston Daily News,* coming home every day with ink-stained hands and clothes and a fresh copy of the newspaper. Hark had spent summers hanging out in the pressroom, and he still loved the rumbling clack-clack-clack of the presses, the smell of freshly inked newsprint, and the crisp smoothness of the newspaper in his hands. At heart, he was a print guy. He was no Luddite, oh, no: he wrote, handled email, and managed business affairs on a computer. But that was as far as it went. He refused to buy an e-reader, and Kindle was a word he associated with book-burning.

Dixon, on the other hand, grew up playing golf at the posh Lakewood Country Club in Dallas, sailing on White Rock Lake, and planning to manage the Dixon family booze distribution business until he was elected to a seat in the Texas Legislature. And why not? Everything was easy for him. Exceptionally bright, he had built a self-designed major in journalism and software design, was elected Delta Tau Delta president, dated several beautiful Alpha Phi girls (all at the same time), married a UT cheerleader named (predictably) Tiffani, and was now (also predictably) divorced. He had taken control of Dixon International and moved into an upscale home in the hills west of Pecan Springs, where (when he wasn't sailing or climbing mountains) he liked to write computer code that would let him do twice as much of whatever he wanted to do *faster.*

Bottom line: Jefferson Davis Dixon III was not the sort of man Hark would voluntarily take on as a partner in the *Enterprise.* Not a man he would trust, come to that. But what other options did he have? Let the bank have the real estate? Turn the *Enterprise* into a weekly shopper?

No. None of it made any sense. The only practical thing to do was swallow his dislike of Dixon and do the damned deal.

So here he was, where he didn't want to be. Parking his banged-up old green Ford truck in the circular drive in front of Dixon's sprawling house. Ringing the doorbell (which naturally played "The eyes of Texas are upon you") at Dixon's massive front door. Following Dixon's pert little uniformed maid through the maze of Dixon's art-lined hallways to the back patio. Greeting Jefferson Davis Dixon III with the closest thing to a smile he could manage.

Because he had to. Because he had run out of options. Because he had no other choice.

"Glad to see you, Hark," Dixon said from a chair beside a round, glass-topped patio table, under an orange-and-white striped umbrella. "Ready to put the deal together?"

A handsome, athletic man in his midforties, Dixon was dressed in crisply pressed white jeans, a burgundy Maison Kitsuné polo shirt, and brown suede Ralph Lauren boat shoes (no socks, naturally). With thick blond hair, very blue eyes in a tanned face, and a lean build, he exuded an easy-in-his-skin confidence. On the table beside him was a pitcher of margaritas, two salt-rimmed glasses, and a plate of sushi, which Hark had never learned to like. Behind him, a musical waterfall splashed across a tier of rough-cut limestone softened with ferns, falling five or six feet into an Olympic-length swimming pool.

"Ready when you are," Hark replied with a resignation that felt closely akin to despair. Dixon's classy appearance made him uncomfortably aware of his rumpled suit jacket, his wrinkled white shirt, and his coffee-stained tie.

"Happy to hear it," Dixon said. He picked up the pitcher. "Open with a margarita?"

Hark would like nothing more than to get this over with. "I'm good," he said, pulling out a chair.

Filling his own glass, Dixon raised an eyebrow. "You're okay with the terms, then? Ready to sign?"

The terms Dixon offered at their first meeting a month before had been a genuine surprise, for they were more generous than Hark expected. In return for picking up the note and keeping the *Enterprise* afloat for another year, the man wanted a 30 percent share of the newspaper, the title of co-publisher, and the role of digital developer.

At first, Hark had balked. He didn't intend to hand over editorial control to anybody, especially not to Jefferson Davis Dixon III, who already had more of everything than anybody could want. Why was he interested in a newspaper, especially one that didn't have much of a shelf life?

But Hark soon realized that Dixon had something quite specific in mind. He was, it seemed, looking for a toy. "I'm fascinated by digital journalism," he'd said at their second meeting. "Journalism online. On the internet."

"We already publish an online replica of our print edition," Hark had said, feeling that — for once — he was up to date with Dixon. "Looks just like the print edition, in fact. Only difference is that people read it on the internet instead of waiting for a copy to land on the front porch." With a feeling of something like satisfaction, he added, "It hasn't brought in enough new subscribers to cover the cost. No future there, I'm afraid."

There was no regret in him. A print guy heart and soul, Hark hated the online edition. It felt like a betrayal of principle. In fact, he had turned it over to Denise Sanger to manage. He rarely looked at it unless Denise brought him a problem to solve.

"I agree," Dixon said, unexpectedly. "No future in the replica. It's impossible to read the damned thing on a phone — and that's where most younger readers would access it."

"Well, then —"

"I'm proposing that we ditch it. And launch a new digital-only edition."

"Digital only?" Hark asked uncertainly. "Which is what, exactly?"

"It's an internet edition that has some of the same content as the printed edition, but many more online features." Dixon spoke with a controlled excitement. "Rolling deadlines, to catch breaking stories. Hot links to stories inside the issue and to internet sites. Search options and bookmarking. Multimedia, with video and animation. Reader-interactive stuff — cooking, crossword puzzles, contests. It would be aimed at a different audience, wider, younger, more diverse." He gave Hark an intent look. "If the *Enterprise* doesn't do it, some competitor is going to do it, and soon, too. When that happens, it will undercut your print edition, and the competition will block that kind of future development for you."

Hark had winced. Competition was something he understood.

"As co-publisher," Dixon had said, "my responsibility would be limited to the digital edition and to the social media side of the newspaper. You're the boss where print is concerned." He gave Hark a sharp look. "The one and *only* boss. Does that satisfy you?"

It hadn't. There was just too damned much uncertainty here. What would happen if Dixon started this fancy new edition with all its electronic bells and whistles — and then lost interest? Or if he decided that digital wasn't enough for him after all, and he wanted to try his hand with print?

Hark had no idea how this was all going to play out. But he knew one thing. Dixon's money was enough to take care of the debt and keep the *Enterprise* going for at least one more year. It wasn't the best solution, not by a long shot. But it was the best he could do.

Dixon was watching him over the rim of his margarita glass. "Ready to sign?" he repeated.

Hark reached into his pocket for a pen. "Let's get this done," he growled.

Fifteen minutes later, when all the documents had been signed and initialed and dated, Dixon smiled. "So it's done. So when do I meet the staff?"

"Meet the staff?" Hark asked blankly. He hadn't thought beyond the agreement they had worked out. He hadn't wanted to consider the unhappy prospect of sharing the title of "publisher" with a guy he didn't much like and wasn't sure he could trust.

"Sure," Dixon said. "That's the next step, isn't it? There have been rumors all over town about the *Enterprise* going under. You must have heard them."

Reluctantly, Hark nodded.

"The employees are bound to have heard them, too. So we'll need an announcement, along with a plan for the new digital-only edition. I've already drawn up an editorial and production schedule for how that's going to work and I want to assemble a team to critique it — a couple of our best reporters, the assistant editor, the features editor. But first we need to tell the staff what's going on. They must be pretty apprehensive."

Hark shook himself. Dixon had plenty of enthusiasm, he had to admit that. So he'd better shape up and take control, or pretty soon the other man would be running the whole show.

"I've already scheduled a staff meeting," he lied. "The newsroom, tomorrow afternoon. Four o'clock."

"Great," Dixon said. "I'll be there." He grinned. "I'm glad to get back in the newspaper game, Hark. It'll be fun." He put out his hand.

The newspaper game? Fun, huh?

Hark shook Dixon's hand, but he only grunted.

CHAPTER FOUR

The Adams County courthouse is a three-story pink granite Classical Revival building that sits like a pink wedding cake on a tidy square of green lawn in the center of downtown Pecan Springs. Across from it is Ranchers State Bank and the Sophie Briggs Museum, with its famous collection of three hundred ceramic frogs and the scuffed cowboy boots that Burt Reynolds wore during the filming of *The Best Little Whorehouse in Texas*. Built in 1900, the courthouse is included on the roster of Texas historic courthouses. But most of the county's civic functions have outgrown its cramped offices and have been moved to the new annex at the edge of town, which also houses the Adams County sheriff's office.

The courtrooms, though, are still in regular use, and their age and early twentieth-century elegance lend the perplexing proceedings of the law a dignity that they sometimes don't deserve. Or so it always seemed to Jessica. Her cops-and-courthouse beat meant that she often spent more of her week in the courthouse than she did in the newsroom. She was on a first-name basis with the bailiff, knew every detail of the carved oak woodwork that framed the bench and the jury box, and had mentally mapped the fissures in the ceiling paint.

Today, a longtime member of the Pecan Springs community, Dr. James Crawley, was being arraigned on a charge of capital murder.* It was a big event in the small town, and nearly every seat was taken, including the wickedly uncomfortable wooden pews along the back wall. A camera crew from KVUE-TV in Austin was stationed out in the hall, and a female reporter was poised to pounce on somebody, *anybody,* for an interview. An NBC news satellite truck with a big dish on top was parked out in the street, and the team was filming on the courthouse steps.

Jessica had staked out a place in the media row, but she'd gotten an important phone

---

* The arraignment is the culmination of the investigation Jessica carried out in *Deadlines,* book 1 in the *Enterprise* trilogy.

call — one she'd been waiting for — and had to go out to the hall to take it. By the time she got back, there was no room left to sit with the other journalists, and she had to find a place in the spectators' seats.

Looking over her shoulder, Jessica smiled at the murder victim's sister, Maggie, and glimpsed many familiar faces — friends and patients of the defendant who refused to believe that the same Dr. Jim who had treated them and their children could have murdered his next-door neighbor. At the *Enterprise,* letters were running six to one in the doctor's favor, and several people had written op-eds attacking the district attorney. There was enormous local interest in the case.

Which is why the spectators were so shocked when Dr. Crawley replied to the judge's "How do you plead?" with his head down and a barely audible "Guilty, Your Honor." A gasp swept the courtroom. Somebody cried "Oh, no!" and others began to weep.

This was followed by some legal back-and-forth about the plea deal that the prosecution and the defense had worked out. The judge announced that the doctor was sentenced to life without parole and remanded immediately to prison. And then the courtroom emptied, the spectators divided between those who thought that the whole thing was criminally unfair and those who felt it was disappointingly anticlimactic. Out on the courthouse steps, Jessica gave Maggie a quick hug and watched her walk away with a new bounce in her step. The family had been spared a long and agonizing trial.

"Charlie told me you had something to do with this case," a voice said behind her, and Jessica turned to see David Redfern.

His dark hair fell in a shock across his forehead, and there was a crooked half-smile on his face. Tall and lean, dressed for court in a navy suit, white shirt, and a tie the same blue as his eyes, he was every inch a "gorgeously hunky guy," as Ruby had called him.

Jessica's heart turned over. Why did he have to look so damned *good*?

"Something, maybe." She managed a modest shrug. "Not much, really."

"Not what Charlie says." His smile widened to a grin. "He says you were the one who got the sister to go for the exhumation and autopsy. That's what nailed the doctor — when they found out that his victim was pregnant. He was lucky to get a plea deal."

She tried not to smile back. "Just doing

266

my job." She moved a step to the side, getting out of the way of a cameraman coming down the steps two at a time. "You know — my job, Counselor? I report on crimes."

"Oh, I remember, all right," he said ruefully. He grinned. "I'm also remembering that we had a nice lunch not long ago. I was all business. You kept a professional distance. Two busy people, a working lunch. But it was fun."

It had been fun, Jessica admitted. They had shared a delicious meal at the new Indian restaurant on the other side of the interstate, and she had discovered that for all David's studious appearance, he had a quirky, half-amused view of his job as an attorney. He took his work seriously, but not himself. For that, she liked him. And besides, he was . . . well, sexy. Very.

"What's more," he went on, "your journalistic integrity and my legal reputation seem to have survived our encounter intact." He bent closer and spoke out of the corner of his mouth, like a movie gangster. "Let's see if we can do that again. Somebody gave me a pair of tickets to *Hello, Dolly!* at the Bass Concert Hall on the UT campus. First balcony center, Saturday night. How would you like to go?"

How would she like to go? *How would she*

like to go?

Jessica caught her breath. Of all the musicals in the world, *Dolly* was her very favorite. She had seen Barbra Streisand's movie a gazillion times. The reviews of the revival were over the top and Betty Buckley, on tour with the show, was said to be magnificent. Jessica had tried to buy a ticket for the Bass performance, but the seats she could afford were already sold out. She hesitated, and he raised his hand.

"I know, I know. I'm a source and you're a reporter and it's against the rules for you to accept anything from me. So how about if I *sell* you one of my tickets — like, for half of what I paid for the pair? We could take separate cars, if you want. Then all you have to do is occupy the seat beside me. No strings attached." He gave her an engaging smile. "If anybody ever asks, we can say it was . . . you know. An accident. A chance encounter. Fate." Smiling, he tilted his head. "That's it. Fate brought us together just for *Dolly.*"

She frowned. "The first balcony? I don't think I can afford that." When she'd looked at tickets online, balcony seats started at a hundred dollars. Center first balcony seats must be even higher.

"I said 'half of what I paid for it,' " he

replied. "Which is nothing." He beamed at her, confident now. "Honest. Not a cent. One of my clients — somebody who's not in jail at the present moment — gave me the tickets. Glad to share."

She shook her head, laughing a little. "David, you are so *bad.*"

But surely an evening at the Bass wouldn't compromise her work. And it was important, wasn't it, to establish a rapport with sources who were critical to your story? Nobody was more critical to her book about Byers' crimes than Byers' attorney. Right?

Right.

And while dating a source was a definite no-no, if they took separate cars and didn't go out for a drink afterward, it couldn't be called a date. And she would insist on paying him for —

No. She straightened her shoulders. *No no no no no.* She really, really wanted to see *Dolly,* but accepting David's offer wasn't smart. And if she were honest with herself, it was just too risky. She had a demanding job and on top of that, an important book contract. She couldn't afford to let herself get emotionally tangled with a source.

She pulled in her breath. And let it out.

"Sorry, David. Thanks for the offer, but I can't do this."

His eyes were intent on hers. "Look, Jessica, I can give you plenty of examples of journalists who date their sources and not only survive but thrive. Andrea Mitchell, for instance, on MSNBC. For years, she filed stories on the Federal Reserve while she was dating the Fed chairman, Alan Greenspan — whom she eventually married. Nobody complained about that. In fact, her editors liked the idea that she had an inside track. It meant they could scoop the competition."

"I know," Jessica said. "But —"

He wasn't done. "The facts that I am Howard Byers' lawyer and you are writing a book on Howard Byers and we are friends do not mean that I am feeding you any information about my client that is not publically available." He looked very stern. "I am bound by attorney-client privilege. I take that seriously."

Jessica sighed. "It's not that you did or you would, David. It's that you *could.* And that people could think that you did."

"I understand. But it doesn't matter what people think. As long as we know —"

She held up her hand. "I want your client's story for my book. But I don't want anybody saying that I dated you for it." She tried to smile. "An editor of the *New York Times* once said, 'I don't care if my reporters are sleeping with elephants, as long as they aren't covering the circus.' Well, I'm covering the circus and you are one of the elephants. Until the circus has left town, I'm not going out with you."

"Sleeping with elephants," David muttered. "I can't believe you said that."

Jessica couldn't, either. But she wasn't sorry. David had to know where she stood. At that moment, her cell pinged. She pulled it out.

"Excuse me," she said, glad for the interruption. "Gotta take this." She turned away.

The caller was Denise Sanger. "Just letting you know that Hark wants us all in the newsroom at four," she said shortly. "Command performance. Whatever you're doing, drop it and get here. Don't be late."

Jessica gritted her teeth. It was almost four now. "Thanks for the heads-up, Denise. On my way." She turned to say goodbye to David, but he was gone.

Oh, hell, she thought. It was the elephants that did it.

CHAPTER FIVE

Wild rumors about the *Enterprise*'s financial dilemma had been flying for weeks, and the anxiety was so high that everybody showed up for the meeting, even the part-time people in production and the community columnists, Jeannine Benson and China Bayles.

China and Will Wagner, the sports editor, were perched on a work table against the back wall, China in her green Thyme and Seasons T-shirt, Will with a Dallas Cowboys cap. Jessica joined them.

"I haven't missed anything, have I?" she asked.

"Nope," China said. "It hasn't started yet."

"What do you think Hark has got for us?" Will asked. "Will this be the final whistle or another inning or two?"

"No idea," Jessica said. She wasn't quite as nervous as everybody else, because her personal situation was a little less precarious. If she watched her pennies, the advance for the Byers book would allow her time to finish the project without having to look for something else. And while reporting jobs were disappearing faster than Greenland ice, the publicity around *Not Only in the Dark* should help. But she hated the thought that the *Enterprise* might go under. Pecan Springs needed its newspaper. The newspaper staff needed jobs.

When Hark came in, a profound silence fell across the room and everyone seemed to stop breathing. But when he announced that he had good news, there was an immediate gusty sigh of relief. The *Enterprise* wouldn't be closing. He had sold a third of the paper to Jefferson Davis Dixon, who came from a well-known Texas family, prominent in both business and politics. They had worked together on the staff of the *Daily Texan,* where they had developed an affection for the newspaper business. Now, Jeff Dixon would be both an investor and a co-publisher. He had a special interest in digital journalism and planned to try some radical tricks to turn the newspaper into the single most important news outlet for the entire I-35 Corridor, San Antonio to Austin and everywhere in between. Hark said this with a diffident grin, as if (Jessica thought) he wanted it to be true but wouldn't bet the farm on it.

Then, with a wave of his hand, he introduced Dixon, a tall, good-looking man of forty-something, self-assured and with a dynamic, confident speaking style. Dixon surprised Jessica by appearing to know who everybody was and what their jobs were. He dug straight into his topic, telling them in detail what he planned to do — and why.

"I want to see the *Enterprise* survive," he said, "because I believe in journalism that matters to the people of the local community. I'm also interested in convergence journalism — the point at which print, the internet, television, and radio all intersect. I am a digital guy and as co-publisher, that's where I'll be concentrating my energies." With a smile, he nodded at Hark. "As I'm sure you know, Hark is a print guy. He'll continue to do his usual fine job of managing the print edition."

Hark put on a smile but it was clear that he wasn't brimming with enthusiasm for his new partner's plans. Jessica, however, had begun to catch the excitement. Dixon sounded to her like someone who had done his homework and was inspired by what he had learned.

And it obviously wasn't going to be business as usual. Dixon was proposing to create a new online edition of the newspaper, which meant publishing breaking news as it happened, stories linked to related stories, and developing stories reported in series, with updates. Reader-oriented columns: cooking, crossword puzzles, contests. An online advertisers' gallery, an active Facebook page, and Twitter, Instagram, and Snapchat links. Media partnerships with Austin and San Antonio television and radio, along with new mobile apps that would give readers what they wanted, whenever they wanted it. There would be more opportunity for more good writing.

And blogs, even. "It'll be a chance for individual reporters and writers to develop your own following," Dixon said. "For instance, those of you who are regular bloggers can integrate some of the stories you're covering into your blogs, where that's appropriate." He pointed at Jessica. "Jessica Nelson, I'm thinking of you. I like what you're doing with your blog. I want to see more. When you have some time, let's talk about that."

Jessica was startled. This guy had been reading *Crime and Consequences*?

He was nodding to Will. "You, too, Wagner. I'd like to see you start a blog covering *all* the sports — especially local area high school sports. Bring in guest bloggers from various communities and you'll bring in readers from those communities. Bring in high-school-age bloggers. Get kids thinking about newspapers before they go to college."

He looked around at the group. "Everybody, you get how this works? Digital gives you a chance, as journalists, to create a personal connection with readers. When you're blogging the story you're covering, the reader gets your story, *plus* your story about covering the story."

Next to Jessica, China seemed to have caught the excitement, too. "What about podcasts?" she asked. "I do a podcast for my customers, on my website. I could easily do one for my Home and Garden column."

Podcasts, Jessica thought excitedly. She could create podcasts of the Byers case for the online edition of the newspaper as she wrote chapters for the book. It would be a way to build her audience.

"Podcasts, absolutely." Dixon looked pleased. "Got a story you really want to dig into? Do a podcast about the process of researching and writing the story. Link it to visuals online and to the print story, but include details that haven't made it into print. Give the readers a sense of what it's like to be on the developing edge of a story, while it's happening. Engage them. Get them thinking about the impact of the story on their lives, on the community as a whole." He spread his arms energetically and looked around at the group. "You see? Everybody see? We're not talking fake news here, folks. You've got the talent. The *Enterprise* has real potential. Let's exploit it!"

Will was frowning. "Who the hell *is* this guy, anyway?" he growled. "He sounds like my journalism professor. Truth is, readers want what they're used to. Sports readers, anyway."

"Sounds like a ton of extra hours to me," Fran whispered, on the other side of Jessica. "Weekends, I run marathons. Hey, I've got a life. I don't have time for a blog."

Perched on a nearby desk, Virgil stuck up his hand. "You know this means putting more resources into photography, right?" he said loudly. "You can't do digital without images. Lots of images, especially video. You ready for that that? It's going to cost some serious money." Jessica was surprised. She'd never heard Virgil challenge anybody, let alone his boss. His *new* boss.

"I'm ready." Dixon folded his arms. "Yeah.

It's going to cost something, Virgil. But it'll be worth it. Come see me. Let's talk about what you think we need."

"Jeff is funding digital," Hark put in. "It's his toy." Jessica thought the remark sounded grudging and wondered how Hark was going to handle his partner's energies. It wasn't going to be easy, she guessed.

"Guy must have friggin' deep pockets," Virgil muttered.

"If he's the Dixon of Dixon Distributors, he does," Will whispered. He held up his phone. He'd been looking at a Wikipedia page. "Family started out in West Texas oil, moved on to beer and wine. They're rolling in dough."

Denise's expression was stormy. "We already have an online edition of the *Enterprise,* Mr. Dixon. Have you looked at that?"

"I have," Dixon replied. "And what I've seen is a static copy of the print edition. Isn't that right?"

Her scowl deepening, she nodded. "Yes, but —"

"So while it shows up on people's phones and desktops, what readers see is the print edition," Dixon said. "It's a digital delivery, that's all. What we're talking about here is an edition that's designed specifically *for* digital. A new kind of storytelling — that's what we're after. *Community* storytelling, where the community plays an active part in the story."

Denise looked flustered. "So you're just going to drop the current online edition? What about the people who have been working on it?"

"She means *her,*" Fran whispered to Jessica. "That's her baby."

"You can move over to the new edition," Dixon said in a reassuring tone. "There will be different skills to learn and different ways to organize the news. It's true that some of us may have to reinvent ourselves. But that will be fun and interesting, right, Denise?" He grinned engagingly. "It's going to be exciting for the team. And productive for us as individuals. We'll come out of this with new skill sets. We're going to *grow,* personally and professionally."

Jessica thought that Denise didn't exactly look thrilled at the idea of reinventing herself. Her mouth was turned down and her eyes were bleak. When the meeting was over, she headed straight for the door without saying a word to anybody.

Jessica wasn't a fan of Denise, but she sympathized. As Hark's assistant editor, Denise had been managing the online replica edition for almost a year. As Fran had said, it was Denise's baby and she was proud of it. Now, Dixon intended to ditch it and Hark wasn't going to do anything to stop him. To build something that was hers, Denise would have to start all over again. Jessica couldn't help wondering how long it would take her to realize that starting over at the *Enterprise* was better than having to look for a new job.

It was true that Dixon had some radical ideas about the newspaper business.

But he also had the money to support them. And right now, the money was talking.

CHAPTER SIX

The meeting had gone on for several hours and it was after six by the time Jessica got home. What she had in mind was a quick, easy supper — a plate of scrambled eggs with mushrooms, tomatoes, green onions, and feta cheese — and after that, a quiet evening with a good book. She was too tired to write, so she would continue reading Billy Jensen's memoir, *Chase Darkness with Me*, about a true-crime writer who had moved from his job as a journalist into a role as a detective and victim's advocate, using the resources of the internet and social media to solve cold cases. She liked what Karen Kilgariff had written in the foreword to Jensen's book. *Good crime journalists offer themselves as a bridge between the worst of humanity and those of us who want to know how bad it can actually be.*

That's what she wanted to be: a bridge. A bridge, or maybe a mirror. A writer who pictured the worst part of the world so that people didn't have to go there to know what it was like. A writer who told the truth about the dark side.

It was seven o'clock and the *NewsHour* was already over when Jessica finished her supper and sat down on the sofa with her book, Murphy purring loudly in her lap. But she found that she had too much on her mind to concentrate on her e-reader.

There was David Redfern, for one thing. She wished she hadn't been so casual and flip with that silly remark about sleeping with elephants. She had offended him, and she was sorry. On the other hand, she had to put a stop to his requests for dates. She couldn't trust herself. She found him far too attractive. If he kept asking, she might say yes. Which would be wrong for her — and wrong for him, too.

Her most recent relationship was a good example. There hadn't been a conflict of interest to keep her and Kelly apart. In fact, they had spent the better part of a year together, until he decided that he was tired of playing second fiddle to her job and specifically, to her investigation of the Angel of Death. In their final stormy encounter, Kelly had growled that she spent every spare minute working on the investigation:

interviewing people, researching records, sending out and responding to inquiries.

"You love this stuff," he had said. "There's no room in your life for anything — or anyone — else."

She hadn't argued with him. Kelly wasn't the first of the men she'd known who had objected to the intensity of her involvement with whatever story she was working on. She didn't want David to join the queue, especially now that she was about to plunge into *Not Only in the Dark,* the biggest story of her life. Even if there were no conflicts of interest — David as Byers' lawyer, she as the journalist writing about Byers' crimes, his trial, and (she expected) his ultimate conviction — it would be wrong of her to let herself get involved with him. Maybe after she finished writing the book . . .

But David wasn't going to wait that long.

Jessica put her e-reader on the coffee table. There was no point in struggling to stay focused on a page when her mind just wouldn't cooperate. There was something else she could do, and now was a good time to do it.

All day, a part of her mind had been puzzling over the conversation she'd had with Ruby and China at lunch in the tearoom, about Ruby's friend, Sarah Gellner, the girl who had vanished. As a journalist, Jessica had a deeply personal interest in the victims of crime — especially the young and defenseless, who couldn't put up a fight against the dark forces that threatened them. And Sarah's story didn't just prick her curiosity, it caught at her heart. A young girl with a bright, promising future to look forward to, just . . . *gone.* Gone without a trace, without a clue. Gone, without anyone ever being held at fault.

What had happened to Sarah Gellner? Had she run away, as the cops thought? Been kidnapped, as Ruby believed? Was she still alive somewhere, like Jaycee Dugard, aching to come back but afraid, or perhaps ashamed? Was she dead? Who remembered her, besides Ruby? Who cared?

Sarah's disappearance would have been covered by the *Enterprise,* and Jessica had intended to search the newspaper morgue that afternoon. There hadn't been time because of the meeting. But there was something she could do tonight.

"Sorry, Murph." She dropped a kiss on one ear and put him on the floor. "Go catch a mouse, sweet boy." On her laptop, she opened a search in one of the online newspaper archives she subscribed to. The *Enterprise* wasn't archived there, but she found back issues from the *Austin American-Statesman,* the *San Antonio Express-News,* and the *New Braunfels Herald-Zeitung.* She typed in Sarah's name and the approximate date range, and within a few seconds, came up with nearly a dozen hits.

Articles about the girl's disappearance had appeared in all three newspapers. Checking the dates, Jessica saw that she had vanished the week after St. Patrick's Day, so they were about to reach an anniversary. All of the stories were similar, but the reporter for the *Express-News* had interviewed Sarah's parents. His stories — there were three of them — were more detailed and personal, and Jessica studied them carefully.

It was a school night, and according to Mrs. Gellner, her daughter had been doing her homework when she got a phone call from a girl named Leslie. Sarah came downstairs and said that she was going to walk over to Leslie's house, a few blocks away, to work on some trig problems. She was wearing jeans, a yellow sweatshirt, and a green fanny pack. She promised to be back in a couple of hours.

Mrs. Gellner wasn't sure who Leslie was, but she was involved in a challenging sewing project and confessed that she hadn't paid much attention. She hadn't worried

about Sarah going out by herself at night.
Pecan Springs was a very safe place for
young people. There had never been any
trouble, and she didn't expect any that
night.

But when Sarah wasn't home by bedtime,
Mrs. Gellner (her husband was out of town)
began to worry. She called Ruby Gifford's
house first — Ruby was Sarah's best friend
— and mentioned that Sarah had gone to
see someone named Leslie. Who was she?
Ruby responded with her name and phone
number.

When Mrs. Gellner reached Leslie, however, the girl said she had spent the evening
at her friend Brittany's house, and that she
hadn't seen Sarah. What's more, Leslie said
that she hadn't made the earlier phone call.
When Mrs. Gellner pressed her, she offered
a different idea.

"Maybe she wanted to . . . you know, meet
somebody," Leslie said hesitantly. "A boy, I
mean. She probably used my name as an
excuse. Not saying she *did,*" she added hastily. "Just saying she might have."

Other girls might have done that, Mrs.
Gellner agreed. But not Sarah. Sarah's
longtime steady boyfriend — Ted Stevens
— had gone to Houston with the debate
team, and Sarah wouldn't have gone out

with another boy. But if she hadn't gone to Leslie's house, where *had* she gone?

It was after eleven now. Panicked, Mrs. Gellner called the police. She gave them Leslie's address, and a pair of officers searched the route between the two houses. They found nothing. Early the next morning, a team of cops began going from house to house in the neighborhood, asking if anyone had seen Sarah.

Several had. An older neighbor reported seeing her walking down the street. "Couldn't miss her, bouncing along in that yellow sweatshirt." Somebody else had seen her talking to a dark-haired boy on a bike. A man out for a walk with his dog hadn't seen Sarah but had seen a pair of older teenage boys in an old red Chevy, cruising along the street. "Didn't come from around here," the man said firmly. "They was scruffier than our boys. Scruffy and long-haired."

There were no eyewitnesses to an abduction, no screams heard in the quiet street, no ransom demand. Just absence. And silence.

The police persisted. They questioned several teens, including Sarah's boyfriend, Ted Stevens, a popular, high-achieving student, also the captain of the high school football team. But it was the older boys in the red car that they focused on. They put out a BOLO for the car, alerting every department in the state to keep an eye out for a pretty, blond sixteen-year-old wearing jeans and a yellow sweatshirt, in the company of two long-hairs in an older-model red Chevy. As far as the cops were concerned, the only question was whether Sarah had arranged to meet the boys, or — having encountered them by accident — whether she had gotten into their car willingly or unwillingly.

The Gellners were frantic to find their daughter. They organized groups of volunteers to comb the nearby woods and then the woods along the river. But their searches turned up nothing, and soon there was nowhere else to look. Weeks went by, and Sarah's name was added to the national list of missing children and her photograph began to appear with others on milk cartons and post office bulletin boards.

Jessica used the clipping tool in the newspaper archive software, clipped the stories, and saved them to a file, noticing that one of the stories included a photo from the school yearbook. That gave her another idea. She typed in the name of the school, the year, and the word "yearbook," and in a moment, she was looking at the Pecan

Springs high school yearbook for Sarah and Ruby's junior year. Flipping open the virtual cover, she saw the class motto, which held a sad irony: "It matters not how long we live, but *how.*"

That was wrong, she thought bleakly, at least where Sarah was concerned. It *does* matter how long we live, for we can't explore the promises of the future if we don't live into the future. Sarah hadn't lived long enough.

Or had she? There was something doubly awful about missing persons, Jessica had discovered. Their stories had no ending, just an ugly, unquiet emptiness. That made them difficult to write. There was no lack of suspense. Will she be found? Will he be found *alive*? Where *are* they? What have they suffered?

But there were no conclusions, no resolutions.

Pecan Springs had been smaller when Ruby and Sarah were juniors. In the yearbook, their class had only about forty kids, all achingly young, the boys with their hair combed and slicked down, the girls with shy smiles and heads tilted just so. Most of the girls were carbon copies of one another, although it was easy to find Ruby, with her hair frizzing in all directions like an Orphan

Annie wig. Beside her was Sarah Gellner, with long, center-parted blond hair framing a wide forehead and delicate features. Ruby was grinning cheerfully. Sarah seemed to be looking into a remote distance, smiling just a little.

Jessica glanced down the orderly, alphabetized rows of black-and-white photos. There was Leslie Newell, the girl Sarah had said she was going to see. Leslie was plumpish and dark-haired, with a round face and a pouty mouth. In the next row, she saw Ted Stevens, who had been identified in the newspaper story as Sarah's steady boyfriend. He was a good-looking boy with large, dark eyes and a cocky, confident smile.

Jessica clicked on the arrow at the side of the screen, and the page flipped. The junior prom. The royal court, posed uncomfortably on a bench in front of a silver crescent moon. The king, Ted Stevens, in a bright plaid jacket, dark tie, and tinfoil crown. The queen —

But Jessica's eye had caught Sarah's name in the paragraph beside the photo. Sarah Gellner had been voted queen of the prom — a foreseeable pairing, with her boyfriend as king. After her disappearance, the runner-up, a dark-haired, intense-looking girl named Brittany, had taken her place.

But Sarah's stand-in interested Jessica less than the six attendants grouped around the king and queen. Among them, she had spotted a familiar face: her friend Fran Fenner, from the *Enterprise,* looking impossibly young.

Fran. *That* was good, Jessica thought with satisfaction. Of course, Ruby would be glad to answer questions. But Ruby was personally involved in the situation, while Fran likely wasn't. What's more, Fran had an eye for detail. A journalist, she loved to tell a story. Fran might remember something that hadn't shown up in the newspaper accounts of Sarah's disappearance.

Jessica copied the page link into an email and mailed it to herself. She would text Fran and see if they could get together for breakfast in the morning before work. They often met at Lila's Diner, which was just down the block from the newspaper. Lila's peach-and-pecan waffles were awesome.

She flipped more pages, seeing the same faces over and over again. Sarah hunched over a typewriter, as editor of the yearbook. Sarah with a camera, taking a photo of herself in a mirror — a primitive selfie, Jessica thought. Ruby in her band uniform, standing behind a xylophone. (An interesting mini-surprise: Jessica hadn't known that Ruby once played the xylophone.) Fran in the orchestra, with a flute. Ted, handsome in suit and tie, accepting a debate award. Ted in his football uniform on the fifty-yard line, the game ball under one arm, the other around Sarah, petite and cute in her uniform as head cheerleader. Sarah again, another cheerleader photo, standing smiling and triumphant on the bent-over backs of two other cheerleaders, Leslie and Brittany, the three of them posed in front of the cheerleading team.

And that was Pecan Springs High the year Sarah Gellner disappeared.

CHAPTER SEVEN

It was close to seven o'clock and the sun was dropping in the western sky when Ruby began looking for a parking space. Tonight was her second counseling session with Dr. Scott at the parapsychology lab. She didn't want to be late.

The university sprawled across several wooded hilltops on the north side of Pecan Springs. The psychology building was on the outer rim of the campus, and Ruby could usually count on finding nearby on-street parking. She located a space, locked her car, and hurried eagerly up the hill.

Everybody joked that it helped to have ESP if you wanted to find the parapsychology lab. It was on the third floor, out of sight at the end of a maze of corridors, behind a windowless door bearing a cryptic sign: PSRP Lab. Appointment only. PSRP stood for the Perceptual Studies Research Program — the intentionally ambiguous name of Dr. Scott's grant-funded project. The lab was deliberately hard to locate, and Dr. Scott never sought publicity for her work. In fact, she went out of her way to avoid it and asked people who used the lab to do the same.

"There's nothing top-secret about what we're doing," she told them. "But people often misunderstand. So let's keep it among ourselves. Okay?"

Her students — especially those who were gifted and knew from experience that their abilities were often misconstrued — had no problem agreeing.

During testing hours, the lab was often busy and Ruby had to wait for her turn at one of the computers. Tonight, the reception area was empty and the offices were dark, except for Dr. Scott's. Her light was on, her door was open, and Ruby could see her hunched over her desk.

She knocked lightly and Dr. Scott looked up. "Oh, hello, Ruby," she said. "It's that time, is it?" She glanced at a clock on the shelf. "Looks like I worked through the supper hour again."

Ruby frowned. "If you haven't had anything to eat this evening, maybe —"

"You're right. I'd better get something to eat." Dr. Scott pushed herself out of her chair. She was wearing black slacks and a black T-shirt with red letters that said Paranormal = Extra + Ordinary. "My intuition tells me that there are some pizzas in the fridge freezer in the lounge. Let's have our session there."

Melissa Scott was in her mid-forties. When you looked at her, the first thing you noticed was her short, dark buzz cut. Then you took in her oddly pale gray eyes behind nerdish dark-rimmed glasses, her symmetrical features, her self-assured bearing. She had a reputation for being brisk and abrupt, but Ruby had learned that when you had her attention, she listened with an absorbed interest and seemed to remember everything you said. Her deliberateness could be off-putting, though, and she had a natural reserve that made her seem withdrawn and aloof. She wasn't currently married (except to her work), had no children, and not many friends. If you walked past the psych building late at night, you'd probably see the light on in her third-floor office.

Dr. Scott's isolation wasn't just personal, it was professional. As Ruby had learned, paranormal psychology — the study of telepathy, psychokinesis, precognition, clairvoyance, near-death experiences, reincarnation, and ghosts — was once accepted as an important field of academic study. Stanford was the first university in America to create an experimental parapsychology lab, in 1911. Duke University followed in the early 1930s, with the establishment of its Parapsychology Laboratory and later, the Rhine Research Center. Princeton was next, with the Princeton Engineering Anomalies Research (PEAR) program. Others followed.

In recent decades, however, parapsychology had become increasingly controversial. The step-child of psychology, it was pushed to the way-out fringe of the scientific world, and most academics now disowned the idea that ESP and other psychic phenomena were worth studying. It had become harder and harder to get papers published in major journals. And even though the federal government — almost exclusively through the CIA and the FBI — had once funded paranormal research at Stanford, Princeton, and Duke, there was no funding now. The centers themselves (except for the privately funded Rhine Center) were closed. People like Dr. Scott were relegated to the margins of their professional world.

The lounge was furnished with a sofa and several comfortable chairs, a fridge, a microwave, and a coffee machine. Dr. Scott opened the refrigerator and took out a packaged pizza.

"Hey, look," she said with a chuckle. "My intuition was right. Want to join me? There's another pizza in the fridge."

"I had a sandwich after work," Ruby said. "But I'll have a cup of coffee. Can I get one for you, too?"

"Absolutely. Mugs are in the cupboard, bottom shelf." Dr. Scott put the pizza in the microwave and closed the door. "I'm sure you're thinking that this baby is loaded with fat and salt," she added, pushing the button. "But that doesn't count when you're hungry."

Ruby smiled. That's exactly what she had been thinking. She found mugs on the shelf and a canister of coffee pods. "Thanks for seeing me tonight," she said, over her shoulder. "I know I'm not one of your university students, but —"

Dr. Scott waved her hand. "Far as this lab is concerned, it doesn't matter whether you're enrolled at the university. We work with gifted people, some of them from the community. And we have projects with psychics from around the country." She leaned against the counter, watching Ruby, her head cocked to one side. "Your ESP test scores are surprising everybody. Did you know that?"

"I thought I flunked." Ruby inserted a cup and pushed the button. "I guessed wrong every time." But the guy who monitored her tests had explained that in ESP testing, a low scorer was as interesting as somebody who scored high. Even more interesting, all things considered.

"It's unusual," Dr. Scott said. "And it definitely matters, but not in a negative way." She folded her arms. "Based on those scores and on the experiences you told me about — especially the role you played in the Montgomery kidnapping last year — I have to say that you are a most unusual person. That's a compliment, from my point of view," she added with a smile. "Seriously."★

"Thank you." Ruby took the first mug of coffee out of the machine. She put in the second, thinking how ironic this was. She had spent her whole life trying to pretend she was just an ordinary person. And now she was being singled out because she was "unusual."

The microwave beeped. Dr. Scott took out

★You can read about the Montgomery case in *NoBODY*, book 1 of the Crystal Cave Trilogy.

her pizza, put it on a paper plate, and carried it to a chair beside the low coffee table. "How's the dream journal coming?" she asked, sitting down.

Ruby made a face. "There have been a lot of dreams lately. I'm getting plenty of practice." She brought the coffee to the table and took the other chair, putting the mugs on the table in front of them. "I've been dreaming about Sarah — my friend, who disappeared when we were in high school."

"Disappeared?"

"Yes. She went out one night and never came back."

Dr. Scott looked interested. "What kind of dreams?"

"Weird ones," Ruby said ruefully. "In one, I had a crowbar in my hands, tearing up a wooden floor. I was convinced that Sarah was hiding under it, like maybe in a cellar. And last night, I saw her sitting in front of an easel, painting a picture." She briefly closed her eyes, remembering. "She wanted me to help her. She wanted me to *find* her."

"Could you see the painting?" Dr. Scott started on her pizza. "What was it?"

"A little house, like a playhouse." Ruby picked up her coffee mug and took a sip. "A tiny house, with ivy growing up one side of it. Blue shutters. And a blue front door. Bright blue. Pretty."

"A blue front door." Dr. Scott's eyebrows went up. "That's vivid. Lots of detail. Was this a playhouse you'd seen before?"

"I'm not sure," Ruby said doubtfully. "Maybe. It was all kind of . . . misty. The next thing I know, I'm trying to open a blue door, but I can't budge it. In the dream, I mean. The knob won't turn. The door's stuck."

"Stuck." Dr. Scott smiled. "That's a dream for you. Misty. And symbolic."

"Symbolic?"

"It may not help to take our dream images literally. They sometimes symbolize things we might not be ready to accept in real life. That stuck door might not be a door at all. It might represent a puzzle you can't solve. Or a place you're forbidden to enter."

"Or something I'm not supposed to know."

Dr. Scott nodded. "So tell me about today. You had an interesting visitor in the shop?"

How did you guess? But Ruby already knew the answer, so she didn't ask the question.

"Yes. Somebody I knew in high school.

Leslie moved away years ago, but she's here because her mom died and she needs to sell the house. She came in the shop and we started talking about Brittany, a girl we both knew. Who killed herself." She shivered. "I can't get it out of my mind."

"Why?"

Ruby thought about that. "Because Brittany didn't start out with a lot of advantages. Her father was gone, her mom had a drinking problem, and her brother was in and out of jail. But she was pretty. Plus, she was whip-smart. And tough." She frowned a little, remembering. "Grasping, maybe. Greedy, some people would say, always wanting things that other girls had. She battled for every chance she got. And when she got what she wanted, she held onto it, hard. She seemed to have gotten what she wanted at last — good-looking husband, kids, upscale house. She's the last person in the world I'd expect to kill herself."

Dr. Scott's brows were up. "What else?"

"Well . . ." Ruby swirled the coffee in her mug, looking into it as if it might hold all the answers. "I keep thinking that Brittany's suicide is somehow connected to Sarah's disappearance. But that's not possible."

"Really?" Dr. Scott took another bite of her pizza. "Why isn't it possible?"

Ruby was surprised by the question. "Well, for one thing, Sarah disappeared twenty-some years ago. I don't know when Brittany killed herself, but it was recently." She shook her head. "I don't know why I'm thinking about her, or about her in connection with Sarah. For that matter, I don't know why I'm dreaming about Sarah. I've thought about her often, of course. But I haven't dreamed about her often, and certainly not on three or four consecutive nights. It's a mystery."

"Doesn't seem very mysterious to me." Dr. Scott finished her pizza and licked her fingers. "Would you like my professional opinion? As a researcher *and* as someone who's psychic?"

"Of course. I mean, please."

"Well, then." Dr. Scott leaned forward, regarding Ruby intently. "I think your abilities — your psychic skills — have matured to the point where they may be an important asset, not just to you but to others. Something you can use. To solve problems. To learn what you need to know."

"An asset?" Ruby frowned. "I'm afraid I don't —"

"Here's the way I understand it, Ruby." Dr. Scott picked up her coffee mug and leaned back in her chair. "Judging from what little I know about you from the testing — and it's not nearly enough — you are an exceptionally strong empath. Of course, most heart-healthy humans have empathy. But you go far beyond that. You have a tendency to absorb other people's emotions, sometimes to the point of being overwhelmed by them."

"That's me," Ruby says ruefully. "My friend China says I always lead with my heart. Gets me into all kinds of trouble."

"That's a good way of describing it. But you are also telepathic and to some extent precognitive — you can see what's ahead. Of course, the future is fluid. It continually shifts and reshapes itself in response to changing events and conditions. It's hard to see through those shifts to the outcomes. You appear to be able to do that, even if you're not consciously aware of the process. But your precognitive ability can make it more difficult for you to manage your empathic skills. It complicates your response to people, since you may have some awareness, however dim, of what's ahead for them."

"But I don't *want* to know what's ahead," Ruby protested. "Really. I have no right to know. And I don't want to get involved."

"Exactly. You don't want to get involved.

But what I'm saying to you is that in many cases — in the *important* cases — you are meant to be involved. Whether you want to be or not."

"*Meant* to?" Ruby repeated. She shook her head. "But growing up, I had to learn —"

"I know." Dr. Scott's smile was sympathetic. "Unfortunately, that happens to almost all psychic children. We learn pretty quickly that parents and teachers and friends get uncomfortable when we know something they don't. So we hide it. We protect ourselves by discounting our skills, or even disowning them. We're like the intelligent young girl who dumbs herself down so the kids at school won't call her a brain and shun her because she's smart. We dumb ourselves down, but psychically, rather than intellectually. And we try to maintain strong buffers — psychological defenses, shields."

"My life in a nutshell," Ruby murmured. "But I do try to set boundaries. I'm afraid of getting sucked into something — or somebody." She shivered. "Of going in too deep. Of not being able to come back out."

"That's understandable. An empath who is also telepathic can be terribly vulnerable. Her knowledge makes her feel exposed." Dr. Scott's face softened. "Unfortunately, being psychic doesn't mean that we always make good choices. If we open ourselves up to another person, we may learn more than we want to know — or give away more than we can afford."

Ruby nodded. "All true. But none of this explains what's going on with the dreams, or with Sarah. And Brittany. Why it's happening, I mean. And why now. After all this time."

"I can't answer those questions specifically without a few more facts." Dr. Scott tilted her head, considering. "But here's my take on it, for the moment. I see you as somebody who was pretty successful in suppressing her abilities — until at some point they simply grew so strong that she couldn't keep a lid on them any longer. Sometimes this process can be triggered by a trauma of some kind."

"A trauma?"

"Most often, a physical trauma. One of my grad students found himself learning to deal with strong telepathic abilities after he was struck by lightning."

"Eek!" Ruby exclaimed with a little laugh. "Thankfully, nothing that dramatic has happened to me." She sobered. "But something *did* happen, actually. Last summer, I rode my bike into a tree and —"

Dr. Scott's eyebrows arched in a silent

question. When Ruby didn't continue, she said, "And . . . what?"

Ruby took a breath. "Just a mild concussion. I felt fine afterward, really." She touched the scar under her hairline. "No broken bones, and I only missed a day or two of work. I really don't think —"

"I do," Dr. Scott said firmly. "Even a transient brain trauma can trigger the emergence of psychic capabilities. One theory is that we're all psychic to some extent, but that a head injury — like a concussion — can enhance those abilities by rerouting some of the brain's electrical pathways." She paused. "You're a strong woman, Ruby, and you've been suppressing some pretty potent abilities for a very long time. I wouldn't be surprised if they unexpectedly emerged. And powerfully. Sort of like shaking a champagne bottle and then popping the cork."

Ruby frowned, not liking the comparison. "But once the champagne starts fizzing out of the bottle, you can't make it stop. Is this going to be like that?"

"It could be. When this happens, empaths often find themselves highly receptive, like a lightning rod, or a radio receiver that's missing its off button. Some of us become more open to negative energies. We may even start broadcasting." Dr. Scott pushed herself out of her chair. "I'm working late tonight, so I'm going to make some more coffee. Want some?"

"No, thank you. I'm as wired as I need to be." Ruby paused, frowning. "Broadcasting?"

"That's when your buffers — your shields — are down and you have so much energy that it's spilling all over the place. It's like you're sending a signal: 'Here I am. Connect with me.' " She inserted a coffee pod into the machine, added water, and pushed the button. "Over time and with practice, you'll learn to be aware of what you're doing and stop doing it, or put up your shields. But in the meantime, there will be moments when you'll be . . . unprotected. Vulnerable to aggressive energies. Psychics who work with law enforcement and come in contact with a lot of negative energy have to be especially careful."

Ruby shivered, remembering her experience of working with Ethan Connors. "It would be better if we knew in advance and could keep those things from happening," she said. "If only I'd known what was going to happen to Sarah, I might have kept her from going out that night. That would be a better use of these . . . abilities, wouldn't it?"

"That's what we would choose, if we could, yes." Sipping her coffee, Dr. Scott fell silent for a moment. "But maybe that wasn't the way it was supposed to happen."

"*Supposed* to happen?"

Dr. Scott nodded. "There are some things we can see coming and can change, yes. But there are others we can't change. Or to put it a different way, we're not meant to change them." She was speaking slowly and emphatically, her eyes on Ruby's face. "There aren't any absolutes, Ruby. We're talking about ambiguities, uncertainties, mysteries. You will learn to use your abilities to the extent that you can, when you can, as wisely as you can. That's all we can ask of ourselves. That's the best we can do."

"Not good enough," Ruby muttered. "But if I'm stuck with being psychic, I need to learn to manage it."

"You will, if that's what you really want to do. But there's a lot to learn, and you'll have to consciously work at it. There will be energies that are far more powerful than yours, and challenges you can't handle. There will be circumstances that defeat you. And even when your psychic skills have matured to their highest level, you will never be quite sure of them. You'll reach inside yourself for an ability and it simply won't be there." She chuckled wryly. "Or it will be so powerful that you'll wish you had an off button."

"You said, 'consciously work at it.' " Ruby frowned. "What does that mean? Do I read books? Do I practice, like here in the lab?"

Dr. Scott finished her coffee and got up to rinse the mug and replace it in the cupboard. "I can set up some exercises for you. They're sort of like mental push-ups, designed to heighten your awareness, strengthen your buffers, direct your energies." She smiled a little. "But if you're serious about this, it's going to take field exercises."

"Field exercises?" Ruby was immediately curious. "Like what?"

"Things that happen in the real world. Events that teach you to recognize and tap into different kinds of energies — energies we can't simulate in the lab." She paused. "They're like assignments. Coursework designed to develop your psychic abilities in specific ways."

"Coursework designed and assigned by the Universe, I suppose," Ruby said a little drily.

"Exactly. But you'll have to figure out the syllabus as you go. Watch and listen. Take good notes. There's no quiz at the end. But it's pass/fail."

Ruby frowned. "Sounds hard."

"It is. Damned hard." Dr. Scott's voice was amused, her glance enigmatic. "We don't always get what we want, you know. But one way or another, we get what we need. It's been my experience that if we ignore one assignment because we don't like it or we're afraid of it, the Universe will send it to us again. And again."

She glanced up at the clock on the wall. "I have to get back to work. Next time you come, bring your notes. I want to know what field exercises the Universe has offered you." She gave Ruby an intense, oddly penetrating look. "As I said, most of the time, our dreams are symbolic. But sometimes a blue door really *is* a blue door. Please think about that." Her gaze was firm and steady, and she wasn't smiling.

"And don't forget that once a door has been opened, you can't always control what might come through it."

CHAPTER EIGHT

But what was there to think about a blue door, Ruby wondered as she unlocked her own kitchen door — painted her favorite sunny yellow — and stepped inside.

She was met by Pagan, who curled himself around her ankles, politely requesting a bowl of milk, please. *And if you could warm it just a little,* he added, *that would be lovely.*

Pagan was the all-black cat who had arrived on Ruby's back porch one dark and stormy night and announced that the Universe had assigned Ruby to his care. He was a polite and gentlemanly cat but unusually assertive, and Ruby didn't even try to say no.

When she opened the refrigerator to get Pagan's milk, it occurred to her that she was hungry, too. When Pagan was taken care of, she toasted half a bagel for herself, slathered it with cream cheese, added thinly sliced onion and a few capers, and topped it with a slice of smoked salmon. Then, feeling celebratory after her intriguing conversation with Dr. Scott, she poured herself a glass of white wine.

Her cell rang — the spooky opening bars from *The Exorcist* — just as she was sitting down. She took a deep breath, counted to three, and let it out again. She didn't need to glance at the display to know that her sister Ramona was on the other end of the line. She also knew that she had let a couple of Mona's messages go to voice mail that evening. If she didn't answer, her sister would just keep calling. She picked up the phone.

"Hi, Mona. How are you this evening?"

There was a high-pitched *ping* and a quick burst of static, and Ruby held the phone away from her ear. Her younger sister had inherited some of the same family gift that had come to Ruby, although for Mona, it took the form of telekinesis. When she got excited, she gave off surges of electrical energy that registered noisily on whatever electronic devices happened to be nearby.

"I'm working on a new idea for our project," Ramona announced. "If you're not doing anything tonight, I'd love to come over and tell you about it."

Ruby glanced up at the clock. "I just got

home, sweetie. I'm tired and I —"

"I tried to reach you earlier," Ramona said accusingly.

"I was in a meeting." Ruby didn't mention Dr. Scott. Her sister had expressed an interest in visiting the lab, which Ruby thought was a terrible idea. "And I'm just about to have a —"

"Bagel," Ramona said. "With cream cheese, onions, and capers. And you didn't invite me." She made a pouty noise. "But I forgive you, dear. Do you want to hear my idea?" Without waiting for Ruby's answer, she went on. "It's about the Psychic Sisters. Remember what I told you about setting up a website?"

The previous fall, Ramona had announced that she and Ruby were going to open a psychic consulting service. They would go into business as professional psychics, helping people use their intuition, develop their psychic energies, and get in touch with their spirit guides. "We can do clairvoyant readings and teach classes and offer phone consultations — all that sort of thing," Ramona had said. "And we can do it all on the internet, in our pajamas, if we like. Don't you think it's brilliant, Ruby? We can make a ton of money."

Ruby did *not* think it was brilliant. But

she knew that saying no to Ramona was a sure way to get her to do whatever you didn't want her to do. So she had been discouraging without being downright negative, hoping that Ramona would get excited about something else and forget about the Psychic Sisters. Unfortunately, she hadn't. Not yet.

Pagan had been sitting on his haunches, watching her with interest. Suddenly, he turned and launched a flying leap onto a pantry shelf, where Ruby had stacked some cans of cat food, soup, and canned soft drinks. He body-slammed the cans onto the floor, where they made a loud clatter.

"Uh-oh," Ruby said hurriedly. "Pagan just made a big mess — stuff all over the floor. Gotta go, Mona. Talk to you tomorrow." Without waiting for her sister's response, she clicked off the phone and went to pick up the cans.

"Thank you, Pagan," she said. "Exactly what I needed, at the moment I needed it. You're a good kitty."

"Mrrrow," Pagan said modestly, and flicked his tail.

CHAPTER NINE

Lila's Diner was on Nueces, just a block east of the newspaper. The Diner, a converted Missouri and Pacific railroad dining car, had been rescued from oblivion and made over by Lila and Ralph Jennings in classic 1950s style, with a red Formica counter, chrome-and-red tables and chairs, and a red-and-white tile floor. Sadly, Ralph had succumbed to his two-pack-a-day habit, but their daughter Docia moved from Dallas to take her dad's place in the kitchen and the Diner just kept on cookin', as Lila liked to put it. It was a favorite breakfast and lunch hangout for the *Enterprise* staff, so when Jessica came in and headed for her usual back table, Lila immediately poured a cup of black coffee and set it in front of her.

"What're you hungry for this mornin', Ms. Jessie?"

Lila spoke over the Willie Nelson ballad, "Always on My Mind," playing on the radio

315

behind the counter. She was fifty-something, as thin as a stalk of Johnson grass, with bleached blond hair. She had grown up in Texarkana, which is as about far east as you can go in Texas without crossing over into Arkansas. You could hear East Texas in her twang.

"Peach-and-pecan waffles for two, please," Jessica said. "And another cup of coffee. Fran will be here in a minute."

Lila nodded and asked her usual question. "Caught 'ny crooks lately?"

Jessica smiled and gave her usual answer. "Maybe today. Working on it."

"You go, girl," Lila said, and patted her shoulder. "You're as good as them cops, any day."

Lila had just brought Fran's coffee when Will Wagner, the *Enterprise* sports editor, came in, wearing an orange University of Texas T-shirt and a white Longhorns baseball cap. He saw Jessica and sauntered toward the table.

"That for me?" he asked, pointing to the coffee.

"Nope. It's Fran's. We're having a meeting."

"Girl talk, huh? Secrets?" He leaned over and spoke in a low voice. "Wonder what you thought about Dixon."

"Dixon?" Jessica asked blankly.

"Jefferson Davis Dixon. Our new boss." His voice became wry. "You know. The guy who wants to yank the *Enterprise* into the twenty-first century. Personally, I figure he'll bomb. Spend a lot of money, have some fun, accomplish nothing much."

"Well, maybe," Jessica said. "But I'd rather try something — anything — than just give up. Did you hear about what happened up in Ohio? The *Vindicator* folded and a hundred and forty-four newspaper people are out of work. In Youngstown, which already has a huge unemployment problem."

"Journalism jobs are scarce everywhere." Will shook his head glumly. "The problem is that Dixon is going all in for that new stuff when readers only want what they're used to. They're not going to sit in front of their computers to read the newspaper, damn it." His face darkened. "Especially sports readers. I'm lucky if I can hold their attention for seven or eight paragraphs. *Short* paragraphs. And that's in print. On screens or in phones, forget it. They'll scan for scores, glance at a few photos, and that's it."

"Hey, guys." It was Fran. She peered at Will. "You're looking gloomy this morning, Sunshine."

"I am the voice of doom." Will straightened and tipped his cap. "You girls enjoy your little talkfest. See you back at the shop." He stuck his hands in his pockets and ambled over to the counter, where Virgil had just come in.

Fran slid into the booth. Her dark hair was pulled into its usual ponytail, the tendrils around her face slightly damp. She was wearing an ivory open-front blazer with scrunch sleeves over a red tank top, jeans, and dark suede boots.

"Did you order for me?"

Jessica nodded. They always had the same thing. "Waffles. Peach and pecan."

"Thanks. I'm hungry." Fran pulled her coffee cup toward her. "Just got back from a run."

Jessica rolled her eyes. "I won't ask."

"Then I won't tell you I ran five miles."

"Before breakfast." Jessica sighed. "I wish you hadn't told me."

The radio switched from Willie to Reba McEntire, an upbeat "I Want a Cowboy." Fran added sugar to her coffee and stirred, singing under her breath about a guy who wore Wranglers and drove a pickup and rode bulls.

"If you had a guy like that, you wouldn't like him."

318

"Who says? You betcha I'd like him. And his Wranglers. His pickup, too. I don't know about the bull."

Jessica pulled out her phone and brought up the photo she had sent to herself the night before. "I want to show you something."

"What've you got?" Fran bent forward, peering at the screen. "Our junior prom court!" she squealed. "Omigod, Jessica. That's *me,* a princess! Jeez, look how young I was. And how *fat.*" She bent closer. "That was before I started running. I must have been carrying thirty pounds of baby fat. No wonder nobody would date me." She took a sip of coffee. "You pulled that out of our high school yearbook, didn't you? Why? What's up with that?"

"Actually, I happened to find your photo when I was looking for Sarah Gellner's," Jessica said. "When I saw it, I realized that you and Sarah were in the same class. I wondered what you remembered about her."

"Oh, poor Sarah." Fran said, with a dramatic eye-roll. She pushed her damp hair back. "Nobody knows what became of her. She went out one night and just — just disappeared." She waved her hand. "Like that. Gone. Nobody ever heard from her ever again. It was a very big deal."

"A big deal?"

"Yeah. Nothing like that had ever happened in Pecan Springs, and it had this huge impact. My parents changed my weekend curfew to nine o'clock, which was impossible, of course. I had my driver's license by that time, but they wouldn't let me take the car unless one of them was with me. They grilled me about where I was going and who I was going with. Everybody's parents acted pretty much the same way, so all the kids were pissed off. And the school?" She rolled her eyes again. "Lordy. It was a crackdown."

Lila appeared with two plates of crisp golden waffles heaped with peach compote and pecans and topped with whipped cream laced with maple syrup. "Bonny appetite, as they say in France."

"Heavenly," Fran said, taking a big sniff. "Thank you, Lila!" She picked up her fork and began digging in.

"Thank Docia," Lila said. "She's the one stood over a hot stove to make that compote last July, when we got a couple of bushels of them Fredericksburg peaches."

"Tell Docia we love her," Jessica said with a smile, and Lila nodded, satisfied. When she had gone, Jessica said, "You were telling me about the school."

Fran spoke around a mouthful of waffle. "The principal — Mr. Mertz — canceled just about everything that was scheduled at night. It was like all of Pecan Springs was on lockdown, because this one girl had disappeared. Ran away, some people said. I think the kids felt like we were being punished just because of her. There was a lot of grumbling, some of it pretty spiteful."

"That wasn't fair," Jessica said, forking up a bite of peach compote. "It doesn't sound like Sarah was the kind to run away. Weren't people . . . well, afraid for her?"

Fran frowned. "You know, I don't think so. Pecan Springs was such a peaceful little town back then. Folks didn't think anything bad could ever happen here. And we were just kids, really. What did we know?" She sighed. "But it was a bad time for this to happen, you see. Especially because of baseball season."

"Baseball? What did baseball have to do with it?"

"The coach rescheduled the night games to the afternoons so kids wouldn't be out after dark. Which meant that the parents couldn't go. Which was bad because high school baseball was huge in Pecan Springs, especially back then, before the internet and

321

cable TV. The games were something the whole family could enjoy."

"And the prom was coming up," Jessica mused, glancing at the photo on her phone, which lay on the table between them.

"Yes, just a couple of weeks after she disappeared." Fran looked up from her plate. "Sarah was . . . well, a little wild, I guess you would say. She was active in everything, and popular — head cheerleader, junior yearbook editor, volleyball captain. She was elected prom queen and her boyfriend, Ted, was elected king. So when she went missing somebody had to decide what to do. Should she be replaced or should they maybe just scrap the court or what?"

"Wait a minute. What do you mean, 'a little wild'? Wild how?"

"Maybe that's not the right word." Fran gestured with her fork. "She was like . . . well, sassy. She talked back. She did things her way, regardless of what people thought. She liked to take chances, you might say. Her parents let her come and go pretty much as she pleased, and sometimes she'd tell these crazy stories about where she'd been and what she'd done. She and Ruby Gifford — Ruby Wilcox, now — were best friends." She frowned. "Ruby was pretty outrageous in high school, too. She and

322

Sarah were quite a pair."

"Being sassy doesn't sound very wild," Jessica remarked. "Or outrageous."

"By Pecan Springs standards? Back in the day?" Fran chuckled. "Believe me, sassy was wild *and* outrageous. And as I said, Sarah was a risk-taker — at least, a lot more than the rest of us." She looked pensive. "But maybe we wished we had the guts to do what she did. Maybe that was why the kids admired her. Or were jealous of her. And maybe why they were so willing to believe she'd gone off with a couple of boys and was having a great time somewhere."

"In that red Chevy," Jessica murmured.

"The cops never located the car." Fran picked up her coffee cup and took a sip. "Anyway, Sarah had a cousin in LA, and some of the kids said she could have gone out there to live. Some even said that maybe Ted had gotten her pregnant and her parents sent her out there to have the baby and give it up for adoption." Over the rim, she added, "Her parents shot that down. They said *absolutely not.* But you know what small towns are like. A lot of people believed that's what happened. If you asked them today, that's probably what they'd say."

"I read the coverage in the *Express-News,*" Jessica said. "I'll go up to the morgue today and see what the *Enterprise* had to say. Maybe I can find a few more details."

"I doubt it," Fran said. "That was before Hark's time, you know. The Seidenstickers owned the newspaper back then, and they didn't print what they thought of as 'bad news.' Or they whitewashed it and *then* printed it." She frowned. "But maybe that's why it was so easy to believe that she had gone off with those guys. We couldn't believe something really bad could happen."

"And then what? As time went on, I mean."

Fran shrugged. "Well, nobody knew anything, really. The thing is, that Sarah was — not forgotten, exactly. I mean, people still thought about her and wondered. But she sort of slipped out of focus, if you know what I mean. Maybe because her parents were killed, which meant that people stopped searching. The investigation was left to the cops, and they had other priorities."

"Her parents were killed?" Jessica asked, startled. She had been thinking of interviewing them. "When? What happened?"

"They'd been to San Antonio to do a TV interview about the search for Sarah. Coming back, they plowed into a jackknifed eighteen-wheeler during a rainstorm. Died instantly, both of them."

Jessica picked up her phone and looked at the yearbook photo. "This girl Brittany — she took Sarah's place on the prom court?"

"Yes. Actually, she was the nearest runner-up to Sarah in the election. So somebody made an executive decision and said she'd be queen — unless Sarah somehow magically showed up. Which of course didn't happen." Fran finished her waffle and leaned back in her chair. "Actually, Brit took Sarah's place. In more ways than one."

"How so?"

"Ted and Sarah had been going steady for about a year. He was out of town when she disappeared, so he wasn't the cops' number one suspect. But they grilled him anyway. He kept telling everybody that Sarah would be back. And when her folks were killed and she still hadn't come back, I guess he sort of gave up. We all did. There was nothing we could do. Now, with Amber Alert and the internet, it might be different. But back then . . ." She shrugged.

Jessica thought of something she had read that week: roughly eight hundred thousand children are reported missing every year, nearly two thousand a day. The numbers might have been less back then, but Sarah would have been just another statistic.

"It must have been especially hard for Ted," she said. "He really was out of town?"

"In Houston, at a debate competition. The team drove over with the debate coach and came back with her, too." Fran pushed her plate away. "He was pretty broken up at first, but after a while, he must have decided to move on. He and Brit started going together on the class trip to Six Flags. Over time, I guess it began to seem really romantic. The king's queen ran away and he married the princess."

"Married?" Jessica was surprised. She looked at the photo again and thought she detected a look of something like triumph on the queen's face. "So Ted and Brittany got married?"

Fran nodded. "Yes. His parents hated it. As far as they were concerned, Brit wasn't the right sort of girl for their son. Her brother was in jail more often than he was out, and her mother was an alcoholic. Nobody knew where her father was. Things were tough for her — but she was tougher." She smiled a little. "Anyway, she got pregnant and Ted insisted on marrying her, over his parents' objections. But it worked out — at least, we all thought it did. He finished college and got through med school and eventually set up his practice outside of Houston." Her face darkened. "Brit didn't get to enjoy that part of it, though. That's the irony in all this."

"Oh?" Jessica finished her waffle and put her fork down.

"Yeah. One evening she drove her Lexus to the nearest railroad crossing, waited until the train was almost there, and stepped out in front of it. *Boom.*" Fran whacked the flat of her hand on the table and Jessica jumped.

"You mean —" Jessica winced. "She *killed* herself?" A train? Oh, god, what a horrible way to die. "Does anybody know why?"

"Pretty awful, huh?" Fran's mouth twisted. "I was surprised when I saw it come over the newswire and realized who it was. 'Why?' was my first question, too. So I phoned Leslie Newell, who knew Brit pretty well back in high school. But Leslie didn't have a clue, either. She said it looked like Brittany had everything she ever wanted. Ted, a couple of kids, a big house next to a golf course, clothes, even that Lexus. She wasn't in ill health, and Ted told Leslie that they were getting along okay, so he didn't think it was his fault. Why would a girl like her do a thing like that? It was *gruesome.* And so far as I know, it's still a mystery."

Her eyes met Jessica's and there was a

challenge in her voice — her reporter's voice. "*Now* will you tell me why you're asking about all this old stuff?"

Jessica cleared her throat. "Ruby Wilcox has mentioned Sarah to me, and I'm . . . well, curious. You know how I am about unsolved mysteries. I get compulsive."

"Yeah." Fran pushed her plate away. "Well, all I can say is that this unsolved mystery is a humdinger. If you're going to get compulsive about it, I can only wish you luck."

CHAPTER TEN

For Ruby, it was a night of restless, uneasy dreams. She was groggy when she woke up the next morning, and her eyes felt as if they were full of sand. She pulled her dream journal out of the drawer of her bedside table, found her pen, and managed to scrawl a few details before the bright morning light washed them out of her mind.

She had dreamed once again of Sarah. This time, her friend was taking photos with her new digital camera, the one she'd been so proud of. Sarah wanted to be a professional photographer when she grew up, so she was always trying out the new developments she read about in camera magazines. This camera had a screen on the back where you could see what the camera saw as you snapped the photo. If you flipped a switch, you could see the photos you'd already taken. Colored photos, every bit as good as the ones you got when you took your film to Walgreen's — but it had no film. These days, of course, everybody had a cellphone camera. Back in the day, Sarah's little digital camera was a new thing.

In the dream, Sarah turned the camera around to show a photo to Ruby. With a toss of her russet curls and that mischievous grin that always tugged at Ruby's heart, she said. *Take a look, Ruby. Take a good look.*

The house was the same one Ruby had seen in her dream of Sarah's painting. A tiny house, the size of a playhouse, in somebody's backyard. It was painted white, with a red roof and purple shutters. And an inviting blue door. Beside the door was a hand-painted sign: *I dream my painting and I paint my dream. Vincent van Gogh.*

Weird enough, Ruby thought. But what was even weirder was what happened next. In Ruby's dream, she was suddenly *inside* Sarah's photograph, standing in front of that blue door, reaching for the doorknob, turning it. Before, the knob wouldn't turn or the door stuck. This time, it swung open easily. But when she was about to step over the threshold, she looked down and saw that there was nothing there. Only a dark, yawning hole, starkly terrifying in its vast emptiness, opening all the way down into the center of the earth. The emptiness was waiting for her. It *wanted* her, and from some-where, as if from a great distance, she heard Sarah's voice. *Ruby,* she called. *Ruby, find me, please!*

Ruby clung to the door frame, fighting the temptation to let go, to step over the thresh-old and fall in. Just fall, fall free, fall forever. The temptation was real, so very *real.* And frighteningly compelling.

Panicked, she slammed the door and stepped back, out of the photograph. But that changed nothing. The hole was still there in front of her, deep and black and threatening, and no amount of wishing would wish it away. She awoke shivering and covered with cold sweat, vividly remember-ing the sign beside the door: *I dream my painting and I paint my dream.* And remem-bering that Vincent van Gogh's dreams had not been pretty or pleasant. He had been tormented by nightmares.

Ten minutes later, as Ruby finished writ-ing in her journal, she was still shivering. The dream had brought with it a strong feeling of *déjà vu,* a feeling she couldn't shake.

That tiny house with the purple shutters and the blue door. She had seen it before, hadn't she, somewhere?

Somewhere, yes. Not in a dream, but in

the real world.

And now that she thought about it, she thought she knew where it was. Or where it *had* been.

Was it still there?

At the shop that day, all day, Sarah's photo stayed with her, the tiny house with the blue door flashing into Ruby's mind every now and then with an oddly increasing urgency, as if the dream — or the house, or the blue door — had a will of its own and refused to let her go. With it came images of Sarah. Lively, feisty, unforgettable Sarah. Sarah the cheerleader, the yearbook editor, the elected prom queen. Sarah, who was always ready to answer back, always larger and brighter and lovelier than life. Always Sarah the friend.

And with it, too, came Dr. Scott's voice. *One way or another, we get what we need. It's been my experience that if we ignore one assignment because we don't like it or we're afraid of it, the Universe will send it to us again. And again.*

And her final admonition: *Most of the time, our dreams are symbolic. But sometimes a blue door really is a blue door. Please think about that.*

But Ruby didn't need Dr. Scott's encouragement, for no matter how hard she tried, she couldn't *stop* thinking about that blue door.

Was this her assignment from the Universe?

If it was, did she have to carry it out all by herself, or could she ask for help?

In the last weeks of March in the Texas Hill Country, it is almost full dark by eight o'clock in the evening. On this particular March evening, the sky was heavily overcast and the clouds were producing a chilly drizzle, so dark had fallen a little earlier.

China Bayles usually finished the evening kitchen chores about this time of the evening, looked over Caitie's finished homework, and joined McQuaid in the living room for a companionable couple of hours with a quiet project: needlework, a good book, or a movie they had been looking forward to. Winchester, the family basset, was usually there, too.

And Mr. Spock, a stunning green parrot with an orange beak and splashes of red and blue under his wings. Spock was the Eclectus parrot that Caitie and China had adopted (whether temporarily or permanently wasn't quite clear yet) from old Mrs. Birkett, who lived down the street from

Thyme and Seasons. Mrs. Birkett had inherited Spock from a neighbor — a Star Trek fan — who could no longer take care of him, but the elderly lady wasn't an enthusiastic audience of his constant chatter. Caitie had a flock of chickens and loved every single feather of them. To her, Spock was an exotic chicken with a sound track. She had fallen in love with him and was spending hours teaching him new words — and cataloging his remarkable vocabulary of Klingon curses.

Tonight, China was looking forward to Amy Stewart's *Wicked Plants,* a reread that she was enjoying as much as any murder mystery. The plants were fascinating. The castor bean, for instance, yielded the deadly poison ricin, which the Soviet KGB had used in the so-called umbrella assassination of Bulgarian journalist Georgi Markov in London back in the 1970s. And the hallucinogenic datura, or jimson weed, which, while it produced gorgeous flowers, could definitely mess with your mind.

But as she sat down and opened the book, her cell phone rang. It was Ruby. Her voice was urgent.

"China, I have to go somewhere and I need you to come with me. Tonight."

"Tonight?" China asked in surprise.

"Gosh, Ruby, I just sat down with a book. Where do you want to go?"

"Boldly go," Spock squawked cheerfully from the ceiling-high cage that currently occupied a corner of the living room. "Final frontier."

"I'd rather tell you when you get here," Ruby said. "Please bring a flashlight. You'll need to wear walking shoes. And something dark — like a dark poncho, maybe. It's drizzling out there."

"But if it's drizzling enough for a poncho and dark enough for a flashlight, why do we have to go out *tonight*? Whatever-it-is can wait until tomorrow, can't it? Or the weekend? Or —"

"Explore strange new worlds," Spock crooned. "Seek out new civilizations."

"Shut up, Spock," McQuaid said from his recliner, where he was reading a magazine, Winchester snugged against him, snoring gently.

Spock ignored him. "Boldly go!" he cried. "Dor-sho-gha!" *Dor-sho-gha,* Caitie had discovered on the internet, was Klingon for something like "Get on with it, damn it!"

"Is that your parrot?" Ruby asked. "Tell him he has the right idea. And don't argue with me, China. I need to do this. If I have to, I'll do it alone. But I want you to come as a . . . as a witness."

A witness? China frowned. This was beginning to sound serious. "Well, okay. But at least tell me what we're doing."

"We're just going to take a little walk," Ruby said. "Only about three blocks. Well, four, I guess. Not far."

China gave in to the inevitable. "I'll see you in about twenty minutes," she said, and closed her book.

McQuaid glanced up from the issue of *Texas Monthly* he was reading. "Ruby's got a burr under her saddle?"

"That's one way to put it," China said. "All she'll say is that we're going somewhere to do something, and I should wear a dark poncho and bring a flashlight. I'm a witness."

"We are the Borg," Spock announced. "Resistance is futile!"

"Sounds like one of her Nancy Drew expeditions," McQuaid said. "Ruby always wanted to be Carolyn Keene."

"Sounds like that to me, too," China said, with one last, longing look at her comfortable chair. Outside, she heard the deep rumble of thunder.

Winchester woke up and draped a paw over McQuaid's knee. McQuaid patted the dog's head and went back to his magazine.

"Have fun," he said. "And don't get shot. Okay?"

"I'll try," China said, wondering if it was wet enough to wear her boots. "Any idea where I'll find the flashlight?"

"Look under the hood, Scotty," Spock said, in a very fair imitation of Captain Kirk.

Jessica was sitting cross-legged on her bed, hunched over her Mac and deep in the second chapter of *Not Only in the Dark*. She looked up as a flicker of lightning flared across her window. It was followed by the grumble of thunder and the sound of rain. From her CD player came the quiet sounds of Julian Bream playing a Bach violin concerto, one of her collection of classical guitar recordings. Beside her on the bed, Murphy purred contentedly, the tip of his orange tail flicking.

Jessica was just thinking how pleasant it was not to have to go out on such a rainy evening, when she heard her cellphone's muffled ringtone: the theme from *The Good, the Bad, and the Ugly*. For Jessica, the ringtone was a crime writer's life, in a nutshell. The good stuff was bad and the bad stuff was ugly. Get used to it.

She groped for her cell hastily, thinking that David might be calling and then hoping he wasn't. When she finally found it under an empty pizza box, a pair of lace panties, and a T-shirt that said *Save a journalist. Buy a newspaper,* the phone had stopped ringing. But she could see who had called, so she called her back.

"What's up, Ruby?" Murphy stopped purring and twitched his whiskers.

"I've got a breaking news story for you," Ruby said brightly.

"Really?" Jessica leaned back against the pillow, thinking that Ruby's cheeriness sounded a little forced. "What kind of story?"

"The cold-case scoop kind. The three-column headline kind. To get it, you'll have to go with me tonight."

"A scoop? Tonight?" Jessica sat up straight. "Go where? Why?"

"Wear a raincoat or a poncho. Something dark-colored. We don't want to call attention to ourselves."

"But I'm working on my book tonight," Jessica protested. As she spoke, she heard another roll of thunder. She glanced toward the windows. "And it's raining." The rain drummed harder. "In fact, it's pouring."

"It's just a shower," Ruby said. "And we're only walking a short way. You should wear boots, though," she added. "It might be muddy."

"Walking?" Jessica asked. "In the rain? Why do we have to *walk*? Why can't we drive?"

"Because we don't want anybody to see us," Ruby said in a reasonable tone, as if they were talking about going to the Dairy Queen for hot fudge sundaes. "A car's headlights would give us away. Anyway, it's not far."

Jessica frowned. "But surely this story can wait until tomorrow. When it's daylight. And it's stopped raining."

"It can't wait." Ruby's tone changed. "Of course, if you're not interested in the scoop, I suppose I could call Fran Fenner. I'm sure she'd be glad to go. She's not the kind to be afraid of a little bit of damp, either. She ran that last marathon when it was pouring rain the whole way. And if Fran's not available, there's that reporter you're always complaining about. What's her name — Heather? You said she was hungry for stories."

"Ruby, this is blackmail," Jessica said between her teeth. "This is totally not playing fair."

"Probably," Ruby said, and her voice dropped. "But I really need to do this. And I need *you,* Jessica. I'm not trying to guilt you, but will you come?"

Jessica paused. She would much prefer to stay home and write, but Ruby was obviously concerned about something. And she had come (and brought the cops) when Jessica desperately needed her. In fact, if Ruby hadn't rescued her the night she was grabbed by the Angel of Death, she might not be sitting here, working on her book about the guy who had tried to add her to his collection of murder victims. It was only right to return the favor. And not out of guilt, either. Out of fairness. Because Ruby was a friend.

"I'm in," she said, forcing herself to sound cheerful. "Be there in a few." She hit the save button and closed her laptop.

On the other end of the line, Ruby gave a relieved sigh. "Bless you, Jess," she said gratefully. "Oh, and if you have a flashlight, please bring it. It's dark out there."

CHAPTER ELEVEN

Jessica pulled into the driveway at Ruby's house, behind China's dinged-up white Toyota. Oh, good, she thought, relieved. There would be three of them on this mysterious rainy-and-dark-as-the-pit expedition.

And China herself was in Ruby's kitchen, sitting at the table with a mug of tea, her maroon poncho hanging, dripping, on a hook behind the door.

"Sit down, Jessie," Ruby said. "We're warming ourselves up before we go out in the rain."

"We are waiting until the rain *stops,*" China corrected her, in a big-sister voice. "Some of us are wondering whether this trip is absolutely necessary."

With a chuckle, Jessica hung up her windbreaker, floppy rain hat, and the waist pack she had brought instead of a handbag. She sat down across from China, while

Ruby poured her a mug of spice-scented tea. Pagan, Ruby's black cat, got out of his basket, stalked across the floor, and jumped into Jessica's lap, sniffing the fabric of her jeans for Murphy's scent. She stroked him, feeling the throaty rumbling of his purr through the tips of her fingers.

After the damp, chilly outdoors, Ruby's kitchen was warm and inviting, with its red-and-white striped wallpaper and watermelon border and red table and red-and-green chairs with little black seeds painted on the seats. There was a watermelon rug under the table and watermelon place mats on the table. Even the pottery mugs for their tea were glazed in watermelon colors, green on the outside, red with small black seeds on the inside.

China was frowning. "You know, Ruby, I still love Nancy Drew. But I've long since lost my desire to *be* her when I grow up. So until you tell us where we are going tonight and why, I am not leaving this wonderful kitchen — except to go back home, where there's a good book and a comfortable chair waiting for me. And a parrot with an impressive vocabulary of Klingon curse words." Her critical tone was softened by a smile. "I sincerely hope we're not going out tonight just because your Ouija board happens to think it might be a really fun thing for us to do."

Ruby poured tea for herself and sat down. "My Ouija board has nothing to do with this."

"Well, then, what?" Jessica asked, still stroking Pagan. "When you called, you mentioned a cold case. Is it Sarah's?"

Ruby sighed. "Yes. It has to do with Sarah."

"And if not the Ouija board," China observed, "then something else must have inspired this expedition. The I Ching? Runestones? What?" As usual, she sounded skeptical.

Ruby squared her shoulders, and Jessica could tell that she had hoped that there wouldn't be any questions. "It was . . . well, to tell the truth, it was a dream."

China rolled her eyes. "A *dream*? We are going for a walk on a dark and stormy night because you had a *dream*?"

"Two dreams," Ruby paused, pursing her lips. "On the same subject but on different nights — which made it more important. Like, if I didn't get the message the first time, here it comes again."

"And the subject?" Jessica asked, trying to remember what she had read about the meanings of dreams.

"A little white house. With a blue door," Ruby added. Half to herself, she said. "The door is important, too."

"Dream doors are supposed to be important," Jessica said. "Tell us, Ruby."

Ruby told them about her first dream: Sarah, painting a picture of a small white house with a red roof and purple shutters and ivy growing up one side — and a blue door. And then the second dream: a digital photo of the same house. This time, there was a sign beside the door, with a quote from Vincent van Gogh: *I dream my painting and I paint my dream.*

"But it's what happened in both dreams that's important," Ruby added.

"What happened?" China asked.

"In the first dream, the house was so real that I reached for the doorknob and tried to open the door. I couldn't. It was stuck." Ruby cleared her throat and added uncomfortably. "In the second dream, I got the door open. But . . ." She shivered, and Jessica thought she looked frightened.

"But what?" China pressed.

"But there was a deep, black hole on the other side." Ruby reached for her mug, and Jessica saw that her fingers were trembling. "It was so deep I couldn't see the bottom. It was . . . waiting for me. That hole, I mean.

It wanted me to fall in. Or jump." Her voice sounded hollow. "I know it sounds crazy, but something down there *wanted* me to jump."

On Jessica's lap, Pagan stirred restlessly, raised his head to yawn, showing a pink tongue and shiny white teeth, and then leapt down to the floor and up onto Ruby's lap. She pulled him against her and buried her face in his fur.

"You must have been frightened," Jessica said.

"I was terrified." Ruby's voice was muffled against Pagan's fur. "But not by Sarah. She was so *real*, you know? In the dream, she wanted me to find her. And it was amazing, Jess. She looked just the way she did the day she vanished. I would have given any-thing for a hug, but I knew if I touched her, I would wake up and she would be gone. And it would be my fault." She looked up, shaking her head. "My fault again, the way it was when she disappeared. I don't think there's any way I can make up for it, but I have to try." She repeated fiercely, "It may sound illogical, but I have to *try.*"

"I've been reading newspaper clips about what happened that night," Jessica said. "You mentioned that Sarah called you and asked you to go somewhere with her. Where

345

was that?"

"She said she was going to Leslie Newell's house," Ruby said. "To work on some trig problems."

Leslie Newell, Jessica thought, thinking back to the newspaper stories she had read. Leslie had claimed that she *didn't* call Sarah that night, hadn't she? She had said that she'd spent the evening with a friend who lived across the street. She had suggested that Sarah might have used her name as an excuse to get out of the house and meet somebody — a boy, maybe.

And Jessie had recently heard Leslie Newell's name in another context, too. Wasn't she the person Fran had called to find out about the woman who stepped out in front of a train? Jessica made a mental note to do some research on Leslie Newell.

"At the time," Ruby went on, "I remember thinking it was a little weird that Sarah said she was going to Leslie's house. Leslie and Sarah were never exactly besties. Sarah made the cheerleading squad every year since middle school, and Leslie didn't. Sarah was editor of the yearbook and Leslie wasn't. Leslie was oozing jealousy." She made a face. "What if I hadn't been grounded? I would have gone with Sarah."

"And Sarah never made it to Leslie's

house?" China asked.

"Right," Ruby said sadly. "You can see, can't you? It *was* my fault. If I'd been able to go, it would have been a different story. Whatever happened to Sarah wouldn't have happened to *two* girls."

"It could have," China said quietly. "And it has. Remember the yogurt shop murders in Austin? There were four girls, not two. It happened to all four of them. And it was the fault of the killers, not the victims — or their friends or their families. 'What if' isn't relevant." She reached for Ruby's hand. "You can't blame yourself, Ruby. It *wasn't* your fault."

Still thinking about Leslie, Jessica frowned. "You believe that the white house in your dream — in both your dreams — is somehow connected to Sarah's disappearance?"

China leaned forward. "And you think you know where it is?"

"Yes and yes," Ruby said. She was still holding China's hand. "Actually, if it's the place I'm thinking of, it's in Leslie Newell's backyard. It was her mother's art studio. That's where we're going tonight."

"But the white house in your dream," Jessica reminded her, "isn't necessarily a *real* house. In fact, it probably isn't. From what

347

I've read, dreams are almost always symbolic. Houses can represent all sorts of things. For instance, parts of ourselves that we haven't yet explored or lived into."

"You said that this one is an art studio?" China asked. "Maybe it's a suggestion that you should explore some new creative venture."

"Like Ramona's idea for the Psychic Sisters?" Ruby asked with a rueful chuckle.

China smiled. "And that terrifying hole represents your fear of falling into a Psychic Sisters pit."

Ruby rolled her eyes.

"Or maybe it's something much simpler," Jessica said. "Maybe Sarah just wants you to know that she's happy and secure where she lives now, in a comfortable, inviting home somewhere — somewhere other than Pecan Springs. She's sending you an image of it, so you won't worry about her."

"I would like to believe that." Ruby squeezed China's hand and let it go. "But sometimes a dream can be literal, you know. A blue door can simply be a blue door. And a hole can be a . . . well, a real hole. In the floor, I mean." She sounded hesitant, and Jessica wondered if there was something Ruby wasn't telling them.

"So that's where we're going, huh?" China

pushed back her chair. "To look at a little house with a blue door and a hole in the floor. And you know where it is."

"I *might* know," Ruby corrected her quietly. "I only saw it once, a long time ago."

"How long ago?" Jessica asked.

"Twelve years? Fifteen?" It was more a question than a statement, and Ruby swallowed. "This was long after Sarah disappeared. I happened to go to a community art show at the house next door to Mrs. Newell's. The little house — it wasn't much bigger than a playhouse — used to be her backyard art studio. Some of her paintings were displayed there, and we were invited to go next door and take a look. The studio was painted white, with a red roof and purple shutters. Like the little house in my dreams."

"And a blue door?" Jessica asked, picturing it.

"Yes," Ruby replied. "A blue door. I don't remember seeing a sign with van Gogh's quote on it, but the door was definitely blue." She took a breath. "I understand that the studio is still there. But it won't be, in just a few days. If we want to take a look, we need to do it soon." Another breath. "Like now. Tonight."

"Why?" China asked, interested. "What's

going to happen to it?"

"Leslie Newell came into the shop yesterday. Her mother died recently, and she's here from out of town, getting the property ready to sell. She happened to mention that the studio is in pretty bad shape, and the realtor suggested that she hire somebody to tear the thing down." She bit her lip. "I don't know much else about it, really. I only know that Sarah — the Sarah I met in my dreams — is telling me that she wants me to see it before it's gone. I don't know why. And I . . . I'm afraid to go there alone." She looked from one of them to the other, and Jessica could see the apprehension on her face. "That's why I asked you to come."

"You didn't think of asking your cop buddy Ethan to check it out?" China asked mildly. "If you think the place might be connected to your friend's disappearance, the police may want to have a look."

"I'll call Ethan if we find anything that might . . . interest him," Ruby said. "But Sarah's disappearance is a very old cold case. I just thought it would be better if we — well, if we checked it out first."

Jessica nodded, understanding that Ruby didn't want to be embarrassed if she dragged Ethan Connors out on a rainy night to take a look and there was nothing to see.

And anyway, what *could* there be? At the best, an old backyard studio, slated for demolition.

"If *we* checked it out first," China repeated significantly. "As in all three of us."

"Yes." Ruby laughed nervously. "I'm not sure whether I'm more afraid of finding something — or finding nothing at all. But either way, there's safety in numbers. I hope you don't mind too much." She turned to Jessica. "And there might be a story here, really, Jess."

"I agree," Jessica said staunchly. "Thanks for letting me in on it."

China stood and went to the window, her hands in her pockets. "Looks like it's stopped raining," she said in a practical tone. "And there's only one way to find out whether this is the real deal or a wild goose chase."

She turned back to them with a grin. "Come on, girls. It's time to pull up our Nancy Drew panties and get a move on."

CHAPTER TWELVE

When they stepped outdoors, Ruby realized that China was wrong. The rain hadn't entirely stopped. But it was very light, almost a mist, and it haloed eerily around the beams of their flashlights as they went through her back gate and into the muddy alley. The March air wasn't terribly chilly and Ruby was wearing a sweater and a windbreaker under her dark blue raincoat. But she shivered, wishing she had dressed more warmly. Or was it apprehension that made her shudder, not the cold?

Ruby closed the gate behind them and turned to the right. "This way," she said, and they set off.

The alley sliced through the middle of the block, between the neatly fenced backyards of two rows of houses. A narrow two-track with grass on either side and a strip of turf down the middle, the alley was primarily used as a service road. It was just wide enough for the truck that picked up the trash once a week, so they walked single file, each holding her flashlight. Ruby took the lead, since she knew where they were going. Jessica was close behind her, and China brought up the rear, a few paces back.

The sky overhead was pitch black, the backyards were dark and deserted, and there wasn't much chance that they would be seen. But they held their flashlights close to their bodies, keeping the beams trained on the ground just ahead.

If they looked furtive, Ruby thought, it's because they were — not because they were doing something terribly wrong but because she didn't want anybody to challenge them and ask where they were going and why. She kept remembering the words from Van Gogh: *I dream my painting and I paint my dream.* That's what she was doing, wasn't it? "Painting" — that is, acting out — her dream, as if it were a field exercise, an assignment from the Universe. Coursework designed, as Dr. Scott said, to help her tap into energies that couldn't be simulated in the lab but that would help her develop her psychic abilities.

But in what ways? How far? By what means?

And what would happen if she failed the test?

Ruby had no answers, and truth be told, the more she thought about this, the more terrified she became. Which was why she had recruited China and Jessica. She didn't consider herself an especially brave person, and she had the terrible feeling that — whatever the lesson the Universe had planned for her — she could flunk.

What's more, there was something *else* going on here. What, she didn't know, but she had the feeling that what they were doing tonight might be both the end of something old and the beginning of something new. She had been afraid before they set out, and the farther they walked, the more anxious and uneasy she felt. Finally, the apprehension translated itself into several physical sensations. The skin along her shoulders began to tingle, her breath felt tight in her throat, and her palms were clammy.

The last hundred yards was even darker, for there were houses on only one side of the alley now. On the other, a silent, shadowy woods sloped away from the alley and down toward a small creek. An owl hooted eerily in the darkness, a small dog yapped in one of the yards as they passed, and somewhere a baby cried. They could hear the occasional sound of a television — canned audience laughter and jumbled fragments of music. But otherwise, the silence was broken only by the splash of their boots in a puddle and the ragged wisps of their breathing.

"We're here," Ruby said finally, and stopped, as the tingle across her shoulders became a distinct and unnerving buzz. "This is the Newell place — the house that belonged to Leslie Newell's mother."

"Where Sarah was supposed to be going the night she disappeared?" Jessica asked.

"Yes," Ruby said. They were standing beside a five-foot chain-link fence that ran along the alley. There was a gate, but when Ruby tried to pull it open, she saw that it was locked with a padlock.

"Rats," she muttered. "I guess we'll have to climb the fence."

Jessica leaned over the fence and shone her light into the yard. "If there's a little house there, I'm not seeing it. Do you know if there's a dog?"

"I don't think so," Ruby said. The tingling had crawled from her shoulders down her arms to her fingers, and her tongue felt numb. Was she slurring her words? "Mrs. Newell died a couple of months ago, and

Leslie is just visiting. She might be staying here, or somewhere else."

"Dog or not, if we go over that fence, we're trespassing," China said in a low voice. "Class B misdemeanor with a fine of up to two thousand dollars and 180 days jail time." At Ruby's glance, she shrugged. "Just sayin'."

"Well, at least we brought our own lawyer along," Jessica said with a nervous giggle.

"Who won't be much help if she's arrested too," China replied. "Or shot. You've heard of the castle doctrine, I suppose."

"I have," Jessica replied. "Somebody who thinks an intruder is about to invade his house can use deadly force to defend it. But we're not invading anybody's house."

"Somebody might think we intend to invade his house *next*," China said. "He might be reaching for his shotgun at this very moment."

"Will you two stop being silly and boost me over," Ruby said. Her voice was light and thready, and she sounded braver than she felt. This was *not* fun.

"Just thought I'd bring it up," China said. "Being silly about being arrested for trespassing is not being silly."

Ruby shivered. The temperature was dropping. They hadn't been here five minutes and she already felt chill and drained. "Well, if you don't want to trespass," she said, "you can just stand here and wait for me."

"Wait for you to do what?" Jessica wanted to know.

"Trespass," Ruby said. "Maybe even break and enter. I'd like to get into the studio and have a look around."

Or maybe not. It felt as if she had already failed this wretched field exercise, and there was no point in bothering with more. They should just go back home, where it was warm and safe.

"Here, sweetie," Jessica said, holding out her hand like a stirrup. "Step in this and I'll help you get over the fence."

China put her hands on Ruby's hips to give her a boost. "Don't rip your jeans," she cautioned. "Once you're over, we'll be next. Won't we, Jess?"

"Oh, you bet," Jessica said drily. "Can't think of anything else I'd rather be doing."

"See?" China asked, as Ruby cleared the fence. "We've got your back, Nancy."

Several moments later, all three of them were over the fence and huddling in the Newell back yard. The two-story house loomed like a bulky black shadow about thirty yards away, but there were no lights in any of the windows. Ruby had the ominous feeling that something was about to happen, something totally unexpected, like lightning on a clear day. Or a gunshot in the dark. Something bad. Very bad.

She looked around. A cluster of trees and a green-painted garden bench stood to their right, along with a small yellow Bobcat tractor with a bucket loader on the front, like a hulking, prehistoric one-clawed creature. It was parked beside a scattering of lumber, red shingles, and white-painted siding boards that gleamed under the moving beams of their flashlights.

Ruby gasped. "The studio is gone!" she exclaimed. "It used to stand right there." She pointed with her flashlight. "But Leslie said it wouldn't be torn down until next week!" Her heart sinking, she stared at the pile of lumber.

"Looks like somebody didn't get the memo," China muttered. She flashed her light across the pile of wet boards. "That Bobcat probably made quick work of the demolition. It couldn't have taken more than a couple of swings of that bucket to knock the studio down." She flicked her flashlight toward a dark square shape a few yards away, and a shovel. "That looks like a pallet of sod over there. Once the grass is growing, it'll be hard to tell there was anything here."

"We'd better be careful with these flash-lights," Jessica cautioned. "Ruby, didn't you say that Mrs. Newell's daughter is in town? If she's staying here, she might be out for the evening. But still, I don't think we want to explain what we're doing in her mother's backyard."

"What *are* we doing here, Ruby?" China asked.

Ruby couldn't answer. She had no clue.

"Oh, look, Ruby," Jessica said, pointing. "There's the sign you told us about. The one you saw in your dream." She bent over to pick it up and held it out, sounding surprised. "Hey! It's actually real. Awesome."

She was holding a hand-painted wooden sign, decorated with flowers and the words, *I dream my painting and I paint my dream — Vincent van Gogh.*

Ruby blinked. She didn't remember seeing the sign when she'd visited the little studio during the neighborhood art show. But that had been quite a few years ago. Had she seen this sign then, but forgotten it? Had Sarah fetched the memory back to her via a dream? But why? What was the connection? What did it *mean*?

The feeling of disorientation heightened,

and the ground under her feet seemed to shift slightly. As if to steady herself, she reached for the sign Jessica was holding. She was suddenly unsure.

What was real and what was a dream? Was she really *here* right now, with China and Jessica? Or was she at home in her bed, dreaming that she was here?

But the sign felt very real as she took it from Jessica and ran her fingers across its rough, splintery surface. "I wonder if Leslie wants this," she said, half to herself. "If she doesn't, I'd like to keep it, if only as a reminder that dreams can help you remember something you've forgotten."

None of this had anything to do with Sarah, did it? And anyway, they were too late. Now that the studio had been knocked down, there was nothing for them to see, nothing they could do. They might as well go home. In the distance, she heard a low growl of thunder, as if the Universe was endorsing that idea. And anyway, that buzzing she'd felt outside the fence — it was getting worse now, much worse. Not just her shoulders were tingling, but her arms as well, and her fingers. She looked down at her hands, realizing that she could barely feel her fingers.

Jessica bent over and moved a couple of

boards. "Look, guys!" she exclaimed. "Here's the door Ruby remembered." She shifted several shingles so they could see what was underneath. "The *blue* door. The one she couldn't open — and then did. We've come to the right place."

Ruby stared. Yes, that's what it was. A blue door. A *real* blue door, just as real as the sign she was holding.

"Looks like your dream got the details right," China pointed out. "The white siding, the red shingles, the blue door, even the painted sign. I wonder where the purple shutters are."

"There's one, over there," Jessica said, her flashlight glancing off it. "And that's where the building stood before it was knocked down. See that patch of dirt?"

Ruby looked toward the spot — a twelve-by-fifteen foot rectangle of bare earth — illuminated by Jessica's flashlight. Nearby, she could see part of what appeared to be part of the floor, a rectangle of plywood upended and leaning against a tree. It looked like the Bobcat operator had just shoved his bucket under one edge of the plywood floor and lifted it, exposing the earth beneath.

China was right, she thought. It would be easy to lay some of that sod over the patch.

Give it plenty of water and it would start growing right away. Nobody would ever know that Mrs. Newell's studio had stood there. Nobody would ever know . . .

But she could scarcely hold her thoughts together. The buzzing had turned into an arrhythmic whisper, a white noise that rippled and swelled, then faded and swelled again.

As if from a distance, she heard China say, "Your dream got one thing wrong, Ruby. There's no hole." She shifted her flashlight toward the end of the rectangle nearest them. "That's where the front door was. You can even see the threshold — it's still there, a board across what was the opening. And beyond that, nothing but hard, flat dirt. You see, Ruby?"

"No . . . hole," Ruby said numbly. Her lips felt almost frozen, the words like cold molasses on her icy tongue. "It's just the dirt. Just the . . ." In her ears, her voice sounded flat and unnatural. "But there's something else. I can hear . . ."

Hear what? What was it? She strained, listening into the dark as the whispering rose all around. Braided into the whispers, in and around and under them, she could almost catch the fleeting, shadowy echoes of words. She listened harder, trying to make them out. What were they? Who was speaking?

find me please find find

A light, thin sound, like a flute, a silvery thread.

"Ruby?" Jessica put an arm around her waist. "Hey, babe, you okay? What's going on?"

"Hush," Ruby whispered, straining to hear. "I'm listening."

i'm here i want to be found i want

Jessica and China exchanged glances. "Listening to what?" China asked. "I don't hear a —"

"Be quiet!" Ruby commanded. China fell silent, staring at her.

to be found i want please just find me find

Ruby took a steadying breath and stepped toward the bare rectangle where the little studio had once stood. Overhead, a flare of lightning flashed, illuminating the scene as if with a strobe.

She raised her arm, pointing toward the back corner of the rectangle, some fifteen feet away. "Over there," she heard herself say. "Wrapped in plastic, just under the surface. You won't have to dig far."

Ruby pulled herself free of Jessica's arm and took a step forward, through the absent blue door and over the threshold, into what had once been Mrs. Newell's pretty little studio.

And then, without a sound, the ground opened up in front of her, an opening so vast and deep and dark and empty that it seemed to have no bottom.

She looked down to see nothing beneath her feet, nothing at all. She took one final step into the emptiness, falling, falling, falling into the center of the earth.

CHAPTER THIRTEEN

Some moments later, Ruby found herself sitting on the garden bench. Her head was on China's shoulder, and China's arms were around her, cradling her. Jessica was standing in front of them, on the phone. Ruby heard Ethan's voice and, with a jerk, realized that he was on the speaker phone with Jessica.

"You're with Ruby?" he was asking. His voice sounded tinny and distant in the darkness. And concerned.

"Yes, and China is here, too," she said. "You'd better come. We've found a dead body."

"A *body*?" Connors asked, startled. "You're freaking kidding me."

"No, not." Jessica looked at China. "What's the address here?"

"I don't know," China said. "Tell him it's the last house on the left in the last block of . . ." She paused. "Damn," she muttered.

"What *is* this street?"

"Mesquite," Ruby said, slurring the word. She raised her voice and tried to speak more clearly. "Tell him it's the last house on West Mesquite, past Llano. I don't remember the number."

"Ruby's back with us," Jessica said into the phone, looking down at her with a worried expression. "But we still need EMS. Last house on West Mesquite, one block past Llano. We don't know the number."

"No EMS." Ruby managed to sit up straighter. "Really, I don't need EMS." She took a deep breath. "You've found a *body*?"

"Yep." China said. "More like a skeleton, actually. A collection of bones wrapped in black plastic. It's obviously been here a long time."

"And since Sarah sent you here in a dream," Jessica added, "we're guessing it's Sarah." She shook her head. "Jeez, Ruby, you promised me a scoop. But I had no idea that *this* was what you had in mind!"

"Hey!" Ethan yelled out of the phone. "Is that you, Ruby?" Jessica held the phone so they could all hear. "Are you okay? What the hell is going on? What's this about a dream? What —"

"I will be okay," Ruby said. "In a minute." The buzzing had stopped. She felt warmer.

Her lips seemed normal, almost, and her arms and fingers had stopped tingling. The whispers had disappeared, and with them, the voice. All it had wanted, she knew now, was to be heard. Once heard, once found, there was nothing more to say.

She looked at Jessica. "Where did you find her?"

"Over there," Jessica replied, with a wave of her hand. "Where the studio used to be. Very shallowly buried."

"Are you listening to me?" Ethan demanded. "If it's a human body, it's a crime scene. Don't touch anything."

"We won't," China said to the phone. "Scout's honor."

"We think it's a girl named Sarah," Jessica said. "A friend of Ruby's. Who disappeared when they were in high school."

Of course it was Sarah, Ruby thought. Who else would it be? It was Sarah who had brought them here. It was Sarah who wanted to be found. She got up from the bench. She wobbled, but she was upright.

China put an arm around Ruby's waist. "There's not much to see at this point, but if you're feeling up to it, dear, we can show it to you."

"I said DON'T TOUCH ANYTHING!" Ethan bawled. "I'm on my way." He cut off the call.

With a chuckle, Jessica pocketed her phone. "I guess we're not supposed to touch anything."

"I want to see," Ruby said. Still feeling wobbly, she was glad for China's arm. "Show me."

A moment later, the three of them, arms linked, were standing beside the back corner of the dirt rectangle. Ruby saw the shovel lying on the ground beside the faint outline of a sunken grave. Enough dirt had been removed to see shreds of black plastic wrapped around . . .

Ruby shut her eyes. "It's Sarah," she said.

She was swept with a wave of black, fierce anger. Someone had robbed Sarah of the full, rich life ahead of her — things she would have done, places she would have gone, people she would have loved. Her killer had stolen her future and left nothing of her past, except in photos and in the memories of a few living people. Her killer had left her here in an unmarked grave, where no one could find her, until Sarah herself —

"How can you be sure?" Jessica asked.

Ruby opened her eyes again. "I just know," she said. She knelt, pressing her hand flat against the earth over Sarah's grave, wishing that Sarah's parents could know, too. But hard on that thought came another. Perhaps they did know. Perhaps in some distant space and time, the three of them were together.

She took a deep breath, and her hand felt warm on the cold earth. She could *feel* her friend, even though she was no longer warm and whole and full of life. But there was no anger in Sarah, no burning desire for revenge or even hope for justice. There was only a kind of peace. Sarah had been found at last, and she could rest. After all these lonely years here by herself, she had been *found.*

"Let's assume you're right." China put her hand on Ruby's shoulder. "Can you tell us anything about who might have put her here? Or how it happened?"

Silently, Ruby pressed the palm of her hand to the ground, listening, feeling Sarah in her own heart, in her bones. After a moment she clambered back to her feet, buoyed by a new confidence.

"I can't tell you," she said. "I can't make out enough of the story to be sure I have it right. But Sarah knows. She'll tell us."

"*She'll* tell us?" Jessica asked doubtfully. She didn't say *But Sarah is dead and dead girls can't talk.*

But Ruby heard it anyway and nodded, confident in what Sarah would share. "She'll tell us," she said, "but not tonight." She smiled a little wryly. "You'll get your story, Jessica. Just be a little patient."

In the distance, Ruby heard the keening wail of a police siren. "Ethan is coming," she said, and sighed. She would be glad to put all of this — Sarah's body, Sarah's story — into his capable hands. But for better or worse, Ethan and the police would take possession of Sarah. She would belong to him, to them. To the police and to the justice system and, through Jessica and the *Enterprise,* to the world. Sarah would no longer be hers.

"Goodbye," she whispered. "Sarah, goodbye."

Tears blinding her, she turned back toward the bench.

Ethan Connors was an experienced professional, Jessica thought, watching him take charge. Within thirty minutes, he had brought in a team of a half-dozen officers, established the perimeter of the crime scene, ordered preliminary photographs, and set up an array of bright lights trained on the rectangle of bare earth where Mrs. Newell's studio had stood.

The rain had stopped, but the air was still cool and damp, and there were halos of mist around the lights. Jessica, Ruby, and China sat on the garden bench beside the yellow Bobcat, staying out of the way until the detective had a few moments to talk to them. Jessica had pulled her notebook from her waist pack and begun taking notes on the scene. The discovery of Sarah Gellner — if that's who it was — would be a big story in the newspaper's next edition, and Hark would expect her to cover it. She thought of calling him, but decided to wait until after she'd talked to Connors. She might get a quote or two for the story.

But in the meantime, she had several questions for Ruby, who told her that the Newells — Leslie and her mother (her parents were divorced) — had lived here when they were in high school. Sarah had lived about six blocks away, on Cottage Hill Drive. Ruby herself, as a teenager, had lived with her mother and Ramona a couple of blocks the other side of Sarah's house. Ruby and Leslie hadn't been close friends, and Ruby couldn't remember ever being in the Newell house during her high school years.

She couldn't tell Jessica when Mrs. Newell built the artist's studio, either. "The first time I saw it — the only time, really — was during that neighborhood art show," she said.

Jessica scribbled a note to herself — *When was the studio built?* — and looked up. "As I remember, Sarah told both you and her mom that Leslie had telephoned and asked her to come to her house. You couldn't go, so she went alone. Do I have that right?"

Ruby nodded miserably. "It was my fault. If I'd only been able to go —" At a look from China, she broke off. "Yes. That's right. But Leslie said Sarah never got here."

"I read in one of the newspaper accounts that Leslie insisted she *didn't* telephone Sarah," Jessica said. "Did anybody ask Mrs. Newell whether she saw Sarah that night?"

"Yes," Ruby said. "Her sister was ill, and she stayed all night with her." She gestured toward the house. "So she wasn't here."

Jessica looked up to see Detective Connors coming toward them. He was wearing jeans and a blue Pecan Springs police jacket. Under the lights the mist glinted in his dark hair.

He nodded curtly to each of them. "Okay," he growled. "I need to know what you three were doing here at this hour. And don't give me any of that 'We were just out for a walk' crap. Normal people don't go out for a walk on a night like this. Not that you are normal people," he added darkly.

Jessica glanced at Ruby, wondering how much she was going to tell the detective about why they had come. He and Ruby had been involved in several situations where, Ruby said, he'd had to suspend his distrust of what he had always thought of as "woo-woo." Like most cops, he preferred to deal with facts, whenever he could get them.

But Ruby had been seeing him since the previous fall, and Jessica knew from a few things she had said that they were romantically involved. So maybe he was beginning to accept Ruby's gift. Or at least acknowledge it.

"Here's what happened, Ethan." Ruby lifted her gaze and met his eyes. Her voice was thin but steady. "I had a couple of dreams about my friend Sarah Gellner, the girl I told you about — the one who disappeared when we were juniors in high school."

"The girl who ran away?" Connors asked.

Ruby hesitated. "The girl the cops *thought* had run away," she said finally. "I dreamed that Sarah was painting a picture of a little house with a red roof and a blue door. In another dream, she showed me a photo of the same little house on her digital camera. I had already seen Mrs. Newell's studio over there." She waved a hand. "I thought it looked like the building Sarah showed me in my dreams. When I heard that it was supposed to be torn down, I . . . well, I wanted to have a look."

"At night?" Connors asked, frowning. "In the rain?"

"I didn't want to attract attention. And I didn't want to come by myself, so I asked Jessica and China to come with me. When we got here, we saw that the studio had already been demolished." Ruby nodded toward the pile of boards and shingles. "And I sort of had the feeling . . . that is, I —" She faltered.

Jessica took up the narration. "It looked like something had been buried," she said helpfully, "Or maybe like somebody was getting ready to lay some of that sod over there."

"There was even a shovel against a tree," China chimed in. "We got curious and decided to take a closer look, but when we saw what it was, we stopped." She gave the detective a disarming smile. "We knew you wouldn't want us to disturb anything."

"Damn straight," Connors said gruffly. He turned and beckoned to a female officer with a notebook. "Officer Grady will take your statements." He gave them a stern look. "One at a time, separately. Then you can go home."

"Got it," Jessica said. Beside her, she could feel Ruby shivering. "But do you think maybe the officer could take us back to Ruby's house and get the statements there? It's pretty chilly out here. And damp."

"We can do that." Connors offered a hand to Ruby, helping her off the bench. "You okay?" he asked, in a lower voice.

"I'm fine," Ruby said. She glanced toward the place where the body was buried. "When you find out for sure that it's Sarah, will you let me know? I —"

Whatever else she was about to say was drowned out by a woman's angry cries.

"What the hell is all this? What's going on back here?" A heavyset woman in dark slacks and a pumpkin-orange sweatshirt was storming across the backyard. "Who *are* you people? What are you doing here? I am calling the *police.*"

A uniformed officer stepped in front of her and said something. The shrieks grew louder. "What do you *mean,* a BODY? What are you doing? Stop that — I won't let you! You can't be digging! You have no right! You have to leave, this very minute!"

"That's Leslie Newell," Ruby said to Connors. "This is — was — her mother's house. Mrs. Newell died a couple of months ago, and Leslie is here for a few days, selling the place. We went to high school together," she added. "I know her slightly. She can be a little . . . excitable."

"Maybe I can calm her down," Connors said drily, and went to meet the woman.

Thirty minutes later, Jessica was pulling her Kia out of Ruby's driveway. Officer Grady had taken all three of their statements and left to rejoin her boss. Now, China was on her way home and Ruby was heading for a hot bath.

But Jessica's evening had just begun. She was, after all, a reporter, and the discovery of the body was going to be an important story. She didn't need a phone call from Hark to tell her that she had to go back to the Newell house and see what was going on with the investigation.

But she got one anyway, before she reached the stop sign at the end of the block. "I just picked up some news on the police scanner," Hark said. "Seems that the cops are digging up a dead body buried in somebody's backyard. I know it's late and the weather is crappy, but there's a story here. I want you to drive over to 2535 Mesquite and see what's going on."

"Been there already and am about to go back," Jessica replied. Somewhat disingenuously, she added, "Actually, I happened to be on scene when the body was discovered, so this story is going to have something of a personal angle."

"On scene?" If Hark was surprised, he didn't show it. "Good," he said. "Then you'd better get back over there before the TV guys get wind of this. With any luck, it'll be a few hours before they pick it up." His chuckle took on a sour edge. "Guess this'll give you something new to blog about. The personal angle, inside the story. That'll please Dixon, I'm sure." He rang off before Jessica could reply.

Jessica frowned. Obviously, the partnership between Hark and Jeff Dixon was in for some seriously stormy weather. She could only hope that the *Enterprise* would survive it. And now that she thought about it, she wasn't quite sure how to write about discovering the body. She'd have to do it without revealing how she and Ruby and China happened to be there, because she couldn't write about Ruby's dreams. They were private — and a bridge too far for most readers.

At the Newell house, Jessica parked along the curb. The street was still full of emergency vehicles, plus a TV truck from KVUE in Austin and another from KSAT in San Antonio. So it was already too late, Jessica thought, frowning. The story would be on their morning newscasts tomorrow. The next edition of the *Enterprise* was two whole days away. Another argument for Dixon's online edition.

Before she got out of the car, she hung her press badge around her neck and pulled her notebook and pen out of her waist pack. The badge would get her past the officer — Sam Gilbert, a young patrolman she had met on a previous case — who was stationed at the gate in the corner of the yard.

Except that it didn't.

"Sorry, Jessica," Gilbert said. "Detective Connors says no press through this gate." He nodded toward the TV trucks. "They're leaving. They got a little pissed off when I told them they couldn't fly their photo drone overhead." As he spoke, both trucks began to drive away.

"But I was one of the people who found the body," Jessica protested.

"Sorry. Detective Connors says he's keeping a lid on the story. No access." He gave her an apologetic smile. "Not even you."

Over Gilbert's shoulder, Jessica could see that a walled tent had been erected over the site of the grave to protect it from the weather, and that a second, larger bank of lights had been added to the first array. The Newell backyard was ablaze with light. The neighbors in the adjoining house were pressed up against the fence, peering out from under their umbrellas at the unusual goings-on.

"That's no way to win friends and influence people," Jessica said lightly, and they both laughed. She added, "Do you know if they've dug up the body yet? On background," she said quickly. "Not for attribution."

The officer shook his head. "They've protected the burial site, but they're waiting for Judge Davidson before they start any serious excavation." He leaned forward and lowered his voice. "For what it's worth, I'm hearing that it's an old skeleton. Twenty years, maybe more." Quickly, he added, "Don't quote me."

Jessica nodded. Adams County didn't have a coroner or a medical examiner, and a justice of the peace was required to be involved with all unattended deaths. This might be a twenty-year-old skeleton, but it still demanded a JP's urgent attention.

"So no ID yet," she said.

"Nope. I heard that Connors is bringing

in somebody from the university," Gilbert said. "The bone lady. Supposed to be some kinda expert on skeletons."

"Oh, Dr. Kenyon," Jessica said. "Rebecca Kenyon." She had interviewed the professor for a story on CTSU's body farm — the thirty-acre outdoor human decomposition research laboratory that Dr. Kenyon managed. In terms of physical size it was the largest in the world.

Gilbert grinned. "Yeah, her. From the body farm. After they get the skeleton out, I hear it's going to Travis. There's no hurry."

Jessica nodded. No surprise there. "Travis" would be the Travis County Medical Examiner's Office on Sabine Street in Austin. The TCME served forty-two counties in Central Texas. Its five full-time examiners were competent and expert, but out-of-county bodies weren't high priority, which usually meant that the autopsy report you wanted yesterday wouldn't be available until next week. Or next month.

But whatever else this was, it was a cold case, and these were old bones. There was no statute of limitations on murder and nobody was in a rush, which meant that this story would be slow in developing. Hark might not like it, but it was a break for Jessica. It would give her time to figure out how to deal with the discovery — and her part in it.

"Thanks, Sam," Jessica said. "See you later."

But Jessica wasn't the kind of reporter who took no for an answer. So, since she wasn't allowed to go through the side gate, she would give the front door a try. Leslie Newell had been here earlier — maybe she was still here.

Jessica went up the steps of the front porch and knocked, then knocked again. She was about to knock a third time when the door was jerked open by the woman in dark slacks and orange sweatshirt. Her eyes and nose were red and she was clutching a tissue in her fist. Her glance went to Jessica's press badge.

"I'm not talking to you," she snapped, and tried to close the door.

But Jessica's foot was already blocking the door. She put on a bright smile. "There will be a story in the next edition of the *Enterprise* about the discovery of the body in your backyard, Ms. Newell. My editor and I understand that you're planning to sell this house, and potential buyers might be put off by what was found tonight. Wouldn't you like to be sure that our readers get the message *you* want them to get?"

"Well . . ." Leslie considered that, hesitating, her mouth working. Finally, she opened the door and stepped back. "Yeah, I guess so," she growled, "since you're doing a story anyway. She waved an arm. "Ignore the mess. I'm organizing Mom's stuff for a yard sale this weekend."

Jessica saw that the hallway was stacked with cardboard boxes, framed pictures, books, piles of folded curtains, and several crates full of kitchen items. She doubted that Ethan Connors would release the crime scene in time for a weekend yard sale, but she didn't say that out loud. Leslie must have already sold some of the furniture, because the living room was nearly empty. It was lit by a single lamp on a small table. Leslie unfolded a pair of metal chairs, took one and pointed Jessica to the other.

"I was sorry to hear that your mother died recently." Jessica sat down, opened her notebook, and began with an easy, nonthreatening question that might lessen Leslie's tension. The woman was wound tight as a spring — understandably, with that body in the backyard. "Someone said that she lived here alone for many years. Is that correct?"

Leslie relaxed a little. "Yes, that's right. Dad died when I was in kindergarten. I lived here with Mom when I was going to middle school and high school, then moved to Fort Worth for college, and after that to Dallas, where I work. I'm here for a week or so, getting the house ready to sell." Her hands were twisting in her lap and there was a nervous tic at the corner of her mouth. "This . . . this thing that's happening in the backyard — it's a nuisance."

You don't know the half of it, Jessica thought. And then: *But maybe you do.*

Aloud, she said, "It must have been quite a shock when the police showed up tonight."

"Oh, it *was,*" Leslie said urgently, leaning forward. "I mean, I just can't *tell* you! I went out to dinner and came back to find the backyard full of police. The detective said they'd dug up a body." She swallowed. "Who was it? Some kind of homeless person or something?"

"I don't think so," Jessica said. "One of the cops said it was buried under a little shed in the backyard. A playhouse, maybe? I saw the Bobcat back there. You had the shed knocked down?"

"It was my mom's art studio." Leslie looked as if she were bracing herself for a root canal. "It's been there since I was in high school, but it was sort of falling down and the realtor who's listing the house said it was an eyesore. So I hired this guy to

383

come in and knock it down next week. Next week — *not* today! He did it while I was gone this afternoon." Her voice was beginning to tremble. "I even bought a pallet of sod, so I could get some grass started where the building stood."

"Well, then, it's a good thing the body was discovered tonight," Jessica said in a practical tone. "You might not have noticed it when you laid the sod. It might have been there forever." Which was exactly what would have happened, if it hadn't been for Ruby's dreams — and her decision to act on them tonight. "Do you have any idea who might be buried there?"

"Me? Not a *clue.*" Leslie wrinkled her forehead as if she were trying to think of possibilities. "But maybe — you know, Mom had a German shepherd that died a few years ago. I never heard what she did with the body. I wonder if that's what they've found. Somebody said it was mostly bones, so it might not be a person at all." Her voice roughening, she clenched her hands. "Who found it, that's what I want to know. And how? That backyard is private property. Somebody was trespassing." Hysteria was edging into her voice and she tried to quell it. "Did they climb the fence to get in? The police ought to be looking for *them,* instead of digging up a damned dog."

"The cops don't think it's a dog," Jessica said, quietly making notes. Without looking up, she added, "I wonder — do you happen to remember when your mom build that studio?"

"When?" More forehead wrinkling. "I don't think I . . ."

"No problem," Jessica said. "We can check with the Pecan Springs building permit office. I'm sure your mom would have had to get a permit for it. I just thought she might have built it while you were living here."

"Probably." Trying to appear cooperative, Leslie gave it some more thought. "Sometime in my junior year," she hazarded. "I seem to remember a lot of construction in the backyard that spring."

"That's interesting." Jessica looked up from her notebook. "Just the other day, I was reviewing a file of newspaper stories about a disappearance that took place around that time, in this neighborhood. A girl named Sarah, I think. Sarah Gellner. Maybe you went to high school with her?"

"Sarah . . . Gellner?" Leslie blinked. "I don't think I recognize —"

"Wait a minute," Jessica broke in. She widened her eyes. "Oh, my gosh! Now I remember! You're Leslie Newell. You're the girl who called Sarah Gellner the night she disappeared. It's in those newspaper stories I read. You asked her to come over and help with homework or something."

"No!" Leslie cried. "I'm not —" White-faced and frantic, she looked around wildly, as if she were hoping for some kind of escape. "I mean, whoever called her, it wasn't me! Sarah made that up — I guess because she didn't want her mom to know she was going off with some boy. I never saw her that night. In fact, we never did anything together. We weren't even friends."

"Oh, that's right," Jessica said. "Sorry. I read that you spent the evening with your friend Brittany, as I remember. Didn't Brittany live across the street?"

"Yes. We were together, Brit and me." Leslie sucked in her breath, obviously trying to calm herself. "And Sarah ran away, you know. Her parents didn't want to admit it, but she left home and went to the West Coast. That was what everybody said. That's what the police finally decided."

Jessica held her gaze. "So if that's Sarah Gellner's body under your mom's art studio, you don't know who put her there?"

"Of course I don't!" Leslie's voice was shrill. "I don't know a thing. And I don't have time for any more silly questions. You'd better not put any of this in your little rag of a newspaper. If you do, I'll sue." She stood up. "You'll have to leave now. I'm tired. I'm going to bed."

"Of course." Jessica closed her notebook. "I'm sure that tomorrow will be a big day for you. What time are you going to the police station for your interview?"

Leslie replied without thinking. "At ten," she said, and then caught herself angrily. "That's none of your damn business," she cried. "Out!"

"Yes, ma'am." Jessica stood. "Thanks for taking the time to talk to me. Mind if I go out your back door?"

"Whatever," Leslie said disgustedly. "Just *go*."

A few minutes later, Jessica was standing next to Ethan Connors in the backyard. He swiveled to face her.

"How did you get past —" he began furiously, but she held up her hand.

"Don't blame Officer Gilbert. He did his job. I came through the house instead." She gave him a hard, straight look. "There's something you need to know about Leslie Newell and Sarah Gellner."

"Thirty seconds," Connors growled, looking at his watch. "I'm tired and I'm wet and you have thirty friggin' seconds before I have you thrown the hell outta here, Nelson."

"If that turns out to be Sarah Gellner," she said, pointing to the area where the tent had been erected, "you need to ask Leslie Newell how she got there. Leslie knows. She may also know, or suspect, why a girl named Brittany — who was with her the night Sarah died — killed herself."

"Whoa," Connors said, holding up his hand. "What the *hell* are you talking about?"

Jessica repeated what she'd said, adding, "Brittany stepped out in front of a train, I understand."

Connors glared at her. "I want the story. All you got and where you got it. Now. From the top."

Jessica's story and the detective's questions took nearly fifteen minutes. Finally, satisfied, Connors nodded. "Okay. I need what you just told me in writing." He fixed her with a glance. "And I do *not* want to see it in the *Enterprise* — at least, not until I give you a green light. It's eighty percent speculation."

"More like sixty percent," Jessica said with a small smile. "Maybe only fifty. Anyway, this is a developing story, so I'll check with you for late details before we go to press."

She looked at him inquiringly. "I hear that Dr. Kenyon is coming. I interviewed her for an article on the body farm recently. Mind if I stick around?"

"I read your story. It was good." Connors gave her a grudging nod. "Yeah, you can stick around. But stay out of the way. And keep your mouth shut."

That's why, for the next couple of hours, Jessica stood in the misty drizzle on the periphery of the circle of light cast by the powerful lamps, watching Dr. Rebecca Kenyon direct a pair of her graduate students and two police officers in the delicate removal of the body that had lain for so many years in the dry, protected space under the floor of Mrs. Newell's tiny art studio.

And why, when the exhumation team had finished its work, she was on hand when the green fanny pack was removed from among the bones and cautiously opened to reveal Sarah Gellner's wallet, with its ID cards still intact.

And Sarah's small digital camera.

CHAPTER FOURTEEN

The drizzle had finally stopped and the night sky was beginning to clear when Jessica parked her car and went into her warm kitchen. Murphy's orange fur was puffed up with a deeply felt sense of outrage — *It's three a.m. Where have you been?* He refused to have anything to do with her until she opened a fresh can of his favorite fishy kitty food and served a long-delayed evening snack. Then she headed for a hot shower and a shampoo, hoping to flush away some of the dark detritus of the grisly night.

But Jessica had covered enough crime scenes to know that hot water, soap, and shampoo couldn't wash the brutal ugliness away. Sitting down at her computer and writing the story would take the edge off, but she would have to live with it until she had lived through it. And sleep would help, too, she reminded herself, as she climbed into bed with Murphy, who smelled strongly of fish and was now quite willing to forgive her.

She was able to get three hours of it — not nearly enough, but it would have to do.

Up at six-thirty, she gobbled a quick bowl of cereal, gave Murphy a consoling hug and a kiss with his breakfast, and was in the Enterprise newsroom by seven-fifteen. Coralee had already made a fresh pot of coffee and Will had stopped at the Diner and picked up a box of Lila's jelly doughnuts (filled with Docia's peach compote), so Jessica sipped and munched while she went through her notes from the night before, then started typing.

She had given quite a bit of thought to the lede, which reported that the discovery of the body came from information provided by a neighbor, avoiding mention of Ruby and Ruby's dream. With luck, that part of the story wouldn't become public.

A neighborhood tip resulted in the discovery of a body buried in the backyard at 2535 Mesquite in Pecan Springs. The police acted quickly to protect the scene from the weather and to facilitate recovery of the human remains.

The house is the former residence of recently deceased Karen Newell. The remains were discovered under the floor of her backyard art studio. It was not immediately clear how long the body had lain in place or how it had come to be there. With the body, investigators discovered a wallet containing identification and a small digital camera. According to PSPD Detective Ethan Connors, however, a final positive identification of the remains will likely be made from dental records. The authorities are withholding the identity until their investigation is completed.

Reached for comment late last night, Leslie Newell said that her mother's studio was constructed some twenty years ago. It had fallen into disrepair and had been demolished shortly before the body was discovered. Assisting in the recovery and dating of the fragile remains was Dr. Rebecca Kenyon, professor at CTSU and an expert in forensic anthropology. According to Detective Connors, an autopsy is planned for next week.

"While this death took place many years ago, we are confident that we will be able to get to the bottom of it expeditiously," Detective Connors said. This is a developing story.

Jessica reread the story carefully, then

added a note to Hark, saying that she would update it when there was news. She sent it off and went to the break room to refill her coffee cup. She was still groggy from lack of sleep, but a quick review of her calendar had reminded her that she had a busy day ahead. There was a hearing in the courthouse this afternoon and a call to Sheila Dawson to see if she'd be willing to give an interview for Fran's magazine feature on the challenges of being a police chief and the mother of a new baby. Plus, there had been another reported rape on campus, and she wanted to talk to the chief of security, who —

"Hey, there."

Jessica looked up. It was Jeff Dixon, handsome and self-assured in a beige cashmere crewneck sweater and khakis, leaning against the door of the break room.

Jessica stirred creamer into her coffee. "Good morning," she said with a smile.

"Hark filled me in on your adventure last night," he said. "It sounds interesting. Are you going to blog about it?" He grinned disarmingly. "*Crime and Consequences* is a great title for a blog, by the way."

"Thanks," Jessica said. "Yes, I plan to write about it — after the police have ID'd the body and given the all clear. Jumping in early with facts they don't want the public to have is a good way to screw up my relationships with the cop shop."

"I get that," he said, picking up a coffee mug and filling it. "I'll look forward to your post. Oh, and I'm moving into the office next to Hark's in a couple of days. Come in and talk when you have time. I'd like to hear what you think we ought to be doing with this new online edition — how you see yourself fitting in, as a crime reporter. And I want to discuss that podcast."

"I'll do it," she said, and met his eyes. "I'm interested in what you said about community journalism. Local news is important here. We can't let Pecan Springs lose its newspaper. But the online edition by itself isn't the answer. We've got to keep the print edition, too."

"I'm with you on that," Jeff said, and smiled at her. "We need *both.*" His smile faded. "I hope I didn't oversell this project the other day. It's not going to be easy. It'll take all hands on deck. And a few lucky breaks."

Jessica couldn't think of what to say, so she just nodded, took her coffee, and went back to her cubicle, where she called Connie Page, Sheila Dawson's assistant, and set up a phone interview with the chief on the feature that Fran wanted her to do. Then she pulled up the dockets of the two judges who were hearing cases that week, calendared the ones she intended to cover, and made a few calls about a flurry of dognapping cases that had occurred in the upscale neighborhood west of Pecan Springs. There was a story there, not a big one, but an interesting one, and publicity might result in the dogs' return to their homes. And then she started to work on the article about Sheila Dawson.

She was still working on the draft when Fran stuck her head into Jessica's cubicle.

"The Diner for lunch?" she asked. "Will and Virgil want to go, too."

"Is it that time already?" Jessica asked, surprised.

"Time flies when you're having fun," Fran said sagely.

Jessica nodded. "You guys go on ahead, though. I have a couple of paragraphs yet to do, and I'll meet you there. Order a BLT for me, will you?"

"You got it," Fran said, and left.

Jessica was writing the very last sentence when her phone rang. It was Ethan Connors.

"I thought I'd pass along some breaking news," he said. "I'm going to make an announcement later today, but I figured you should get a heads-up, since you played a pretty big part in what went down last night and this morning."

Jessica saved her story, closed the file, and opened a new file. "On the record?"

"On the record, but don't release it until I give you the go-ahead. This isn't public yet, and there will be more to come." He paused. "Remember the camera we found with the body?"

Of course she remembered. Dr. Kenyon had been extremely slow and careful in the removal of the body, reduced now to skeletal remains and fragments of clothing. A green canvas fanny pack — waterproof, luckily — had been buried with the body. Inside it was a wallet, a tube of lipstick, some loose coins, and a digital camera.

"Yes, I remember it," she said — and remembered that Ruby had mentioned it earlier. Sarah was looking forward to a career as a professional photographer. It was Sarah's camera,

"It's a Casio," Connors said. "One of the early digital cameras. I had one myself, years ago, when they first came out. It was quite a change from film, and while the resolution wasn't all that great, it was a nice little camera for its time. Pretty reliable, too.

Still, given that it's been buried for a couple of decades, I didn't have much hope that the images — if there were any — would survive. But the burial site stayed dry, and the camera still worked. We used a cable to download the flash memory to a computer and retrieved a couple of dozen photos." He paused. "Six of them were date- and time-stamped on the night Sarah Gellner disappeared."

Jessica's fingers had been flying across the keyboard. Now she stopped. "Photos of — ?"

"Three girls, teenagers. I emailed copies to Ruby. She ID'd one of the girls as Leslie Newell, another as Brittany Morrow, who lived across the street from the Newell house. And Sarah herself, of course. She's in two of the photos, one with Leslie, the other with Brittany. They were taken in a room we've identified as Leslie's bedroom, upstairs in the Newell house."

Jessica had gone back to her typing. "But Leslie told me — and others, too, at the time — that she and Brittany never saw Sarah that night."

"She tried to tell us that, too," Connors said. "Until she saw the date- and time-stamps on the photos. They were quite a shock. To her, I mean. Especially since the last photo appears to be Sarah's body, partially wrapped in plastic. When she saw that, and when she heard that we found her prints on the camera — well, she went to pieces."

"Omigod," Jessica said, half under her breath. "Did you get a confession?"

"Leslie volunteered a story," Connors said. "How well it holds together remains to be seen. According to her, the murder was Brittany's fault. It was Brittany who came up with the idea and told Leslie what to do. It was Brittany who showed up with the date rape drug that she got from her brother. It was Brittany who gave it to Sarah, in a soft drink. When Sarah passed out, it was Brittany who smothered her with a pillow."

"And Leslie didn't call for help?"

"She panicked and tried to stop her, she says, but Brittany threatened to implicate her. After all, Leslie was the one who invited Sarah to her house. The murder took place in Leslie's bedroom, on Leslie's bed. And they buried Sarah's body under the studio that was being built in Leslie's backyard. She says the carpenter finished the floor the next day and never noticed a thing. The next night, Brittany brought over a bottle of champagne and they celebrated. They thought they'd gotten away with it."

Jessica had known that Leslie must have been involved, but to hear the details was breathtaking.

"Why?" she managed. "Why did they do it?"

"Classic motive, jealousy. Brittany had the hots for Ted Stevens, Sarah's boyfriend. And Leslie was pissed off because Sarah was elected yearbook editor and head cheer-leader — which Leslie wanted for herself. She got both, after Sarah was out of the way. And Brittany got Ted."

Jessica's fingers slowed. "Did Leslie tell you about Brittany's suicide?" she asked.

"Yes," Connors said. "She showed us a text she had saved on her phone. It was from Brittany, saying that she couldn't live with herself because she had killed Sarah."

"Mmm," Jessica said. "I suppose that with Brittany gone, Leslie thought there was no danger that Sarah would ever be found — especially after she finished laying that sod over her grave."

No danger, that is, until Ruby dreamed of a little white house with a blue door. And a hole in the floor.

"You got it," Connors said. "I'm on my way over to the DA's office right now. Leslie is talking to her lawyer. We'll probably hear from him in an hour or two, looking for a deal."

"What kind of a deal?"

"It's a second-degree felony to tamper with or conceal a human corpse," Connors said. "So even if there's no murder charge, Leslie is still vulnerable. A second-degree felony conviction could get her up to twenty years and a ten thousand dollar fine. Given the photographs and the fingerprint evidence, her lawyer will advise her to plead. The camera, after all, doesn't lie."

Jessica chuckled wryly. "But it was all Brittany's fault. And Brittany's dead."

"Yeah, right. It's always somebody else's fault." Connors paused. "I won't pretend to understand that dream thing, but I've already thanked Ruby for orchestrating the discovery of the body. I'm thanking you for connecting the whole thing to Leslie as quick as you did."

Jessica knew that Leslie would have been his prime suspect as soon as he saw those photos, but she accepted his thanks. "You're welcome. You'll let me know when you and the DA come up with the charges?"

"I'll text you as soon as that happens, and you can come over to the DA's office and get a quote from both of us."

"Thanks," Jessica said.

"Don't mention it," Connors replied, and cut the connection.

Jessica had just pocketed her phone when it rang again.

"Where *are* you?" Fran demanded crossly. "We're here and your BLT is getting cold. Log off that computer and get your tail over here, girl. Right now."

"On my way." With a little smile, Jessica closed the file, turned off the computer, and stood, reaching for her jacket, feeling grateful.

The *Enterprise* might not have a very secure future, and the past was still littered with ghosts. But she had a job to do, stories to tell, and a book to write. She had friends.

What else could she want?

■ ■ ■ ■

FIRELINES:
BOOK THREE

■ ■ ■ ■

We all live in a house on fire, no fire department to call; no way out, just the upstairs window to look out of while the fire burns the house down with us trapped, locked in it.
— *Tennessee Williams,*
The Milk Train Doesn't Stop Here Anymore

A NOTE TO READERS

This third book in the *Enterprise* trilogy continues the ongoing story of a newspaper that is battling to serve a community only half-aware of the challenge it faces: what to do if the local newspaper disappears and the town becomes another "news desert."

Firelines also continues the story of Jessica Nelson, whose career as a journalist began in *Mourning Gloria* (China Bayles book 19). In this novella, Jessica begins to piece together the facts about the arson murders of her family and to learn more about the psychological scars she has carried through the years since the tragedy. In *Firelines,* Jessica is faced with the task of resolving the cold-case mystery of her family's deaths and confronting her crippling fear of fire. She is helped in this by an experienced firefighter, an attractive man (an *older* man, which in itself presents a problem for Jessica) who knows a thing or two about wildfires and is willing to teach Jessica.

Somebody asked me recently if there will be more of these linked stories. As a reader, I find something very satisfying in a form where themes and issues are braided into several narratives, appearing and reappearing in different transformations, and where an ensemble of characters act and interact with each other to help (and sometimes hinder) their own growth and understanding. In the *Enterprise* trilogy, I haven't tried to resolve the major issues of the newspaper's storyline. (Is there *any* answer to the conundrum of disappearing newspapers? What's going to happen to the newspaper in your home town?) And there are still plenty of questions to be asked and answered about Pecan Springs, as Jessica and her journalist colleagues dig deeper into what's-happening-now in their community. But the answer to "will there be more of these stories?" depends on you.

If you like them, yes, there'll be more.

After all, you are the reader. It's all because of *you*.

Susan Wittig Albert

PROLOGUE

When Jessica Nelson was a girl, Georgia Shores was a tiny hamlet wedged contentedly between the placid blue waters of Lake Georgia and the dense greenbelt of Lost Pines, the seventy-five-thousand-acre stretch of loblolly woodland that marks the far western edge of the great southern pine forest. Genetically unique and adapted to the drier conditions of this Colorado River region, pines have been permanent dwellers there for over eighteen thousand years.

But some ten thousand years ago, humans arrived and claimed the territory. In the beginning, this was benign. Small bands of nomadic Tonkawa and Karankawa roamed the area until it was claimed as part of Mexico by Spain and settlers began straggling in. To keep an eye on things, Spanish soldiers built a fort where the Old San Antonio Road crossed the Colorado River, and tiny settlements began to grow up along the margins of the forest. Ships brought immigrants from Germany and Eastern Europe and the railroad brought Yankee farmers from the East Coast and the North. And since the pines were the major source of lumber in all of Central Texas, much of the forest was cut for construction in the fast-growing nearby cities: Austin, San Antonio, and even Houston.

The Tonkawa and Karankawa are gone now, the Spanish fort is long forgotten, and the settlements have grown into attractive little towns. Dozens of historic courthouses, picturesque churches, and centuries-old cemeteries are scattered through the remaining loblolly stands, over six thousand acres of which is officially protected by a pair of adjacent state parks. Towns like Georgia Shores, Bastrop, and Giddings promise residents a relaxing life, good schools, and a "small-town experience," while tourists are guaranteed scenic landscapes and a richly diverse cultural history.

To its residents, Georgia Shores must have seemed a perfect small retreat, with everything that promised a quietly happy life. But a few years before this story begins, a tragic wildfire — the most destructive in Texas' recorded history — rampaged through the area. The town itself was spared, but the area around it was devastated. Sparked by power lines downed in a red-flag wind and feeding on drought-starved trees, the Lost Pines fire destroyed nearly seventeen hundred homes and burned thirty-four thousand acres of forest, including all but one hundred acres of the old-growth trees in Bastrop State Park. The massive wildfire killed five people, displaced thousands, and burned for over a month, causing air pollution all over Central Texas and leaving behind a charred and ashen landscape.

Several years later, the blackened wreckage is brightened with the cheerful green shoots of young trees — hackberry, juniper, blackjack oak, mesquite — and if you look closely, you can see signs that the forest understory is rejuvenating. The slower-growing native loblollies are another matter. A massive replanting effort has been underway since the fire, but foresters caution that it will take good rains (never a sure thing in this part of Texas) and a generation or more for Lost Pines to recover from this catastrophic wildfire.

And the people who lost loved ones and friends, lost their homes, their businesses, their jobs? They may recover, but their lives will never be the same.

They will always live with the scarring memory of fire.

CHAPTER ONE

Jessica Nelson had been in college when the disastrous Lost Pines fire swept the area, and she made every effort *not* to go anywhere near it. She had never been back to Georgia Shores, either. She had lost her entire family in a terrible house fire there when she was just a teenager, and for some fifteen years, she hadn't been able to bear the thought of returning.

But here she was, going back for the first time. Unavoidably, her route that June afternoon took her through the burned-over forest, a landscape much altered from the green, pine-scented woodlands she remembered from her childhood. There hadn't been much rain all spring. Summer had arrived early, with temperatures in the nineties and a hot, dry wind that prompted a rash of red-flag warnings from the National Weather Service. A tropical storm — it would be called Debby when it grew to name-size — was pumping itself up out there in the southern Gulf of Mexico, the Bay of Campeche. The forecast track was still uncertain, but winds from the storm were already pushing inland, bringing wind warnings that everybody had learned to take seriously. Increased wind meant increased fire danger.

As she rounded a curve, she noticed a large swath of burned-out timber and a prominent sign posted beside the road:

THIS WAS AN ARSON FIRE. Up to $10,000 reward for information leading to the arrest and grand jury indictment of person(s) responsible. Call Texas Forest Service.

There was an 800 number.

Jessica shuddered. You'd think, after the big Lost Pines fire, anybody with an urge to strike a match would have seen the enormous damage it could cause. And this burn looked recent, too, not a trace of new green life poking up from the ashes.

She was still thinking of this as she passed the Georgia Shores high school and then the little park where she and her twin sister Ginger had spent the summer of their eleventh year learning to play tennis. Her heart twisted as she saw a couple of girls in shorts and T-shirts on the court now, slamming a ball across the net. There was a dog with them, too — a shaggy black dog that reminded her of Rascal. He had loved to play tennis as much as they had. Whenever one of them hit the ball out of bounds, it was his job to fetch it.

The pain was sharp and she turned her gaze away quickly. She had already made up her mind not to drive past the place where her family's house had once stood. She knew that would hurt more than she could bear. Her heart flipped over at the thought, and her breath caught in her throat. For a moment, she wondered whether she had made a mistake coming back here again. What had happened in the past was buried in the past. Maybe it was better to leave it there.

But she was already here, she had an appointment to keep, and despite the reminders of her past, Georgia Shores had definitely changed since her childhood. Driving down Main Street toward the lake, she saw a few familiar buildings — Parker's Drugstore, where she had bought her first lipstick. The bank where she and Ginger had stashed their babysitting money.

And ahead, where the street dead-ended at the lake, was Scott's Landing, the little marina where the locals docked a few boats and the tourists rented canoes and kayaks and went out with fishing guides. The sparkling blue waters of Lake Georgia, glimpsed through the masts of sailboats moored at the docks, brought another sharp twist to her heart. She and Ginger had all but abandoned the tennis court for the lake. They taught themselves to sail the little Sunfish that Dad and Mom had bought them for their twelfth birthday, learning to manage the fleet little boat with the rainbow-hued sail. The days on the water had been glorious, their bikini-clad bodies lean and agile and athletic, their tans a gorgeous golden-toast.

But the past was irretrievable, and she was glad that there were new sights to pull her mind away from what was too painful to remember. There were new sidewalks on both sides of the street. A new Popeyes Louisiana Kitchen occupied the corner of Main and Pecan, and there was a Jack in the Box and a Subway on the opposite corners. A sprawling HEB supermarket had replaced the little mom-and-pop grocery on Pecan, next to the town's Carnegie library, one of the only three or four Texas Carnegies that still served as libraries. Across the street, she could see an AT&T store, a tattoo and piercing parlor, and Sweetie Pie's Ice Cream Shoppe.

Tattoos and piercings made Jessica smile. There had been nothing like that when she lived here. She had been in middle school and her first year of high school then, when getting your ears pierced was hugely adventurous, much less your nose or belly button or (heaven help you) getting a tattoo, like the roses she wore on her left shoulder now, under her red sleeveless blouse. Cell phones hadn't yet been invented (there had been a laundromat where the AT&T store was now located), and Sweetie Pie's was called Dopey's Ice Cream. It was the hangout for all the teens in town.

Another twist of the heart. Both of them had loved Dopey's banana splits. Even more, Ginger had adored the boy behind the counter, the one with the curly blond hair and the cute butt. Sean, his name was, Jessica remembered. His dad owned the marina, and he was always hanging around the dock on those summer days when they took their Sunfish out. The rest of the year, he worked weekends at Dopey's, where he treated them with double helpings of maraschino cherries and whipped cream. So whenever they had a couple of dollars to spend on a Saturday afternoon, they had ridden their bikes to Dopey's for banana splits, their goofy Lab, Rascal, running alongside, ears flopping and pink tongue happily hanging out.

But Ginger was gone, and Jessica's mother and father, and Rascal. All had died in the savage fire that swept their two-story house on Marigold Lane one night when Jessica was in Austin with the school debate team. The fire had been arson, and the volunteer fire department had gotten there too late to save anyone. The police had never found the person that set it. It had left her orphaned — abruptly, appallingly alone in a world forever filled with the awful absence of everyone and everything she had ever loved.

Two weeks after the fire, Jessica had gone to live with her grandmother and attend high school in Louisiana. The challenge of getting used to a new school had kept her focused and for the next year or so, she had coped with her loss fairly well. She saw a school counselor who helped her with her grief. She made a couple of close friends who, while they couldn't replace Ginger, had eased some of the pain.

But as time went on, she began to experience occasional panic attacks when she was around fire. Candle flames and gas burners on the kitchen stove were manageable, but a neighbor's bonfire or flames in somebody's living room fireplace or the sudden blare of the fire alarm at school — even when she knew it was a drill — could push her panic button. She would start to hyperventilate, then feel unsteady and dizzy. Her heart would jump into her throat and her pulse would race.

When this happened, she would try to control her breathing, square her shoulders, and tell herself, very sternly, not to be silly. Yes, there was a fire, but it was absolutely nothing to be afraid of. This was just her — nobody else was having this reaction. She would get over it. And in a moment, the dizziness would subside, her breathing and heart rate would return to normal, and she could go on with what she'd been doing.

But after a while, being stern with herself didn't fix things. The panic attacks became more frequent and more severe. The smell of smoke and the sight of open flames — even film footage of a California wildfire on television — could make her feel breathless, lightheaded, faint. It was a little inconvenient, certainly, but as long as it didn't get any worse, she thought she could handle it.

By this time, she had come back to Texas, to Pecan Springs, where she enrolled at

Central Texas State. She loved her classes and the social life, but she tried to avoid fire whenever she could, especially the big homecoming bonfires and the Fourth of July celebrations.

But then something happened that she couldn't avoid. Midway through her sophomore year, the pizza shop next door to her apartment building caught fire while she and her boyfriend Charlie were studying together late one evening. It was a two-alarm fire and the manager of her building ordered all the residents to evacuate. She and Charlie joined the crowd of spectators on the sidewalk. While Jessica was frightened and shivering in the chilly night, she was pretty much okay — until she looked up and saw the flames arching into the sky over her head and a heavy billow of black smoke blanketing the street.

Terrified, she found herself breathing fast and hard. Then dizzy, and suddenly faint, she turned to try to get away from the smothering smoke. But before she could take a step, the dark closed all around her and she felt herself falling. She was dimly aware of Charlie easing her to the sidewalk, cradling her in his arms.

"You okay, Jess?" he asked urgently. He

bent over her. "What happened? What can I do?"

She opened her eyes and tried to breathe without taking in a lungful of smoke. "I'm okay," she said after a few moments, and struggled to sit. "Really, I'm fine," she said, although her head was whirling. "I think I can get up if you'll give me a hand."

"Are you sure?" he asked anxiously, brushing the hair out of her eyes. "You're awfully pale. There's an EMS crew parked down the block. Why don't I ask them to —"

"I'm *sure*," she said, hating the feeling of being helpless. "Please. Just give me a hand."

"Well, okay," Charlie said, putting his arm around her waist. But as he was helping her to her feet, she fainted again. This time the blackness was complete, as if she had entirely left the world. She came to only slowly, lying on a gurney with an EMS tech giving her oxygen and preparing to bundle her off to the hospital.

She managed to convince them that she'd just had a simple panic attack. All she needed was to get away from the fire and the smoke and she would be fine. Just. Fine. Really.

Charlie took her to his place to spend the night and in the morning she was her usual self again. But after that, she noticed that he kept a solicitous, almost proprietary eye on her. He was constantly asking her if she was feeling okay, or if he could get her something, anything. It was as if he thought she might faint at any moment and it was his job to be there and take care of her when it happened — the man in charge.

For Jessica, Charlie's feeling of being in charge made *her* feel that her independence was compromised. She didn't like feeling helpless. And that spelled the end of the relationship. She told Charlie she couldn't see him again. Not his fault, just . . . well, not his fault.

And with that, Jessica realized that she couldn't go on letting herself be ambushed by her fears. On the recommendation of her friend China Bayles, she went to see Dr. Pam Neely, a psychotherapist. It was exactly the right choice.

When she heard Jessica's story, Dr. Neely was sympathetic. "Given what happened to your family," she said, "your fear is quite understandable. We may not be able to get rid of it altogether, but we can at least make the experience less terrifying." She prescribed journal writing and a series of "therapeutic exposures" — short sessions with small, carefully controlled fires that let

Jessica experience her distress in a safe environment. Over the next couple of years and with a lot of diligent work, she gradually lost most of her fear of fire.

Most, not all. Dr. Neely said that she would probably always feel anxious and physically uncomfortable around open flames. But the situation had improved to the point where she could get a good whiff of smoke without her pulse going into hyperdrive or feeling as if she might faint.

For Jessica, life was pretty much back to normal. She finished her undergrad program, got a masters in journalism, and landed a full-time job — her dream job as a crime reporter — at the Pecan Springs *Enterprise.* There, she discovered that she could even cover a structure fire when it was assigned to her, like the laundromat fire a few months ago. She knew she would always be a little apprehensive, but fires were part of her cops-and-court beat. That was her job. She could do it.

It wasn't her job as a crime reporter that was taking Jessica to Georgia Shores today. This was a deeply, intensely *personal* trip. There might be a new development in the arson fire that had killed her family some fifteen years before. She was here to learn more about that new development — if

423

somebody in the police department would come clean with her.

Well, if that happened, Jess thought wryly, it would be a first. In the years since the fire, the cops had never come up with a single clue to the identity of the arsonist, whether because they hadn't looked very hard or because whoever-it-was had done a good job of covering his tracks.

But she had to admit that it was a tough case. Her father, Major Nelson, had been a legal officer — an Army judge advocate, stationed at Fort Sam Houston in nearby San Antonio — and there had been any number of people who might have had a grudge against him. The cops had interviewed a handful of possible suspects, but there'd been no arrests. Jessica knew that arson was a tough crime to prove and that nationwide, fewer than 30 percent of residential arson fires were cleared. In Texas, there was a seven-year statute of limitations on arson. There was no limit on murder, so theoretically the case was still open.

Jessica had finally accepted the fact that she would never know who the killer was, and she had poured all her need for answers into her work as a journalist. Practically speaking, she could do nothing about the crime that destroyed her family, but she could help readers understand the impact of crime in their community, on their streets, and in their lives, every day of every year. It had become her motivation, the source of her energy, the power that compelled her. The idea that there might finally be a break in the case was frigging exciting — and damned scary, too.

What if she were to learn who had done it and why?

What if the cops were about to *catch* him?

What if —

Jessica pushed the questions out of her mind as she turned left at the corner of Main and Pecan, checking the address on her cellphone's map app. The Georgia Shores PD had moved to a new police station since she'd left. It was two blocks down on the right, in a modern two-story building constructed of sand-colored brick. The heat hit her when she parked in the lot and got out of the air-conditioned car, and with it came the familiar scent of pine resin that would forever remind her of the summers she had spent here when she was a girl.

And smoke. She sniffed. Was that smoke she smelled?

Her diaphragm muscles tightened — an involuntary response she had not yet learned to control — and she took a calming breath.

She straightened her red blouse and short khaki skirt, glad that she was bare-legged and wearing sandals. Hose and heels would have been too much on such a hot day. She slung her bag over one shoulder and threaded her way between cars to the building.

Behind double glass doors, the lobby was lined with large framed color photographs of local scenery — sailboats on the serene blue lake, a regal red-shouldered hawk, a picnic table and a yellow pop-up tent under a tall green pine — and featured a chest-high counter in one corner. The uniformed officer sitting behind the counter looked up from his paperwork.

"Jessica Nelson to see Beverly Loomis," she said. "I have an appointment."

The officer gave her an appraising glance, then turned to his computer to confirm the appointment. "The reporter from the *Enterprise,* over in Pecan Springs. Working on a story, huh?" Without waiting for an answer he said "I gotta take a look at your bag."

Refraining from saying that she was here on personal business, Jessica handed over her shoulder bag for the officer's inspection and pinned on the visitor's badge he gave her. He thrust a flyer at her as he handed back her bag.

"Whatever you're working on, you oughta do a story on the PD's pie supper, too," he said. "Proceeds go to Blue Santa." He grinned. "We're always glad for a little extra publicity."

She smiled. "Good idea," she said, and followed his directions — down the corridor to the left, third door on the right.

Chapter Two

Seated behind a gray metal desk littered with papers, Beverly Loomis was a pretty, soft-voiced brunette in a khaki uniform. She wore her dark hair almost as short as Jessica's own blond boy-cut. She had been working on a computer, but she stood, smiled, and held out her hand as Jess introduced herself. "Good to meet you," she said, and gestured to the visitor's chair.

With a growing sense of anticipation mixed with a visceral uneasiness, Jessica sat down. Loomis had not been the first person from the GSPD to contact her. Back in February, she had picked up an unexpected and deeply disturbing call from a man who identified himself as Officer Walter Riley. There was a possibility, he said, that the Georgia Shores police might reactivate the investigation into the Nelson House Fire — the name the cops had given to her family's cold case. He had asked Jessica several questions about local friends of her mother and father and then asked specifically for the names of boys who might have been interested in her or Ginger. Boys they might have gone out with.

"Gone out with?" She was startled. "We'd just started our freshman year in high school. Neither of us were dating yet. There wasn't anybody."

"Well, think about it," he'd said, sounding disappointed. "I'm looking into a new lead. I may want to talk to you again." He promised to get back to her as soon as he had anything to report. "But don't get your hopes up," he added. "It might not work out."

Trembling, Jessica clicked off the call. Losing everything she loved in a single horrible night had opened up a dark void at the center of her life, leaving her with only a phobic fear of fire and anguished, unanswered questions.

Who had done it? Who and why? Why, why, *why*? Was it possible that her questions might be answered at last? And then what? A splinter of hope had jabbed at her, hard and sharp, like the point of a knife. Could they actually find the person who had done it?

But Riley hadn't gotten back to her as he

promised, and when she tried to get in touch with him, she was shocked to learn that he was dead. Officer Loomis — the woman sitting across the desk from her this afternoon — told her on the phone that he had been shot and killed in a routine traffic stop. The shooter, a parole violator, was caught after a chase at a nearby Dairy Queen and was now in jail, charged with capital murder and unable to make a half-million-dollar bond. Riley's death was all the more tragic because he had left a young wife and a three-year-old son.

Jessica had told Officer Loomis about Riley's phone call and his report of a possible lead in her family's arson deaths. New in the department, Loomis had seemed both interested and sympathetic. She had heard about the Nelson House Fire, but not that the case was being reopened.

"I'll check with Riley's partner, Officer Hapgood," she'd said. "He's out this week, but he might know something."

Jessica had heard nothing for quite a while, until finally Loomis called her to say that Jim Hapgood remembered his partner talking on the phone to somebody about the Nelson fire. He hadn't found any notes, but he would keep looking. If he found anything worth sharing, they would be in touch.

And then nothing again — until the day before yesterday. Loomis called to say that they had found a notebook containing a few of Riley's notes, pulled out of his pocket at the hospital, misplaced there, now finally returned to the police. The notes were sketchy at best, but if Jessica was still interested, she was welcome to come to the station to have a look.

Still interested? Of course she was still interested. And in spite of her stern admonitions to herself, she couldn't help feeling hopeful. Riley must have dug up something or he wouldn't have sounded so optimistic when he phoned her.

Which was why Jessica was here this afternoon, sitting across the desk from Officer Loomis.

Loomis gave her a considering look, then reached into a drawer and pulled out a file folder, pushing it across the desk.

"Officer Riley's notes," she said. "There's not much here, but maybe something will ring a bell." She shoved her chair back and stood. "I'm going for coffee. Can I get you one?"

"That would be great," Jessica said, reaching for the folder. "Black, please."

Loomis was right when she said there wasn't much in the folder. When Jessica opened it and began to read, her hopes faded. There were copies of three small notebook pages, each one covered with cramped, almost illegible handwriting. It was, Jessica decided, Riley's notes on a telephone call from someone — an anonymous woman, it seemed — who claimed to have information about the fire. She had overheard somebody bragging that he had set the fire at the Nelson house back when he was a kid. He did it because he was pissed off at one of the twins, who was too stuck up and la-di-dah to go out with him. The woman remembered the fire, she said, because at the time, her father had worked at Fort Sam Houston with Mr. Nelson. Her father and mother had gone to the funeral.

On the last page, Riley had written a cryptic note to himself: "Has more to say, wants to talk but running out of cell juice. Getting her phone # changed tomorrow. Will call back with new #." One final note, underlined and circled, "Call Jessica Nelson, *Enterprise.* Maybe she remembers the kid?"

When Jessica finished reading, her heart was hammering and her palms were sweaty. The woman who had talked to Riley — her parents had actually gone to her family's funeral. That little small-world detail made the whole thing seem incredibly *real.* And painful.

But stuck up and la-di-dah? Whoever said that didn't know what he was talking about. Neither she nor Ginger —

"Make out his hen scratches, can you?" Loomis asked sympathetically, putting a white foam cup on the desk in front of Jessica. "Riley's writing is a little hard to read."

Jessica looked up from her notes. "So what's the story here, Officer Loomis? Did Riley find out who the woman was? Did he follow up? What —"

"Whoa." Loomis sat down in her chair. "First off, I'm Beverly, Jessica." She sipped her coffee. "Second, I checked with Officer Hapgood. Maybe you know that he was in charge of the original investigation?"

"Okay, Beverly. But actually, I didn't know." Jessica made a note of his name. "I was just a kid. And I went to live with my grandmother right after the fire."

"Well, he was. But he doesn't know anything about Riley's informant, which isn't a surprise, I suppose." She made a little face. "And third, Walt Riley liked to work on his own. That's usually not a problem in a small department, where we all live in one another's laps most of the time. In fact, getting involved in something outside the box is usually good for us. But in this case . . ."

She shrugged, almost apologetic. "Fact is, we don't know anything more than what's in that file, plus what you say Riley told you over the phone. He was killed just a couple of days after he talked to you, so there wouldn't have been much time for him to dig any further. And those are the only notes we've found. Hapgood says that if there was any more contact with that informant, we don't know about it." She hesitated. "Maybe I ought to add that Officer Hapgood is within a couple of weeks of retirement."

Retirement. Which probably meant that he'd been mailing it in for several months. Jessica let out her breath. It sounded like another dead end. Beverly Loomis might be sympathetic, but it was clear that the Georgia Shores police weren't exactly falling all over themselves to follow up on the lead that had landed in Riley's lap.

She shifted the subject slightly. "I understand that Officer Riley left a family."

"Yeah. Wife and a little boy about three years old. Tough for her now — especially because she's six months pregnant. And it'll get tougher when Riley's killer goes to trial and she has to live through the thing all over again." Beverly planted her elbows on the desk and leaned on them. "Look, Jessica. I know it's been a long time. You were just a kid when that fire happened." She narrowed her eyes, considering. "But not quite a kid, I guess. You were, what? Fourteen? Old enough for boyfriends. At least, that's what the woman said to Riley."

Jessica looked back down at Riley's notes and her heart twisted. *He did it because he was pissed off at one of the twins.* It hadn't been her, she knew that much. Of the pair, she'd been the introverted one, the one who'd rather read a book than hang out at Dopey's. No boy had ever asked her out or even acted like he was the slightest bit interested. Ginger, on the other hand, had been lively, outgoing, fun. She liked being with friends, talking on the phone about boys and clothes, passing notes in class. Still, her twin had never had a *real* boyfriend. There was only that kid at Dopey's, and that was mostly make-believe. At least, she didn't *think* there had ever been a real boyfriend.

Staunchly, she said, "Ginger and I spent all our time together. That summer, we rode our bikes, we sailed our Sunfish, we climbed trees. Ginger had a one-way crush on a boy who worked at Dopey's. But they never went out together. I'm sure he never knew how she felt."

"And you?"

A hard lump rose in her throat, the sudden sadness sweeping over her like a tidal wave. "Being a twin pretty much takes care of your need for companionship, for friendship — for anything, really." She swallowed. "Ginger was enough." Ginger was all.

"So you can't tell me anything about what that caller claimed to have overheard — that the fire was set by somebody who was pissed off at you or your sister for being stuck up. La-di-dah, I think was the word. You can't come up with a name?"

"Sorry," Jessica replied, feeling vaguely guilty. "I would if I could. There just wasn't anybody."

"What about the boy your sister was interested in? You said he worked at Dopey's. Where was that? What was his name?"

"Dopey's was an ice cream parlor — where Sweetie Pie's is now," Jessica said. She frowned. "The guy's name was Sean. Ginger thought he had a cute butt," she added, with a sad little chuckle. "He did."

"Sean what? Did he have a last name?" Beverly was making notes.

"Sean Scott," Jessica said. "His dad and mom owned the marina, which was pretty small back then. He was older. Sixteen,

436

maybe seventeen, so he didn't pay any attention to us."

She paused, thinking. She had never wanted to see the police report on the fire — she had always felt that the details would be too painful. Now, that struck her as an evasion. She *should* see it, however she felt about it. There might be something in it that would jog her memory.

She cleared her throat. "The original report on the fire that killed my parents and my sister. How can I get a copy of that?"

Beverly didn't answer. Instead, she looked down at her notes, then back up again. "This woman who called Riley. She says her mom and dad went to the funeral. Any idea who she might have been?"

Jessica shook her head. "Not a clue." She considered repeating her question about the report again, but another had occurred to her. "Was Riley using a departmental cellphone? If so, you might be able to track her down."

Sheila Dawson, the Pecan Springs chief of police, had recently purchased phones that her cops were required to use for departmental business. Jessica knew this, because she had written a story about it. The officers found them a nuisance to use. Which phone is ringing? Which phone do you reach for first? Do you get them mixed up? But even those who didn't like it had to admit that the liability of using a personal phone for police business was just too great. You might end up having your cell subpoenaed in a court case.

"We don't have departmental phones here yet," Beverly said. "All of us use the department landline or our personal cellphones. Riley likely used his cellphone. Anyway, as you can tell from his notes, the caller said she was going to change the number. The one she was calling from would be disconnected."

That was true, Jessica thought, although most disconnected numbers could be traced. But there was something else. "The phone," she said. "Do you think Riley's wife might have it?" She took out her own notebook. "What's her name?"

"Everybody calls her Cam, but I think it's Cameo." Beverly turned down her mouth. "Gotta feel sorry for her, you know? Being a cop's wife is bad enough. Being a cop's widow is a damn sight harder."

"Cameo?" Jessica was startled. "There was a girl named Cameo in the class ahead of ours. Her last name was Schneider, I think. Or Snider. I wonder if it's the same person."

"Dunno," Beverly said. "I grew up in

Houston. I've only been here a couple of years." She gave Jessica a speculative look. "Cam has red hair and lots of freckles — naturally red hair, I mean. Not sandy, not orange, real *red.* If that's any help."

"It's an unusual name," Jessica said. "And the Cameo we knew was a redhead with *lots* of freckles. The kids used to be pretty mean about that. Must be the same girl."

"Guess I'm not surprised. Lots of families seem to stay here — or the kids come back, after they're grown." Beverly was regarding her speculatively. "If you know Cam, maybe you could stop by their place and talk to her. It's possible that Riley mentioned something about the case." She reached for a pad and pencil, jotted down an address, and handed it to Jessica. "It's only a couple of blocks."

Jessica took the address. "The original police report on the fire," she said again. "Where do I go to get a copy?"

Beverly hesitated. "I'm afraid there's a problem. You see —" She was interrupted by a tinny chirp. She pulled a cellphone out of her pocket and checked the caller ID. "Hang on," she said to Jessica. And "What's up, Jim?" into the phone.

Then, her voice rising, "Another one? Jeez, when is this going to *stop*?" She swiveled to the computer, keyed in a string of words, and said, "Yeah, I see the location on the map. Millersville Road, south of Hobart's Corner. Forest Service on it?" Another pause. "Understand. On my way."

She clicked off the phone and stood. "Sorry to cut this short, Jessica, but I've got to go. We've got another wildfire to deal with. The Forest Service already has a crew on scene and I'm needed for traffic duty." Her gear belt was hanging on a wall rack behind the desk and she buckled it on. "You can keep the copies in that folder."

Jessica remembered the smoke she had smelled when she got out of the car. "*Another* wildfire?" She put the folder in her bag and stood.

"The third," Beverly said flatly. Off the wall rack, she took a dark blue billed cap with POLICE in white letters across the front. "The first two were arson fires, both started with the same type of ignition devices. You can't blame folks around here for being a little spooked, given what happened with the Lost Pines fire a few years ago." She tugged the cap down on her head. "Pretty windy out there today, too, with that storm blowing up in the Gulf. It was Tropical Storm Lee that whipped the Lost Pines fire into an inferno." She looked questioningly at Jessica. "You're going to see Cam — Mrs. Riley?"

"Yes," Jessica said without hesitation. "That's where I'm headed next." She took a breath. "That report. Where can I get a copy?"

"You can't." Beverly put her cap on her head. "Sorry. It's not available."

"Not available?" Jessica frowned. "I suppose you've heard of the Freedom of Information Act." She had used it often enough to know that it worked. Even the most recalcitrant of bureaucrats understood that they had to yield to the FOIA. It was the law.

"It's not available because it's lost," Beverly said shortly. She took out her gun, checked it, holstered it again. "I know this because I looked for it myself."

Jessica wasn't sure she'd heard right. "Lost? How long has it been lost? Who lost it? Why?"

"If I knew, I'd tell you," Beverly said, with the hint of a smile. "But I don't. That's it. Sorry. We'll keep looking."

"Yeah," Jessica muttered. "Thanks."

That wasn't the end of it, as far as she was concerned. Not by a long shot.

Chapter Three

The temperature on her phone's weather app registered 98 degrees when Jessica parked her Kia in front of the Riley house on Sherman Street. Even with the air conditioner on, her red sleeveless blouse was sticking to her back. When she got out of the car and locked it, the wind was lashing the leaves of a nearby green live oak and the smell of smoke was stronger than before. In spite of the heat, she shivered. The town must be downwind of the wildfire, she thought, and wondered how far away it was.

The house was a one-story white-painted bungalow with blue shutters. A multi-trunked pecan tree shaded a wooden playground set and a trucktire sandbox, with a red tricycle parked nearby. A calico cat lounged lazily on the porch swing, and a black cat lay on the mat before the front door.

The woman who answered the doorbell

was wearing pedal pushers and a green T-shirt, her feet bare. She was taller than Jessica remembered and clearly pregnant. Her face was lined, too. She looked tired and there were dark circles under her eyes. But the red hair — now worn long and in a single braid over her shoulder — was the same. And the freckles.

"Yes?" she asked through the screen door. "What can I do for you?" Then her blue-green eyes widened and she gasped. "Wait," she said. "I know you. But you're . . ." Her voice trailed off.

"I'm Jessica Nelson," Jessica said. "I'm not sure you'll remember me, Cameo. My twin sister Ginger and I went to school here in Georgia Shores until —"

"Of course," Cameo said, and rolled her eyes. "For a minute there, I thought — I mean, you look just like — Oh, hell," she said abruptly. "I might as well just come right out with it. I thought you were your sister. Or her ghost. You two looked enough alike to be —"

She broke off again, took a breath, and said, half-apologetically. "Sure. I remember, Jessica. I don't think I ever got the chance to say how sorry I was, back when it happened. The fire, I mean. Your house." As if trying to explain, or excuse herself, she

443

added, "You didn't come back to school."

Jessica nodded, half-smiling at the idea that Cam might have thought she was Ginger, come back from the dead. "We didn't have any family here in town, so I went to live with my grandmother in Louisiana. Now, I'm over in Pecan Springs." She hesitated, not quite knowing what to say. "And I'm sorry, too, Cam. About your husband, I mean."

"So we're both sorry." Cam's voice was steady but her eyes were bleak. "There's plenty to be sorry about, wouldn't you say? But that's life. We just have to get through it the best we can." Somewhere in the distance, a fire siren sounded, then a second. She raised her head and sniffed the air. "Smoke. Must be another one of those fires. I wonder where it is."

"On Millersville Road," Jessica said. "Somewhere near Hobart's Corner. Beverly Loomis and I were talking when she got called out to handle traffic."

"That's maybe four-five miles away," Cam said. "South around the lake, which is why we're smelling the smoke. Another arson fire, I suppose." Her voice grew bitter. "I hope they catch the rat, whoever he is." She pushed the screen door open. "We could talk out here on the porch, but it's too hot and smoky for me. Come in where it's cool and we'll have some iced tea."

"Sounds wonderful," Jessica said gratefully, and followed her into the house and down the short hallway. In the kitchen, a radio on the counter was playing Janis Joplin's "Me and Bobby McGee," and Cam abruptly switched it off.

"A voice out of the past," Jessica said. "Joplin, I mean. Austin, back in the seventies."

Recently, David Redfern had at last talked her into going out with him on a real date. They had gone to Threadgill's, the converted gas station on North Lamar where the gritty-voiced singer-songwriter had gotten her start. Jessica had resisted David's invitations for months because he was the defense attorney for Howard Byers, the serial killer who called himself Azrael, the Angel of Death. She had played a major role in Byers' capture and would be a witness for the prosecution. She was also under contract with St. Martin's to write a book called *Not Only in the Dark,* about Byers' string of murders. Dating David was complicated and presented some serious ethical issues. But she found him attractive and she'd agreed to go out with him in spite of herself.*

" 'Bobby McGee' was Walt's favorite song," Cam said, her voice thin. "I can't listen to it. Not yet, anyway." She took a pitcher out of the refrigerator. "Sugar?"

"Pink stuff, if you've got it, please," Jessica said, taking a stool at the counter. The kitchen was small and old-fashioned, featuring yellow-painted cabinets and hen-and-chicks wallpaper. But clean and neat, with a child's crayon drawings covering the refrigerator door and a cotton apron and a straw garden hat hanging from yellow pegs on the wall. She gestured at a red plastic fireman's helmet lying on the floor.

"Beverly Loomis said you have a little boy."

"Bobby." Cam smiled. "Yeah. Like the song. He's three, going on thirteen." She glanced at the clock as she put two frosty glasses on the counter and took a stool on the opposite side. "He's asleep. If we're lucky, he'll stay that way while we're talking. If not —" She shrugged. "He's having

* The story of Jessica's part in the Angel of Death investigation is told in *Out of BODY,* the third novella in the Crystal Cave trilogy. There's more about her relationship with David Redfern in *Firelines* and *Fault Lines.*

a hard time right now. He doesn't understand why his dad doesn't come home. And he keeps wanting his little sister to come out and play with him." She patted her belly. "This is Angel."

Jessica smiled sympathetically. "It must be hard to carry a baby in the summer time. When are you due?"

"The end of September. I'd like to go back to the classroom in the spring. I teach middle school. But I think it would be better for the kids — mine, I mean — if I took the year off."

Jessica picked up her glass and sipped her iced tea. Loomis was right. Being a cop's widow was difficult, especially with two young children. But Cameo seemed like the kind of woman who would be okay, once she got through this catastrophe.

She put down her glass. "Your husband and I talked on the phone a few days before he was killed," she said slowly. "He told me he was working on something that might lead to whoever caused the fire. My family fire, I mean. The Nelson House Fire."

"He told me about it," Cam said, wrapping her hands around the cold glass. "Both of us remembered the fire from when we were kids, you know."

"Really?" Jessica was surprised. "Your

husband grew up here, too?"

"Oh, you bet. He was a couple of years ahead of me in school. High school sweethearts and all that. We went over to Pecan Springs for college, then back here to live. We wanted to raise our kids in a small town." Cameo gave Jessica a curious look. "I read the stories you wrote in the *Enterprise* last year, about that serial killer. And your reporter's blog. *Crime and Consequences.* Isn't that the name of it?"

"That's it," Jessica said. Jeff Dixon, the new editor at the *Enterprise,* was pushing the reporters to do more with their blogs. She liked the idea. But blogging would take time away from her reporting and from *Not Only in the Dark,* which wouldn't be finished until early the next year.

Cameo sighed. "I envy you, Jessica. It must be totally exciting, being a newspaper reporter — especially a crime reporter. You get to go everywhere, talk to interesting people. Crooks, I mean. And cops."

"Sometimes it's exciting," Jessica said with a little smile. "Sometimes it's frustrating. Endlessly following leads and never getting anywhere." She hesitated. "I wonder —" She paused again, hearing the light ping of her phone in her bag. But the text would have to wait. She took a breath.

"Your husband told me that he was following some sort of new lead. I understand that it was a phone call from an anonymous tipster, a woman. I wonder — did he happen to mention the call to you?"

"Yeah, he did," Cam said, drawing wet circles on the counter with the base of her glass. "In fact, he got it here at the house. During Bobby's birthday party. He told me about it that night while we were cleaning up." She rolled her eyes. "Thirteen preschool kids, a piñata, a birthday cake with blue frosting — Bobby's favorite color — and blue Kool-Aid. It took us *hours.*"

"I can only imagine," Jessica said with a shudder. "What did he tell you about the call?" She took her notebook out of her bag. "Okay if I make a few notes, just for the record?"

"Sure. But there isn't much to tell, I'm afraid. Walt just said it was a woman, and that she knew something about the Nelson fire." Cameo related the same story Jessica had read in Riley's notes: that the caller had said she'd overheard a guy talking about setting the Nelson fire because he was annoyed at one of the twins, who wouldn't go out with him. "Or maybe it was both of the twins." She wrinkled her nose. "I think maybe it was both."

And then she added a detail that wasn't in the notes. "The guy said he set the fire in the garage. He said he was a kid then, didn't know from fires. He had no idea it would spread to the house. Walt was going to try to get in touch with you. Maybe you would remember who it might have been — somebody that you or your sister refused to go out with." She chewed on her lower lip. "That kind of jolted me. You and your sister were just a year behind me in school. I mean, it had to be somebody we *all* knew. Like, somebody from one of our classes."

Jessica looked up from her shorthand, which was a mashup of the Gregg she'd learned in high school and her own private code. "When did he get the call?"

"Like I said, on Bobby's birthday."

"Which was . . ."

"February thirteenth. Just a few days before he was killed." She sighed heavily. "Things don't always happen the way you want them to, do they." It wasn't a question.

"No, they don't," Jessica replied ruefully. She was remembering that Riley had called her on Valentine's Day. "I understand that your husband took the call on his cell." When Cameo nodded, she said, "I hope you don't think I'm being nosey, Cam, but I

450

wonder if you still have his phone."

"Well . . ." Cam said it hesitantly. "I don't really think I should —"

Jessica interrupted. "I would really like to find the woman who made that call. I want to talk to her, find out where she overheard this conversation, under what circumstances. Ask her if she's seen the guy again and where. She's the only one who has that information. And the only way to connect to her is through that call."

"I get that," Cam said. "But the phone's not going to help you. Walt said the woman was having her number changed and would get back to him. She never did." She reached down and pulled out a drawer under the counter. "But I do have his phone. You can take a look, if you want to." She took the phone out of the drawer, clicked to the call records, and studied the screen. "She called about six o'clock on Bobby's birthday, which would make it . . ." Her voice trailed off as she scrolled down through the data. "I hope he didn't delete it."

Jessica watched, holding her breath, thinking that she had never been so close to a piece of information that — if she was really, really lucky — might take her to the arsonist who killed her family.

Finally, Cameo said, "I think this might

be it. The time looks about right, anyway. And the only other call was a lot later." She handed Jessica the phone.

The number Jessica was looking at was a 737 area code, so it was local — although the woman might have called from the other side of the globe. She added the number and the date and time to her notebook.

Cameo frowned. "But the number's no longer in service, right?"

"That doesn't necessarily mean it can't be found," Jessica said. People thought that once they changed their number, the record was deleted. But it wasn't. Service providers retained subscriber information for up to ten years and call records for up to seven, which meant that the disconnected number was still traceable. She had used a reverse-search service before and was always surprised at the information she turned up: name, location, occupation, present and past addresses, marital status, current phone number, and so on. It was a valuable research tool that every investigative reporter learned how to use.

She navigated to the settings of Riley's phone and noted down its number before she handed it back. "Did your husband say anything else about the call?"

"Well, he seemed excited about it," Cam

said slowly. "I think he thought it would be a feather in his cap if he solved the case. It was the biggest thing that ever happened in this little town — until the Lost Pines fire, anyway. Everybody knew your mom. I remember how shocked my parents were — both of them — when it happened. My mother cried when she heard it. She worked with your mother on some big PTA committee or something."

Jessica smiled sadly. "Mom always liked to be involved." She felt proud when she thought of her mother, who, like Ginger, had been an outgoing person with a generous spirit. The family had followed Jessie's father to several different Army bases, but no matter where they lived, her mother immediately became an active member of the community. By the time they'd been in Georgia Shores a couple of years, she was volunteering for the food pantry, the library board, and the PTA governing committee.

"Probably fewer knew Dad, though," Jessica added thoughtfully. "He worked in the judge advocate's office at Fort Sam. In fact, the cops thought it was probably somebody over there who set the fire — somebody with a grudge against him for something related to a legal case he was working on. So that's what I've always assumed. That it might have been connected to us — to Ginger or me — is a totally new idea. I still don't quite believe it. Neither of us had a boyfriend, I mean. But at least it's a *lead.* Something to go on."

"And it makes a certain sense, I guess," Cam said. "If something like that could ever make any kind of sense." She tilted her head. "Some teenage boys are pretty fragile, you know. Rejection seems to make them question their manhood. Sends them off the deep end. Maybe you didn't even know you'd rejected him because he was too insecure to let you know he liked you."

Jessica nodded. "Remember Dopey's? Ginger was hot for a cute guy who worked there. Sean, his name was. Sean Scott. He had no idea, of course. After all, he was older."

"Remember Dopey's?" Cam threw back her head and laughed. "Oh, do I! Walt and I once had a fight there, and I threw my milkshake in his face." She dropped her voice, biting her lip. "What wouldn't I give to be there again, with him?" With a sigh, she went on. "Sean Scott is still around, though. Not as hot as he used to be, and on his second divorce — or maybe his third. I've lost track. His dad and mom owned the marina, you know. Scott's Landing."

"Yes, I remember. Ginger and I used to sail our Sunfish there."

"Well, both Mr. and Mrs. Scott died a couple of years ago, first one and then the other. Sean's running the place now. It's a much bigger operation than it was when we were kids. A lot more boats, more fishing, tourists, stuff like that." Cameo smiled crookedly. "But I doubt that Sean Scott's ego was terribly fragile. Back in the day, every girl in town was after him. Dopey used to say that after Sean graduated and went off to college to play football, he lost half his customer base."

"Mommy?"

Jessica heard a whimper and turned to see a tow-headed toddler, barefoot and wearing rumpled shorts and a yellow T-shirt with a big red slice of watermelon on it. He was rubbing his eyes and clutching a green plush dinosaur with an orange crest.

"Hey, sweetie," Cameo said. "Wake up and have a cookie. Quick, before it gets away." As she reached into a ceramic frog cookie jar, the little boy ran to her and clambered up into her lap.

"Cookie!" he cried, and then, cagily, "Dino wants one, too, Mommy. He's *hungry.*"

"Of course he is," his mother said. "Dino

455

is always hungry. And he can certainly have one — as soon as you've found your sandals and put them on."

Jessica wrote *Sean Scott — Scott's Landing* in her notebook and flipped the cover closed. She glanced up, suddenly aware of the tenderness in Cameo's voice and the way she held her small son close, against the daughter who was still a part of her body. *I envy you,* Cam had said.

But for just this moment, it was Jessica who envied her, and the pain she felt was as sudden and sharp as a punch in the gut. This woman's husband was gone. But she had his children, and they would comfort her for the rest of her life. Jessica, who was just her age, had her career. But she was alone and often — too often — lonely. It wasn't a recognition she admitted to very often. It came now, unbidden. And unwelcome. She didn't want to think about it.

She put her notebook in her bag and stood. "It's time for me to be on my way. Thank you, Cam. I'm very grateful for your help." She nodded at the phone lying on the counter. "It's possible that your husband's cellphone may become important. Please keep it safe."

"It's not going anywhere," Cam said, and dropped it into the drawer. "Look, I hope

456

you won't take this the wrong way, Jessica. Back in the old days, the cops here in Georgia Shores sort of went with the flow, you know? I don't mean they were lazy or anything. But nothing like that fire had ever happened here, and they just . . . Well, Walt said they didn't have a clue about investigating it." She gave a little shrug. "It took something for him to say that, you know. He knew the officer in charge of that investigation — Pete Remmick."

"Pete Remmick," Jessica repeated thoughtfully. "He's still on the force?" It might be a good idea for her to talk to him, especially since it didn't look like she was going to be able to read the police report. Lost, was it? How convenient.

"Nope. Pete died last year," Cam said. "Alzheimer's."

"Oh, too bad." Another roadblock, Jessica thought. Wasn't she going to get a break?

"That's for sure. Pete was a nice guy. Walt said that if he'd had some of the forensic tools they have now, the guy who killed your family would have been caught and convicted. He felt bad about that." Cameo's mouth softened. "And the call from that woman seemed like it was a shot in the arm, kinda. It got him thinking about reopening the case and maybe even bringing the killer to justice. If he had lived . . ."

Tears flooded her eyes and she tightened her arms around her son. She raised her voice, steadying it. "If Walt had lived, I think he would have done that. I *know* he would have tried."

"I think you're right," Jessica said quietly. "Thanks for your help, Cam. I appreciate it very much."

"Yeah." Cam managed a tremulous smile. "I hope you find what you're looking for, Jessica."

Jessica nodded. "So do I, Cam. So do I."

Chapter Four

Phone me when you can — story assignment. Jeff

The text Jessica had missed was from Jefferson Davis Dixon, the new co-editor and co-publisher of the *Enterprise.* Jeff (he insisted on first names with the reporters) was responsible for the newspaper's just-launched digital edition. He had stepped into the role back in March, when he bought a third of the newspaper, rescuing it from the brink of bankruptcy. What he demanded in return for his buy-in? That he would be named as editor/publisher of the newspaper's new digital edition: *Pecan SpringsEnterpriseOnline.com.* It was online now in a skeletal format, with new developments in the works and plenty of promotion (99-cent trial subscriptions, for instance) to attract new readers.

It was an open secret that Hark Hibler,

who had owned and published the *Enterprise* for the past five or six years, was a print guy to his bones. He had grown up with newspapers and loved the smell of fresh ink and the crinkle of newsprint in his fingers. He'd been reluctant to take Dixon's money and even more reluctant to allow him to push the *Enterprise* into digital publishing, which he regarded as about as risky as trying to cross I-35 at the height of rush hour — blindfolded. If you wanted to be an idiot you were welcome to try, but you'd get flattened. And even if you made it to the other side, what you gained in the attempt wasn't worth the doing.

But it wasn't just Hark's preference for print that accounted for his reluctance. He and Dixon had worked together on the staff of the *Daily Texan,* the student newspaper at UT Austin, and Hark remembered the guy — the scion of the powerful Dixon political family and heir to the multinational Dixon beer and wine distributorship — as bright and enthusiastic but a dilettante and playboy.

He also suspected that Dixon intended to use the *Enterprise* as a way into political office: a seat in the Texas Legislature or even the governor's mansion. "Pour enough Dixon money onto the playing field," he'd told Jessica, "and anything is possible."

But when push came to shove, Hark knew he had no options. He hadn't been successful in finding other investors, and Dixon's large cash infusion into the newspaper's bank account would keep it from going belly-up for at least another year. With every fiber of his being, Hark believed in the importance of community journalism: a local newspaper committed to providing news and information to the local community. Some people wouldn't miss the *Enterprise* until it was gone, but he knew that the newspaper's failure would tear a big hole in the town's heart. What's more, newspapers were failing all over the country, and jobs in journalism were as few and far between as winning lottery tickets. He had to think of the loyal staff he'd built and the good work they'd done together.

So Hark took Jeff Dixon's money and told him he could do whatever he wanted with the dot-com edition, and Jeff's online *Enterprise* had launched this past week. With a lot of help from the newsroom, Jeff and his small team — Don Seibert, web designer; Denise Sanger, assistant editor; and Sarita Hernandez, advertising and social media — had published the first issue, with twice-daily news updates and features from the newsroom. According to the press release (written by features editor Fran Fenner) the digital edition would "showcase the breadth of the *Enterprise*'s community coverage in a format that is as easy to read and share as the print edition that has kept Pecan Springs informed for over a century." The release optimistically concluded: "We believe a platform for sharing local news is critical to our community. We're glad you think so, too."

Of course, nobody could predict how successful the online edition was going to be. But the staff of the *Enterprise* knew that their journalistic futures depended on it, and they had their collective fingers and toes crossed. Hark knew it, too, so they weren't surprised to see that he had added his signature to Dixon's on the rah-rah email urging them to do everything they could to make it work:

```
While we need to serve the many
regular readers who remain com-
mitted to print, the new digital
edition offers us an outstand-
ing opportunity to expand our
readership. But to make the best
of it, we'll need all hands on
board, 24-7. We're depending on
```

each one of you to keep your eyes and ears open for breaking news, unusual events, and human-interest stories. Please study the new website and apps and bring us your ideas. Let's make this a success!

Jeff Dixon
Hark Hibler

Before Jessica drove to the Riley house that afternoon, she had texted Dixon about the wildfire outside of Georgia Shores, thinking that it would make a good story for the online edition. She wasn't eager to cover it herself, for she could still remember the bone-melting terror that had seized her the evening of the pizza shop fire, when she was still in college. This new wildfire was bound to be larger and perhaps even more terrifying, and she didn't want to go there again.

But it sounded like the wildfire was arson. Arson was a crime and crime was her beat and that made it *her* story. Like it or not, she had to cover it. And she was on the scene. Well, almost.

Now, as she unlocked her car, she sniffed the air. She was close enough to smell the smoke, anyway. And the smell was stronger than it had been before she had gone into the Riley house, maybe because the wind had increased. The Texas flag on the house across the street was flapping wildly. She tried to quash her uneasiness. With this wind, the fire would be ramping up.

She opened the Kia's door to let out the heat. Leaning against the car, she dialed Dixon's cell number. He picked up on the second ring.

"You're still in Georgia Shores?" He had asked reporters to sign out and in on the board by the newsroom door, so the editors would know where everybody else was in case a breaking story needed to be covered. Jessica wasn't on a story, so she had taken the afternoon as personal time — just a few of the dozens of hours she'd accumulated over the past year. But she had still signed out on the board, noting that she was going to Georgia Shores.

"I'm about ready to head back to Pecan Springs." She slid into the driver's seat, started the car, and turned on the air conditioner, which produced a hot breeze. It always took a while for the Kia's AC to cool things down. "Were you texting about that wildfire?"

"Yeah. I heard on the scanner that the Pecan Springs FD is sending an engine. They're saying it looks like arson — the third arson wildfire in that area in the past couple of weeks. The Forest Service has set up a mobile command post on Millersville Road at — Hang on. I've got it here somewhere." He paused, and Jessica heard papers rustling.

"Hobart's Corner," Jessica said, redirecting the AC away from her face. She was already hot enough.

"Right. Hobart's Corner. You somewhere close?"

"Four or five miles. It's a bad day for a fire — lots of wind, with that storm whipping up in the southern Gulf. You want me to run the story down?"

"Yeah. See what you can pick up, especially on the arson angle. You have a video camera and a mic? If you can get some footage of the fire, we could run a clip on the homepage. That'll bring eyes and ears to the story."

As a print reporter, video had never been a part of Jessica's assignments, so getting footage was a new challenge. But she had already given some thought to this.

"I've got a good smartphone camera with a selfie stick, a jack, and a clip-on mic," she said. "I also have a handheld with a wind shield. I think I'm all set for an interview — if I can get one. Depends on who's in charge and how close I can get to the action."

Dixon chuckled. "We'll make a TV reporter out of you yet, Jessica. If you get something you think we can use, email it pronto. Anything up to three minutes will work without edits." He paused. "We've missed the three p.m. website update, but we can upload the story when we get it and run it as breaking news, with an email alert to all subscribers." He sounded pleased. "Your byline, of course."

Jessica understood Hark's commitment to print, but the online edition was better at getting the word out fast. Anybody reading their email would get the news of the fire as soon as it was posted.

"On it," she said. She knew she sounded braver than she felt.

Millersville Road was a two-lane asphalt lined on both sides by dense stands of tall green loblollies. In the distance, Jessica could see a plume of dark gray smoke blown nearly horizontal by the brisk wind. But it was several miles away, so she pulled her attention back to the road and concentrated on the traffic, which seemed to be stopped ahead at a checkpoint. It looked like most vehicles were being instructed to detour. Would she be turned back?

But when she reached the barricade, she saw that the officer handling the traffic was Beverly Loomis. She opened her window, held up her press pass and said, "I'm on assignment for the Pecan Springs *Enterprise,* Beverly. Any chance I can get through to the command center at Hobart's Corner?"

Beverly looked sweaty and stressed, but she nodded. "You're in luck. I just got word that Mark Hemming — he's the incident commander on this one — is about to do a briefing." She gave Jessica a questioning look. "You get to talk with Walt Riley's wife?"

"I did," Jessica said.

Beverly waited a beat. "And?"

"And yes, she's the same girl I knew back when," Jessica said.

Beverly rolled her eyes. "That's it? No luck with Riley's informant."

"That's it," Jessica said.

She was still stewing over the idea that the police report on the Nelson fire was "lost." That certainly seemed strange. And if either Jim Hapgood or Beverly Loomis had bothered to ask, Cameo Riley would likely have given them the anonymous caller's number from her husband's cellphone, just as she had given it to Jessica. But they hadn't. If the information led somewhere important,

Jessica might be willing to share — later. For now, Cam Riley was *her* source, and she was in the habit of protecting her sources.

Resigned, Beverly sighed. "The command center is half a mile on the right, at the Exxon station." She moved the barricade to let the Kia through. "Drive carefully."

A half mile later, Jessica saw the gas station where the fire's mobile command center was set up in the parking lot. There were a dozen cars and trucks in the lot, several of the trucks belonging to the Texas Forest Service, with the maroon A&M logo on the doors. Other reporters were already here, she saw, as she parked beside a blue KXAN news van with a transmission dish on the roof.

Hurriedly, she attached her cellphone to her selfie stick, set the rear camera on the phone, and checked to make sure it was working. Hanging her press badge around her neck and propping her large red-lettered PRESS sign on the dash, she grabbed her shoulder bag and got out of the car.

The Forest Service mobile command truck was parked at the back of the lot. About as big as a mid-size RV, the truck bristled with antennas and satellite and microwave dishes. A pair of doors on the side were open, displaying a computer screen, a whiteboard, and a big map of the area. Clustered around the display was a group of fifteen or so — a few in khaki Forest Service uniforms, some in firefighters' yellow shirts and white hardhats, others in street clothes with cameras and broadcast equipment. All but one of them were male. The group was mostly silent, listening to the briefer, whom Loomis had identified as Mark Hemming. Jessica joined them, moving to a spot where she could get a good video shot of the man who stood beside the map, holding a laser pointer.

Hemming had thick dark hair under a yellow cap, a strong nose, and a cleft chin — not a handsome face, but one with a definite rough-edged masculinity. His face was sweat-streaked and dirty, and it looked like he'd just come in off the fireline to do the briefing. He wore sunglasses and a firefighter's bright yellow Nomex shirt with smudges of dark ash on one sleeve, and jeans tucked into scuffed brown boots. He held himself with the dynamic strength of a man sure of who he was, what he had done, and what he could and *would* do if he had to.

A strikingly sexy man, Jessica admitted to herself, although he was older — forty, maybe? Whatever age he was, he was intimidating. Definitely not her type.

She stepped closer, pressed the video button on her phone and held it up. Hemming noticed what she was doing. She couldn't see his eyes behind his sunglasses, but he glanced down at her press badge, nodded, and went on with what he was saying, using his laser to point out areas on the map, his words crisp, his tone all business.

"For now, the Hobart's Corner Fire has been designated a Type Three incident. It's located on the east side of the Millersville Road, between Oak Creek — here — and the KOA Campground — here. It has the potential to burn to this northeastern perimeter — here — which would make it about 350 acres. There are no threatened structures."

Somebody's cell phone dinged and the owner, also wearing a press badge, hastily stepped away from the group. Overhead, Jessica could hear the slap-slap-slap of a helicopter rotor and in the distance, a shrill siren, then another. There was no visible smoke, but she could taste it at the back of her throat, and she swallowed, shifting uneasily. How close was the fire? Was it coming in their direction?

The sirens grew louder and Hemming raised his voice. "Bottom line, this isn't just one fire. There appear to have been three separate ignition points set about a half mile apart at the foot of a slope, all on the same side of the road. The ignition devices themselves have not been located yet, but several areas have been marked for searching. The wind is . . ." He turned to squint at the computer screen. "The wind isn't helping us out today, with the tropical storm brewing in the Gulf. It's south-southeast at eighteen, gusting to twenty-two. This area has never been subject to prescribed burning, so there's plenty of fuel: dense standing pine, dry understory shrubs, thick pine litter on the forest floor. The terrain is a challenge — steep upslope to a ridgeline. But while it's intense, the fire is relatively small. We're working to contain it quickly."

Jessica finished shooting her video as Hemming turned back to the map. "Two brush trucks from Bastrop are on the western perimeter, along with a Smithville engine and two from Georgia Shores. We've got a five-person hand crew working the northern perimeter. Pecan Springs is sending an engine with another five-person hand crew to join them. That helicopter you heard a moment ago belongs to the Texas Forest Service. It's carrying a Bambi bucket — picking up water dumps from the lake."

He glanced at Jessica. "Media folks, there are photos of the area on the Forest Service website."

"A *Bambi* bucket?" the other woman asked, giggling. Jessica recognized Marla Cohen, a KXAN-TV reporter. Her cameraman was standing beside her, a bulky TV camera on his shoulder.

Somebody laughed. "Named for a waitress at a bar up in Idaho. The helicopter guys love to fly it."

"Named for its manufacturer," Hemming said shortly. "This one holds about a hundred and sixty gallons."

"Containment estimate?" another firefighter asked.

"The two earlier fires in this series were not carefully set and we were able to contain them in several hours each. It looks like the firestarter understands the way a slope can boost the fire." Hemming pulled off his cap and rubbed sweat off his forehead with the back of a hand. "Best guess, we should be able to get around this one tonight sometime. As I said, all three fires were set at the foot of a slope, so the blaze is moving uphill pretty fast. However, at the top of the slope, the terrain levels out and there's a gravel road that looks like a pretty good fireline. As I'm sure you know, containment is always a crapshoot, especially in fire weather like today's. But when all the crews are in place, it's likely that we'll have this one fifty percent contained by twenty-two hundred hours. That's ten p.m." He picked up a black marker and wrote a web address on the whiteboard. "You can get detailed fire updates at this URL. Or you can check our Facebook page." He added that address to the board.

"You said this is the third fire in the area," Jessica said. "In how many weeks?"

"Right. The third in a little over three weeks. So far, we've been lucky. Lost just one structure — a garage — in the two previous burns." Hemming smiled crookedly, and Jessica noticed that he had dimples. "You can tell your readers that this firestarter isn't somebody who's had a few too many beers and figures it'll be fun to go out and set the woods on fire. This is definitely one of a series, not a one-off. And once a serial arsonist gets started, he doesn't stop until he's caught."

Marla spoke up. "Dr. Hemming, you're saying 'he.' Aren't you jumping to conclusions here? Couldn't the arsonist be a woman? Seems like setting a fire would be an easy thing to do. Just toss a match into the brush along the road. Doesn't require a lot of muscle."

Dr. Hemming? Then Jessica understood. In addition to his work with the Forest Service, this man must be a professor at Texas A&M, where the Forest Service was headquartered. He must do research and teach courses on fire management.

Dr. Hemming spoke patiently. "Could be a woman, yes. It's been estimated that two or three out of ten firestarters are women. Mostly, though, female arsonists torch dwellings — individual, specific dwellings — and usually out of jealousy or revenge. They do it to get even with somebody. They're not serial arsonists. The fire is a one-off."

Jessica shivered, feeling cold in spite of the hot afternoon sun. If Riley's anonymous tipster was to be believed, the person who had torched her family's house was a *guy* who had acted out of revenge, because he'd been ignored by her or her sister. But their fire hadn't been one of a series.

Or had it? Maybe she should look into that. Georgia Shores didn't have a news-paper now, but it had one — the *Georgia Shores Weekly Beacon* — when she was a girl. If there had been other fires, somebody at the *Beacon* would have covered them. She took a breath. And what kind of ignition device had been used to set her house ablaze? That piece of information must have been in the police report that Beverly Loomis said was lost. Or maybe it was mentioned in the newspaper coverage — if she could find it.

Dr. Hemming looked at Jessica, then at the KXAN reporter. "Media people, we would appreciate it if you would publicize the Texas Forest Service arson report line." He picked up the marker and wrote an 800 number on the board. "It's just a matter of time before this arsonist strikes again. The next time, he could kill somebody. We need to catch him."

There were a few more questions, but Jessica had pulled out her notebook and was scribbling rapidly, making a note to check the Georgia Shores library for issues of the *Beacon* around the time her family's house had burned. What's more, a story idea had just occurred to her: a multipart crime story about wildfire arson. It was a subject the *Enterprise* hadn't covered, and one that many readers might find interesting.

There was a ping on her phone and she saw that the *EnterpriseOnline* had just sent out a "breaking news" email to all its subscribers:

The Texas Forest Service and crews from nearby towns are fighting a wildfire in the Lost Pines near Lake Georgia. The fire, off the Millersville Road in Bastrop County, may be arson-caused, according to officials. More details coming soon.

As the others left, Marla and the KXAN crew began a short television interview with Hemming. When they were finished, Jessica went up to him, introduced herself, and showed him the *Enterprise* email alert on her phone.

"Just as soon as I get your story written, we'll be running it in our new online edition," she said. "We'll certainly emphasize the arson angle and publish your tip line number." She took a breath and got to her request. "I'm wondering if there's any chance I can get close enough to the fire to get some footage. My editor is asking for a video clip with the story."

Listening to the briefing had made the wildfire seem much more immediate and real, and she definitely wasn't crazy about getting the video Dixon wanted. The thought of being close to that out-of-control wildfire made her throat tighten and her insides feel queasy. She wondered whether she could actually do this.

Hemming pulled off his sunglasses, folded them into his shirt pocket, and gave her a long look. He was taller by a head, lean-hipped but with the broad shoulders and muscular frame of a man who worked on the firelines with the rest of the crew, even if he was a professor. Up close, his features were rugged, his mouth was hard, and she could see the jagged slash of a two-inch scar across his jaw under the shadow of a dark beard. He smelled — strongly — of sweat and smoke.

Smoke. Her pulse speeded up. She felt breathless.

"No," he said shortly. "No way." His eyes were a pale steel gray, flecked with green. He looked at her press badge, then back to her face. "I'm sorry," he added, a fraction less abruptly. "I can't let you do that, Ms. Nelson."

He didn't sound sorry, though. It sounded like he knew he was in charge and he intended to keep it that way. But it wasn't cockiness, and he wasn't patronizing. He was just supremely self-assured, confident. He assumed that he knew what was best. That all he had to do was tell her what to do and she would do it.

"Jessica," she said, trying to appear casual. Of course, if this had been a different situation — a car wreck, a shooting, a crime scene — she would have stood her ground as a reporter. And she knew all the arguments, for she'd had plenty of opportunity to use them. The story was important. Her editor was waiting. The public had a right to be informed. And getting close to the action, even when it was risky, was a journalist's job.

But they were talking about a *fire.* The queasiness was there, definitely, and she was beginning to feel distinctly shaky. She swallowed. She couldn't argue about access when she couldn't keep her fear in check.

"Jessica, then," he said, and the corners of his mouth tipped up. He gave her another look, perhaps not quite so stern, but direct, measuring, assessing.

She felt herself coloring. Standing close to him, she was once again aware of the strong, mixed scents of male sweat and smoke that clung to his clothing. She felt her belly muscles tighten against the danger.

Wait. Whoa, she thought. *Danger?* She bit her lip. She must be reacting to the smoke. It couldn't be the effect of the man's physical presence, for she had always been attracted to guys her own age. This man must be eight or ten years older than she, maybe more. There were crow's feet at the corners of his pale eyes, his sun-browned face testified to days spent outdoors, and there was even a touch of silver at his temples. And older men always had baggage, sometimes very difficult baggage. The thought of it unsettled her, and reflexively, without intending to do it, she dropped her glance to his left hand. He wasn't wearing a wedding ring.

When she looked up again, there was a glint of something like amusement in his eyes and his mouth had softened. She bit the inside of her cheek, thinking he had noticed her glance, but he didn't remark on it. He took out his phone and thumbed the screen, scrolling through emails.

"Tell you what, Jessica. The helicopter copilot just sent me about two minutes of . . ." He clicked, tapped, and handed her his phone. "Here. If this aerial footage will work for you, you can post it with your story."

Jessica was looking at an overhead sequence of bright orange flames licking fiercely at a stand of pine trees. The camera swiveled through a cloud of billowing smoke to show that the flames had left nothing behind but a wide swath of ruined forest. It was a dramatic, frighteningly vivid picture of wildfire in action. Her chest tightened, and she felt her breath coming faster. Before she started to work with Dr. Pam, a video like this would have had almost the same effect as the real thing. It would have sent her spiraling into one of her panic attacks.

"Thank you," she managed with a shiver. She bit her lip. "That helicopter shot is better than anything I could have gotten on the ground. My editor will love it." She handed the phone back quickly, grateful that he had turned down her request for access. Getting anywhere close to that horrifying monster was *not* a good idea — not for her, anyway.

He took the phone from her, and as he did, his fingers brushed hers. She felt something like a spark and hastily pulled her hand back.

"Static electricity," he remarked casually. "Happens when the air is super dry. In the wrong place — at a fuel pump, say — it can start a wildfire." He was watching her, one eyebrow cocked, and she wondered if he had guessed at her fear. When he spoke, his voice was less brusque.

"I teach fire ecology, Jessica. How fire behaves in an ecosystem, how it functions in ecological succession, when and why it's necessary, how to work with it. This fire may not be all that big as wildfires go, but it's plenty scary up close." He gave her a crooked smile. "Firefighters are always afraid, whether we acknowledge it or not. When we work on the firelines, we have to learn to respect fire — and respect our fear of it. Once we stop being afraid, we start being careless. When we get careless, fire can kill us. Fast."

Yes. He had noticed her reaction. She swallowed, once again conscious of that potent scent of him, of mixed sweat and smoke. And danger.

He glanced at the card she had given him, then input her email address into the phone and hit the send button. "Video clip coming your way," he said briskly. "Appreciate it if you'd credit the Texas Forest Service, A&M University."

"Glad to," she said. She took a breath. "Thanks, Dr. Hemming."

"Mark," he said, slipping his phone into his pocket. He met her eyes.

"Mark." She blushed and looked quickly down at her own phone, as if she were checking to be sure that she had received his email and attachment.

He waited. "Got it?"

"It's downloading now." There was one more thing, and she took a deep breath. "During your briefing, I thought of an idea

481

for expanding this story for our new online edition. I'm going to need a bit more background, though. For example, information about the other two fires that may have been set by the arsonist who set this one. About wildfire arson in general, and whether that's a problem here in Texas. Oh, and about the Texas Forest Service, too. I'd have to pitch it to my editor, but I think he'll go for it." She hesitated, not wanting him to think this was personal. That she might be angling for an opportunity to see him again. "We could do the interview by email if you like. Or by phone. It needn't take much of your time."

From somewhere nearby came the sound of a truck motor and loud male voices. Mark bent over to pick up a backpack that was leaning against the mobile command center.

"Or you could come over to our headquarters in College Station," he said. "I'm always glad to talk to reporters. We need you to get the stories out there." He shrugged into the backpack. "My phone number is in the email I just sent. Text or email me, phone, whatever. We'll find some time to get together."

"Hey, Mark." A man in jeans and a yellow shirt came around the command center.

"The rest of the team is here and the truck is loaded. You ready to head up to the fire?"

"On my way," Mark said. He resettled a backpack strap on one shoulder. "You'll be in touch, Jessica?"

At the sound of her name on his lips, Jessica caught her breath. "I will," she said. "Good luck. And be careful. I'm sure it's dangerous up there — Mark."

He smiled and gave her a quick thumbs-up. This time, she didn't need the touch of fingers to feel the electricity.

It was after five when Jessica got back to Pecan Springs, and the usually busy newsroom was mostly empty. This suited her just fines. She had a story to file.

She checked her notes, pulled up a Google map to confirm the fire's location, and began typing. It took about twenty minutes to draft the five-paragraph story for the online edition, including several minutes of lookup time to pick up references to the previous two fires believed to be set by the arsonist. She also included a link that explained why the Texas Forest Service was a part of Texas A&M University (because the legislature had said so, back in 1915), and another link that explained the term "Bambi bucket."

From her phone, she added the video she had shot at the briefing and the helicopter footage Mark Hemming had emailed, knowing that Jeff Dixon would edit the clips if he needed to. She paused over the video of the briefing. Mark Hemming wasn't handsome, not by a long shot. His mouth was too hard, his features too rugged. But he was an expert at what he did and incredibly . . . what was the word? She considered *dynamic,* then *forceful,* and ended, ruefully, with *sexy.* Not to mention *dangerous.* A relationship with him would be a risky affair. So did he have a steady girlfriend? A string of them?

But those were irrelevant questions. Pushing them out of her mind, she typed both Jeff's and Hark's names in the address line and added the subject. Jeff would do a quick edit and upload the story to the website, with the footage. Hark might ask her to expand it for the print edition — she had a couple of quotes from the briefing that she could add, plus copy for a sidebar on Bambi buckets. He could probably pull a good still photo or two out of the helicopter's aerial sequence.

Before she hit the send button, she glanced up at Dixon's glassed-in office next to Hark's, overlooking the newsroom. His office light was on and she could see him hunched at his desk, staring into a computer monitor. Maybe now would be a good time to pitch that story.

By the time she got to his office, he had

already opened her story file, read it, and made two small changes. "Good work, Jessica," he said as she came in. He was still looking at the two videos she had attached, but he took a break to listen to her pitch.

"Sounds like a promising story to me," he said when she had finished. He clasped his hands behind his head, leaned back in his chair, and stretched his legs. A good-looking, athletic guy with carefully styled blond hair and shrewd blue eyes in a tanned face, Jeff was dressed in pressed khakis, a red Maison Kitsuné polo shirt, and St. Laurent loafers. "Especially with wildfire season ahead of us. Got some stats?"

Jessica had Googled a few of the important facts before she left her cubicle. "On the list of states at high-to-extreme wildfire risk this year, Texas is second only to California. Last year, though, Texas was ahead of all the other states in the *number* of wildfires reported." She paused for effect. "Over ten thousand."

Jeff whistled under his breath. "How many of those were arson fires?"

"Still working on that," Jessica said. "The guy I met at the Hobart's Corner Fire this afternoon — Dr. Mark Hemming — has agreed to be interviewed. He's with the Forest Service and also teaches at A and

M. He'll be able to point me to more information." She paused. "It's your basic Smokey the Bear story about preventing wildfires, only this one will have the arson angle. Plus the tie-in to the Lost Pines fire."

"Smokey the Bear, huh? Maybe include a sidebar about his history? He was a real bear, you know."

"Sure, I can do that," she said. "I'll dig up a photo of him, too."

"Great. I remember Smokey from when I was a kid. 'Only you can prevent forest fires.' " Jeff dropped his hands, leaned forward, and hunched over the computer again. "Go for it, Jessica. It's all yours." He frowned. "But go home first. You've put in a long day. Get some rest before you dig into another one."

"Thank you," she said, glad to have his approval. And although she didn't take the time to examine the feeling, Jessica was also glad that the story gave her a reason to see Mark Hemming again.

Late last year, Jessica had moved from her upscale condo to a smaller house with a big yard in an older part of Pecan Springs. She had liked the condo well enough, but the investigation she'd worked on for much of the year had ended when the killer she was tracking, Howard Byers (aka the Angel of Death) had broken into her condo and attacked her. If it hadn't been for Ruby Wilcox and Ethan Connors, Byers probably would have killed her.*

Jessica had the locks changed, but she hadn't felt safe in the condo after that. And anyway, she had felt for some time that the place was too impersonal. The condo residents, most of them single and obsessed with their careers, had little inclination to be neighborly. Jessica wanted to live in a real house in a neighborhood where people noticed. And cared.

It took a while to find the right place. Her small house had a big yard shaded by live oak trees, a little herb garden beside the kitchen door, and a front porch with an old-fashioned white-painted porch swing and honeysuckle growing up the trellis. Inside, there were wood floors, a red-brick fireplace (with a tidy little gas log that didn't much resemble a real fire), and a pleasant sunporch off the kitchen, where she hoped her collection of houseplants might feel more at home than they had in the condo. To celebrate, she bought a sweet-smelling rose

* You can read the story in *Out of BODY,* the third novella in the Crystal Cave trilogy.

488

geranium, putting it where it could get plenty of sun.

The condo had forbidden pets, but now that she had her own house, there was no reason she couldn't have a cat. At the Humane Society one Saturday, she was adopted by a large orange tabby cat who went by the name of Murphy. Murph had very decided views on a cat's responsibility for his human. When the human was in the house, the cat should always be nearby (preferably in his human's lap), in case he was needed. A cat should definitely be needed. A cat should notice and care.

The neighborhood noticed and cared, too. Mrs. Robertson, an elderly widow with two iguanas and a cockatoo, lived in the tiny cottage on the left and regularly baked bread and made desserts that she shared with Jessica. The seven Knights (two parents, three adopted kids, plus two fosters) lived in the larger house on the right, with a red rooster and a half-dozen Barred Rock hens in the backyard. The hens laid so many eggs that Mrs. Knight was happy to share with Jessica, while the rooster, for his part, was glad to broadcast his dawn song to the whole neighborhood.

Elsewhere on the block lived a Latina nurse, a single mom with a teenaged son named Julio who had his own lawn-mowing business and who offered to mow Jessica's lawn — a big job — for half the cost of a lawn-care service. Across the street was a gray-bearded Harley jock with a plumpish Italian wife named Antonella and an elderly English bulldog named Victoria, both of whom (Antonella and Victoria) liked to ride in the Harley's sidecar. Antonella tended a large backyard garden, and Jessica could be sure of a daily basket of veggies on her porch during growing season.

This evening, Antonella's basket contained three svelte zucchini, two juicy tomatoes, and a sprightly bunch of green onions. There were several large brown eggs in the fridge, thanks to Mrs. Knight's diligent hens, and Mrs. Robertson had recently left her a loaf of the rosemary bread she baked in her slow cooker, to cut down on the heat in her kitchen. With all those goodies, supper was easy and quick: an omelet with zucchini and onions, sliced tomatoes, warm bread and butter, and a glass of wine. Murphy enjoyed a dish of kibbles in his corner of the kitchen, then joined her on a chair at the kitchen table, purring loudly while she ate. And all this while, outside the window, Julio was mowing the yard with an old-fashioned push mower that whirred and didn't spit out any engine exhaust.

"Nothing wrong with this picture," Jessica remarked to Murph. Nodding, Murph turned up the volume of his purr. He obviously agreed.

Supper over, the table cleared, and the grass cut, she paid Julio, adding a nice tip and praising him for a job well done. Then she brewed a cup of coffee, retrieved her notebook from her shoulder bag, and set up her laptop on the kitchen table. There was a little breeze and the evening had cooled off enough to leave the door and windows open. Jessica could smell the pleasant fragrance of fresh-cut grass. One of the Knights' hens was cackling triumphantly and the Harley guy across the street was revving his motorcycle — comforting noises that reminded Jessica that it was nice to live in a real neighborhood, surrounded by real people.

Five minutes after she sat down, Jessica had logged into the telephone search service and keyed in the disconnected phone number she'd found in Officer Riley's cellphone. Ten minutes and another couple of easy searches later, she was scrolling through a website that belonged to the anonymous caller who claimed that she had overheard somebody bragging that he had set the fire that killed Jessica's family.

The woman lived on a farm called Merry Llama Meadows on a country road about halfway between Pecan Springs and College Station. The website featured a calendar of farm events, testimonials praising the farm's owner, and photos of a dozen handsome llamas with names like Mama Mia, Merriweather, and MaryNelle. Their owner bred and raised them and harvested and sold their wool and her weaving in an online shop and on Etsy.

Her name was Claire Mercer.

CHAPTER SIX

Early the next morning, Jessica logged onto the Facebook page that Mark Hemming had mentioned and saw that the Hobart's Corner Fire was now fully contained, which meant that the incident commander was probably off the fireline and back at his desk. She texted him that her editor had approved her story idea and asked if he was available that afternoon. When he texted back that he could see her after he finished grading summer term exams, about one o'clock, she tried to stifle her pleasure. She didn't want to admit that it wasn't just the story that was taking her to College Station.

Which was definitely *not* a good idea, Jessica reprimanded herself, as she pulled on a blue blouse, ivory-colored slacks, and sandals. Dr. Hemming — Mark — had a decade more life experience than she'd had, plus a marriage, probably, maybe two, and maybe as many divorces. More to the point, there was something deeply unsettling about him. She hadn't seen enough of him to make a good judgment, but he seemed very different from Charlie (when she was a student), Kelly (her boyfriend of the previous year), and David Redfern (the lawyer she shouldn't be dating now). Mark wasn't just older. He was more mature, more experienced, more sure of himself, tougher, more in charge.

When it came to relationships, Jessica had always been pretty levelheaded. It was like setting off on a journey, she thought. It was good to know where you were going and what you were going to do when you got there. She had the feeling that a relationship with Mark Hemming would mean that *he* would be doing the driving and his partner would be along for the ride. That's probably why this felt . . . well, dangerous. It wasn't the smell of smoke, although maybe that triggered it. It was something more fundamentally threatening.

But she wasn't going to get involved with him. Number one, he was too old for her, by *several* years. And number two, it was entirely likely that he was already involved with somebody else. So there probably wasn't any harm in admitting to herself that there was something undeniably compelling about the man. She stared at her reflection as she put on some makeup, remembering what had happened when their hands touched.

But she wasn't going to linger on that. This morning, she had to focus on learning whether Claire Mercer was the woman who had called Officer Riley. And if she was, persuading her to disclose what she might have told Riley if the man had lived.

But Riley was dead, and the Georgia Shores cops had other things on their minds.

If anybody was going to investigate the fire that killed her family, it would have to be *her*.

As a reporter, Jessica had learned a long time ago that the trick to interviewing somebody who might not be especially keen on being interviewed was to show up on their front doorstep and start asking questions. This strategy wasn't always entirely comfortable. In fact, it had proved downright hazardous a time or two. But she learned much more when she caught people by surprise and they didn't have time to plan their answers. What she got was worth the risk, whatever it was.

Jessica's destination was about twenty-five

miles east of Pecan Springs. She turned west at a cluster of antique shops, barbecue joints, and a Fourth of July fireworks stand draped with red, white, and blue bunting and flying a Stars and Stripes almost as big as a bed sheet. Just past it: an official sign cautioning that the county was under a burn ban. Did people buying fireworks stop to wonder whether it was legal to shoot them?

Her route took her down a winding two-lane road that led deep into a mature stand of loblollies. It was just after ten in the morning when she drove past the farm's painted wooden sign (Turn Here for Merry Llama Meadows) and followed the gravel drive until it came to a dead end in front of a two-story farmhouse — old, but freshly painted white with jaunty blue shutters, a fire-engine-red front door, and pots of bright marigolds and daisies on the porch steps. Its old-fashioned charm was enhanced by a tangle of pink roses that tumbled across the porch roof and a cottage garden that filled the front yard with hollyhocks, zinnias, and lavender. Behind the house, Jessica could see a large red barn, and off to one side was a fenced pasture — presumably, the outdoor home of the merry llamas.

Jessica drew a deep breath, slung her bag over her shoulder, and got out of the car, feeling both apprehensive and eager. This visit could be a massive waste of time. But if Claire Mercer *was* the anonymous woman who had telephoned Riley, and if her claim was true, the odds of finding the arsonist who killed her family might have improved — dramatically. The thought that she might be closer to that discovery made Jessica's mouth go dry and her heart pound.

The front door opened and a woman came out on the porch, an alert-looking black-and-white border collie at her heels. She appeared to be a couple of years younger than Jessica, in her mid-twenties. Of slight build, she was dressed in green bib overalls, a yellow T-shirt, and work boots. Her long, taffy-colored hair was tied back in a bouncy ponytail and freckles — attractive freckles — were scattered across her nose.

"Hello, Ms. Carter," she called cheerfully as she came down the path. "I wasn't expecting you for another few hours, and the llamas are still in the pasture. We can walk down there to meet them, but I'd rather show you the studio first."

The border collie, interested in Murphy's feline scent, was sniffing around Jessica's shoes. The woman frowned at the dog. "Stop that, Minx. Ms. Carter doesn't want to be sniffed." The dog sat on her haunches as the woman bent over and peered into Jessica's car. "Your photographer didn't come with you?" She sounded disappointed. "I thought we were going to do a photo shoot."

Jessica put on a pleasant smile. "I'd love to see the studio, Ms. Mercer. And meet your llamas, too. But I'm not Ms. Carter, and I don't have a photographer." She could hear the nervousness in her voice and hoped it wasn't obvious to the other woman. "I'm here because you told a Georgia Shores police officer that you overheard a guy bragging that he'd set the fire that killed three members of the Nelson family in Georgia Shores over twenty years ago." She held out her hand. "I'm Jessica Nelson. Officer Riley told me about your call."

The young woman put out her hand automatically, and then dropped it. "Jessica . . . *Nelson*?"

"Yes. The people who were killed in that fire were my mother and father and twin sister, Ginger — our dog, Rascal, too. I was away on a school trip that weekend, so I was spared. But I've lived with the fire every day since it happened. I'm hoping you can help me find out something more about the arsonist."

Claire's eyes widened. "Your *twin*? Your mom and dad and —" She glanced at her dog. "Oh, good lord," she whispered. "I never thought — I mean, I didn't —" She broke off, staring at Jessica. "Wait a minute. Jessica Nelson. I think I've seen you on TV. Aren't you the reporter who's been writing about that awful serial killer? And didn't you actually *nab* him?"

"The police nabbed him," Jessica said. "But yes, I worked on the investigation. And you probably saw my interview on KXAN when he was arrested. But I'm not here as a reporter. This thing about the fire — it's very personal. Our conversation today is totally off the record. And confidential."

"That's good, I guess. But I still don't —" Claire looked puzzled. "Hey. I changed my cell number and I didn't give that cop my new one. How did you find me?"

"I spent a few minutes doing research online." Jessica was always surprised when people failed to understand just how much of their personal information could be found on the internet. She gestured toward the house. "Could we go inside and talk?"

"I don't know whether that's such a good idea." Claire bit her lip apprehensively. "It might not be . . . healthy. For either of us."

"Not healthy?" Jessica raised both eyebrows. "What makes you say that?"

Claire stuck her hands in her pockets. "Look," she said. "I really don't think we ought to be doing this. In fact, maybe you ought to just leave. I'm sorry you got involved."

"Why shouldn't we be doing this?" Jessica was startled. "What are you afraid of?"

"Are you friggin' kidding me?" Claire demanded gruffly. "That cop I talked to — Riley, his name was. He got killed, didn't he? Shot to death, right there on the street in Georgia Shores, just a couple of days after I talked to him! I mean, I don't know any of the gory details, but I saw part of it on TV. The guy was definitely *dead.*"

Jessica shook her head. "I hear what you're saying, but —"

Claire raised her hand. "My phone ran out of juice when I was talking to him. I really did intend to call him back and give him my new number. But when I heard what went down, I was glad I hadn't. I don't know about you, but I don't aim to get *shot.*"

"But Riley's shooting had absolutely nothing to do with your telephone call," Jessica protested. "It was an entirely different thing — some guy went psycho at a traffic stop and started shooting. What's more, the man who shot Riley can't make bond. He'll stay in jail until his trial. And after he's convicted — well, shooting a cop is capital murder in Texas. He'll be over in Huntsville. On Death Row."

"Oh." Claire looked at Jessica. "This is all straight up? You're telling me the truth?"

"Scout's honor." Jessica held up three fingers. "Call Officer Loomis — Beverly Loomis — over in Georgia Shores. She'll verify. Riley's killing had nothing to do with your phone call."

There was a moment's silence. Then: "Duh." Claire made a face. "Guess I jumped to conclusions. Stupid me."

"Not at all," Jessica said. "It could have been bad reporting, you know." She grinned slightly. "Reporters don't always get the facts right. And it's not surprising that Riley's murder got connected — in your mind — with your phone call. I don't blame you for feeling scared."

"Well, maybe." Claire shook her head, looking disgusted. "Or I could be watching too many cop shows." She gave Jessica a crooked smile. "There's lemonade in the fridge. Come on in." She looked down at the dog. "You, too, Minx."

Trailed by Minx and with Jessica following, Claire kept up a chatter as they went into the house. She had inherited the farm from her grandmother, who had also been a weaver and spinner. But the llamas were *her* idea, and she hoped someday, when she had a little more money to invest in a stronger herd sire, that she could build a better breeding program.

"Since it's just me, I live upstairs," she said with a wave of her hand. "I use the whole first floor of the house — with the exception of the kitchen, of course — as my spinning and weaving studio."

They paused in the door of what had once been the dining room, where Jessica spotted a spinning wheel beside a chair at the sunny window, surrounded by baskets of roving and batts of fluffy carded fleece in a rainbow of colors. A rack on one wall held a dozen hand spindles, and another wall was papered with photos of Claire's llamas, along with a dozen blue and red show ribbons. Through the open door into another room, Jessica could see a pair of weaving looms, one portable, the other quite large and heavy. Skeins of hand-dyed yarn and samples of Claire's weaving and knitting hung on every wall. To Jessica's eye, the young woman was extremely talented, and she said so.

"Thanks." Claire grinned briefly. "The llamas get credit for it, too, you know. I just wish there was more money in it. I'd love to do it full time."

On a first-name basis by this time, they took their glasses and a pitcher of lemonade and settled down in comfortable chairs on the screened-in back porch. A mesquite tree with delicate green leaves and ivory-colored blossoms stood just outside. The tree was covered in bees, and Jessica could hear them buzzing as she sat back in her chair. Minx flopped at Claire's feet.

"Okay if I take notes?" Jessica asked, pulling out her notebook. "Still off the record," she added. "Just for me."

"I get that this is personal to you," Claire said slowly. "But what are you going to do with the information? That fire happened a long time ago. Riley seemed interested, but he's dead."

Jessica had already thought about this. "I'll keep on working on it. When I've gotten to the point where I think it's time to involve the police, I'll connect with Officer Loomis. I know it's a cold case, but there's no statute of limitations on murder."

Feeling more confident now that she understood the story, Claire answered Jessica's questions, slowly at first and then without hesitation. The llamas were the love of her life and Claire considered them —

and her spinning and weaving — to be her day job. But they couldn't begin to bring in enough money, and while she was hoping to build up the demand for raw fiber and handspun yarn on Etsy and in her new online shop, she had to have other work. She enjoyed waitressing, and she could make a little extra with tips. So she worked two or three nights a week in Pecan Springs, in the restaurant that was part of the Old Firehouse Dance Hall.

"Oh, sure," Jessica said. "I know that place. I've been there dozens of times." The Old Firehouse used to be a real firehouse, back when Pecan Springs was smaller. Across the street from Bean's Bar and Grill, it was famous for its cleverly named burgers (The Arsonist, Hook and Ladder, Firestorm, Platoon Meltdown) and for the country music bands that played at the dance hall on weekends. Lyle Lovett, Joe Ely, Garth Brooks — at one time or another they had all played to the dancers who packed the Firehouse floor.

"I overheard this guy talking about the fire when I was doing their table," Claire said. "They'd had supper and a few beers. He was telling his friend that he was the one who set the fire at the Nelson house in Georgia Shores."

Jessica held her breath. She was looking at a woman who had actually *seen* the killer.

"He was just a kid when it happened," Claire went on, "and he didn't mean to burn down the house." She took a sip of her lemonade. "He only meant to set fire to the garage."

Only. Jessica could feel her pulse racing. "His intention doesn't count," she said softly. "He's a murderer. My family is dead and he's still free."

Claire leaned forward and put a sympathetic hand on Jessica's arm. "I am so sorry, Jessica. I can't imagine how awful it must have been. You were just a kid yourself."

"I'm an adult now and it's still pretty awful," Jessica said. She swallowed hard. This part held an unexpected hurt. "In his notes on your phone call, Riley wrote that you heard the guy say *why* he decided to burn the place."

"Yes. He said he did it because he was pissed off at one of the twins." She squeezed Jessica's arm and pulled her hand away. "He didn't say which twin. He just said that she was too la-di-dah to go out with him. That she only had eyes for a friend of his, some guy who worked at the ice cream parlor."

"The ice cream parlor?" Jessica asked sharply. "He must have been talking about

505

Sean Scott, who worked at Dopey's. Sean was a couple of years older, and really cute. Ginger had a thing for him, although I doubt that he had a clue." She made a face. "He seemed to be into cheerleaders in a big way."

But if the arsonist and Sean had been friends, or even just acquaintances, Sean would surely know who he was. And Jessica knew where she could reach Sean — at the marina in Georgia Shores.

"This guy you overheard — did you recognize him? What does he look like? Does he have a name?"

Claire shook her head. "I'd never seen him before. The man who was with him called him Shorty, but I didn't hear a last name. They paid cash for dinner and drinks — no credit card."

Shorty. Not enough, but it would do for starters. "Description?" Jessica was taking rapid notes.

"Oh, gosh." Claire rolled her eyes. "Well, he was kind of a little guy, I guess you'd say. Not much of a build. Pretty skinny. I didn't see him standing up but I'd guess that he wasn't any taller than me."

"And you are —"

"Five-five in my sandals."

"His hair?"

"Sort of a muddy blond. A little long around the ears. He wasn't the kind of guy who stands out in a crowd." She snapped her fingers. "But actually there was something, come to think of it. He had a tattoo on his neck — his shoulder and arm, too, maybe. He had on a blue work shirt so I couldn't see that part. I did see it on his neck, though."

"What kind of tattoo?"

"Flames. Red, mostly. Red and yellow. Some blue." Claire pulled up one leg of her jeans and stuck out her ankle proudly. "See the heart tattoo I got last year? I really like it, and I've been thinking of getting another. But not fire." She shook her head. "Not for me."

"Which shoulder?"

"The left one."

"And you saw this guy when?"

Claire furrowed her brow, thinking. "The first or second weekend in February. I thought about it for a couple of days, wondering what I should do. Then I called the Georgia Springs police. That's how I got connected with Officer Riley."

Jessica remembered that Riley had called her on Valentine's Day, so the timing fit. "The two guys. Are they regulars at the Firehouse? Had you seen either of them before? Have either of them been in since?"

"They're not regulars, no." Claire shook her head. "I might not recognize the other guy. But I'm sure I haven't seen Shorty again. He's not much to look at, but I'd notice his tattoo." From inside the house came the chiming of a clock, and she looked startled. "Oh, gosh. I forgot about Ms. Carter. She's coming to interview me and take some pictures. She'll be here in a few minutes and you haven't met the llamas yet." She put her glass down. "Ready?"

"You can't think of anything else?" Jessica asked, closing her notebook. "Something that might help me find this guy?"

"If I do, I can text you, can't I?" Claire stood up. "Come on, Jessica. I know you will *love* the llamas. They are such gentle souls."

CHAPTER SEVEN

She did enjoy meeting the llamas. They were friendly and interesting — especially Mama Mia, who allowed Jessica to hug her. It would have been fun to get acquainted and to see more of Claire's spinning and weaving work. And fun to connect her with Lori Lowry, a textile artist who had a studio in the loft above China's and Ruby's shops back in Pecan Springs. Maybe Claire could sell some of her yarn there, or offer a guest workshop on spinning or weaving. And maybe this could turn into a feature story about a weaver-spinner who used the fleece from her own herd of llamas. She would suggest it to Fran, for the *Magazine.* And Jeff would probably want it for the online edition.

But Claire was obviously thinking about her next appointment. And it was time that Jessica headed for College Station and the campus of Texas A&M University, where she was to meet Mark Hemming. Claire's help had been unexpectedly valuable, and when Jessica left, she knew a great deal more than when she'd arrived.

Most importantly, she knew the man's nickname, Shorty, and that he wore a fire tattoo on his right shoulder and neck. Had he chosen that image because of what he had done to her family? She also knew that Shorty knew Sean Scott — or at least, that the two had known one another when they were in high school. Which suggested that Sean should be able to tell her Shorty's full name and where she could find him. Sean might even have some information about the fire — rumors, if nothing else.

In fact, Jessica was tempted to call Mark Hemming and cancel their appointment, then turn around and drive straight to the marina at Georgia Shores for a serious conversation with Sean.

No, she wasn't going to do that. Jeff Dixon was expecting to see the story she had pitched him. She would get the Hemming interview done and start on the wildfire arson story before she took another step in her own investigation.

But to tell the honest truth, she couldn't be sure whether it was the story she was pursuing — or Mark Hemming.

■ ■ ■ ■

Jessica picked up a quick fast-food lunch, then headed for Hemming's office, which was on the west side of the sprawling A&M campus — at over five thousand acres, one of the largest in the United States. Following her GPS through a maze of inner-campus roads, Jessica found what she was looking for: the rectangular, many-windowed, sand-colored Horticulture and Forest Science Building, surrounded by well-tended research gardens and an expansive greenhouse complex. She parked, got out, and headed for the building. She was fifteen minutes early, but if he wasn't ready for her, she could wait.

Hemming's office was on the third floor, on a balcony that overlooked a lofty, light-filled atrium. The door was closed, but his name was on it, so she knew she was in the right place. She hesitated before she knocked, bracing herself — against what? Really, she was being very silly. This was only an interview, and interviews were her forte, weren't they?

What's more, there was nothing especially daunting about this one. Mark Hemming was a source, that's all. She had already made up a list of questions she wanted to ask him for the story she had outlined in her mind — the usual Smokey the Bear fire-prevention story, with an arson twist. Wild-fires were bad for the environment and bad for people. Arsonists were truly evil and had to be caught.

She pulled in her breath and rapped.

A deep male voice barked, "Door's open. Come in."

Surrounded by messy piles of books and papers on every available flat surface, Dr. Hemming was sitting in his chair with his feet up on his desk, his back to the door. He was reading a blue exam booklet.

"Grab a seat." He spoke without looking up. "Gotta finish this last one."

Feeling like a student, Jessica sat, watching him. He was dressed in faded jeans, a plaid shirt with the sleeves rolled to the elbows, and a pair of scruffy-looking, ash-streaked boots that looked as if he'd worn them on the fireline. His dark-rimmed reading glasses had slid to the end of his nose. He hadn't shaved since yesterday, but she could still see the jagged scar on his jaw.

In fact, everything about the man was rugged and rough-edged. Not cute and sweet and mostly manageable like Charlie and Kelly or handsome and sophisticated and gallant like David Redfern. He was . . . older. He was strong and hardened and experienced, as if he'd been to the wars and back more than once and was ready to go again, whenever and wherever he was needed.

Which of course he had been doing just the day before. Fighting fires must be a lot like fighting a war, Jessica thought. Fire was the enemy, a terrible enemy that had to be defeated every time it blazed up. The fire-fighters were soldiers in the battle.

Liking the sound of that, she pulled out her notebook and jotted it down. She glanced around the office, quickly making notes for the story: overflowing bookshelves, a cork bulletin board filled with photos and tacked-on notices, a large poster of a raging forest fire that made her shudder. There were several photographs on his desk. An older couple sitting on a porch — his parents? A smiling boy in his teens, wearing climbing gear and perched on a rock. His son, maybe? She looked for a photo of the boy's mother but didn't see one.

He slapped the booklet shut, scrawled a large red D+ on the cover and tossed it on the stack. "Hell's bells, Jake," he growled, "you'd think these kids could at least read the assignments."

She couldn't think of anything to say except "I'm not Jake."

He dropped his boots to the floor and spun his chair around, scowling. "You sneaked up on me, Jessica." He looked up at the clock over the bulletin board. "And you're early."

"You told me to come in and grab a seat," she said, feeling even more like a student, and not a very bright one at that. But at least he'd remembered her name.

There was a brief silence. Then, "Yeah. I thought you were the guy from the office next door, returning a book. Sorry about growling at you." He glanced at the exam. "For me, the worst damned thing about teaching is marking the finals. I hate to see how I failed some of these kids. Makes me cranky."

"*You* failed them?" She was surprised. How did that work? "I thought it was the other way around."

He shook his head. "They're all capable of doing well, but I didn't make them care about the subject. Which is a friggin' shame, don't you think? Everybody on the planet ought to care about forests." He took off his reading glasses and dropped them on the desk. "Anyway, today is the last day of the first summer term. All I have to do is turn in my grades and I'm done until August. Done shaving until August, too," he muttered, rubbing a hand over one cheek. "I can get out into the field."

She wondered how he would look in a beard, then pushed that silly, irrelevant thought away. " 'Everybody ought to care about forests,' " she said. "Can I quote you on that, Dr. Hemming?"

"Thought I told you to call me Mark," he said gruffly. "But sure. Quote me on that. Caring about forests is the sermon I preach all day long." He cocked his head to one side, looking at her. "So tell me what you pitched to your editor."

Jessica briefly outlined the story for him — a straightforward piece of reporting that used Smokey the Bear, the disastrous Lost Pines fire, and the current series of arson fires to illustrate the central premise: that Texas wildfires are a genuine threat and must be suppressed.

"Except that they aren't, really." He clasped his hands behind his head and leaned back in his chair.

"Wait — what?" Jessica said. "What did you say?"

"What I'm about to say," he replied, "is that fire is a natural and essential part of an ecosystem's development. Many plant species in fire-affected environments require fire to germinate and reproduce. Wildfire suppression not only eliminates these native species, but also the animals that depend on them." He was watching her. "Forests need fire. Prairies need fire. Texas needs fire."

"Hang on." Jessica was writing as fast as she could, but it was hard to keep up. "Texas needs fire? Is that what you said? That's not what I —"

"I know." He dropped his arms and leaned forward, an amused expression on his face. "It's what we've all been taught, right? 'Only you can prevent forest fires.' Smokey the Bear says so."

"Exactly," Jessica said, scribbling faster. "Most readers will remember Smokey from the time they were kids. He's the first thing everybody learns about forest fires."

"Of course. The trouble is that Smokey taught everybody that fire is always harmful. It's an enemy we have to wipe out."

"It . . . isn't?" she asked, staring at him.

"It *isn't,*" he repeated firmly. "The PR campaign that produced Smokey has led to decades of fire suppression and fuel-filled forests and infernos fierce enough to wipe out entire human settlements. Every time we put out a small fire, we're kicking the can down the road. We're creating the potential for a fire that can grow to unimaginable strength." He frowned accusingly at her. "Your eyes are glazing over."

Jessica shook her head. "Actually, it's my hand, not my eyes. It just can't keep up. If you're going to keep on lecturing, would you mind if I recorded you?"

He laughed comfortably. "You caught me. It's my regular rant. But sure. Go ahead and record, so you can get it right."

He waited until she pulled out her phone and set it for recording. Then he said, "Look. What I'm saying is that the old ideas about managing the environment are based on the notion that any disruption in an ecosystem — fire, for instance — unbalances things, throws nature out of kilter. But in many natural habitats, fire isn't disruptive at all. The environment is created and sustained by fire. The plants and animals that live in those habitats have adapted to fire and in some cases actually *need* it. Lodgepole pine cones, for instance, can't open unless they're exposed to fire temperatures. Eucalyptus, too. Fire destroys the old trees and prepares the way for new ones."

"Wait." Jessica held up her hand. "You're saying that suppressing fire is *bad*? We need to forget about Smokey?"

"What I'm saying is that suppressing fire results in more unforeseen consequences for natural ecosystems than anybody imagined back when Smokey earned his badge and fire shovel in 1944. In fact, a few years ago, Smokey's message got tweaked. Now, instead of 'Only you can prevent forest fires,' it's 'Only you can prevent *wildfires.*' "

"That's a pretty subtle difference." Jessica wrinkled her forehead. "What's it supposed to mean?"

"Yeah. Subtle is the word for it. They're trying to make a distinction between bad fires — wildfires that are intentionally set or occur because of somebody's carelessness — and naturally caused or controlled burns that promote healthy forests. But that still leaves us with a flock of head-scratching questions. Set aside the question of how the fire got started. Once it starts burning, should it be contained or should it be allowed to burn? Protecting human life goes without saying. But if somebody chooses to build a house in fire country, at what cost should it be protected?"

He paused and grinned, and his dimples flashed. "There. Deep background, as you journalists say. So let's hear your questions."

Jessica stared at him, distracted by the dimples, which made him look younger, almost boyish. But he was saying something that bothered her. Bothered her very much.

"*Allowed* to burn? You're not talking about . . . houses, are you?"

"Of course not. We can't stand back and let people's houses and businesses and schools and churches burn. That's off the table. But maybe those houses shouldn't have been built there in the first place. Should restrictions be placed on where people can build? But here's the thing —"

He broke off abruptly, pursing his lips and glancing critically at her feet. "Nice-looking sandals. But I don't suppose you've got a pair of sneakers in your car."

Taken aback, Jessica stammered, "Well, yes, actually. My tennis shoes are in the —"

"Fine." He got up. "Bring your stuff and come on."

"Where are we going?" She turned off her phone and closed her notebook. Her mouth felt dry and her breath was uneven. Excitement?

Yes. But she was apprehensive, too. He was so . . . take-charge. Authoritative. Sure of himself. Not at all like —

"You'll see, Jess." Already at the door, he spoke over his shoulder. "You'll learn something. And it'll be an adventure. Guaranteed."

■ ■ ■

It was. An adventure, that is.

And she did learn something — quite a lot, in fact.

Mark (it still felt strange to call him by his first name) drove an almost new light blue Dodge Ram crew cab pickup, about twice as long and high as her Kia, with a camper shell over the truck bed. Jessica climbed into the passenger's seat and settled back. The electronics in the dash and overhead console looked like they belonged in the cockpit of a two-engine aircraft: GPS and weather radar display, computer, dash cam system, flasher light, satellite radio, CB radio, even a police scanner.

"Wow," she said, glancing around. "Do you have to take flying lessons before you can get out on the road with this baby?"

"Yeah." Mark chuckled as he started the motor. "There's a lot. But everything has its uses, believe me." He tipped his head toward the rear. "I keep my gear in the back, so I'm ready to jump in and drive off when there's a fire or when I can get a couple of days away from the desk for research. I can sleep back there, too. Saves on motel bills, gives me more hours to work."

Behind the wheel, Jessica thought, Mark seemed . . . well, different. Take-charge, yes. Mature and experienced, yes. Expert in his work, definitely. But older? Not so much. In fact . . .

She stole a glance at him. He was so *macho,* his shoulders and arms muscled under his plaid shirt, his slender hips, his thighs —

Her face flushing, she pulled her glance away quickly and concentrated on the road unwinding in front of them.

They drove out to what Mark called the "burn lab," some twenty miles south of the campus on a narrow, badly rutted dirt road that wound through two starkly different landscapes. On the south side of the road, to her right, she could see nothing but the charred ghosts of a burned forest, blackened hulks in a blistered landscape.

Mark slowed the truck to a crawl. "That fire was caused by arson two years ago. It was a high-intensity, active crown fire that burned so hard and so hot that it destroyed most of the loblolly seed cones, sterilized the surface layers of the soil, and volatized the organic nutrients. It was classified as a severe burn, which means that loblolly regeneration won't occur naturally. Left to itself, the area will eventually be repopulated with hackberry, blackjack oak, juniper, and mesquite. But loblolly, no." He pointed. "And see that gulley over there? It formed in a recent flash flood event. Before natural reforestation can take place, erosion can completely alter an area like this one."

On the left side of the road, the view was altogether different. This forest, too, had been burned, and Jessica could see the skeletons of dead trees. But the landscape was a lively green. The forest floor was alive with plants and shrubs and understory trees. And when Mark stopped the truck and they got out to walk, Jessica saw plenty of young green pine trees — loblolly pines, Mark said — pushing out of the ground.

"We did a prescribed burn in this section of the forest three years ago," Mark said, "the year before the big crown fire across the road. It was a low-intensity burn that crept through the litter on the forest floor, taking out a lot of brush, shrubs, small trees, and the lower limbs on the pines." He bent over and gently lifted a thorny vine. "The burn also encouraged the new growth of native vegetation, like these little wild blackberries here, which are eaten by squirrels, raccoons, and skunks — birds, too. What's more, the fire killed off several non-native invasives, such as Japanese honeysuckle and giant reed. And this burned-over area served as a barrier against the further spread of the fire on the other side of the road."

They walked deeper into the green forest, which held a residual coolness even in the very hot afternoon. As they walked, Mark talked, and Jessica found herself grasping a little of his passion for his work. He was an ideal interview subject, she discovered. He liked nothing better than answering an intelligent question, often 'at great length. Then he would break off with a quick, self-deprecatory "Pardon the rant. I get carried away."

The afternoon sped by quickly, and by the time they were back in the truck, her notebook was full and her phone held dozens of photos and more than an hour of recorded conversation. But she still had a couple of questions, and she asked them as they headed back to the campus.

"The fire yesterday," she said. "The one at Georgia Shores. You were doing the briefing, but you're a professor. So how come?"

"I regularly work with the Forest Service on prescribed burns. Yesterday, the guy who normally does the briefing was needed on the fireline. I was at the site, so I stood in for him."

"You said it was an arson fire, one of a series. How do you know? That they're a series, I mean."

"Because this arsonist is using a similar device in every fire. It's a layover device made up of a cigarette — Lucky Strikes for this guy — with five or six Diamond matches laid across it. As the cigarette burns down to the matches, they ignite, one after the other. It's pretty damned effective, especially when it's planted in a patch of dry grass." He paused, giving her a sidewise glance. "But that's off the record, Jessica. We don't want to alert him to what we know about his methods. And we don't want to encourage copycats."

"I get that." She paused. "Any chance of finding DNA on any unburned cigarettes or matches?"

He eyed her approvingly. "Good question. The arsonist who started the 2006 Esperanza Fire was convicted on DNA found on an ignition device — got a death sentence, too. Twenty counts of arson, seventeen for the use of incendiary devices, plus five counts of first-degree murder. I was in California at the time. I saw that fire. It was apocalyptic. Something like that can change you forever."

"I know," Jessica murmured, turning her

head so he could not see the sudden tears that had come to her eyes. But he appeared not to notice.

"So DNA is always a possibility," he went on. "Nothing so far, I'm afraid. But this morning, investigators were able to find two of the ignition devices used in the fire you saw yesterday. They're being tested now, by a forensic arson tech at the DPS Crime Lab in Austin."

It was nearly five when they reached the A&M campus, and Mark pulled up alongside Jessica's Kia. He turned off the motor and smiled at her. "You've been a good sport this afternoon, Jessie. I hope you got what you needed for your story."

"I did," she replied. "More than I expected. And I enjoyed it. Thanks for all the information."

He grinned. "Even the lectures? Sorry. I get all fired up." Realizing his pun, he chuckled ruefully. "Apologies. It's just that . . . well, fire's my passion. Wasn't always, but it is now."

For a moment, she hesitated. She was suddenly tempted to tell him that her interest was more than academic and that it had less to do with the story she was writing and more to do with her own personal tragedy. That she had lived with the fear of fire her whole adult life.

But she held back. For one thing, she didn't know how he would respond. He was accustomed to working with fire, to using it, to seeing its beneficial side. He would probably think that her fear was just silliness. Anyway, what had happened to her was so intensely personal that she had rarely shared it with anyone who didn't already know the story. She barely knew this man. She had actually been intimidated by him — by his air of authority, his self-confidence, his self-assurance. Why would she even consider sharing her story with him?

He was turned toward her, an arm draped over the steering wheel. "Hey, I was just thinking. I'm doing some work over on the CTSU campus tomorrow, in Pecan Springs." He gave her a boyish, tentative grin that revealed his dimples. "I wonder if you'd maybe like to go out to dinner together."

Jessica stared at him in silence as her heart went into hyperdrive. She had met Mark Hemming only the day before. Now, here he was, asking her for a date. She bit her lip. Or maybe it wasn't a date he had in mind. Maybe he was thinking of finding himself in Pecan Springs on an evening when he had nothing special to do and he just wanted some company, a couple of hours with —

But she had hesitated a little too long. He frowned uncertainly. "Oops, sorry. I'm probably stepping into something here. I should have guessed that you're seeing somebody. Forget I said anything."

"No, wait." Jessica took a breath. "I'm not seeing anybody." Remembering her recent date with David Redfern and feeling that for some reason she needed to be honest with this man, she amended her answer. "Not exclusively, I mean. That is, I —"

She met his eyes. Another breath. It felt like stepping through a door. Or off a cliff. "Yes. I'd like to have dinner with you, Mark."

"You . . . would?" His gray eyes were on hers with an intensity that surprised her. "Awesome," he said, and smiled as if he meant it. "I'm not sure what time I'll get finished on the campus — it depends on a couple of other people over there. How about if I text you in the afternoon? We can figure out what time and where we'd like to eat." He put up a hand and rubbed his cheek. "Guess I should shave, too," he muttered. "I don't always look this scruffy."

"Oh, don't," Jessica heard herself say, with some surprise. "Remember? You're on vacation until August." She smiled as she opened the door. "And besides, I like it."

CHAPTER EIGHT

It was one of those you-have-to-be-there-to-believe it mornings. The Texas sky was a cloudless, crystalline blue, and the temperature was a moderate eighty-one, with the promise of the mid-nineties by mid-afternoon. Tropical Storm Debby was still hanging off the coast east of Brownsville, which meant that there would be plenty of wind again today. An ideal sailing day, Jessica thought, as she parked her Kia at Scott's Landing just after eleven. Her heart wrenched as she remembered the many beautiful mornings, just like this one, when she and Ginger had pushed their Sunfish into the water and sailed out onto the lake.

She had gone into the newsroom early that morning to write the first of the three stories she planned from the material she had gathered from Mark and supplemented with online research into the history of Texas wildfires. As usual, the place was alive

529

with the buzz of voices on phones, the noise of the copy machine, and the low mutter of a pair of TVs on the wall, one tuned to CNN, the other to Fox, a third, in the break room, to MSNBC. They were a *newsroom,* Hark had always insisted. What happened to DC and New York and Chicago and Los Angeles happened to Pecan Springs, too — just not right away. It was their job to be ahead of the curve.

But for a change, there had been no apparent crises or emergencies, unless you counted the impending threat in the Gulf east of Brownsville. Debby's forecast track was uncertain, though, and tropical storms were notoriously unpredictable. It could blow inland into Texas or head north toward Louisiana. Nobody knew, so there wasn't any point in getting excited about it yet.

Jessica submitted her story, checked her inbox, her calendar, and the assignment board, and chatted briefly with Jeff Dixon to make sure she had covered everything. Tomorrow, there were a couple of court hearings she had to attend and a press conference the DA had just scheduled, but there was nothing urgent going on for the rest of the day. Glad that she had worn casual clothes — khaki slacks and sandals, a teal blue tank, and a loose mesh see-through cardigan in shades of brown and blue — she had signed out, taking the rest of the day as personal time and noting her destination as Georgia Shores. With luck, she would be able to connect with Sean Scott. There was a good chance that he knew Shorty, the guy Claire Mercer had told her about. The guy who had bragged about torching her house.

When Jessica was a girl, Scott's Landing had been a sleepy little marina, with only three or four short, narrow wooden docks, a few small motorboats and sailboats moored alongside. A dozen kayaks and canoes had been stacked beside the bait shop, along with a couple of the paddleboats that were always popular with tourists. In the bait shop, Mrs. Scott had sold live bait and fishing tackle and was always glad to direct an out-of-town fisherman to the fishing guide service offered by Pete Lemke, who lived a couple of blocks away on Main Street, behind the barber shop. Lake Georgia was famous for its striped bass, and Mr. Lemke had a reputation for finding trophy fish. Jessica remembered when he'd hooked a thirty-two-pound striper, the record for the lake. The *Beacon* had run a front-page story with a three-column photo of a proud Mr. Lemke and his impressive fish.

The bait shop was still there, Jessica saw, although it was now called the Ship's Store and offered snacks, soda, beer, and ice. You could also buy boating accessories and life jackets, as well as fuel, bait, and fishing tackle. There were twice as many canoes and kayaks on their racks, the paddleboat fleet had tripled, and a double-decker party boat with powerful twin motors was moored at the end of one of the docks, for rent by the day or half-day.

And at the top of the asphalt ramp that used to slope down to the free public boat launch, there was now a locked gate. It bore a large sign: MEMBERS AND GUESTS ONLY. Underneath, in smaller letters, *For Day Use or Sail-In Docking Fees, Check with Manager.* Through the gate, Jessica could see ten or twelve long wooden piers jutting out into the blue water, each one berthing a couple of dozen boats — small sailboats, yachts, and motorboats of all sizes. Down the shore to the left, she saw a covered dock, so the more expensive yachts berthed there were out of the rain. Scott's Landing had obviously undergone some major upscale changes over the years since Jessica and Ginger had launched their little Sunfish from a nearly deserted public ramp.

There would be plenty of wind for sailing

today. The morning was filled with the sound of waves slapping boat hulls, halyard fittings clanking against aluminum masts, and the shrill cries of gulls high overhead. Several sailors in shorts and swim trunks were rigging their boats to go out, and on the water, a pair of sailboats were beating into a hard breeze.

Jessica looked around and saw a sign pointing to the manager's office, a small, white-painted frame building near the Ship's Store. The door was open and she knocked on the doorframe. A man sat at a desk in front of a wide window, giving him a good view of the marina's docks. There was a computer on one side of the desk, and he was running a calculator, expertly. Hearing her knock, he turned around.

"Yeah?" he said amiably. "How can I help you?"

Sean Scott had changed even more than his marina. Still tall and blond, he was attractively dressed in yacht-club whites: white pants, epaulettes on his white short-sleeved shirt. But the lean teenager with the cute butt had disappeared and in his place was a man who was carrying an additional sixty or seventy pounds. His cheeks were round and flushed, his arms were fleshy, and a ponderous belly overlapped his belt. It wasn't lunchtime yet, but there was a bottle of Coors at one elbow. At the other, half a glazed doughnut and a thick ham sandwich with one very large bite missing.

"Hi, Scott." Jessica smiled. "I'm not sure you'll remember me. When we were kids, my sister and I used to sail our Sunfish out of your marina. And you used to make banana splits for us at Dopey's."

Scott's mouth fell open. "Jeez," he whispered, staring at her. "You're . . . But I thought you were . . ." His voice trailed away uncertainly. His eyes were round.

Half amused, Jessica let his unfinished question hang in the air, waiting to hear if he was actually going to say "I thought you were *dead.*" After a moment, she said, "I'm Jessica. Ginger was my twin. She's the one who died in the fire." She said it deliberately, watching him.

He exhaled noisily. "Jeez," he said again, reaching out with a pudgy hand and picking up the Coors. "Man, for a minute there, you got to me. I thought you were a ghost. You look exactly like I figured you'd look if you hadn't —" He stopped, looked at the bottle, and put it down again, shaking his head.

"Except maybe prettier," he finished awkwardly. He jerked a thumb toward a metal folding chair. "No point in standing. Pull up a chair and have a seat."

"I'm surprised that you remember," Jessica said, putting the chair beside the desk where she could see his face. "Ginger and I were just a couple of little kids to you, I'm sure. We were at least two years younger, maybe three. You never seemed to pay attention."

"Remember you?" He raised both eyebrows at the question, sounding halfway indignant. "Damned straight I remember you. Summers, you two girls were always out there rompin' around in your skimpy little red bikinis. Hot as a pair of firecrackers. Boobs and bottoms round like —"

The flush on his face deepened and he looked away. "Sorry," he muttered. "No offense. Just sayin', you know. You might've been only kids, but you was pretty good at handling that little Sunfish." He gave her a self-conscious grin. "I was probably trying to play it cool, but yeah, sure, I remember you."

It was almost funny, Jessica thought. She remembered Sean from Dopey's, standing behind the counter in a white apron and a white paper soda-jerk hat. He remembered them in their bikinis.

"Ginger's was blue," she said.

"Blue, was it?" He seemed to have regained his composure. "It's the red one sticks in my mind. That's how come you got the extra cherry on your banana split. Whipped cream, too."

"On *my* banana split?" Jessica asked in surprise. "I thought that was for Ginger."

"Oh, hell, no. *You* were the one I had my eye on. But I couldn't just give extra to you, now could I?" He leaned back in the chair, his appraising glance moving over her. "I reckon this is your first time back to Georgia Shores. I woulda noticed you, if you'd been around."

She nodded and repeated what she had told Cam Riley about going to live with her grandmother in Louisiana, then going to college in Pecan Springs. She didn't mention the *Enterprise*.

"Actually, I'm here about the fire," she said, watching his face closely. "The fire that killed Ginger and my parents." She took a breath. "Maybe you remember it?"

"Nobody's ever forgot it." He gave her a sober glance. "Awful thing. Did they ever figure out how come it got started?"

"Not yet." She folded her arms. "But I heard yesterday that some guy has been talking about it."

"Talking about it?" Sean narrowed his

536

eyes. "Talking like how? Who? Where?" Was there something sinister in his voice?

"Like how he set the fire, when he was a kid." She didn't answer his other questions. "I came to you because I thought you might know him, Sean. He goes by the name of Shorty. He has a fire tattoo on his right shoulder."

Sean blinked. "You're sayin' that some kid . . . that this guy Shorty says he set the fire?"

"Yes. He set fire to the garage. He didn't mean for it to spread to the house, but it did. That's his story, anyway." She paused. "Do you remember a kid called Shorty?"

"Not that I can recall." He frowned. "What makes you think I would?"

"Because between working at Dopey's and here at the marina, you probably knew every kid in town." She was watching him, thinking that — whatever else he might be concealing — he seemed to be telling the truth about this. "And because he mentioned you."

"Me?" His mouth tightened and he held up both hands, palms out. "Now, hang on just a damned minute there. You're not accusing me of —"

"Nobody's accusing you of anything, Sean." Jessica took a deep breath. "This guy

537

says he torched the garage because he was pissed off at one of the twins. He said that she was too la-di-dah to go out with him. That she only had eyes for his friend." She paused. "The friend who worked at the ice cream parlor."

"She only had eyes for —" He narrowed his eyes. "But I wasn't the only guy working there, you know. Dopey used to hire any kid who was dumb enough to work for seventy cents an hour. That guy could have been talking about half-a-dozen of us."

"I know that," Jessica said evenly. "But *you* were the one Ginger had a thing for, Sean. She was too shy to let you see it, but I saw it. Shorty must have seen it, too, and it made him jealous. And angry. He set the fire to get even."

"Hell's bells." Sean had been staring at his beer bottle. Now, he picked it up and took a swig. "I had no idea your sister had the hots for me." He squinted at her — or was that a leer? "You were the one I had my eye on. You and that red bikini."

Jessica didn't know what to say. *She* was the one Sean had been interested in? Her mouth was suddenly dry and her chest felt tight. Did that mean that she might be the twin whose imagined rejection had sparked enough anger to kindle the fire?

And she was the twin who had survived. It had never seemed fair. She shivered. Now it seemed even more unfair. Was her fire phobia a punishment for being both the cause and a survivor?

"About this Shorty guy." Sean put the beer down again. "What does he look like?"

"Around five-five, maybe." Claire had only seen him sitting down. "Slight build, muddy blond hair. He has a tattoo. A fire tattoo, on his right shoulder and up his neck."

Sean shook his head. "Not ringing a bell. I didn't know anybody who had a tattoo in those days, except maybe things kids would draw on their arms with ballpoint. Seems like there was several short guys who hung around Dopey's, and maybe half of them was blond. And no, in case you've got a different idea in your head, I never heard nobody bragging about doing it. Setting the fire, I mean."

He leaned forward, elbows on his knees, now deeply earnest. "You listen to me, Jessica. What happened back then, it was damned awful — the fire, I mean, your family bein' dead. The whole town talked about it for months. Hell, for *years*. There'd never been nothing like it in Georgia Shores. It was a first. And I never knew a thing about it except what people said or what I read in the *Beacon*. You got that? I never heard of no Shorty or what he said or anything else. I don't know nothin'."

Jessica took a breath. "So was there a second?"

"A second?" He rubbed his chin, confused. "A second what?"

"A second fire. You said it was a first. Were there any others?"

Sean sat back in his chair. "If you mean, did anybody else die," he said slowly, "the answer is no. But was there more fires?" He furrowed his brow. "Well, yeah, there was the landfill fire, although the sheriff said that could've been spontaneous combustion, or maybe just a cigarette or some smoldering ashes that caught fire. I don't recall anybody saying for sure it was arson."

"When was that?"

"When? Best I recall, a couple of months after your fire. Burned all summer and it was still burning weeks after school started. Smelled awful. Real bad for my mom, who had asthma." He paused. "Come to think of it, though, the kayaks were before that."

"The kayaks?"

"Yeah." He pointed out the window, toward the stack of colorful kayaks. "The kayaks we've got now are made out of fiberglass, but back in the day, they was made out of marine plywood. Pops had six of 'em stacked up next to the bait shop, out of the way. One night, somebody pushed a pile of brush and trash under the stack and lit a match. Whole thing went up fast, made a big blaze. Would've made an even bigger blaze if it'd caught the bait shop, but old man Lemke and a couple of his buddies was coming back from night-fishing on the lake and saw it burning. They got to the payphone we used to have down there by the dock and woke up the volunteer fire department. The chief said another few minutes, we could've kissed the bait shop goodbye. And back then, Pops didn't have no insurance."

Jessica was making mental notes. "When was that?"

Sean tugged at his upper lip. "Three, four weeks after your house burned, as I remember it." He stared at her. "Wait a minute. Are you sayin' that whoever set your fire set them others, too?"

"I'm just asking. *You're* saying."

Jessica regarded Scott steadily, wondering if he would make the connection: that the arsonist had torched the Nelson house because of Ginger's interest in him. And then torched the kayaks at his family's marina because of jealousy toward Scott. But

541

he only gave her a blank look.

"Anything else?" she asked.

"Fires, you mean?" He shook his head. "If there was, I'm not remembering. And no Shorty, neither. Coupla short kids, but no Shortys." He paused, reflecting. "Unless he went by another name back then. I'd have to think about that."

Jessica was disappointed, but she wasn't leaving empty-handed. The kayak and landfill fires might be the work of the same arsonist. She jotted her private email — not her *Enterprise* address — on a piece of paper and put it on the desk. "Let me know if you think of something that might help fill in some of the blanks." She got up. "Okay?"

"Yeah, sure." He eyed her up and down, his glance lingering on her breasts, then stood, hitching up his white pants. "Listen, Jessica, I got me a real neat Rhodes 19 with a fixed keel — real neat little one-design racer. I keep it in a wet slip so it's ready to launch any time. How about if we take it out. Sunday afternoon, maybe?" He grinned jauntily. "It'll be fun, big time. I guarantee."

"Thanks for the invitation," she said. "I'll keep it in mind."

"Good. I'll drop you an email, see if we

can set us up a date." His grin widened. "If you've got a red bikini, wear it."

Jessica had never considered her red bikini at all sexy. It was just what she wore when she went sailing, and when she moved to Louisiana, her grandmother had thought it was immodest. She'd never owned another after that.

And she'd had no idea that *she* was the intended beneficiary of all those extra cherries and whipped cream. That *she* might have been the twin whose fancied slight had prompted the arsonist to do what he did. The thought of it made her feel sick.

She was still thinking about this when she parked her car in front of the library and got out, bending into the hot wind, which seemed to be blowing harder than ever. The American flag beside the library steps was streaming straight out. She would have to check to see if the forecast had changed. Maybe Debby was heading inland. If so, Hark would put the newsroom on alert. Tropical storms could bring flash flooding. People died in flash floods.

The Georgia Shores Carnegie Library was one of the few buildings in town that looked exactly the way she remembered it: a red-brick building with a red-orange tile roof, a double front door, and four white arch-topped windows across the front. It had been built in 1914 for the grand sum of $7,500, designed and paid for by the Carnegie Corporation. In that library, Jessica and Ginger had met Nancy Drew and the Baby-Sitters Club and Elizabeth and Jessica (of course!), the Sweet Valley twins. There, they had graduated to *Anne of Green Gables* and *Pride and Prejudice* and *To Kill a Mockingbird.* In fact, the library's copy of *Little Women* had gone up in flames with their house. The day before she'd left for Louisiana, she had paid Mrs. Sanders, the head librarian, $2.35 for the lost book.

Mrs. Sanders no longer sat behind the checkout desk in the hushed main room, but to Jessica's surprise, she recognized her replacement, an attractive young woman her own age with shoulder-length dark hair and round, gold-rimmed glasses that gave her a bookish look.

"Hazel?" Jessica asked. "Aren't you Hazel Gorrell?"

"Oh, my golly, it's one of the Nelson twins!" the young woman exclaimed in a breathy voice. "You must be —" She stopped, frowning. "I guess I don't remember which one . . . ." She didn't finish her sentence.

544

Jessica regarded her for a moment, waiting. "It was Ginger who died," she said finally. "I'm the other one. I'm Jessica."

"Oh." Hazel wrinkled her nose, trying not to look embarrassed. "Oh, sure. Jessica. Well, gosh." She gave Jessica a half-accusing glance. "The thing was that you left town so quick, you know? You didn't come back to school. None of us kids had the chance to say goodbye or sorry or anything. And most of us didn't really know . . . like, which one of you was . . ." She swallowed. "Dead, I mean."

For an instant, Jessica was tempted to tell Hazel that it was Jessica who had died and she was really Ginger. Or that both Jessica and Ginger had died, and she was their composite ghost — which in a way might be closer to the truth than she liked to think. She swallowed the impulse.

"It wasn't my idea to leave," she said with a rueful smile. "I didn't have any family left here, so I had to go live with my grandmother. It was a really hard time."

"Well, it's not like it was your fault or anything," Hazel said, trying to be reassuring. "You had to do what you had to do." She paused. "Are you in town on a visit? Looking for something specific? Maybe I can help."

Jessica had already decided that it wasn't a good idea to be specific with Hazel. "I understand that the *Beacon* folded a while back," she said. "But I was thinking that the library might have some of the old issues on microfiche."

"Oh, sure," Hazel said brightly. "We've got all of them, from way back when, from the beginning, I guess. But not on microfiche. We're not that up to date. They're just the old newspapers, in the basement." She pointed off to the right. "Take the stairs over there, and when you get down to the bottom, it's the shelves on the right." She opened a drawer and pulled out a small flashlight. "It's kinda dim down there, so when I have to look for something, I take this. Oh, and watch out for spiders. It's spider territory down there."

Jessica accepted the flashlight. "Is there a machine to make copies, if I find something interesting?"

"Sure." Hazel opened the drawer again and pulled out a counter. "The copier is at the bottom of the stairs, to the left. It's sorta old and creaky, but it usually works. Plug this in and it'll count your copies. You can leave the money in the box on top — twenty cents apiece. If the thing gives you trouble, bang it real hard on the right side, just above the switch. Or whistle and I'll come down-stairs and give it a good hard kick."

The basement smelled like damp mold and was, indeed, badly lit, with fluorescent bulbs that did little more than cast flicker-ing shadows. The *Beacon* had been a weekly, and all fifty-two issues in a given year were bound into a single leather-covered volume. Jessica used Hazel's flashlight to search for the year she wanted, which she located on a bottom shelf near the basement's back wall. The year was stamped on the cover in gold, and one corner had been thoroughly chewed by a mouse. She carried it to the back-corner table, sat down in a rickety wooden chair, and opened the cover.

She found her family's fire easily, for the story occupied the full front page of one of the March issues. Tears flooded her eyes and she had to catch her breath when she saw the photographs of the burned house and pictures of her parents and Ginger. But if she'd been hoping for details about the fire or its investigation — the ignition source, for instance, or any suspects the cops might have questioned — she was disappointed. It was the kind of superficial write-up that any cub reporter could have whacked out in half an hour. The only thing of interest was the comment by the chief of the volunteer fire department that the fire started in the garage, in a pile of gasoline-soaked rags. The next week's coverage, on page two, was briefer and no more detailed. By the third week, the story had drifted to page three.

There was much more information about the kayak fire at Scott's Landing — a pair of before-and-after photos as well as several quoted comments from the VFD chief, who said that the fire had been intentionally started by a cigarette "carefully placed" on top of a pile of flammable trash under the kayaks. It was a "delaying arrangement," the chief said, that allowed the arsonist to be "at least a couple of blocks away by the time the fire got good and started."

A delaying arrangement, Jessica thought, thinking of the ignition device Mark had described at the fire scene a couple of days before. She also remembered what he had said about the wildfire arsonist. "Once somebody like him gets started, he doesn't stop until he's caught."

The story about the landfill fire was even more detailed, because (although Sean hadn't remembered this), the guy who was supposed to manage the dump had seen somebody in an old blue truck — he didn't get a license plate number — dumping a load of trash at the place where the fire flared up overnight. It began in mid-June and burned until late September, and the *Beacon* reported on it each week. The cause? Nobody was willing to say for sure, and the VFD's fifty-dollar reward was never claimed.

So what about the Georgia Shores arsonist, if there was one? *Had* he stopped? Sean had remembered only three fires, including hers, but were there others? Jessica went through the rest of the *Beacon*'s issues in that year's volume. In November, just a little over a month after the landfill fire was out, there was another blaze, set in one of the outbuildings at the high school. Again, according to the VFD chief, the arsonist had used a "delaying device" — a candle this time.

She pulled the next year's volume of *Beacons* from the shelf and leafed quickly through it, but that was it. Four fires. Not proof, exactly, but a trail of events that suggested that the fire that killed her family had been one of a series, maybe — or maybe not — the fist, but apparently not the last.

She sat for a few moments, thinking. Mark had said that a serial arsonist doesn't stop until he's caught. But this guy *hadn't* been caught. So why had he stopped setting fires in Georgia Shores? Had he moved on? Had he continued to set fires, somewhere else?

Out of a reporter's compulsion to document her findings, meager as they were, she turned on the copier, inserted the counter, and copied the articles about her family's fire, the first and last pieces on the landfill fire, and the stories covering the other two. She replaced the volumes, dropped three dollars into the box on top of the copy machine, and climbed the stairs.

"Hope you got what you were looking for," Hazel said cheerily, when she returned the flashlight.

"Yes, thank you," Jessica said. She half-turned to go, then hesitated. "I was wondering, Hazel — do you remember a boy called Shorty? He might have been a couple of years ahead of us."

"Shorty?" Hazel screwed up her face, thinking. "Well, there was this guy that a few kids called Shorty. Most everybody called him Peewee, though. He was pretty skinny." She smiled a little. "We used to give him a hard time."

"What was his last name?" Jessica asked. Peewee wasn't exactly Shorty, but the meaning was similar. It was a place to start.

"Last name?" Hazel pulled down the corners of her mouth. "Oh, gosh. You *would* ask that. He was in my brother's class — a sophomore when I was in eighth grade. He moved away someplace, California, maybe? But he's back. I saw him over at Sweetie's the other day. If you'll wait, his last name is right on the tip of my tongue." She pushed her tongue out and licked her lips, as though to prompt her memory. "Peewee . . . Peewee . . ." she muttered.

Jessica picked up a scrap of paper from the desk and wrote her private email address on it. "If you think of it, maybe you could drop me an email," she said.

"How come you're asking?" Hazel asked, tucking the scrap into a pocket. "I mean, school was a long time ago."

"Oh, just curious," Jessica said vaguely, and turned to go. She was almost to the door when Hazel raised her voice.

"Hey, I remembered it," she called. "Paine."

Only half-hearing what Hazel had said, Jessica turned. "Sorry," she said. "What was that?"

"Peewee's last name," Hazel said. "I remember it because the kids used to tease him about being a pain in the butt. He was Paine, with an *e* on the end. Peewee Paine."

CHAPTER NINE

Jessica opened the door of her Kia and held it, letting the heat spill out in an almost visible flood. Then she tossed the copies onto the back seat and slid under the wheel. It was the middle of the afternoon and she hadn't had any lunch. Maybe a sandwich from Subway? She put the key into the ignition. While she ate, she could strategize ways to locate Peewee Paine, assuming that's who she was looking for.

And then she had to head back to Pecan Springs. She hadn't yet gotten a text from Mark about plans for that evening — something she had tried her best not to think of all day. The man was terribly attractive, yes. She had to admit that.

But in spite of the pleasant hours they'd spent together yesterday afternoon, there was still an aura of something like danger around him. It was like trying to balance on a narrow ledge, with a long way to the ground. Was it his age, and the baggage that came with the years — a marriage or two, maybe, a son. Or maybe his work with fire. Fire was his *thing,* wasn't it? He didn't just teach it, he lived it. She shivered. Maybe it wouldn't be smart to go out with him. Maybe she should just —

Her thought was interrupted when she looked up and saw something that caught her attention. Across the street from the library, sandwiched between Sweetie Pie's (which used to be Dopey's) and the AT&T store, she saw a small shop. On the front window was painted, in large, elaborate gold letters, *The Final Frontier Tattoos and Piercings.*

Tattoos. Shorty sported a fire tattoo on his shoulder.

Startled, Jessica pulled the key out of the ignition, remembering that she had noticed the shop when she came to the police station to talk to Beverly Loomis, just the day before yesterday. Then, of course, she'd had no idea that it might be significant.

Was it significant. There was only one way to find out. Her heart beating fast, she got out of the car and walked across the street.

The Final Frontier was open and brightly lit, with walls painted a rich gold and hung with dozens of colorful, fanciful photos of tattoos, framed like pieces of art. On one side of the room, two brown leather sofas sat facing each other across a coffee table stacked with art books and tattoo magazines, with a coffee bar and a large rack of piercing jewelry nearby. On the other side, there were two small privacy cubicles, just large enough for a brown leather recliner, a small table holding a tray filled with tattoo and piercing instruments, and a work chair and a magnifying lamp. Beyond them, a larger cubicle with a table, like a massage table.

As Jessica paused, a door at the back of the room opened and a young woman came out, smiling. She wore her brown hair in a buzz cut and was dressed in black leggings and a tight-fitting, short-sleeved black top that showed off her tattooed neck and floral sleeves. She smiled brightly.

"Hi. I'm Candy. Are you thinking of getting some piercings? Or maybe a tat?"

"I have a tattoo," Jessica said. "See?" She pulled aside her mesh cardigan to display her roses.

"Very nice," Candy said appreciatively.

"I like it." Jessica gazed at Candy's arms, covered with elaborate red and yellow flowers, green leaves, and brown vines trailing down the backs of her hands and onto her fingers. "It's not as impressive as yours, though."

Which was definitely true. Candy's tattoos were an attractive advertisement for what she was selling. She held out her arms, turning them so Jessica could admire.

"Carl did them," she said. "He's one of our tattoo artists. Does awesomely *epic* work, don't you think?"

Jessica nodded. "Do you think maybe Carl could do something for me? I saw a guy the other day — Shorty. Flames on his left shoulder and on his neck. Maybe something like that?"

"Oh, sure," Candy said easily. "Carl actually specializes in flames. Let me show you." She led the way to a group of framed photographs. In a practiced tone, she slipped into what was obviously her sales pitch.

"Fire is a natural element that symbolizes destruction, renewal and rebirth, and secret knowledge. It can blaze out of control like a wildfire — like passion. Or it can be warm and comforting, like a fire on the hearth. Lots of guys like fire tats, of course, but flames can be a *very* meaningful tattoo for a woman." She gave Jessica a searching look. "Just imagine what a flame tat would say about *you*."

Jessica bit her lip. What would a flame tattoo say about her? Would it signify renewal and rebirth, the way Mark Hemming obviously thought of fire? Or would it be an eternal reminder of how fire had destroyed the three people she loved? Finding no answer to those questions, she looked at the tattoo photographs, all in full color — red and orange flames, mostly, some blue. There were all sizes, from quite small to very large, some encircling arms and legs. One amazing blaze even covered the person's entire bare back, buttocks, and legs.

"Wow," Jessica breathed, in genuine astonishment. "Just. Wow." Why would anybody decorate his — or her — body in such an *invisible* way? Invisible to others until you took your shirt off. Invisible even to the person who was wearing the artwork. The only way you'd see it was by looking in a mirror.

"Yeah," Candy said proudly. "Carl does simply amazing work. I'm sure you'll be pleased."

Jessica took a breath. "I wonder if maybe he did Shorty's fire tattoo," she said. "It's really outstanding."

"Shorty?" Candy tilted her head. "I don't remember a client by that name."

"I met him over in Pecan Springs, but he's

from this area," Jessica said. "I can't remember his last name." She hesitated. "Paine, maybe?"

"Oh, sure," Candy said immediately. "That's Wendell Paine — and yes, he's pretty short, for a guy. He moved back here from San Diego last fall and Carl did a fire tat on his shoulder." She picked up a photo album and began to page through it. "I think there's a photo here. Wendell says he's going to make it a full sleeve when he can. Large tattoos take time, you know." She turned a page. "Yeah. Here it is. Wendell and his fire tat. Cool, isn't it?"

Wendell Paine. The photo showed a man, seated, his face turned halfway away, the flames licking up his bare shoulder onto his neck. Jessica's knees felt suddenly wobbly. Had she finally found the arsonist who killed her family? Was *this* the man? She took a breath, steadying herself, trying to sound casual.

"Yes, cool," she said. "He was a couple of years ahead in school, so I didn't really know him. He's living in Georgia Shores now?"

"Yeah, with his dad, Wendell Senior. Poor old guy's got cancer. Wendell came home to take care of him." Remembering her job, Candy went on. "Of course, Wendell's tattoo is really great, but you'll want something that's uniquely *you.* When would you like to get started?"

"Not this week, I'm afraid. I have to —" Jessica heard the ping of her cell phone and pulled it out of her purse. It was a text. From Mark. Without reading it, she thrust the phone back into her bag.

"Oops, gotta go," she said. "Give me a card and I'll call you for an appointment when I can spot a free afternoon on my calendar."

"Easy peasy," Candy said with a bright smile, and picked up a business card from a holder on the table. "Just give me a call, and we'll set it up."

"Will do." Jessica took the card and turned to go. "Thanks for your help, Candy," she added, over her shoulder. "I'll be back."

As she left, she was determined to do just that. And when she did, she would ask Carl to give her another tattoo, someplace where *she* could see it. But whether it would be a flame or something else, she hadn't decided.

Back in the library parking lot, Jessica got into her car and checked her phone. The text from Mark was short and to the point.

Beans @7? Need address 2 pick u up.

He didn't mean that they would be eating beans for dinner, of course. He was telling her that they would be eating at Bean's Bar and Grill, the most popular place in Pecan Springs. Jessica felt her breath come faster, although she couldn't have said whether it was from anticipation or anxiety — or a mix of both. She thought for a moment of simply ignoring his text. But that wasn't quite fair, was it?

She pondered for a moment, then texted back.

ok but meet u there @7:30.

It was already almost four o'clock, and she needed to go to the newsroom before she went home to change. She'd be cutting it close. Anyway, driving her own car would give her more flexibility. It meant that she wouldn't have to depend on him to take her home after dinner. It would send him a message.

What message, exactly?

She started the car. She didn't want to think about that right now.

By the time Jessica got back to the *Enterprise* newsroom, the place had almost emptied out for the day, except for Will Wagner, who was still on the telephone. And Jeff Dixon, who could be seen in his glassed-in office above the newsroom. Denise Sanger was leaning over his shoulder — a little close, Jessica thought — and he was pointing at something on his computer monitor. It looked like Denise — dressed uber-stylishly today — might be up to her old flirtatious tricks with the new boss.

Jessica gave Will a hello wave and settled into her cubicle to check her mail (mostly junk) and clean up her email (nothing very important). That done, she checked the assignment board and the Pecan Springs and Adams County arrest blotters, both of which listed only the usual DWIs, family violence, and a residential break and enter. There was nothing more on the tropical storm and nothing much else going on. It had been a slow news day, except for a nasty three-car pileup on I-35, and Heather and Virgil had covered that. Tomorrow, a couple of court hearings and a press conference would keep her busy. But the next hour-and-a-half belonged to *her,* and she put it to good use.

Tracking Wendell Paine, aka Peewee and Shorty, might have been difficult for the average person, someone without a newspaper's investigative resources. But Jessica was an experienced reporter who knew how to use the search tools on her phone and computer. It didn't take long to dig up the man's essential information.

High school was easy. A photo of Wendell Paine ("Peewee" to his high school friends) appeared in the Georgia Shores high school yearbook, archived online. Paine had a pimply, unmemorable teenaged face, brown hair swept back to reveal a distinct widow's peak, and narrow, girlish shoulders. In a lineup of the varsity basketball team, he was easily the shortest boy in the photo. Jessica studied his face, finding nothing familiar in it. She had no memory of him at all. And to think that he'd torched their house because he thought she — or Ginger — had rebuffed him. The pointlessness of it made her feel sick.

But Wendell appeared in the school yearbooks only in his freshman and sophomore years. If he was ever questioned about any of the fires in Georgia Shores, that fact was lost in the mists of time — at least in this initial search. He turned up again on the other side of the country, as a junior in the accounting program at San Diego City College. He was living with his mother in Escondido, one of the city's suburbs, and earning recognition for his academic performance by Beta Alpha Psi, the national financial services fraternity.

In his next public appearance, Paine was featured in a page-two story in the *San Diego Union-Tribune*. He rescued three young women trapped in a mountain campground surrounded by a raging wildfire — with only one road in and out. He showed up on the front page a couple of months later, accepting an award for the rescue. She paused over that story, wondering about the coincidence of a suspected arsonist who rescued somebody from a fire. Whatever that connection, a year after the award, he and one of the young women he'd rescued were married in a ceremony that the *Union-Tribune* covered as a news event, on page three.

After that, the tracking got a little more complicated. Having finished college, Paine found a job in the accounting department at Qualcomm, a major San Diego employer, commuting from Escondido. But his real passion seemed to be moonlighting as a firefighter in the county's volunteer program.

She blinked. *Wendell Paine, with his possible connections to the fires in Georgia Shores, had become a firefighter?* Had the man reformed and decided to dedicate himself to the service of the community? In any event, before long, he was taking courses — and doing quite well — at a regional emergency training center, where he gained National Fire Protection certification. He even earned enough certifications to qualify as an instructor in the center's programs and gain some featured coverage in the local paper.

But at home, things weren't going so well. Jessica turned up a couple of reports of police summoned to the Paine home and then, a divorce, in which Wendell's ex-wife was granted custody of their two young children. After that, for a period of four years or so, Paine no longer seemed to be working at Qualcomm, and she could find no evidence that he was serving as a firefighter, paid or volunteer. He had disappeared — until he showed up back in Georgia Shores the previous autumn and began living with his father, Wendell Paine, Senior, in a duplex on MacArthur Street. He did not appear to be employed.

Jessica glanced up at the clock on the newsroom wall. It was almost seven, and she had filled in everything but that puzzling gap of several years in Wendell's personal and professional history. She had already given up her earlier plan of going home to change clothes. What she was wearing — her casual khaki slacks, teal tank, and mesh cardigan — would do for Bean's, which was a down-home place. She would have to leave in a few minutes if she didn't want to be late, so there wasn't time to open a more extensive background check search program that would yield all of Paine's past addresses, the names of his relatives and their contact information, his marital history, and any bankruptcies or criminal history.

But there was time for one more quick search. And that was when she found it, on the San Diego NBC Channel 7 site. A terse and intriguing three-sentence paragraph buried in the middle of a four-year-old story headlined "Looking for Answers in the San Diego Wildfires":

On Friday, 31-year-old Wendell Paine of Escondido pleaded guilty to three counts of attempted arson in connection with three small fires he set in the hills near Escondido. Paine, a volunteer firefighter and instructor in the regional emergency center, was fined $10,000 and sentenced to three years in prison. Police found no evidence linking him to the half-dozen other fires in the Escondido area in the past three months.

Jessica shook her head. Three years for attempted arson? It sounded as if the California courts were serious about punishing arsonists. And while the cops couldn't link him to the half-dozen other fires around Escondido, that didn't mean he hadn't set those, too — and others over the years, along the way.

But if Wendell Paine was the Georgia Shores firestarter, he had obviously *not* reformed. How often did firefighters become arsonists? It seemed quite incredible to her.

Still, he had been arrested and convicted. She looked again at the date on the article. If Paine had been imprisoned in California right after he was sentenced, he would have been released sometime last fall, which was just about the time he returned to Texas to live with his cancer-stricken father, acquire a flame tattoo at The Last Frontier, and confess to a friend, in Claire Mercer's hearing, that he had torched the Nelson house.

Jessica logged off and shut down her computer, remembering that Claire Mercer's testimony was hearsay evidence and admissible in court only as an exception to the hearsay rule — an exception that was highly unlikely. So how could she connect Paine to the murders of her family, so many years ago? There had to be another way, but what was it? What *was* it?

Still asking herself that question, she left the newsroom and was hurrying to her car when her cellphone dinged. The call was from Beverly Loomis, the police officer from Georgia Shores.

"Jessica, I'm glad to tell you that we've found the Nelson House Fire case file," she announced, sounding elated. "One of the officers stumbled over it in the records room. It was misfiled."

Misfiled! Startled, Jessica leaned for a moment against her car, trying not to over-react. "That's great," she said cautiously. "Is there . . . is there anything useful in it?"

"Maybe," Loomis said. "Photographs of the scene, investigator's notes, interview statements. Oh, and a matchbook. In an envelope."

Jessica unlocked the door and got in. "A *matchbook*?"

"Yeah. Along with a note about where it was found — in a tin can several feet from the ignition point. There's a photo of the can with the matchbook in it."

"Does the matchbook have any advertising?"

"Yes," Loomis said. "It's from Scott's Landing. And it still has traces of fingerprint powder on it."

"Which means that it was fingerprinted?" Jessica hazarded.

"Yes, exactly!" Loomis said. "There's also a copy of a fingerprint in the file. Pete Remmick — he was the investigator — must have lifted it from the matchbook." The exultant note in her voice grew stronger. "And there's more, Jessica. Not long after the fire at your house, a stack of kayaks were torched next to the bait shop at the marina. After that, a fire in an outbuilding at the high school. The notes are in the file, too. It looks like Remmick suspected Sean Scott, but didn't have enough evidence to charge him."

"The fingerprint isn't Scott's?" She thought of her conversation with Sean, who had replied to her probing questions without any evidence of guilt. And of Wendell Paine. Had she jumped to too many conclusions about him?

"Apparently not." Loomis sounded a bit deflated. "But there may be another print there that a more modern technology will turn up."

"But *why*?" Jessica asked. "The marina belonged to Sean's family. And the school — why in the world would Sean do it?"

"Remmick found out that Sean and his dad had had a big argument and the kid had been grounded — just before the kayak fire. Plus, Sean had had a run-in with the school principal. He couldn't handle authority, seems like." She paused. "Anyway, you'll be glad to hear that we're bringing Sean in for an interview. We'll print him again, and get the matchbook tested for latents. For DNA, too. That kind of testing wasn't available to Remmick back then, but a lot of cold cases are being solved that way now." She gave a satisfied chuckle. "I'm betting that we can connect that matchbook to Sean. And when we do, we'll have our guy."

"Hang on a minute, Beverly. I've been doing some digging and I —"

Loomis broke in. "I knew you'd want to hear this so I called you right away. Keep a lid on it, though. This is all off the record for now. I'll call you the minute we have more information. Goodnight."

And she clicked off.

CHAPTER TEN

In Jessica's current state of mind, it was amazing that she was able to find her car and drive to the restaurant without causing an accident. As it was, she was ten minutes late when she opened the door and stepped inside, her heart still hammering.

Bean's Bar and Grill (named for the notorious Judge Roy Bean, who once claimed to be the "only law west of the Pecos") was Pecan Springs' favorite place for barbecue and Tex-Mex food. It was crowded tonight, as usual, with people lined up at the old-fashioned saloon bar and filling more than half of the tables. The air was rich with the spicy smell of grilled cabrito and the mellow sound of George Strait on the jukebox, singing "This Is Where the Cowboy Rides Away." Bean's was the right place for a private conversation, as long as you sat shoulder-to-shoulder with your friend and talked under the music, the buzz of loud voices, the clatter of dishes, and the sharp crack of cue balls from the pool tables in the back room.

It was a few moments before Jessica saw Mark sitting in a corner, a beer on the table in front of him. He stood when he saw her and put up a hand. He was wearing a black blazer, a black T-shirt, and black jeans. He still hadn't shaved, so there was a dark stubble across both cheeks. The sight of him made her catch her breath.

"Sorry to be late," she said breathlessly, sliding into the chair he held for her. It was an unexpected courtesy. Kelly and David had never held her chair. "I got caught up in some research."

"Oh, yeah?" He pulled his chair closer to hers, smiling. "Must have been something pretty intense. You're flushed." He grew serious, his eyes searching her face, as if he were reading her thoughts. "You look like you could use a drink. What can I get you?"

"I'll have a margarita," she said shakily, and looked up to see Bob Godwin, Bean's owner, coming in their direction.

"Hey, Jessica," Bob said. He grinned at Mark, and Jessica understood that they knew one another. "You buyin' for this pretty little lady, Hemming?"

On an ordinary day, Jessica (who counted

Bob among her friends) would have reminded him, teasingly, that she was taller than he by about two inches and not much of a lady, either. But tonight, frazzled, she let it go.

To Bob, with an easy grin, Mark said, "Yep, I'm buying. She'll have a margarita." He gave Jessica a concerned glance and added, "And we're taking it slow this evening. Give us a plate of nachos and another ten or fifteen minutes before we order."

When Bob had gone, he reached across the table and put both hands firmly over Jessica's fingers. Under the warmth of his hands, hers felt icy cold.

"Something's happened to upset you," he said in a low voice. His pale gray eyes were on her face. He wasn't smiling. "I'd like to help if I can. Want to tell me about it?"

Suddenly, she did. His concern was warm and his maturity and age, instead of seeming threatening, calmed and steadied her. As he held her hands, the whole story came tumbling out in a rush. About the fire that killed her family when she was a girl, and the marina and landfill and school fires that followed. About Officer Riley's telephone call last Valentine's Day, and his death. About her visit with Beverly Loomis, her talk with Riley's pregnant wife, and her search of Riley's phone records. About what she had learned from Claire Mercer at the llama farm, from Sean at Scott's Landing, and from her afternoon visits to the library and the tattoo parlor — all of which had led to Wendell Paine.

At that point her margarita arrived. "Drink," Mark directed, releasing her hands. "You'll feel better."

Still shaky, she took several grateful sips of the salty-sweet-sour drink, then a deep breath and another sip. Bob Godwin appeared with a plate of hot nachos: corn chips topped with seasoned ground beef, refried beans, onions, tomatoes, jalapeño peppers, shredded cheese, and sour cream — served with bowls of guacamole and pico de gallo.

"Time to eat," Mark commanded. "Don't talk."

Fortified by several nachos, she said, "There's more to the story." She took a deep breath and began again.

More slowly and deliberately now, she told him what she had discovered that evening in her online search. About Wendell Paine's move, with his mother, to California, his rescue of the young women trapped by the wildfire and his marriage to one of them, his work as a volunteer firefighter, his divorce, his arrest for arson, his prison sentence, and his return to Georgia Shores. And then about Loomis' call, the recovered police report, the matchbook and fingerprint. By the time she finished, Jessica's heartbeat had slowed, her breath was under control, and she was almost calm again. The only thing she had left out were her panic attacks. At this point, her fear of fire somehow didn't seem to be an important part of the story.

But there was something else. "Loomis says they're bringing Sean Scott in for questioning," Jessica said. "I tried to tell her about Wendell Paine, but she was in a hurry to end the call. I'm afraid they'll get stuck on Sean and won't want to take a look at Wendell Paine."

From the beginning, Mark had been listening with an intense interest. Now, his jaw tightened and he wore a darkly serious look. "Sounds like your guy Paine is the real deal, Jessica. Real and *dangerous.* Are you going to tell Loomis what you know about him?"

Dangerous. There was that word again, although this time, in a different context with a very different significance. But what *was* she going to do?

Jessica let out a long breath. Now, with

her steadiness somewhat restored, she said, "I understand that Paine is living in Georgia Shores with his father. Tomorrow, I'll phone Beverly Loomis and tell her what I know. Maybe she'll —"

"Uh-uh." Mark's eyes had darkened and he was shaking his head firmly. "Tonight. Call her tonight." He paused, considering. "Better yet, let's go see her."

She stared at him. "You want to go with me?"

"Sure. It's not that late, if we leave right away. She needs to hear what you've found out."

That wasn't the point. Jessica frowned. "Why do *you* want to be involved?"

He leaned closer and took her hand again. "Remember the Hobart's Corner Fire, where we met?"

"Of course." She was very aware of his fingers, firm and hard, surrounding hers. Her heart fluttered. "What about it?"

"It was the third fire — so far. You've just told me about a serial arsonist who may have set three or four fires, maybe more, when he was a kid in Georgia Shores. He grew up to be a firefighter arsonist out in California, and now he's come back. He —"

Jessica stopped him. "Wait. A firefighter arsonist? It seems contradictory."

"It happens," he said flatly. "They come into the fire service to be as close as possible to the action. Some of these guys are thrill-seekers looking for excitement. If there aren't enough fires, they start a few. Some are looking for attention — they want to be heroes. And there are still others who are looking for paying work. In fact, that kind of fire happens so often that it has a name. Job fires."

He let her hands go but he held her eyes. "What I'm saying is that there's a chance — a damned *good* chance, Jessica — that Wendell Paine is setting these local wildfires."

Jessica stared at him. "I should have thought of that," she muttered.

"What's more," he went on, "I got word this afternoon that the state forensic arson investigator was able to get some DNA off one of the ignition devices. I don't know if a case can be made against anyone for the arson-murder of your family — the evidence may not exist. But if Paine is our wildfire arsonist, we may be able to nail him for this current series." His voice became urgent. "This can't wait, Jessica. Loomis needs to hear it. Tonight."

Jessica looked at him for a long moment.

Then, understanding that Mark had a stake in this, too, she reached for her phone.

They didn't order dinner. Bob Godwin boxed up their nachos and Mark paid the bill. Jessica left her Kia in the parking lot at Bean's and they headed for Georgia Shores in Mark's truck.

It was well past eight by this time. Twilight was falling across the Texas landscape, and a bank of clouds had piled up against the eastern horizon, its lavender shading to deep purple. The National Weather Service had issued their latest forecast for Debby, predicting that the storm would move inland a few miles and then north, which meant that there would be high winds tonight and a chance of storms.

They munched as they drove, the nachos on the console between their seats. Mark turned the CB radio and the police scanner off when they started out, and the two of them were mostly silent, for which Jessica was grateful. She was occupied with her thoughts, which ranged from her long-lost family to arsonists to somebody named Shorty with a flame tattoo. And to a guy who was several years too old for her.

She was glad, though, when at one point Mark reached across the by-then-empty nacho box, took her left hand, held it tight for a moment, and then let it go.

"You okay?" he asked.

"Not so much," she said. "But I'll survive." She would, she knew. It wasn't a matter of being tough, but of being strong enough to carry on long enough to get the job done, whatever it was. She could collapse later, when there was time.

He kept his eyes on the road. "Actually, I'm impressed," he said quietly.

She was startled. "Impressed? By . . . what?"

"By the way you put this all together. All the clues, like pieces of a puzzle. The way you're *holding* it together, too. You know, if I were you — if that was my dad and mom and sister — I'd be bouncing off the walls. I would hate the guy who torched my house. I'd want to kill him."

"Oh, I've been there," Jessica said emphatically. "I've been there. Believe me."

It was true. She had hated and grieved and the hatred and grief had been braided together so tightly that she had thought it could never be pulled apart. How could it? It had all happened so long ago, in a distant past that was remote, inaccessible, out of reach.

But maybe that wasn't true. Maybe the

summer days with the sailboat on the lake and tennis in the park were lodged in the *present,* in her heart. And Rascal running alongside their bikes and ice cream at Dopey's and Dad and Mom in the kitchen, collaborating on a family picnic. These images weren't buried in a dead past, they were with her now, right now, comforting her and holding her together.

In the half-dark, she stole a look at Mark. Lit by the green dash lights, his expression was grave. His mouth was set hard, and she could see the jagged line of the scar on his jaw. There were definitely crow's feet at the corners of his pale eyes and the glint of silver at his temples. Yes, he was a decade older than she, maybe more. But now he didn't seem at all . . . dangerous. And while he might have baggage, that no longer unsettled her — at least, not so much.

She had baggage, didn't she? Of course she did — and plenty of it.

Come to think of it, everybody had baggage. You couldn't go through life without collecting the complications of mothers and fathers and sisters and brothers and lovers and children and friends. And the sadness of tragedies and the pain of difficult experiences, some bad, some worse, some terrifying.

It was all just . . . life. That's what it was.

And once you accepted that and understood what it meant, the rest might not be so hard.

Beverly Loomis met them in her small office at the police station, where she listened to Jessica's story without comment or question. Then to Mark's, tapping a pencil on her desk as he spoke.

When he was done, she asked. "Did I hear you say that you've got DNA on the guy who's setting the wildfires?"

"The state's forensic arson lab has it," Mark said. "What we need is a sample from Paine. Here." He scribbled something on a piece of paper. "If we can get a sample, it needs to go to this guy."

Loomis tucked the paper into her shirt pocket and leaned back in her chair, her expression unreadable. "Well, I happen to know where he goes for breakfast. I'll see what I can do."

Jessica stared at her. "You actually *know* Wendell Paine?"

"I know who he is. His dad lives across the street from me. Poor old guy's got lung cancer. He doesn't have much more time left. Before Wendell came back, a couple of neighbors and I took turns doing Mr.

Paine's grocery shopping. Now, Wendell — Shorty, his dad calls him — does it."

Jessica was amazed. It really was a small world. But of course, it was a very small town.

"Where does Paine go for breakfast?" Mark asked.

"Jack in the Box." Loomis smiled crookedly. "The court says we don't need a warrant to grab a fork or a cup that somebody's tossed. We'll see if we can get a match to the DNA you have." She looked at Jessica. "I met with Chief Sheridan this evening, after you and I talked on the phone. We're reopening your cold case. A tech at the DPS Crime Lab in Austin will be taking a look at that old fingerprint we found in the file. And at the matchbook, too, to see if there are latent prints that didn't turn up when Remmick dusted it."

"You're reopening the case!" Jessica exclaimed. "That's terrific news!"

Loomis nodded. "I appreciate your digging up the information on Paine's California prison time. His prints will be on file in AFIS — the Automated Fingerprint Identification System. The tech will do a comparison, and we'll see." She set her jaw. "And if it's not Paine, I can promise you that we'll keep on looking. I'm talking to Sean Scott tomorrow."

"It's been such a long time," Jessica murmured, fighting back the sting of unexpected tears. She tried to swallow the huge lump that blocked her throat. "And there were so many pieces to this. If it hadn't been for Claire Mercer calling Officer Riley . . ."

Loomis leaned forward and her face softened. "That's where it began. But if you hadn't kept the ball rolling, we could never have come this far. This one's on you, Jessica. You're the one who pulled it all together."

With a smile, she pushed herself out of the chair. "And I'm actually looking forward to dropping in on Jack in the Box in the morning."

CHAPTER ELEVEN

Back in Mark's truck, in the darkness, a jolt of anguish shot through her and Jessica gave in to the wracking sobs she had been holding back.

Mark leaned over the console and pulled her into his arms, just holding her, saying nothing. Her face against his shoulder, she let herself lean against him. His arms felt . . . safe, somehow, and after a while, her sobs subsided.

"I'm sorry," she muttered. "I'm really sorry."

"Don't be." He let her go and pulled a tissue out of a box under the dash.

"Thank you." She blew her nose. "Thank you for . . . everything."

He shook his head. "I didn't do anything. Loomis is right, you know. *You* were the one who pulled all this together." He put the key into the ignition. "It was quite a trick, actually. If I were grading this investi-

"gation, you'd get an A plus."

"Thanks professor," Jessica said, managing a faint smile. "Although I'm not sure how many investigations you've graded."

"You might be surprised." He hesitated, his hand on the key. Then he dropped it and turned toward her. "There's something I have to say, Jessica, and it's time I said it. Past time, probably."

She was startled by the gravity of his tone. "Something —"

He held up his hand. "Just let me say it, please. I'm aware — very aware — that I'm a decade or so older than you. I want you to know that I've made it a practice not to date students at the university, whether they were in my classes or not." He spoke heavily, as if this was something he had thought deeply about. "In fact, I was glad when the university decided to ban even consensual relationships between faculty and undergraduate students. Some of us are beginning to realize that consent is complicated. It isn't just not saying no, especially when the woman is . . . quite a bit younger. So if the age difference . . ." He paused. "I guess I'm not saying this very well. I just mean that . . ." Another pause. "Look. If you're not interested in getting together again, it's okay. My feelings won't be hurt."

Jessica took a breath. It was ironic, wasn't it? She had thought that *she* was the one most concerned about the difference in their ages. She hadn't imagined that he would be uncomfortable with it. Thoughts and feelings crowded her heart, but all she could think of to say was, "I'm younger, yes. But I'm not a student."

"And I'm damned glad you're not. But I'm aware that age and experience can seem to convey a certain . . . well, maybe 'authority' is the best word." He stopped and cleared his throat. "My wife and I were equal partners in everything. If I was out of line, she told me about it. If she had a problem, I helped her deal with it. It didn't matter that she was five years older." He let out a breath. "That's the kind of relationship I'm looking for. Does that make sense?"

"Your . . . wife?"

His voice was gruff. "Rachel was killed in the Lost Pines fire. We had just celebrated our twelfth wedding anniversary."

"Oh." Jessica's eyes widened and her hand went to her mouth. "Oh, I'm so sorry, Mark."

"Yes. Tore my heart out." He paused. "There have been one or two other women since Rachel. But it hasn't been easy to move on. Now, maybe it's time. Anyway, what I'm trying to say is that I don't want you to think I'm an authority, because I'm older or . . ." He grunted. "Or because I look like I've been to a few rodeos. I just wanted to have that out in the open. Between us." His eyes were on her face. "Just in case. Does that make sense, Jessica?"

She thought of asking *Just in case of what?* and *Where do we go from here?* But she only nodded, wordlessly. She didn't need to ask the questions. She already knew the answers.

"Good," he said with satisfaction. "I'm glad we got that cleared up. Just one thing more . . ." He leaned across the console and kissed her. It was a testing, tasting kiss, his mouth gentle on hers. But she could sense the passion he was withholding and she leaned into him, embraced by his warmth and energy. After a moment, as if they had both learned what they wanted to know, they pulled apart and he started the truck.

Jessica settled back into the seat, smiling in the dark. Who could have guessed, just a few days ago, that something like this might happen? That she might have solved the central mystery of her life. And that she might have found the person she had been looking for — without even knowing it.

She was still smiling as Mark drove back

toward Pecan Springs. It was just ten o'clock. They could probably get back before Bob Godwin closed the kitchen at Bean's and have a late supper before she picked up her car and drove home.

But things didn't turn out that way.

They weren't quite ten miles outside of Georgia Shores when Jessica looked out of her window and saw a small orange flicker in the darkness at the foot of the hill off to her right. She thought at first it was a lantern, swinging in the wind, then a pair of lanterns, then three or four. And then she realized it wasn't lanterns at all, but —

"Stop, Mark!" she said urgently, and put her hand on his arm. "There's a fire! Down there!"

Mark muttered something under his breath and braked hard, pulling the truck to the side of the road. Leaving the engine running, he yanked up the console top and pulled out an odd-looking pair of binoculars, putting it to his eyes.

"Night-vision scanner," he muttered. "I'm trying to see . . ."

While he was doing that, Jessica pulled out her phone and clicked on the compass app. A few seconds later, their GPS coordinates came up. When he dropped the binoculars back in the console and reached for the CB radio, she held out the phone. "Here's our coordinates, if you need them."

"Quick thinking," he said approvingly. In a moment, he was talking to a Forest Service dispatcher, whom he obviously knew. "Hemming here, Harley. Reporting a fire on FM 281, nine miles north of Georgia Shores." He read the coordinates off Jessica's phone. "Fire's in three patches, in tall dry grass and brush at the foot of a twenty-degree slope. About a half-acre, maybe, but growing, headed for a dense stand of loblolly about fifty yards uphill on the other side of a gully. I can't see any structures in the immediate area. Wind is gusty and variable." He paused. "Possible arson. No power lines in this area, no lightning."

"Ten-four," the dispatcher replied. "Stand by, Hemming." Forty seconds of empty silence, and then: "Georgia Shores Engines Fifteen and Two Five Seven, en route. ETA to your coordinates, sixteen minutes."

"This one could be a problem if this wind holds," Mark said into the mic. "Better wake up the Bastrop boys. We could use their brush truck."

A moment later, Harley was back. "Bastrop ETA twenty-two minutes. Five on their four-by-four."

"That should do it for now. I have a passenger with me — Jessica. She'll stay with the truck. I'm going to work on the fire. I'll keep her posted via cellphone and she can relay to you."

She'll stay with the truck? Jessica tensed. She had been watching the fire as it grew into a half-dozen broad ribbons of flame flickering up the hillside toward the pines at the top. She swallowed, feeling a little light-headed, her pulse beating erratically.

Mark had his hand on the door. "I've got my phone," he said, his voice clipped. "Keep your cellphone out, in case I call. Oh, and you'd better take the driver's seat. I'm leaving the key in the ignition, in case the wind shifts and the fire blows back in this direction. If it does, drive forward as far as you have to, to get out of the fire."

He was getting out of the truck but he paused, his eyes on her. "You okay, Jess? I realize fire has been a problem for you, but we don't have a lot of options here."

The thought of the fire coming in this direction had pinned her to the seat, her heart hammering in her chest, but she knew she had to respond.

"I'll be okay," she managed weakly. "Yes, I can move the truck. You . . . you're going to . . . to work on the fire?" Whatever that meant.

"Good girl." He stepped out of the truck and stripped off his black blazer, reaching over the seat and pulling out his yellow Nomex shirt, the one she had seen him wear at the briefing. "Yeah. I'm taking my drip torch down there to set a backfire along the north flank."

Set a backfire? Her breath caught as she watched him suiting up. He could be in the middle of it, between two fires. The thought of it clutched at her throat and she shuddered. But the fear that froze her — the fear of *this* fire — wasn't for herself. It was for him. This was dangerous, dangerous work. Firefighters died. Even in small fires, if they got trapped in the wrong place and couldn't get out, they died. But she didn't want him to see her fear, or worry that it might disable her. He had to know he could count on her to do what had to be done.

She took a breath and lightened her voice. "Be careful up there, you."

"Always." He took a headlamp out of the console and put it on, then picked up his helmet and heavy leather gloves from the back seat. "Always careful." He leaned across the driver's seat, put a hand on her face, and kissed her quickly. "Especially now."

And then he was gone into the dark, toward the fire.

The night was a cacophony of sound and motion and color slashing through the darkness. As the fire grew larger and more violent, it perversely grew more beautiful, blooming into glowing, pulsing billows of red, rose, orange, and yellow flame as it raced across the brush-covered hillside toward the loblollies. Mark had disappeared into the darkness. But when she picked up the night-vision binoculars, she could see him drawing a line of fire across the hillside, as if he were etching the dark ground with flame. She watched, biting her lip, now so concerned for him that she forgot to be afraid for herself.

At last, after what seemed like hours, she heard sirens from the direction of Georgia Shores. One truck, then a second, pulled in along the road just ahead of her, red and blue lights flashing. Yellow-shirted, helmeted men jumped off the trucks, pulling a couple of hundred feet of hose. Within moments, a stream of water was arcing into the heart of the fire while a trio of men carrying shovels and wearing orange backpack fire pumps were scrambling around the perimeter to catch the flames as they advanced up the hill.

A third truck — the brush truck from Bastrop — came from the opposite direction, turned, and drove straight down the hill, bouncing as it went. At the foot, it stopped and a firefighter grabbed a hose and shot a stream of water onto the fire. When water hit the flames, smoke geysered upward. Fans of flaming brush were pulled up by the wind and tossed into the dark sky while fiery cartwheels rolled across the hill, sparking new fires and chased by men on foot.

Jessica had slid into the driver's seat, where, with her heart in her throat, she watched the fire. Even with the truck windows closed, the smoke seeped in and the air grew heavy with it. Smoke had often triggered her panic before, but now she fought back, reminding herself that she was safe in the truck and could drive away if she had to, while Mark was on the fire line, in the middle of the worst of it. She felt even better when she realized that a big story was happening right in front of her and that she was the only one who could capture it. What in the world was she waiting for?

She reached for her cellphone and began dictating the details of the scene playing out on the hillside beneath her. When she finished, she opened the door and stepped out into the road, taking photos and video of the fire and the fire trucks and videoed quick, forty-second interviews with a couple of the firefighter. Back in the truck, she emailed the story she had just dictated, along with the photos and the video, to both Hark and Jeff. Hark might be able to use one or two of the photos in the print edition. Jeff would likely post everything she had just sent online, even the raw video. With the flames illuminating the sweaty, ash-streaked faces of the men she interviewed, and the fire crackling in the background, the scene had all the power of real and unrehearsed immediacy. It was a story she could be proud of.

She had just gotten back behind the wheel when her cellphone dinged. Mark said, "This thing is just about contained and we're doing mop-ups now. You okay?"

"Yes," she said without hesitation. "I'm fine." And for the first time in more years than she could count, she *was*.

"Good," he said with a smile in his voice. "Sit tight. I'll be back at the truck in another twenty minutes or so."

But it was well past midnight when Mark opened the passenger door. "Sorry," he said, pulling off his gloves and wiping the sweat off his soot-stained face. "There were some stubborn patches. It took longer than we expected." He tossed his gloves and his helmet into the back of the cab.

Relief flooded through her in a great wave. "Glad you're back," she said. "You're okay?"

"Yeah, just tired. And glad to cool off. That was hot work." He unsnapped his Nomex shirt and tossed it after his gloves and helmet. That was followed by his black T-shirt, so heavily soaked with sweat that it clung to his skin.

"Apologies for stripping down on our first date, but I plead extenuating circumstances," he said, climbing bare-chested into the passenger seat.

"Not a problem," Jessica murmured. The mingled smell of smoke and sweat was nearly overpowering, but she suddenly discovered that she didn't mind it so much, or maybe not at all. Certainly there was nothing dangerous about it — except, perhaps, the startlingly intense, undeniable physical attraction of his muscled body.

Up ahead, the hoses and other equipment were being loaded into the fire truck. Emerging out of the darkness, a grimy firefighter smacked the hood of Mark's truck with the flat of his hand and flashed a grin and a thumbs-up. Returning the gesture, Mark unhooked the CB mic and spoke into it.

"We're a hundred percent contained, Harley. Georgia Shores is packing up to leave, but Bastrop will hang out here for another couple of hours, watching for hot spots. We ID'd two ignition points — more of those Lucky Strike layover devices — and secured them for the arson investigator. He's on his way, but I'm heading out. It's been a long day."

"Sounds right," Harley said. "Have a beer and get some sleep."

"Roger that," Mark said. He keyed off and clipped the CB mic in the hanger.

"How do you ID an ignition point?" Jessica asked.

"Put a roasting pan over it," Mark said, buckling his seat belt. "Top the pan with a rock so it doesn't blow away. You want to keep it from getting trashed or watered down until the investigator can have a look at it." With a sigh, he stretched out his legs and closed his eyes. "I am bushed. Think you can drive this baby back to Bean's? You need to pick up your car."

The truck was twice as big as her Kia and Jessica wasn't sure she could handle it. But she didn't intend to let Mark know that.

And she had already made up her mind about the car.

"I'll drive," she said. "To my house."

Mark opened his eyes. "Your house?"

She fastened her seat belt. "All we had for dinner was a few nachos, and that was hours ago. I'll scramble some eggs and sausage while you take a shower and your clothes go into the washer. You can borrow my bathrobe until your things come out of the dryer." She checked the mirror and pulled out into the road. "My car will be fine where it is for tonight."

"Got it," Mark said, and closed his eyes again.

CHAPTER TWELVE

"And then what happened?"

China picked up the pitcher and poured hibiscus tea over the mint ice cubes in Jessica's glass. They were sitting on the front porch at China's house on Limekiln Road, where the midsummer twilight was rich with birdsong and the scent of honeysuckle. In the distance, toward the old stone wall that divided the yard from the woodland beyond, a doe and two fawns were browsing.

And then what happened? Remembering, Jessica colored, then smiled. "Well, what do you think?"

China chuckled. "I think you . . . got better acquainted." She put the pitcher on the table in front of them and leaned back in her deck chair. "You've stopped worrying about the difference in your ages?"

From his perch in the corner of the porch, Mr. Spock gave a long, low wolf whistle.

"Hello, sweetheart," he cooed. A bright green parrot with a Day-Glo orange beak and red and blue feathers that flashed when he raised his wings, Spock belonged to Caitie, China's adopted daughter. He had been named by a previous owner who had taught him a full vocabulary of Star Trek words.*

"The longer I know Mark, the more comfortable I am with him," Jessica said, replying to China's question. "I'm not totally there yet, although I'm getting closer. But then I see him in one of his professional situations — on a fire, or giving a lecture — and I see how everybody looks up to him. Which reminds me again that he's older." She wrinkled her nose. "Which makes me feel *younger.* Like one of his students. Sometimes I'm okay with that. Sometimes, not so much."

"I know." China put her hand on Jessica's. "Professional people sometimes have a very strong professional persona. Out there in the world, on the job, they're different from the way they are at home, with family. But when it's quitting time, they have to be able to leave that persona. At home, it's the *personal* that counts."

* You may remember meeting Mr. Spock in the last chapters of *A Plain Vanilla Murder*.

"It's the personal that seems to be working," Jessica said with a little smile.

Spock ruffled the feathers on his neck. "Wanna grape." He clicked his beak. "Deserve a grape."

"I bet you do." Laughing, China picked one from the bunch on the table and gave it to him.

"Love a grape," he said, holding it in one claw and nibbling around it. "Thank you, Mom."

"You're welcome." To Jessica, China said, "I loved it when Brian and Caitie felt like calling me Mom." The two had come late into China's life, after she married McQuaid. "I'm not sure how I feel about being called Mom by a *parrot*."

"Set phasers to stun," Spock snapped. "Engage!"

Jessica sipped her tea. "Maybe Fran ought to do a story on Spock. How about if I pitch it to her for her weekend *Magazine*? She could include a video clip of you and Spock having a conversation. I'll bet our *Enterprise* readers would love it."

"Sounds like fun — but it should be Caitie and Spock," China said. "He's her bird. And I'm sure she'd love it."

"Love Caitie," Spock said indulgently. "Love love love." He lapsed into a series of kissing noises, punctuated by whistles and coos.

China picked up her iced tea glass. "So what's the latest from Georgia Shores?"

"That's what I came to tell you." Jessica put her glass down and leaned forward. "Remember the fingerprint on the matchbook? The one in the police file that was lost for years and years?"

"Sure, I remember. What about it?"

Jessica took a steadying breath. "Beverly Loomis called this afternoon to tell me that they've matched it. The print belongs to Wendell Paine. He will be charged with the murders of my family." At last, after all these years. She could hardly believe it.

"I'm glad to hear that." But China was frowning. "Not to throw cold water on your cop buddies, but I hope they have more than a single fingerprint on an old matchbook with a questionable custody record. 'Lost for years and years'?" She scoffed. "A good defense attorney will wipe her feet on that." China had been a criminal defense attorney before she moved to Pecan Springs and opened her herb shop. She knew what she was talking about.

"The police *do* have more," Jessica replied. "They have a statement from Shorty's friend, the guy he bragged to that evening at the Old Firehouse. Loomis says it's almost as good as a confession. Plus, Claire Mercer has made a corroborating statement."

"Better," China acknowledged cautiously. "Best would be a confession to the *cops*."

"They're working on that. According to Loomis, the prosecutor is talking with Paine's lawyer about a plea deal." Jessica paused. "It looks like they've got him on a couple of those recent arson wildfires, too."

"No kidding." China raised both eyebrows. "Well, that's good to hear. How'd they do that?"

"The forensic tech in the arson lab was able to pull DNA from two of the ignition devices that Paine used to set fires along the highway. It matches the DNA on the empty foam coffee cup that Loomis picked up from his breakfast table at Jack in the Box."

"DNA." China whistled between her teeth. "Lucky break. And good police work."

"Fascinating," Spock said, in perfect imitation of his namesake, and added a whistle just like China's.

"There's his past criminal record, too," Jessica added, and explained what she had discovered when she researched Wendell Paine's California history. "He was convicted and imprisoned — for arson."

600

"Maybe admissible, maybe not," China said. "Depends on the circumstances, and on the judge. But the prosecutor likely won't need it. Paine was a juvenile when he committed the crime, so he may not face capital murder charges for what he did to your family. But the potential prison sentence is usually enough to leverage a plea, and his attorney has probably told him he ought to take whatever he can get." She looked thoughtful. "Which is not altogether a good thing, in my opinion. Prosecutors often use a plea deal to coerce defendants to forfeit their right to a fair —"

Jessica raised her hand. "I'd like to hear more about that, China. But not this evening. Wendell Paine is paying a long overdue debt. I don't want to think about that man and his rights until I have to."

"I totally get that," China said. She shook her head admiringly. "You worked this whole thing out like a charm, Jessica. When are you going into the PI business? Mc-Quaid says he'd be interested in bringing you into his firm. He has a case that could use a woman's special insights."

"Wow. McQuaid said that? That's a huge compliment, coming from him." Jessica laughed. "But please tell Mike that being a crime reporter is enough of a job for me.

I'm covering two developing stories for the *Enterprise* right now, not to mention the looming deadline on my book manuscript."

She had appointments all next week with people she was interviewing for *Not Only in the Dark* — including one with David Redfern, which might be a little uncomfortable now that she was seeing Mark. It was a reminder that the warning against getting too close to your journalistic sources was just good common sense.

"Speaking of the newspaper," China said, "I sent Jeff Dixon an email about last week's coverage. I told him I thought it was excellent, especially that video clip of the chief of police — Smart Cookie — telling the city council about the new body cams. And the fire footage you filmed was outstanding."

Jessica smiled. "The online edition is doing better than anyone expected, I'm glad to say. Subscriptions are growing every week, and advertising is up by five percent overall. Hark is even beginning to smile once in a while, which must mean that the bottom line is improving. I don't think we're out of the woods yet, but maybe there's hope." Her smile grew into a grin. "Did you see my blog? I wrote about working on *Not Only in the Dark*. I've been getting a lot of email about it."

"I enjoyed it," China said. "That was an important investigation, and I can't wait to read your book. I hope it's a bestseller."

"A bestseller would be great," Jessica agreed. She made a face. "But right now, I'm just focused on getting the darn thing *written.*"

China gave an approving thumbs-up. "Good plan. And I'm betting that there are a lot more great stories out there after you've finished that one."

tters and the Texas Literary Hall of Fame. She has three children and eight grandchildren. She and her husband Bill live on thirty-one acres in the Texas Hill Country, where she gardens, tends chickens and bees, and indulges her passions for reading and writing.

ABOUT THE AUTHOR

As a young child growing up on a farm on the Illinois prairie, **Susan Wittig Albert** learned that books could take her anywhere, and reading and writing became passions that have accompanied her throughout her life. She earned an undergraduate degree in English from the University of Illinois and a PhD in medieval studies from the University of California at Berkeley, then turned to teaching. After faculty and administrative appointments at the University of Texas, Newcomb College/Tulane University, and Texas State University, she left her academic career for full-time writing.

There are over four million copies of Susan's books in print, including mysteries, memoirs, biographical fiction, fiction for young adult readers, and nonfiction. She is the founder of the Story Circle Network, a nonprofit organization for women writers, and a member of the Texas Institute of Letters and the Texas Literary Hall of Fame. She has three children and eight grand-children. She and her husband Bill live on thirty-one acres in the Texas Hill Country, where she gardens, tends chickens and geese, and indulges her passions for needle-work and (of course) reading.

Visit Susan on her website:
www.susanalbert.com
and on social media:
Pinterest:
www.pinterest.com/susanwalbert
Instagram:
www.instagram.com/susanwittigalbert
Facebook:
www.facebook.com/susan.w.albert
www.facebook.com/susan.w.albert.author
www.facebook.com/ChinaBayles